The Stone Raft

ALSO BY JOSÉ SARAMAGO

JOSÉ SARAMAGO

The Stone Raft

Translated from the Portuguese
by Giovanni Pontiero

A HARVEST BOOK

HARCOURT BRACE & COMPANY

SAN DIEGO   NEW YORK   LONDON

This translation of A *Jangada de Pedra* has been made possible, in part, by a grant
from the Instituto da Biblioteca Nacional e do Livro.

Library of Congress Cataloging-in-Publication Data
Saramago, José
[A Jangada de pedra. English]
The stone raft/José Saramago; translated from the Portuguese by
Giovanni Pontiero.
A Harvest book
p. cm.
ISBN 0-15-185198-0
ISBN 0-15-600401-1 (pbk.)
I. Pontiero, Giovanni. II. Title.
PQ9281.A66J313 1995 94-49622
869.3'42—dc20

Designed by Lori J. McThomas
First Harvest edition 1996
Printed in the United States of America
D F G E C

Every future is fabulous.

—ALEJO CARPENTIER

The Stone Raft

When Joana Carda scratched the ground with the elm branch all the dogs of Cerbère began to bark, throwing the inhabitants into panic and terror, because from time immemorial it was believed that, when these canine creatures that had always been silent started to bark, the entire universe was nearing its end. No one remembers any longer the origin of this deep-rooted superstition, or firm conviction, in many cases these are simply alternative ways of expressing the same thing, but as so often happens, having heard the story and now passing it on with fresh distortions, French grandmothers used to amuse their grandchildren with the fable that in the times of the ancient Greek myths, here, in the district of Cerbère in the Eastern Pyrenees, a dog with three heads and the above-mentioned named of Cerberus had barked when summoned by its master, the ferryman Charon. We are equally unclear about the organic change this legendary howling canine must have undergone to acquire the historically proven muteness of its degenerate one-headed offspring. Nevertheless, and this is a point of doctrine known to almost everyone, especially to those of the older generation, the dog Cerberus, as written and pronounced in English, guarded with ferocity the gates of hell, so that no soul would dare try to escape, and then, perhaps as one final act of mercy on the part of the moribund gods, all the dogs fell silent for the rest of eternity, perhaps hoping that their silence might erase the memory of the infernal regions. But since the everlasting does not last forever, as the modern age has clearly shown us, it sufficed that a few days ago and hundreds of kilometers from Cerbère, somewhere in Portugal, in a place whose name we shall record anon, a woman named Joana Carda scratched the ground with an elm branch whereupon all the dogs came onto the streets howling, dogs, let me remind you, that had never barked before. Were someone to ask Joana Carda what had possessed her to scratch the ground with an elm branch, more the gesture of a moonstruck adolescent than that of a mature woman, if she had not thought of the possible consequences of an act that seemed meaningless, and these are the most dangerous acts of all, perhaps she might reply, I don't know what came over me, the branch was lying on the ground, I picked it up and drew a line. She had no idea that it might be a magic wand. It seemed rather big for a magic wand, and besides I've always heard it said that magic wands are made of shimmering gold and crystal and have a star on top. Did you know it was an elm branch. I know very little about trees, they told me afterwards that wych-elm is the same as wych-hazel, botanically known as *ulmus*, none of these having supernatural powers, even when they change their names, but in this case I'm sure that a matchstick would have produced the same effect, Why do you say that, What must be, must be, and there's no way around it, I've heard the old people say this a thousand times, Do you believe in fate, I believe in what has to be.

In Paris they had a good laugh at the appeal made by the *maire*, who appeared to be telephoning from a kennel at the hour when they were feeding the dogs, and it was only at the insistent pleading of a member of parliament born and bred in the commune, and thus familiar with local legends and tales, that two qualified veterinary surgeons of the *Deuxième Bureau* were dispatched to the south, with the special mission of investigating this unusual phenomenon and presenting a report and a plan of action. Meanwhile, the desperate inhabitants, reduced to near-deafness, had crisscrossed the streets and squares of the agreeable resort town suddenly transformed into a hellhole, setting out dozens of poisoned meat pies, a method of supreme simplicity and one whose effectiveness has been confirmed by experience in every age and latitude. As it happened, only one dog died, but the lesson was not lost on the survivors, who soon disappeared, yelping, barking, and howling, into the surrounding fields, where, for no apparent reason, they fell silent within a few minutes. When the veterinary surgeons finally arrived, they were presented with the sad Medor, cold, swollen, so different from the contented animal who accompanied his mistress when she went shopping, and who, old dog that he was, liked nothing better than sleeping peacefully in the sun. But since justice has not yet entirely abandoned this world, God decided, poetically, that Medor should die from eating the meat pie cooked by his beloved mistress, who, let it be said, had meant the pie for a certain bitch of the neighborhood who never left her garden alone. The older of the veterinary surgeons, confronted by that sad corpse, suggested, Let's hold an autopsy, which was pointless, for any inhabitant of Cerbère could, if he or she so wished, testify to the cause of death. But the hidden intention of the Faculty, as it was referred to in the jargon of that secret service, was to proceed in secrecy to an examination of the vocal cords of an animal that, between the quietude of death, which was now definitive, and its lifelong silence, which had seemed eternal, had finally enjoyed a few hours of speech like any other dog. Their efforts were futile, Medor did not even have any vocal cords. The surgeons were amazed, but the *maire*, giving his official and judicious opinion, said, That's not surprising, for centuries the dogs of Cerbère have not barked, their vocal cords had wasted away. Then why the sudden change, I don't know, I'm not a veterinary surgeon, but our worries are over, the *chiens* have disappeared, from wherever they are they cannot be heard. Medor, dissected and badly stitched up again, was delivered to his weeping mistress, as a living reproach, which is what reproaches are even after they are dead. On the way to the airport, where they were about to catch a plane to Paris, the veterinary surgeons agreed that they would omit from their report the curious business about the missing vocal cords. And to all appearances definitive, for that same night there was Cerberus himself out prowling, an enormous dog as tall as a tree, three-headed but mute.

About the same time, perhaps before Joana Carda had scratched the ground with the elm branch, perhaps after, a man was strolling along the beach, it was toward evening, when the noise of the waves,

3

brief and restrained like an unprovoked sigh, can scarcely be heard, and that man, who will later say that his name is Joaquim Sassa, was walking above the tidemark that distinguishes the dry sands from the wet, and from time to time he bent down to pick up a shell, a crab's claw, a strand of green seaweed, we often while away the hours in this way, and this solitary passerby was doing likewise. Since he had neither pockets nor sack to hoard his findings, he put the lifeless remnants back in the water when his hands were full, let the sea have what belongs to the sea, let the earth remain with the earth. But every rule has its exceptions, and Joaquim Sassa picked up a stone he had seen ahead, beyond the reach of the tides, a stone as large and heavy as a discus and irregular in shape. If it had been like the others, light, with smooth outlines, like those stones that fit easily between the thumb and the index finger, then Joaquim Sassa would have skimmed it on the surface of the water, watching it bounce, childishly satisfied with his own ability, and finally sink, the impetus gone, a stone that appeared to have its destiny traced out, dried by the sun, dampened only by the rain, but now finally sinking into the dark depths to wait a million years, until this sea evaporates, or, receding, brings the stone back to land for another million years, allowing sufficient time for another Joaquim Sassa to come down to the beach and unwittingly perform the same gesture and movement, let no man say I will not do it, for no stone is secure and firm.

On the southern shores, at this tepid hour, there is someone having one last dip, swimming, playing with a ball, diving under the waves, or taking it easy on an air mattress, or feeling the first waft of the evening breeze on his skin, or shifting his position to receive one last caress from the sun that is about to settle momentarily on the sea, the longest moment of all, for we look at the sun and the sun allows itself to be watched. But here, on this northern shore where Joaquim Sassa is carrying a stone, so heavy that his arms are already tiring, the breeze is chilly, the sun is already halfway down, and there is not a sea gull in sight flying over the waters. Joaquim Sassa has thrown the stone, expecting it to fall a few paces away, not very far from where he's standing, each of us is obliged to know his own strength, there were not even any witnesses there to mock the efforts of the frustrated discus thrower, it was he who was prepared to laugh at himself, but things did not turn out as he expected, the stone, dark and heavy, went up into the air, came down and hit the surface of the water, the impact sent it back up in a great flight or leap, and down it came again, and then up, and finally it sank in the distance, unless the whiteness we have just seen some distance away is not just the froth of a breaking wave. How did that happen, Joaquim Sassa mused in bewilderment, how could I, weak as I am, have thrown such a heavy stone so far, way out on that sea that is already darkening, and there is no one here to say, Well done, Joaquim Sassa, I'm your witness for the *Guinness Book of Records*, such a feat cannot be ignored, what rotten luck, if I were to tell people what has happened, they would call me a liar. A towering wave came in from the open sea, foaming and gushing, the stone finally dropped into the water, this evokes the rivers of childhood, for anyone who had rivers in his childhood, this concentric undulation caused by stones thrown into the water. Joaquim Sassa ran up the shore, and the wave broke on the sand, dragging with it shells, crab's claws, green algae, but also other species, gulfweed, coralline, sea-tangle, and a small stone, light, of the type that can fit easily between the thumb and the index finger. How many years since it has seen the light of the sun.

Writing is extremely difficult, it is an enormous responsibility, you need only think of the exhausting work involved in setting out events in chronological order, first this one, then that, or, if more conducive to the desired effect, today's event before yesterday's episode, and other no less risky acrobatics, presenting the past as if it were something new, or the present as a continuous process with neither beginning nor end, but, however hard writers might try, there is one feat they cannot achieve, and that is to put into writing, in the same tense, two events that have occurred simultaneously. Some believe the difficulty can be solved by dividing the page into two columns, side by side, but this proposal is too simple, because the one will have been written first and the other afterwards, nor may we forget that the reader will have to read this one first and then the other one, or vice versa. The people who come off best are the opera singers, each with his or her own part to sing, three, four, five, six in all among the tenors, basses, sopranos, and baritones, all singing different words, the cynic mocking, for example, the ingénue pleading, the gallant lover slow in coming to her aid, what interests the operagoer is the music, but the reader is not like this, he wants everything explained, syllable by syllable, one after the other, as they are shown here. That is why, having first spoken of Joaquim Sassa, only now will we mention Pedro Orce, when in fact Joaquim Sassa threw the stone into the sea and Pedro Orce rose from his chair at the very same instant, although according to the clocks there was an hour's difference, because the latter happened to be in Spain and the former in Portugal.

It is common knowledge that every effect has its cause, and this is a universal truth, but it is impossible to avoid certain errors of judgment, or of simple identification, for we might think that this effect comes from that cause, when after all it was some other cause, beyond any understanding we possess or any knowledge we think we possess. For example, there appeared to be proof that if the dogs of Cerbère barked it was because Joana Carda scratched the ground with an elm branch, and yet only a very credulous child, if any child has survived from the golden decades of credulity, or an innocent one, if the holy name of innocence can thus be taken in vain, only a child capable of believing that by closing its hands it has trapped the sunlight inside would believe that dogs could bark that had never barked before, for reasons as much historical as physiological. In these tens and tens of thousands of hamlets, villages, towns, and cities, there are many people who would swear that they were the cause or causes of the barking of the dogs and of all that was to follow, because they slammed a door, or split a fingernail, or picked a fruit, or drew back the curtain, or lit a cigarette, or died, or, not the same people, were born, these hypotheses about death and birth would be more difficult to credit, bearing in mind that we are the ones who would have to propose them, for no child comes out of its mother's womb speaking, just as no one speaks any more once he has entered the womb of the earth. And there is no point in adding that any one of us has reasons enough for judging himself the cause of all effects, the reasons we have just mentioned as well as those that are our exclusive contribution to the functioning of the world, and I should dearly like to know what it will be like when people and the effects they alone cause will exist no more, best not to think of such an enormity, for it is enough to make one dizzy, but it will be quite sufficient for some tiny animals, some insects, to survive for there still to be worlds, the world of the ant and the cicada, for example, they will not draw back curtains, they will not look at themselves in the mirror, and what does it matter, after all, the only great truth is that the world cannot die.

Pedro Orce would say, if he so dared, that what caused the earth to tremble were his feet hitting the floor when he rose from the chair, great presumption on his part, if not ours, since we are frivolously expressing doubt, if every person leaves at least one sign in the world, this could be that of Pedro Orce, which is why he declares, I put my feet on the ground and the earth shook. It was an extraordinary trembling, so much so that no one appeared to have felt it, and even now, after two minutes, as the wave on the beach began to recede and Joaquim Sassa said to himself, If I were to tell anyone they would call me a liar, the earth still vibrates just as the chord continues to vibrate although it can no longer be heard, Pedro Orce can feel it in the soles of his feet, he continues to feel it as he leaves the pharmacy and steps out into the street, and no one there notices a thing, it's like watching a star and saying, What lovely light, what a beautiful star, without knowing that it went out in mid-sentence, and your children and grandchildren will repeat the same words, poor things, they speak of what is dead and say that it is alive, this deception is not confined to the science of astronomy. Here precisely the opposite happens, everyone would swear that the earth is firm and only Pedro Orce would say that it is trembling, just as well he kept his mouth shut and did not run away in terror, besides the walls are not swaying, the lamps hanging from the ceiling are as straight as a plumb line, and the little caged birds, who are usually the first to sound the alarm, doze peacefully on their perches, each with its head tucked under one wing, the needle of the seismograph has traced and continues to trace a straight horizontal line on the millimetric graph paper.

The next morning, a man was crossing an uncultivated plain, part scrubland, part swampy pasture, he was making his way along paths and tracks between the trees, poplars and ash, as elevated as the names by which they are known, and clumps of tamarisks, with their African scent, this man could not have chosen greater solitude or a loftier sky, and overhead, making the most incredible din, a flock of starlings followed him, so many of them that they formed a huge dark cloud, like the prelude to a storm. Whenever he paused the starlings began to fly in a circle or swooped noisily to roost in a tree, disappearing amid the branches until all the leaves were shaking and the crown echoed with harsh, strident sounds, giving the impression that some ferocious battle was being fought inside. José Anaiço started walking again, for that was his name, and the starlings took sudden flight, all at once, *vruuuuuuuuu*. If we did not know this man, and started guessing, we might decide that he was a bird-catcher by trade or, like the snake, had the power to charm and entice, when, in fact, José Anaiço is as puzzled as we are about the reason for this winged festivity. What can these creatures desire of me, do not wonder at this archaic phrasing, for there are days when one does not feel like using commonplace words.

The man was traveling from east to west, for this was the route he favored, but, forced out of his way by a great reservoir, he now turned south around the bend, hugging the water's edge. By late morning the temperature will soar, but meanwhile there is a fresh, clean breeze, what a pity one cannot store it in one's pocket and keep it there until it is needed once the heat builds up. José Anaiço was turning these thoughts over in his mind as he walked, vague and involuntary as if they did not belong to him, when he suddenly became aware that the starlings had stayed behind, were fluttering over where the road curves to skirt the reservoir, their behavior was quite extraordinary, but when all is said and done, whoever goes, goes, whoever remains, remains, good-bye little birds. José Anaiço had now circled the lake, an awkward journey that took nearly half an hour, amid thistles and nettles, and he picked up his original route, proceeding as he had begun, east to west like the sun, when suddenly, *vruuuu*, the starlings reappeared, where had they been hiding. Well, here's something for which there is no explanation. If a flock of starlings accompanies a man on his morning stroll, like a dog faithful to his master, and waits for him the time it takes to go around a reservoir, and then follows him as before, one doesn't ask him to explain or investigate their motives, birds don't have reasons, just instincts, often vague and involuntary as if they were not part of us, we spoke about instincts, but also about reasons and motives. So let us not ask José Anaiço who he is and what he does for a living, where he comes from and where he is going, whatever we find out about him, we shall only find out from him, and this description, this sketchy information will also have to serve for Joana Carda and her elm branch, for Joaquim Sassa and the stone he threw into the sea, for Pedro Orce and the chair he got up from, life does not begin when people are born, if it were so, each day would be a day gained, life begins much later, and how often too late, not to mention those lives that have no sooner begun than they are over, which has led one poet to exclaim, Ah, who will write the history of what might have been.

And now this woman called Maria Guavaira, such a strange name, who climbed up into the attic of the house and found an old sock, of the real old-fashioned kind that were used to keep money as safely as in any bank vault, symbolic hoardings, gratuitous savings, and upon finding the sock empty she set about unraveling the stitches to amuse herself, having nothing else with which to occupy her hands. An hour passed and another and yet another, and the long strand of blue wool is still unwinding, yet the sock does not appear to get any smaller, the four enigmas already mentioned were not enough, which shows us that at least on this occasion the contents can be greater than the container. The sound of the waves does not reach this silent house, the shadow of passing birds does not darken the window, there must be dogs but they do not bark, the earth, if it trembled, trembles no more. At the feet of the woman unraveling the thread is the mountain that goes on growing. Maria Guavaira is not called Ariadne, with this thread we shall not emerge from the labyrinth, perhaps it will help us to succeed at last in losing ourselves. Where is the end of this thread.

*T*he first crack appeared in a large slab of natural stone, as smooth as the table of the winds, somewhere in these mountains of Albères, which, at the eastern end of the Pyrenees, slope gently down to the sea and where the ill-starred dogs of Cerbère now rove, an allusion that is not inappropriate in time or place, for all these things, despite their appearances, are interconnected. Excluded, as has been stated, from any domestic sustenance, and consequently forced by necessity to recall in his unconscious memory the skills of his predatory ancestors in order to catch some stray rabbit, one of those dogs, Ardent by name and endowed with the acute hearing characteristic of the species, must have heard the stone cracking, for, although incapable of sniffing, the dog approached the stone, dilating his nostrils, his hairs bristling as much from curiosity as from fear. The crack, ever so fine, would remind any human observer of a line drawn with the sharpened point of a pencil, altogether different from that other line made with a branch on hard soil or in the loose, soft dust, or in the mud, should we choose to waste our time on such daydreams. But as the dog was approaching, the crack grew bigger, grew deeper and began to spread, splitting the stone up to the edges of the slab, and then all the way across, there was room to put a hand inside, a whole arm in width and length, had there been any man around with enough courage to cope with this phenomenon. The dog Ardent prowled around, agitated, yet unable to escape, attracted by the snake of which neither the head nor the tail could be seen, and suddenly he was lost, not knowing on which side to stay, whether in France, where he now found himself, or in Spain, no more than three spans away. But this dog, thanks be to God, was not one of those creatures who adapt to situations, the proof being that, with a single jump, he leapt over the abyss, if you'll pardon the obvious exaggeration in this expression, and ended up on this side, he preferred the infernal regions, and we shall never know what longings influence a dog's soul, what dreams, what temptations.

The second crack, but for the world the first, appeared a considerable distance away, toward the Bay of Biscay, not far from a place called Roncevalles, alas all too famous in the history of Charlemagne and his twelve Paladins, where Roland died when he blew on Oliphant, without Angelica or Durandal to come to his assistance. There, descending along the northeastern strip of the Sierra Abodi, runs the River Irati, which, originating in France, flows into the Spanish Erro, in its turn an affluent of the Aragón, which is a tributary of the Ebro, which, bearing all their waters, will finally deposit them in the Mediterranean. At the bottom of the valley, on the edge of the Irati, there is a town, Orbaiceta by name, and upstream exists a dam, or weir, as it is called in those parts.

It is time to explain that what is reported here, or may come to be reported, is the truth and nothing but the truth, as you may verify on any map, provided it is sufficiently comprehensive to include certain details that might seem insignificant, for that is the virtue of maps, they show what can be done with limited space, they foresee that everything can happen therein. And it does. We've already mentioned the rod of destiny, we've already shown that a stone, even if it be removed from the highest tidemark, can end up falling into the sea or make its way back to the shore, now it is the turn of Orbaiceta, where, after the salutary upheaval caused by the construction of the dam many years ago, calm had been restored, a city in the Province of Navarre and dormant amid mountains, now thrown into turmoil once more. For some days Orbaiceta became the nerve center of Europe, if not of the world, invaded by government ministers, politicians, civil and military authorities, geologists and geographers, journalists and mineralogists, photographers, film and television crews, engineers of every kind, inspectors and sightseers. But Orbaiceta's fame will not last for long, a few fleeting days, not much longer than the roses of Malherbe, and how long could the latter, grown on poor soil, have lasted, but we are talking about Orbaiceta, nothing else, until some more notable event is reported elsewhere, which is what happens with notable events.

In the history of rivers there had never been anything like it, water flowing eternally and suddenly it flows no more, like a tap abruptly turned off, as when someone is washing his hands in a basin after shutting off the tap, he pulls the plug, the water drains away, goes down the pipe, disappears, what has remained in the enameled basin will soon evaporate. To put it more aptly, the waters of the Irati retreated like waves that ebb from the shore and vanish, leaving the riverbed exposed, nothing but pebbles, mud, slime, fishes that gasp as they leap and die, then sudden silence.

The engineers were not on the spot when this incredible event took place, but they noticed that something abnormal had occurred, the dials on the observation panels indicated that the river had stopped feeding the great aquatic basin. Three technicians set off in a jeep to investigate the intriguing development, they made their way along the edge of the weir, considered the different possible hypotheses, they had plenty of time to do so for they traveled almost five kilometers, and one of those hypotheses was that a subsidence or landslide on the mountain might have diverted the river's course, another was that it might be the work of the French, typical Gallic perfidy, notwithstanding the bilateral agreement about fluvial waters and their hydroelectric uses, yet another hypothesis, and the most radical of all, was that the source, the fountainhead, the spring, had dried up, the eternity that appeared to exist but did not exist after all. On this point, opinions were divided. One of the engineers, a quiet man, the thoughtful type, and someone who enjoyed life in Orbaiceta, feared that they might send him to some remote place, the others rubbed their hands with glee, perhaps they might be transferred to one of the dams on the Tagus, or closer to Madrid and the Gran Vía. Debating these personal worries they reached the far end of the reservoir, where they found a drainage ditch but no river, nothing but a thin trickle of water still seeping from the soft earth, a muddy swirl that would not have enough power to turn a toy waterwheel. Where the devil can the river have got to, exclaimed the driver of the jeep, and he couldn't have been more forthright and explicit. Puzzled, amazed, uneasy and concerned, the engineers once more began discussing among themselves the various hypotheses mentioned earlier, and when they saw that there was nothing to be gained from this discussion, they returned to the offices attached to the dam, then went on to Orbaiceta where the administrators awaited them, having already been informed of the river's mysterious disappearance. There were recriminations, exclamations of disbelief, telephone calls to Pamplona and Madrid, and the final outcome of these exhausting discussions was expressed in an order of the utmost simplicity, broken down into three successive and complementary stages, follow the course of the river upstream, find out what happened, and say nothing to the French.

Next morning before sunrise, the expedition set out for the frontier, keeping alongside or in sight of the parched river, and when the inspectors arrived, weary, they realized that there would be no more Irati. Through a crack that could not have been more than three meters wide, the waters rushed into the earth, roaring like a tiny Niagara. On the other side, the French had already started to gather, it would have been sublimely naive to think that their neighbors, astute and Cartesian, would have failed to notice the phenomenon, but at least they showed themselves to be as amazed and dumbfounded as the Spaniards on this side, and all brothers in ignorance. The two sides got around to speaking, but the conversation was neither wide-ranging nor profitable, little more than exclamations of justified alarm, a tentative airing of new hypotheses on the part of the Spaniards, in short, a general atmosphere of irritation that could find no obvious target, the French were soon smiling, after all they continued to be masters of the river down to the frontier, they would not need to modify their maps.

That afternoon, helicopters from both countries flew over the area, took photographs, observers were lowered with windlasses and suspended over the cataract, they looked and saw nothing, only the black gaping hole and the curving line and the shining surface of the water. In order to make some useful progress, the municipal authorities of Orbaiceta on the Spanish side, and of Larrau on the French side, met near the river under a tent set up for the occasion and dominated by the three flags, the Spanish bicolor and the French tricolor alongside the flag of Navarre, with the intention of examining the tourist potential of a natural phenomenon that must certainly be unique in the world, and how it might be exploited to their mutual advantage. Having considered the inadequacy and undoubtedly makeshift nature of the methods of analysis at their disposal, the gathering failed to draw up any document defining the obligations and rights of each party, so a joint commission was nominated and entrusted with preparing an agenda for another formal meeting, with all possible haste. At the last minute, however, a complication arose that upset the relative consensus they had reached, this being the almost simultaneous interventions, in Madrid and Paris, of the two States' delegates to the permanent commission charged with settling boundary disputes. These gentlemen expressed grave misgivings. The first thing to do was to see where the hole was opening up, whether toward the Spanish side or toward the French side. It seemed a trivial detail, but once the essentials had been explained, the delicacy of the matter became clear. It was clearly beyond question that from now on the Irati belonged entirely to France, under the jurisdiction of the district authorities in the Lower Pyrenees, but if the crack was entirely on the Spanish side, in the province of Navarre, further negotiations would be needed, since both countries, in a sense, would bear an equal share. If, on the other hand, the crack extended to the French side as well, then the problem was entirely French, just as the respective primary resources, the river and the gaping hole, belonged to them. Faced with this new situation, the two authorities, concealing any mental reservations, agreed to keep in touch until some solution could be found to this crucial problem. In their turn, with a joint declaration that had been laboriously drafted, the two nations' Ministries for Foreign Affairs announced their intention of pursuing urgent talks within the scope of the aforesaid permanent commission for boundary matters, to be advised, as one would expect, by their respective teams of geodetic experts.

It was about this time that vast numbers of geologists from all over the world began to appear on the scene. Between Orbaiceta and Larrau there were already a considerable number of foreign geologists, if not quite as many as suggested earlier. But now all the wise men of this and other lands began to arrive in force, the inspectors of landslides and natural disasters, erratic strata and blocks, each carrying a tiny hammer in one hand, tapping on everything that so much as looked like stone. A French journalist called Michel, something of a wit, quipped to a Spanish colleague, a serious fellow named Miguel, who had already reported to Madrid that the crack was de-fi-nite-ly Spanish, or, to speak in geographical and nationalist terms, Navarrese, Why don't you people just keep it, was what the insolent Frenchman said, if the crack gives you so much pleasure and you need it so badly, after all, in the Cirque de Gavarnie alone we have a waterfall four hundred and twenty meters high, we don't need any inverted artesian wells. Miguel could have replied that on the Spanish side of the Pyrenees there are also plenty of waterfalls, and some of them very fine and high, but the problem was different here, a waterfall open to the sky presents no mystery, always looks the same, in full view of everyone, while in the case of the Irati, you can see where the crack originates, but no one knows where it ends, just like life itself. But it was another journalist, a Galician, moreover, who was passing through, as often happens with Galicians, who came up with the question that had yet to be asked, Where does this water go. This was at a time when geologists in both camps were engaged in scientific discussions, and the question, like that of a timid child, was barely heard by the person who is now putting it on record. Since the accent was Galician, therefore discreet and cautious, it was drowned out by Gallic rapture and Castilian bluster, but then others arrived to repeat the question, proudly claiming to have thought of it first, but then no one pays any heed to tiny nations, this is not a persecution mania, but a historical fact. The debate among the wise men had become almost incomprehensible for the layman, yet two basic theories emerged nonetheless from their discussions, that of the monoglaciologists and that of the polyglaciologists, both inflexible, and soon in opposition, like two conflicting religions, the one monotheist, the other polytheist. Certain statements even sounded interesting, such as the one about deformations, certain deformations that might be due either to a tectonic elevation or to an isotonic compensation for erosion. All the more so, they added, since our examination of the actual forms of the cordillera allows us to conclude that it is not old, that is to say, not old in geological terms. All this, probably, had something to do with the crack. After all, when a mountain is subjected to such play of traction, it is not surprising that there comes a day when it finds itself obliged to give way, to splinter, to collapse, or, as in this instance, to crack open. This was not the case with the great slab lying inert on the mountains of Alberes, but the geologists had not seen it, the slab was far away, in a remote spot, no one came near it, the dog Ardent chased after the rabbit and did not return.

After two days, the members of the commission for boundaries were engaged in field work, taking measurements with their theodolites, checking against their tables, calculating with their instruments, and comparing all these data against the aerial photographs, the French somewhat disgruntled because there was no longer any doubt that the crack was Spanish, as the journalist Miguel had been the first to argue, when suddenly there was news of another fracture. No more was said about tranquil Orbaiceta nor about the River Irati, now cut off, *sic transit gloria mundi* and of Navarre. The journalists, some of whom were women, swarmed on to the crucial site in the Eastern Pyrenees, fortunately endowed with excellent means of access, so many and so excellent that within a few hours everyone who mattered was assembled there, people had even come from as far away as Toulouse and Barcelona. The highways were congested, and by the time the police on both sides of the border intervened to divert the flow of traffic it was much too late, the cars stretched for kilometer after kilometer, mechanical chaos, it soon became necessary to take drastic measures, to make everyone turn back in the other lane, which meant pulling down barriers, jamming the sides of the road with cars, an inferno, the Greeks had good reason to locate hell in this region. Particularly useful in dealing with the crisis were the helicopters, those flying constructions or airships capable of landing almost anywhere, and, whenever it proves impossible to land, they imitate the hummingbird, drawing close until they almost touch the flower, the passengers do not need a ladder, a little jump and that is all, they enter the corolla at once, amid the stamens and pistils, breathing in the aroma, frequently that of naphtha and charred flesh. Heads lowered, they set off running, anxious to find out what has happened, some of them have come straight from the Irati, already experienced in structural geology, but not equipped to cope with anything quite like this.

The crack cuts across the road and the entire parking area and runs on, thinning out on both sides, heading toward the valley, where it disappears from sight, and winding up the mountain slope, until it finally vanishes among the bushes. We are standing right on the frontier, the real one, the line of separation in this nameless limbo between the stations of the two police forces, the *aduana* and the *douane*, *la bandera* and *le drapeau*. At a prudent distance, for one cannot rule out the possibility of a landslide if the edges of the ruptured area should cave in, technicians exchange phrases devoid of any meaning or purpose, one cannot refer to that babble of voices as dialogue, and, to make matters worse, use loudspeakers to hear each other better, while the experts, inside the pavilions, speak on the telephone, one minute among themselves, the next with Madrid and Paris. No sooner have they landed than the journalists are off to discover what happened, and they all pick up the same story with some embroidered variants, which they will embellish further with their imagination, but in simple language, the person who vouched for the occurrence was the motorist who, passing through as darkness fell, sensed his car give a sudden lurch, as if the wheels had bounced across a pothole in the middle of the road, and he got out to see what it was, thinking they might be resurfacing the road and had unwisely forgotten to put up a warning sign. By this time, the crack was half a span wide and at most some four meters long. The man, who was Portuguese, called Sousa, and traveling with his wife and parents-in-law, went back to the car and told them, It looks as if we're already in Portugal, would you believe it, there's an enormous pothole in the road, it's a miracle it didn't flatten the tires or snap the axle. It was no pothole, nor was it enormous, but the words, as we have written them, have one real advantage, simply because they are exaggerated, they allay fear, calm the nerves, why, precisely because they dramatize. The wife, without paying much attention to what he said, replied, You'd better take a look, and he decided to heed her advice, although that was not her intention, the woman's words were more an exclamation than an order, one of those exclamations that often serve as a reply, he got out of the car again and went to check the tires, fortunately there was no apparent damage. Within the next few days, back in his native Portugal, he will become a hero, be interviewed on radio and television, make statements to the press. You were the first to see it happen, Senhor Sousa, give us your impression of that terrible moment. He will repeat his story countless times, and he will always finish off his embroidered version of events with an anxious, rhetorical question, calculated to make the listener shudder as he himself shudders with delicious ecstasy. Just think, if the hole had been bigger, as they say it now is, we would have fallen in, God knows how far down, and the Galician must have been thinking more or less the same when he asked, as you may recall, Where does that water go.

How far, that is the crucial question. The first practical step would be to examine the damage, to check the depth, and then to study, define, and put into operation the appropriate measures in order to fill in the breach, no word could be more apt, it is universal, after all, and one is tempted to believe that someone thought of it one day, or invented it, so that it could be fittingly invoked whenever the earth should crack open. The investigation, once completed, registered a depth of little more than twenty meters, of no real significance, given the resources of modern engineering in carrying out public works. From Spain and from France, from near and from afar, concrete mixers were brought in, those interesting machines that with their simultaneous movements remind one of the earth in space, of rotation, of removal, and upon reaching the spot they poured out the concrete, torrential, measured to achieve the right effect with great quantities of rough stones and fast-setting cement. The filling-up operation was well under way when one imaginative expert suggested that they should attach some clamps, a method once used to heal human wounds, large clamps made of steel, which would secure the edges, assisting, as it were, and speeding up the process of closing the breach. The idea was approved by the bilateral commission coping with the emergency, the Spanish and French metallurgists immediately began carrying out the necessary tests, checking the alloy, the thickness and the section of the material, the relationship between the size of the spike that would be driven into the ground and the space covered, in short, technical details intended for the specialist and here mentioned somewhat superficially. The crack swallowed up the torrent of stones and gray sludge as if it were the River Irati pouring into the depths of the land, deep echoes could be heard coming from the earth, it was even speculated that there might be some gigantic hollow down below, a cavern, some kind of insatiable gorge, And if this is the case, there is no point in carrying on, you simply build a bridge over the gap, probably the easiest and most economical solution of all, and bring in the Italians, who have a great deal of experience when it comes to building viaducts. But, after God knows how many tons and cubic meters had been poured in, the sounding line registered a depth of seventeen meters, then fifteen, then twelve, the level of the concrete went on rising, the battle was won. The technicians, laborers, and policemen embraced each other, flags were waved, the television an- nouncers, excited, read the latest bulletins and gave their own opin- ions, praising this titanic struggle, this collective victory, international solidarity in action, even from Portugal, that tiny country, a convoy of ten concrete mixers set out, they have a long journey ahead, more than one thousand five hundred kilometers, an extraordinary achieve- ment, the cement they are carrying won't be necessary, but history will remember their symbolic gesture.

When the gap had finally been filled in, the general excitement exploded into wild euphoria, as if this were another New Year's Eve, with fireworks and the bullfight of São Silvestre. The air vibrated with the horns of the motorists who had not budged from the spot even after the roadways had been cleared, the trucks let off the hoarse bellowing of their *avertisseurs* and *bocinas*, and the helicopters hovered triumphantly overhead, like seraphim endowed with powers that were probably far from celestial. The cameras clicked incessantly, the television crews, overcoming their fears, moved in, and there, close to the edges of the crack that no longer existed, they filmed great layers of the rough concrete, the evidence of man's victory over the vagaries of nature. And this was how spectators, remote from the scene, in the comfort and safety of their own homes, were able to see pictures transmitted directly from the Franco-Spanish frontier at Coll de Pertus, laughing and clapping their hands and celebrating the event as if they themselves had been responsible for its success, this was how they saw, unable to believe their own eyes, the concrete surface, still moist, begin to shift and sink, as if the enormous mass were about to be sucked under, slowly but surely, until the gaping breach became visible once more. The crack had not widened, and this could only mean one thing, namely that the depth of the hole was no longer twenty meters, as before, but much deeper, God alone knew just how deep. The workers drew back in horror, but a sense of professional duty, which had become second nature, kept the cameras turning, shaking in their holders' hands, and the world could now see faces change their expression, in the wild panic shouting could be heard, cries of horror, there was a general stampede, within seconds the parking area was deserted, the concrete mixers were abandoned, here and there some were still working, the drums turning, filled with concrete that three minutes ago ceased to be necessary and was now quite futile.

For the first time, a shudder of fear went through the peninsula and nearby Europe. In Cerbère, not very far away, the people, running impulsively out into the streets like their dogs before them, said to each other, It was written, whensoever they should bark, the world would end, but it was not quite like that, it had never been written, but great moments call for great words and it is difficult to say why this expression, It was written, figures so prominently in books recording prophetic statements. With greater justification than anyone else, the terror-stricken inhabitants of Cerbère began to abandon the town, migrating en masse onto firmer soil, in the hope that they would be safe there from the world's encroaching end. In Banyuls-sur-Mer, Port-Vendrès, and Collioure, to mention only the villages and hamlets dotted along the coastline, there was not a living soul to be seen. The dead souls, having died, stayed behind, with that persistent indifference that distinguishes them from the rest of humanity, if anyone ever said otherwise, or suggested, for example, that Fernando Pessoa visited Ricardo Reis, the one being dead and the other alive, it was his foolish imagination and nothing else. But one of these dead men, in Collioure, stirred ever so slightly, as if hesitating, shall I go or not, but never into France, he alone knew where, and perhaps one day we shall know too.

Amid the thousand items of news, opinions, commentaries, and roundtable conferences that occupied the press, television, and radio the following day, the brief statement by an orthodox seismologist passed almost unnoticed. What I should dearly like to know is why all this is happening without so much as an earth tremor, to which another seismologist, of the modern school, pragmatic and flexible, replied, All will be explained in due course. Now, in a village in southern Spain, a man, listening to these conflicting opinions, left his house and set off for the city of Granada, to tell the television men that he had felt an earth tremor more than a week ago, that he had not spoken up sooner because he feared that no one would believe him, and that he was now here in person, so that people could see how a simple man can be more sensitive than. all the seismologists in the world put together. As luck would have it, a journalist listened to what he had to say, either out of heartfelt sympathy or because he was intrigued by the unusual occurrence, and this latest scoop was summed up in four lines, and, although there were no pictures, the news was given on television that night, with a cautious smile. Next day, Portuguese television, lacking any material of its own, took up the man's story and developed it further by interviewing a specialist in psychic phenomena who, to judge from his one important statement, could add nothing to what was already known on the subject, As in all situations of this kind, everything depends on one's sensibility.

Much has been said here about causes and effects, taking great care to weigh the facts, proceed logically, be guided by common sense, and reserve any judgment, for it must be clear to all that you cannot make a silk purse out of a sow's ear. It is only natural and right, therefore, that we should doubt that the line drawn on the ground by Joana Carda with an elm branch was the direct cause of the Pyrenees' cracking open, which is what has been insinuated from the beginning. But one cannot deny this other fact, which is entirely true, that Joaquim Sassa went off in search of Pedro Orce after having heard his name mentioned in the evening news bulletin, and having listened to what he had to say.

A loving mother, Europe was saddened by the misfortune of her westernmost lands. Along the entire Pyrenean cordillera, the granite split open, the cracks multiplied, other roads appeared to have been severed, other streams and torrents sank into the depths until they disappeared. Seen from the air, a continuous black line suddenly opened up on the snowcapped peaks like a trail of dust, where the snow was sliding and disappearing with the white sound of a tiny avalanche. The helicopters came and went incessantly, observing the summits and valleys aswarm with experts and specialists of every kind who might prove to be useful, geologists, these present of their own accord, although their habitual domain was currently obstructed, seismologists, perplexed, because the earth insisted on remaining firm, without so much as a tremor, not even a vibration, and also volcanologists, secretly hopeful, despite the clear sky, free of any signs of smoke or fire, the perfect, blue glaze of an August sky. The trail of smoke was merely a comparison, and we should never take comparisons literally, this or any other, unless we learn to treat them with caution. Human strength could do nothing on behalf of a cordillera that was opening up like a pomegranate, with no apparent suffering, and simply, who are we to know, because it had matured and its time had come. Only forty-eight hours after Pedro Orce had said what he said on television, it was no longer possible to cross the frontier at any point from the Atlantic to the Mediterranean, either on foot or by surface transport. And in the low-lying coastlands, the seas, each from its own side, began to find their way into new channels, mysterious unknown gorges, increasingly deeper, with those sheer walls, dropping vertically all the way, the clean cut exposing the arrangement of ancient and modern strata, the synclines, the intercalations of clay, the conglomerates, the extensive concretions of soft limestone and sandstone, the beds of shale, the black, siliceous rocks, the granites, and all the rest, which cannot be listed here because of the narrator's lack of knowledge and time. Now we know what reply should have been given to the Galician who asked, Where does this water go. It ends up in the sea, we should tell him, transformed into the finest rain, into dust, into a waterfall, depending on the height from which it drops and on the amount of water, no, no we are not talking about the Irati, that is some distance away, but you can be sure that everything will end up by conforming to the laws of nature, as jets of water, even as a rainbow, once the sun is able to penetrate the somber depths.

On both sides of the frontier, along a narrow strip extending about a hundred kilometers, the population abandoned their homes and withdrew to the relative security of the interior, but matters were complicated in the case of Andorra, which we were inexcusably forgetting, that's what tends to happen to little countries, which could just as easily have turned out to be bigger. At the beginning, as there was great uncertainty about the final outcome of the cracks, they existed on both sides, on the two frontiers, and also because some of the inhabitants were Spanish, others French, and yet others Andorran, each one gravitated to his native soil, so to speak, or was influenced by what seemed right or in his best interests at that moment, even if it meant breaking up families and other relationships. Finally, the continuous line of the fracture settled once and for all on the French border, several thousand French nationals were evacuated by air, in a brilliant rescue operation that was given the code name Mitre d'Evêque, a name that incurred the grave displeasure of the Bishop of Urgel, who unintentionally provided the inspiration, but this did not detract from his satisfaction when he realized that in future he would become the sole overlord of the principality, provided that the latter, barely encircled by the Spanish side, did not end up in the sea. All that was left in the desert created by the general evacuation were some military detachments who went around with a prayer on their lips, under the constant surveillance of the helicopters hovering overhead, ready to gather up personnel at the slightest sign of any geological instability, and, as one might expect, the inevitable looters, generally alone, for catastrophes always bring snakes out of their lairs, or their eggs, and who, in this case, just like the soldiers who shot them without pity or remorse, also went around with a prayer on their lips, just which prayer depended on the faith they professed, every living being has the right to the love and protection of his god, bearing in mind, in allowance and defense of the robbers, that one could argue that those who have abandoned their homes do not deserve to live there and enjoy them, besides, as the proverb rightly says, All birds eat corn, only the sparrow pays, let each of you decide whether there is any connection to be found between the general principle and this particular case.

This might be the moment to express our regret that this true story is not the libretto of an opera, for if it were we would stage an ensemble the like of which has never been heard before, with twenty voices comprising lyric and dramatic sopranos of every timbre, one by one, or in chorus, in succession or simultaneously, trilling their parts, namely the joint sessions of the Spanish and Portuguese governments, the total disruption of the electric transport system, the resolution adopted by the European Community, the stand taken by the North Atlantic Treaty Organization, the flight of tourists in panic, the attacks on airplanes, the congestion of traffic on the roads, the meeting between Joaquim Sassa and José Anaiço, their encounter with Pedro Orce, the agitation of the bulls in Spain, the nervousness of the horses in Portugal, the disquiet on the coasts of the Mediterranean, the disturbance of tides, the flight of the rich and their fortunes, shortly there will be no singers left onstage. Those who are curious, not to say skeptical, will want to know what is causing all these serious developments, as if the simple breaking up of the Pyrenees were not enough for them, with rivers turning into waterfalls and tides advancing several kilometers inland, after a recession that has lasted millions of years. At this point the hand falters, how can it plausibly write the words that are about to follow, words that will inevitably throw everything into jeopardy, all the more so since it is becoming extremely difficult, should such a thing ever be possible in life, to separate truth from fantasy. But now we must finish off what has remained in suspense, by striving to transform with words what can probably only be transformed with words, the moment has arrived, it has finally come, to reveal that the Iberian peninsula has suddenly broken away, all in one uniform piece, leaving a gap of ten whole meters, who would believe it, the Pyrenees have opened up from top to bottom as if some invisible ax had descended from on high, penetrating the deep cracks, clawing stone and earth down into the sea. Now we can certainly see the Irati dropping a thousand meters, falling headlong into infinity, the Irati opens to the wind and sun, a crystal fan or the tail of a bird of paradise, the first rainbow poised over the abyss, the first vertigo of the hawk hovering with drenched wings, tinged with seven colors. And we should also be able to see the Visaurin, Monte Perdido, the peaks of the Perdiguere and of Estats, two thousand meters, three thousand meters of steep slopes unbearable to behold, you cannot even trace their descent, because of the misty atmosphere in the distance, and then fresh clouds will appear as the gap widens, as certain as the existence of destiny itself.

Time passes, memories fade, we can scarcely perceive any longer the truth and the truths, once so clear and defined, and then, wishing to confirm what we ambitiously call the accuracy of the official version, we consult the evidence relating to the period, the various documents, newspapers, films, video recordings, chronicles, private diaries, parchments, especially the palimpsests, we question survivors, with much good will on either side, we even succeed in believing what some old man claims to have seen and heard as a child, and from all of this we shall have to draw some conclusion, in the absence of any convincing certainties one has to pretend, but what appears to be beyond question is that until the electric cables burst apart there was no real fear in the peninsula, although it has been stated to the contrary, of course there was some panic, but not fear, which is emotion of another order. Obviously, there are many people who retain a clear picture of the dramatic scenes at Coll de Pertus when the concrete disappeared from the sight of those who were shouting, We are winning, we are winning, but the episode only made an impression on those who were actually there, the others looked on from a distance, sitting at home before their own little stage, their television set, in that small rectangle of glass, that courtyard of miracles where an image sweeps away the previous one without trace, everything is on a reduced scale, even emotions. And those sensitive viewers, for they still exist, those viewers who start shedding tears at the slightest pretext and to disguise the lump in their throat, did what they usually do when they cannot bear it any longer, confronted by famine in Africa and other such calamities, they turned their eyes away. Besides, we must not forget that in vast areas of the peninsula, in the heart of the countryside where newspapers do not arrive and the television reception is poor, there were millions, yes, millions of people who did not see what was happening, or had only a vague idea, formed from words whose meaning they had only half digested, perhaps not even that, an idea that was so unreliable that there really was not much difference between what some people thought they knew and what others did not.

But when all the lights in the peninsula went out at the same time, a blackout they later referred to as *apagón* in Spain, *negrum* in a Portuguese village that still invents words, when five hundred and eighty-one square kilometers of land became invisible on the surface of the earth, then there was no longer any doubt, everything was coming to an end. It was just as well that the entire power cut lasted no more than fifteen minutes, then emergency connections were rigged that put domestic energy resources into action, scant at this time of the year, the height of summer, mid-August, dry, low reservoirs, a shortage of power stations, and these cursed nuclear installations, but the pandemonium was truly peninsular, demons on the loose, cold fear, bedlam, even an earthquake could not have had a worse effect on morale. It was night, the beginning of night, when most people have retired indoors, they are sitting watching television, in their kitchens the women are preparing dinner, one particularly patient father is helping, somewhat tentatively, with the solution of an arithmetic problem, there does not appear to be much happiness, but it soon became clear just how much this terror meant, this pitch-darkness, this ink stain that had fallen on Iberia. Do not take away the light, O Lord, let it return, and I promise you that until my dying day, I shall ask for nothing else, this was what penitent sinners were saying, but then they always exaggerate. Anyone living in a valley would have imagined himself to be inside a covered well, anyone living higher up would have climbed to the top and, for many leagues around, failed to see a single light, it was as if the earth had changed its orbit and was now traveling in a space without any sun. Trembling hands lit candles in the houses, flashlights, paraffin lamps kept for an emergency, but not like this one, brought out candlesticks in wrought silver, those in bronze that were used only as ornaments, brass candlesticks, long-forgotten oil lamps, dim lights that filled the darkness with shadows and allowed one to catch a glimpse of startled faces, as distorted as reflections on the water. There were many women shouting, many men were shaking, as for the children, all one can say is that they were all crying their hearts out. After fifteen minutes, which, as the saying goes, seemed like fifteen centuries, although there was no one who had lived the latter and was thus able to compare them with the former, the electricity came back, little by little, intermittent, the lamps were like sleepy eyes casting surly looks everywhere, ready to fall asleep again, until they could finally stand the light and hold it there.

Half an hour later, radio and television stations went back on the air, gave reports about the blackout, and so we learned that all the high-voltage cables between France and Spain had blown up, some pylons had collapsed, through some inexcusable oversight none of the engineers had remembered to disconnect the lines since it was impossible to cut them. Fortunately, the fireworks caused by the short circuits did not claim any victims, a most selfish way of putting it, for while it is true that no human lives were lost, one wolf, at least, did not escape the electrical discharge and was reduced to smoking cinders. But the blowing up of the cables was only one half of the explanation for the blackout, the other half of the explanation, despite the garbled form in which it was, deliberately, expressed, soon became clear, each man spelling things out to his neighbor, What they don't want to admit is that it's not just the cracks in the ground, otherwise the cables wouldn't have broken. Then you tell me, friend, what do you think happened, It's white and the hen lays it but this time it wasn't an egg, the cables broke because they were stretched, because the earth was pulled apart, that's what happened as sure as God is my Maker, You don't tell me, I'm telling you, I'm telling you, just you wait and see, they'll end up spilling the beans. And they did, but only the following day, when there were so many rumors flying about that one more, even if true, could not have added to the confusion, but they did not explain everything, or put it very clearly, they simply announced, and these were the exact words, An alteration in the geological structure of the Pyrenean cordillera has resulted in a continuous rupture, in a disjunction of physical continuity, and for the moment all communications by road between France and the peninsula are interrupted, the authorities are carefully monitoring the situation, air connections are being maintained, all airports are open and fully operational, and as from tomorrow the number of daily flights is likely to be doubled.

And how badly they were needed. When it became clear and beyond question that the Iberian peninsula had separated completely from Europe, as people began saying, The peninsula has broken away, hundreds of thousands of tourists, for as we know this was the peak season, hastily left their hotels, pousadas, paradores, inns, hostels, pensions, rented houses and rooms, camping sites, tents and caravans, without paying their bills, suddenly causing the most colossal traffic jams on the roads, which grew even worse when cars were left abandoned everywhere, it took some time but then it was like a lit fuse, people are generally slow in recognizing and accepting the seriousness of situations, the futility of having a car, for example, once the roads to France were cut off. Littered around the airports, like a flood, stood masses of cars of all sizes, models, makes, and colors, obstructing the roads and access ramps, all bunched up, completely disrupting the life of the local communities. The Spaniards and the Portuguese, having recovered from the frightening experience of finding themselves in a blackout, *apagón* or *negrum*, looked on in panic, thought it absurd, after all there had been no loss of life, Ah, these foreigners, take them out of their routine and they lose control, that's the price they pay for being so advanced in science and technology, and after passing this damning judgment they went off to choose, from among the abandoned vehicles, the ones that appealed to them most and best reflected their aspirations.

In the airports, the airline counters were assailed by the excited multitude, a furious babel of gestures and shouting, unheard-of bribes were offered and accepted in exchange for a ticket, people were selling and buying everything, jewels, cameras, clothes, drugs, these now being peddled quite openly, My car's outside, here are the keys and the papers, if you can't get me a seat to Brussels I don't mind going to Istanbul, even to hell, this tourist was one of the distracted ones, he couldn't see the forest for the trees. Overloaded, their bloated memories nearly saturated, the computers wavered, mistakes were multiplied, until the entire system was paralyzed. Tickets were no longer sold, the planes were stormed, such ferocity, the men first because they were stronger, then the fragile women and innocent children, a great many women and children were left crushed between the terminal gate and the boarding steps, these were the first casualties, and then there were a second and a third cluster of casualties when someone had the tragic idea of forcing his way through, brandishing a pistol, only to be tackled and knocked to the ground by the police. There were other weapons in the crowd and they were fired, there is little point in stating in which airport this disaster occurred, an abominable affair repeated in several other places, although with less serious consequences, for eighteen people died there.

Suddenly, someone remembered that you could also escape from seaports, this sparked another rush for salvation. The refugees turned back, once more in search of their abandoned cars, sometimes they found them, sometimes they did not, but what did that matter, if there were no keys or they could not be used, people soon put two and two together, anyone who did not know quickly learned, Portugal and Spain were transformed into an earthly paradise for car thieves. When the desperate tourists arrived at the ports they went in search of a small boat or canoe to carry them, or, better still, a trawler, a tugboat, a fast rowboat, a sailboat, and in this way they abandoned their last possessions in this cursed land, they departed with the clothes they were wearing and little else, a grubby handkerchief to blow their nose, a lighter without value or fluid, a tie no one had ever liked, it's not right that we should have profited so outrageously from the misfortune of others, we were like brigands from the coast robbing castaways of everything they possessed. The poor wretches disembarked wherever they could, wherever they were swept, and some were left on Ibiza, Majorca, or Minorca, on Formentera or the islands of Cabrera and Conejera, in the hands of fate, the hapless creatures were stuck, in a manner of speaking, between the devil and the deep blue sea, so far there is no evidence that the islands have moved, but who can tell what tomorrow may bring, the Pyrenees appeared to be solid for all eternity, and look what happened. Thousands upon thousands of refugees ended up in Morocco, having fled from the Algarve or from the Spanish coast, in the latter case from below the Cape of Palos, anyone who might have been north of the cape preferred to be taken straight to Europe, if at all possible, and they would ask, How much do you want to take me to Europe, and the first mate would cock an eye, purse his lips, look the refugee up and down assessing his means, You know, Europe is a hell of a long way from here, it's really halfway around the world, and there was no point in arguing. Such exaggeration, it's only ten meters by water, once when a Dutchman dared to advance this bit of sophistry, and a Swede backed him up, they were cruelly told, Oh, so it's only ten meters, then why don't you swim across, and they were forced to apologize and pay twice as much. The bartering flourished until the various countries jointly agreed to provide shuttles to transport their citizens en masse, but, even after this humanitarian measure got under way, certain sailors and fishermen continued to make a fortune, one must not forget that not all travelers are at peace with the law, some who were not were prepared to pay through the nose, not that they had any choice, for the naval forces of Portugal and Spain were patrolling the coasts assiduously, on full alert and under the discreet surveillance of naval squadrons of the other powers.

Some tourists, however, decided not to leave, they accepted the geological fracture as an irreversible act of fate, saw it as an imperious sign of destiny, and wrote to their families, at least they showed some consideration, to say that they no longer thought about them, that their world had changed, and their way of life, they were not to blame, on the whole they were people with little willpower, the sort of people who cannot make up their mind, leave everything for tomorrow, to-morrow, but this does not mean that they do not cherish dreams and desires, the sad thing is that they die before achieving or knowing how to achieve even a small part of them. Others opted for silence, they simply disappeared, they forgot and allowed themselves to be forgot-ten, well, any one of these cases by itself could make a novel, the story of how it turned out in the end, and, even if there is little or nothing to relate, no two human stories are ever the same.

But there are those who carry heavier burdens on their shoulders, burdens from which they cannot escape, so much so that when the nation's affairs are going badly we immediately start asking, Hey, what are you going to do about it, what are you waiting for, these outbursts of impatience are in some measure quite unjust, after all, poor things, they can't escape their destiny either, at best they can go to the Pres-ident and tender their resignation, but not during a crisis, for that would bring them into dishonor, history would judge severely any man in public life who took such a decision at a time like this when, strictly speaking, everything is going under. On both sides of the frontier, in Portugal and in Spain, the governments began making reassuring state-ments, they formally assured us that the situation does not give cause for any grave concern, a curious way of putting it, and that all the necessary steps are being taken to safeguard people and their property, finally the heads of government appeared on television, and then, to pacify troubled minds, their King also appeared over there and our President over here, *Friends, Romans, countrymen, lend me your ears*, they said, and the Portuguese and the Spaniards, gathered in their forums, replied with one voice, Of course, of course, *words, words, nothing but words.* Faced with the hostility of public opinion, the prime ministers of the two nations met at a secret location, first on their own, then accompanied by members of their respective governments. Jointly and separately, they held two days of exhaustive talks, before finally deciding to set up a joint committee to cope with the crisis, whose main objective would be to coordinate civil defense operations in the two countries, which would muster their respective resources, both technical and human, for mutual benefit, and use every expedient in order to deal with this geological challenge that had distanced the peninsula ten meters from Europe. If it doesn't get any worse, people whispered in corridors, the whole thing won't be too serious, you could even say that it will be one in the eye for the Greeks, a channel bigger than that of Corinth, so widely renowned. Even so, we cannot ignore the fact that our problems of communication with Europe, already so complicated in years gone by, will become explosive. Okay, so let's build some bridges, What worries me is that the channel will become so wide that ships will be able to navigate it, especially the tankers, that would be a severe blow for Iberian ports, and with consequences just as important, *mutatis mutandis*, of course, as those that resulted from the opening of the Suez Canal, in other words, northern and southern Europe would have a direct link, and be able to avoid the Cape route. And we end up watching the ships, a Portuguese commented, the others took him to mean the ships that would be passing through the new channel, but we Portuguese know perfectly well that the ships to which he was referring are altogether different, they carry a cargo of shadows, longings, frustrations, delusions and deceptions, their holds filled to the brim, Man overboard, they shouted, but no one went to his assistance.

During their meeting, as had been agreed beforehand, the European Community issued a solemn declaration, whereby it was made clear that the displacement of the Iberian countries toward the west would not jeopardize the agreements in force, all the more so since the separation was nothing more than a few meters, minimal, really, when compared with the distance that separates England from the continent, not to mention Iceland or Greenland, which have so little in common with Europe. This declaration, with its clear objectives, was what resulted from a heated debate among the members of the commission, during which some delegates displayed what can only be called a detached attitude, there is no more precise adjective, even going so far as to suggest that if the Iberian peninsula wished to go away then let it go, the mistake was to have allowed it to come in. Naturally, this was all said in fun, a *joke*, in these awkward international gatherings people also have to amuse themselves, there has to be more than just work, work, work, but the Portuguese and Spanish members strongly objected to this blatantly provocative remark, so anti-community in spirit, each quoting in his own language the well-known Iberian proverb, A friend in need is a friend indeed. A declaration of Atlantic solidarity was also requested from the North Atlantic Treaty Organization, but the reply, without being negative, came to be summed up in an unpublishable phrase, *Wait and see*, words, moreover, that didn't quite express the whole truth, considering that the bases of Beja, Rota, Gibraltar, El Ferrol, Torrejón de Ardoz, Cartagena and San Turjo de Valenzuela, not to mention smaller installations, had all been put on alert as a precautionary measure.

Then the Iberian peninsula moved a little farther, one meter, two meters, just to test its strength. The ropes that served as evidence, strung from one side to the other like those used by firemen when walls develop cracks and threaten to cave in, broke like ordinary string, some of the stronger ones uprooted the trees and posts to which they were tied. Then there was a pause, a great gust of wind could be felt rushing through the air, like the first deep breathing of someone awakening, and the mass of stone and earth, covered with cities, villages, rivers, woodlands, factories, wild scrub, cultivated fields, with all their inhabitants and livestock, began to move, a ship drawing away from harbor and heading out once more to an unknown sea.

This olive tree is *cordovil*, or *cordovesa*, or *cordovia*, what does it matter, for these three names are used indifferently on Portuguese soil, and the olive fruit it produces, because of its size and beauty, would be referred to here as the queen of olives but not as Cordovan, although we're closer to Cordoba than to the frontier beyond. These seem superfluous details of no real importance, melismatic vocalizations, the ornamental artifices of a plainsong that dreams of wings of sonorous melody, when it is much more important to speak of the three men seated beneath the olive tree, one of whom is Pedro Orce, the second Joaquim Sassa, the third José Anaiço, what prodigious events or deliberate manipulations could have brought them together in this place. But calling the olive tree *cordovil* will at least serve to show just how remiss the Evangelists were, when, for example, they confined themselves to writing that Jesus cursed the fig tree, this information should be enough for us but it isn't enough, no sir, after all, twenty centuries have passed and we still do not know whether the cursed tree produced white or black figs, early or late, of this or that variety, not that Christian doctrine is likely to suffer because of this omission, but historical truth most certainly suffers. Anyhow, the olive tree is *cordovil*, and three men are sitting under it. Beyond these hills, and invisible from here, there is a village where Pedro Orce once lived, and by a strange coincidence, the first of them, if this is the first of several coincidences, he and the village bear the same name, a fact that neither diminishes nor increases the verisimilitude of the story, a man can be called Metcalfe or Merryweather without being a butcher or a meteorologist. As we have already observed, these are coincidences and manipulations, but made in good faith.

They are sitting on the ground, in their midst can be heard the nasal twang of a radio that must have weak batteries, and the announcer is making the following statement, According to the latest measurements, the velocity of the peninsula's displacement has stabilized at around seven hundred and fifty meters per hour, more or less eighteen kilometers per day, that may not seem a lot, but if we work it out carefully, that means each minute we move away twelve and a half meters from Europe, and while we should avoid giving way to panic and despair, the situation is truly worrying. And it would be even more worrying if you were to say that we are talking about just over two centimeters and a bit per second, remarked José Anaiço, who was quick at making mental calculations, but incapable of carrying the computations out to tenths and hundredths, Joaquim Sassa asked him to be quiet, he wanted to listen to the announcer, and it was worth his while, According to the latest reports we have received, a great crack has appeared between La Línea and Gibraltar, therefore it is feared, bearing in mind the irreversible outcome of the fractures so far, that El Peñon may end up isolated in the middle of the sea, if this should happen there is no point in blaming the British, we are to blame, yes, Spain is to blame for not having known how to recover in good time this sacred piece of the fatherland, now it is too late, El Peñon itself is abandoning us. This man is an artist with words, said Pedro Orce, but the announcer had already changed his tone, had overcome his emotion. In Great Britain, the Prime Minister's office has issued a statement whereby the government of Her Majesty the Queen reaffirms what is referred to as British rights over Gibraltar, which have now been confirmed, we are quoting, by the incontrovertible fact that El Peñon or The Rock has detached itself from Spain, and all the negotiations that were proceeding toward an eventual, if somewhat problematic, transfer of sovereignty are thus unilaterally and definitively suspended, There are still no signs of the British Empire's imminent end, quipped José Anaiço. In a statement read in the House of Commons, Her Majesty's Loyal Opposition demanded that the north side of the island be fortified without delay, so as to transform the steep rock all around its perimeter into the wall of an unassailable fortress, proudly isolated in the middle of the now widened Atlantic, as a symbol of the enduring power of Albion. They're mad, Pedro Orce muttered, contemplating the heights of the Sierra de Sagra rising before him. For its part, the government, attempting to reduce the political impact of any claim, replied that Gibraltar, in its new geostrategic conditions would continue to be one of the jewels in the crown of Her Britannic Majesty, a formula that like the Magna Carta has the magnificent virtue of satisfying everyone, this ironic conclusion was provided by the announcer, who took his leave by saying, We'll be back with more news in an hour's time, barring any unforeseen circumstances. A flock of starlings flew past like a hurricane passing over a bare mountain, *vruuuuuuuuu*, Are they yours, asked Joaquim Sassa, and, without even turning around, José Anaiço replied, They're mine, he ought to know, for ever since that first day, amid the green fields of Ribatejo, they have scarcely ever been apart, only to eat and sleep, a man does not nourish himself on worms and scattered grains and a bird sleeps in the trees without any bedclothes. The flock flew around in a wide circle, fluttering, wings trembling, beaks drinking in the air and sunlight, the few clouds, white and piled high, navigated through space like galleons, the men, these like all others, looked at the different things, and, as usual, did not really understand them.

It certainly was not to listen to a transistor radio in one another's company that Pedro Orce, Joaquim Sassa, and José Anaiço gathered here, having traveled from such different places. For the last three minutes we have known that Pedro Orce lives in the village that lies hidden behind these hills, we have known from the outset that Joaquim Sassa came from the shores of northern Portugal, and José Anaiço, we now know for certain, was strolling through the fields of Ribatejo when he came across the starlings, and we would have guessed as much had we paid sufficient attention to the details of the landscape. What remains to be known is how the three men met one another and why they are hidden away here under an olive tree, unique in this spot, among rare and unruly dwarf trees that cling to the white soil, the sun is reflected on all around the plains, the air shimmers, this is the heat of Andalusia, and although we are surrounded by mountains, we suddenly become conscious of these material things, we have entered the real world, or it has forced its way in.

If one thinks about it, there is no beginning for things and persons, everything that began one day had begun before, the history of this sheet of paper, for example, just to take an item at hand, in order to be true and complete, would have to date back to the origins of the world, the plural has been used here deliberately instead of the singular, yet even so, we could ask whether those first origins were not simply points of transition, sliding ramps, this poor head of ours, subject to such exertions, an admirable head, nevertheless, which for all sorts of reasons is capable of going mad, except for this one.

There is, then, no beginning, but there was a moment when Joaquim Sassa left the spot where he found himself, on a beach in northern Portugal, perhaps Afife, that beach with the enigmatic stones, or better still A-Ver-o-Mar, which means Seaview, to arrive at the most perfect name imaginable for a beach, poets and novelists could not have invented anything better. From there Joaquim Sassa came, having heard that a certain Pedro Orce from Spain could feel the ground shaking beneath his feet when there were no tremors, this is the natural curiosity of someone who threw a heavy stone into the sea with a strength he didn't possess, all the more so since the peninsula wrenched itself away from Europe without any shock or pain, like a hair quietly falling, simply because it was willed by God, as the saying goes. He set out in his old Citroën Deux Chevaux, he did not say good-bye to his family, alas, for he has no family, nor did he give any explanation to the manager of the office where he works. This is vacation time, you can come and go as you please, now they don't even ask to see your passport at the frontier, you simply show your identity card and the peninsula is yours. On the seat, beside him, he carries a transistor radio, distracts himself by listening to music, the prattling of the announcers, sweet and soothing like an acoustic cradle, suddenly irritating, that was in normal times, now the ether is rippling with febrile words, the news coming in from the Pyrenees, the exodus, the crossing of the Red Sea, Napoleon's retreat. Here on the roads of the interior, there is little traffic, nothing in comparison to the Algarve, all that bustle and turmoil, or with Lisbon, and the highways going north and south, Portela airport looks now like a besieged stronghold, an invasion of ants, iron filings attracted by a magnet. Joaquim Sassa rolls peacefully through the shady lanes of La Beira, heading for a village called Orce, in the Province of Granada, on Spanish soil, where the aforesaid man lives who spoke on television. I'm going there to see if there is any connection between what happened to me and this business of someone who can feel the ground shaking under his feet, once you start imagining things, you start putting two and two together, more often than not you were mistaken, sometimes you hit the nail on the head, a stone thrown into the sea, the earth shaking, a cordillera that has split open. Joaquim Sassa is also traveling amid mountains, even if they can't be compared with those Titans, but suddenly he feels uneasy. Suppose the same thing were to happen here, suppose A Estrela were to crack, the Mondego to sink into the bowels of the earth leaving the autumn poplars without a mirror in which to reflect themselves, his thoughts have become poetic, the danger has passed.

At this moment, the music stopped, the announcer began to read the news, there was nothing fresh to report, the only item of any interest, was a bulletin from London, the Prime Minister had gone to the House of Commons to state, categorically, that British sovereignty over Gibraltar warrants no discussion, whatever the distance separating the Iberian peninsula from Europe, to which the leader of the opposition had added a formal guarantee promising the most loyal cooperation from his fellow members and party, At this great moment in our history. But he then introduced a note of irony into his solemn speech, eliciting laughter from all the honorable members, The Prime Minister committed a serious mistake by speaking of a peninsula when referring to what is now unquestionably an island, although by no means as solid as our own, *of course.* The members of parliament cheered this closing remark, exchanging complacent grins with their opponents, and to be sure, there is nothing like the national interest to unite politicians of opposing tendencies. Joaquim Sassa also grinned, Such a comedy, and then suddenly he caught his breath, the announcer had spoken his name, Senhor Joaquim Sassa, who is traveling somewhere in the country, is kindly requested, we repeat, Senhor Joaquim Sassa is kindly requested, they were asking him kindly to present himself as soon as possible to the nearest officials, in order to assist the authorities with their investigations into the causes of the geological fracture observed in the Pyrenees, for the competent bodies are convinced that the aforesaid Joaquim Sassa can give them information of national interest, we repeat our appeal, Senhor Joaquim Sassa is requested, but Senhor Joaquim Sassa was not listening, he had been obliged to stop the car in order to recover his composure, his sangfroid, so long as his hands continued to tremble like this he would not even be able to drive, his ears were roaring like a seashell, Good heavens, how did they find out about the stone, there wasn't another soul on the beach, at least as far as I could see, and I didn't say a word to anyone, for they would have called me a liar, but someone somewhere must have been watching me after all, although no one usually pays any attention to someone throwing stones into the water, yet they spotted me at once, rotten luck, and then you know what happens, one person speaks to another and adds on what he thought he saw but could not have seen, when this story reached the ears of the authorities, the stone must have been as big as I am, at the very least, and now what am I going to do. He would not answer the appeal, he would not present himself to any civil or military official, just imagine what an absurd dialogue that would be, behind closed doors, the tape recorder playing, Senhor Joaquim Sassa, did you throw a stone into the sea, I did, How much would you say it weighed, I don't know, perhaps two or three kilos, Or more, Yes, it could have been more, Here are some stones, try holding them, and tell me which one comes closest in weight to the stone you threw, This one, Let's weigh it, like so, all right now, please check the weight with your own eyes, I'd never have thought it could weigh so much, five kilos, six hundred grams, Now tell me, have you ever experienced anything like this before, Never, Are you certain, Absolutely, You don't suffer from any mental or nervous disorders, epilepsy, somnambulism, trances of any kind, No sir, We'll take an electroencephalogram later, for the moment try your strength on this machine over here, What is it, A dynamometer, put as much pressure on it as you can, This is all I can do, Is that all, I've never had much strength in my arms, Senhor Joaquim Sassa, you couldn't possibly have thrown that stone, I'm inclined to agree, but I did, We know that you threw it, there are witnesses, persons of the utmost reliability, so you must tell us how you managed it, I've already explained, I was walking along the beach when I saw the stone, I picked it up and threw it, That's impossible, The witnesses can confirm it, True, but the witnesses cannot say where that strength came from, only you can tell us, I've already told you I don't know, The situation, Senhor Sassa, is very serious, I'd go so far as to say exceedingly serious, the rupture of the Pyrenees cannot be explained by natural causes, otherwise we would be in the midst of a planetary catastrophe, it was on the basis of this evidence that we began to investigate certain unusual events that have taken place in recent days, and yours is one of them, Surely throwing a stone into the water couldn't cause a continent to crack up, I have no desire to engage in idle philosophizing, but do you see any connection between a monkey's descending from a tree twenty million years ago and the making of a nuclear bomb, The connection is, precisely, those twenty million years, Good answer, but now let's suppose that it might be possible to reduce to hours the time between a cause, which in this case would be the throwing of a stone, and an effect, such as the peninsula's separation from Europe, in other words, let us suppose that, under normal conditions, that stone thrown into the sea would only produce its effect twenty million years hence, but that, under other conditions, precisely those of the phenomenon we are now investigating, the effect is observed some hours, or days, later, That's pure speculation, the cause might well be something else, Or a combination of this and another, concurrent, event, Then other unusual events would have to be investigated, That's what we're in the process of doing, and the Spaniards, too, as in the case of the man who could feel the earth shaking, By adopting this method, once you have examined the unusual events, you will have to proceed to the usual ones, The what ones, The usual ones, What do you mean by usual, Usual is the opposite of unusual, its antonym, If necessary, we shall pass from the unusual to the usual events, but we must discover the cause, You have a lot of investigating ahead of you, We're making a start, tell me where you found the strength. Joaquim Sassa made no reply, he silenced his imagination, all the more so since the dialogue was threatening to go around in circles, now he would have to repeat, I don't know, and the rest would be as before, with some minor variations, albeit mostly of form, yet this was precisely where he would have to be careful, because, as we know, through form one arrives at the substance, through the wrapping at the contents, through the sound of the word at its meaning.

He put his Deux Chevaux into gear, into step, if such a thing might be said of a car, he wanted time to think, he needed to give the matter some serious thought. He had been an ordinary traveler heading for the border, a simple man with no particular qualities or importance, that was no longer so, at this very moment they were probably printing posters with his photograph and vital statistics, *Wanted* in big red letters, a manhunt. He looked into his rearview mirror and saw a police car, it was coming so quickly that it looked as if the car were about to come through the back window, They've caught up with me, he accelerated, then quickly slowed down without braking, all quite unnecessary, the police car overtook him in a flash, it must be rushing to some emergency, they did not so much as look at him, if only those speeding policemen knew who was driving along there, but of course there are lots of Deux Chevaux on the road, the expression is awkward but there is no mathematical contradiction. Joaquim Sassa took another look in the mirror, this time to have a good look at himself, to acknowledge the relief in his eyes, the mirror reflected little else, a tiny bit of his face, which makes it difficult to know to whom the face belongs, to Joaquim Sassa, as we already know, but who is Joaquim

Sassa, a man who is still young, in his thirties, closer to forty than to thirty, the day inevitably comes, his eyebrows are black, his eyes brown like those of most Portuguese, his nose sharply outlined, his features really quite unexceptional, we shall learn more about him when he turns toward us. For the moment, he thought to himself, It's only an appeal over the radio, the worst is still ahead of me, at the frontier, and as if that weren't enough, there's this name of mine, Sassa, which unfortunately means stone, when what I need right now is to be any old Sousa, like that other one from Coll de Pertus, one day he consulted the dictionary to see if the word existed, Sassa, not Sousa, and what did he find, he discovered that it was a massive tree from Nubia, that's a pretty name, Nubia, a name for a woman, near the Sudan, in West Africa, page 93 in the atlas, And tonight, where am I going to sleep, certainly not in a hotel, where people are always turning the radio on, by this time every hotel in Portugal must be looking out for hotel guests who request a room for one night, the refuge of the persecuted, you can imagine the scene, Let's see now, yes sir, we have an excellent room available, on the second floor, Room 201, Pimenta, please show Senhor Sassa to his room, and no sooner is he resting on the bed, still fully clothed, than the manager, nervous and flustered, is on the telephone, He's here, come quickly.

He parked Deux Chevaux at the side of the road, got out to stretch his legs and clear his mind, which, instead of giving him good advice, came up with a dubious proposition, Stay in a bigger city, somewhere where there's plenty of nightlife, look for a brothel, spend the night with one of the prostitutes, you can bet they won't ask to see any identification as long as you pay, and if under the circumstances you don't feel like gratifying your flesh, at least you'll be able to get some sleep, and you'll pay less than you would in a hotel, How ridiculous, said Joaquim Sassa in reply to this suggestion, the solution is to sleep in the car, by the side of some quiet road off the beaten track. But suppose some tramps or gypsies came along, they might attack you, rob you, maybe even kill you, It's peaceful around here, But suppose some arsonist or madman were to set the pine forests on fire, there's a lot of those around these days, you would wake up to find yourself surrounded by flames, end up being burned to death, that must be the worst way to die, from what I've heard, just think of the martyrs of the Inquisition. How ridiculous, Joaquim Sassa repeated, I've made up my mind, I'm going to sleep in the car, and he made the image disappear, easy enough if one is strong-willed. It was still early, he could cover some forty or fifty kilometers along these winding roads, he would camp near Tomar, or Santarém, in one of those dirt roads that open onto cultivated fields, with those deep furrows once made by ox-drawn carts and nowadays made by tractors, no one passes at night, Deux Chevaux can be hidden anywhere around here, I might even sleep out in the open, the night is so warm, his mind did not react to this idea and clearly disapproved.

He did not stop in Tomar, nor reach Santarém, he dined incognito in a town on the banks of the Tagus, the local inhabitants are inquisitive by nature, but not to the extent of saying, point-blank, to the first traveler who arrived, Tell me, what's your name, but if he were to linger here, then certainly they would very soon start asking questions about his past life and his plans for the future. The television was on, as he ate his dinner Joaquim Sassa watched the last part of a documentary about underwater life, with numerous shoals of tiny fishes, undulating rays and sinuous moray eels, and an ancient anchor, then came the commercials, some fast-moving, built of images in dazzling montage, others deliberately, voluptuously, slow, like some achingly familiar gesture, there were children's voices shouting loudly, the insecure voices of adolescents, or of women who were somewhat hoarse, the men were all virile-sounding baritones, at the back of the house the pig grunted, fattened on slops and leftovers. At last the news came on, and Joaquim Sassa shuddered, he wouldn't stand a chance if they showed his photograph. The appeal was read, but no photograph appeared, they were not pursuing a criminal, after all, they were simply requesting, with polite insistence, that he make his whereabouts known, thus serving the highest national interest, no citizen worthy of the name would shrink from fulfilling such a duty, would fail to appear before the authorities, who simply wished him to make a statement. Three other guests were eating dinner, an elderly couple, and at another table the usual man, sitting by himself, of whom one always says, He must be a commercial traveler.

The conversation ceased when they heard the first news from the Pyrenees, the pig went on grunting but no one paid any attention, and, all this in an instant, the landlord got up on a chair to turn up the volume, the girl who waited on the tables stood wide-eyed, the guests carefully rested their silverware on the edge of their plates, and little wonder, on the screen they were showing a helicopter that was being filmed from another helicopter, both were entering the fearsome channel, and then they showed the towering walls, so tall that the sky was scarcely visible overhead, the merest thread of blue, Good heavens, it's enough to make you dizzy, the girl said, and the landlord snapped, Be quiet, now extremely powerful floodlights were showing the gaping hole, this is what the Greeks' notion of the entrance to hell must have looked like, but where Cerberus would have barked, a pig is grunting, mythologies aren't what they used to be. These dramatic pictures, the announcer reeled off, were taken under hazardous conditions, human lives were at risk, the voice became husky, muffled, the two helicopters transformed themselves into four, the phantoms of phantoms, Damned aerial, the landlord muttered.

By the time sound and picture were once more stable and intelligible, the helicopters had disappeared and the announcer was reading the same old appeal, now addressed to the public at large, Anyone who may know of any strange events or inexplicable phenomena, of anything that seems suspicious, is requested to inform the nearest authorities at once. Prompted by these words addressed directly to her, the girl remembered how people had gossiped locally when a kid had been born with five legs, four black and one white, but the landlord shot back, That was months ago, you fool, kids with five legs and chicks with two heads are nothing out of the ordinary, now what's really odd is this business of the teacher's starlings, What starlings, what teacher, Joaquim Sassa asked, The local teacher, his name is José Anaiço, for some days now, wherever he goes, he is followed by a flock of starlings, as many as two hundred of them, Or more, the commercial traveler corrected him, only this morning I saw them as

I was arriving, they were circling above the school, and the racket they were making, flapping their wings and screeching, was unbelievable. At this point the elderly man interrupted, Unless I'm mistaken, we should inform the mayor about the starlings, He already knows, the landlord observed, He knows all right, but he doesn't connect the one thing with the other, he can't tell his ass from his elbow, if you'll forgive the expression, Then what should we do, Let's go and talk to him tomorrow morning, besides it would be good publicity for the region if the story were on television, it would be good for our economy, But let's keep it a secret among ourselves, not tell anyone, And that teacher, where does he live, Joaquim Sassa asked as if he were not really very interested in the answer, so the distracted landlord was not in time to prevent the girl from blurting out, He lives in the teacher's house right next to the school, there's always a lighted window even late at night, there seemed to be a note of sadness in her voice. Furious, the landlord scolded the poor girl, Shut your mouth, imbecile, you'd better go and see if the pig needs feeding, hard to imagine a more foolish command, for pigs do not eat at this hour, they are usually asleep, perhaps the landlord's angry outburst was caused by worry, for here, too, in the stables and paddocks around the countryside, the mares neigh and shake their heads, nervous, restless, and in their impatience they paw the loose gravel on the ground, tear at the straw. It must be the moon, in the opinion of the foreman.

Joaquim Sassa paid for his dinner, said goodnight, left a generous tip in recompense for the information the girl had given him, the landlord might pocket it, out of pique rather than greed, people's generosity is no better than their deepest selves, no less subject to eclipses and contradictions, rarely constant, as in the case of this girl, scolded and abruptly dismissed, now trying unsuccessfully to feed a pig that is not hungry, scratching its forehead between the eyes. The evening is pleasant, Deux Chevaux is resting beneath the plane trees, refreshing its wheels in the water that runs idly from the spring, and Joaquim Sassa lets it stay there, goes on foot to look for the school and the illuminated window, people cannot hide their secrets even though they may say they wish to keep them, a sudden shriek betrays them, the sudden softening of a vowel exposes them, any observer with experience of the human voice and human nature would have perceived at once that the girl at the inn is in love. The town is nothing but one large village, in less than half an hour you can walk past all the houses from one end to the other, but Joaquim Sassa will not have to walk quite so far, he asked a little boy he met where the school was and could not have found a better-informed guide, You take that street there, you come to a square, you see a church, you turn left, then you keep to the right, you can't go wrong, you'll see the school right away, And does the teacher live there, Yes sir, he does, there's a light in the window, but there was no hint of love in any of these words, the boy is probably a bad pupil and school is his first experience of purgatory, but his voice suddenly became cheerful, children are never resentful, that is their saving grace, And the starlings are always flying overhead, and they're always screeching, if he does not abandon his studies too soon, the boy will learn to shape his sentences without repeating the same constructions so insistently.

There is still a clear patch in one half of the sky, the other half has not completely darkened, the sky is blue as if dawn were about to break. But inside the houses the lights are already on, the tranquil voices of weary people can be heard, quiet sobbing from a cradle, people are really so lacking in awareness, you put them out to sea on a raft and they go on living their lives as if they were still on terra firma, babbling like Moses when he floated down the Nile in a little basket made of rushes, playing with the butterflies, so blessed that even the crocodiles could not harm him. At the end of the narrow street is the school, surrounded by its walls, had Joaquim Sassa not been warned he would have thought the house was just a house like any other, at night they all look drab, by day some are still drab, meanwhile darkness has started falling, but some time remains before the street lamps will light up.

In order not to contradict the girl at the inn and the little boy who kept his feelings to himself, there is a light in the window, and Joaquim Sassa goes and knocks on the pane, the starlings are not so noisy after all, they are settling down for the night, with their habitual squabbling and neighborly disputes, but it will not be long before they calm down beneath the enormous leaves of the fig tree where they are roosting, invisible, black amid the inky darkness, only later will the moon rise, some will stir at the touch of its white fingers before going back to sleep, they do not know how far they will have to travel. From inside the house came a man's voice, Who is it, and Joaquim Sassa replied, If you don't mind, magic words that substitute for any formal identification, language is full of these and other more perplexing enigmas. The window has opened, against the light it is not easy to see who lives in this house, but as if in compensation Joaquim Sassa's face is perfectly clear, some of his features we described earlier, the rest conform, dark brown hair, smooth, sunken cheeks, the nose quite commonplace, the lips full only in speech, Forgive me for disturbing you at this hour, It isn't late, said the teacher, but he had to raise his voice because the starlings, now disturbed, sent up a chorus of protest and alarm, It's really because of them that I'd like to talk to you, Them, who, The starlings, Ah, And about a stone I threw into the sea, much heavier than I can manage, What is your name, Joaquim Sassa, Are you the person they keep mentioning on the radio and on television, That's me, Please come in.

They have spoken about stones and starlings, now they are speaking about decisions taken. They are in the yard behind the house, José Anaiço is seated on the doorstep, Joaquim Sassa in a chair since he is a visitor, and because José Anaiço is sitting with his back to the kitchen where the light is coming from, we still do not know what he looks like, this man appears to be hiding himself, but this is not the case, how often have we shown ourselves as we really are, and yet we need not have bothered, there was no one there to notice. José Anaiço poured a little more white wine into their glasses, they are drinking it at room temperature, which is how it should be drunk, in the opinion of experts, rather than this modern fad of chilling the wine, something in any case out of the question here, because there is no refrigerator in the teacher's house. That's enough for me, said Joaquim Sassa, after the red wine I had with dinner, I've already passed my limit. Let's drink to the trip, replied José Anaiço, and he smiled, showing the whitest of teeth, a detail worth noting. It makes good sense to go off in search of Pedro Orce, since I'm still on vacation, no commitments, Me too, and for much longer, until the schools reopen at the beginning of October, I'm on my own, So am I, It wasn't my intention to come here to persuade you to accompany me, I didn't even know you, I'm the one who's asking you to take me along, if there's room in your car, but you've already agreed and you can't go back on your word now. Just imagine all the excitement there'll be when they discover you've gone, most likely they'll call the police at once, start thinking you're already dead and buried, hanging from some tree, or lying at the bottom of the river, obviously they'll suspect me, the stranger with superhuman strength who turned up from nowhere, asked some questions, and disappeared, it's like something out of a book, I'll leave a note on the door of the town hall saying that I had to leave unexpectedly for Lisbon, I hope no one remembers to go and ask at the station if anyone saw me buy a ticket.

For several moments they remained silent, then José Anaiço rose to his feet, took a few steps in the direction of the fig tree as he drank the rest of his wine, the starlings kept on screeching and began to stir uneasily, some had awakened as the men spoke, others, perhaps, were dreaming aloud, that terrible nightmare of the species, in which they feel themselves to be flying alone, disoriented and separated from the flock, moving through an atmosphere that resists and hinders the flapping of their wings as if it were made of water, the same thing happens to men when they are dreaming and their will tells them to run and they cannot. So we'll leave an hour before sunrise, José Anaiço said, and now we must get some sleep. Joaquim Sassa rose from his chair, I'll sleep in the car and come to get you before dawn, Why don't you sleep here, I've only one bed but it's wide, there's plenty of room for both of us. It was a clear night, the vast expanse of the sky dotted with stars, so close, it seemed, that they might have been magically suspended motes of glass dust, or a snow-white veil, and the great constellations shone dramatically, the morning star, the two Bears, the Pleiades, a fine shower of tiny crystals of light fell on the two men's upturned faces and clung to their skin, got caught in their hair, it was not the first time this phenomenon had occurred, but suddenly all the murmurings of the night fell silent, above the trees the first light of the moon appeared, now the stars must go out. Then Joaquim Sassa said, On a night like this, I might even sleep under the fig tree, if you can lend me a blanket, I'll keep you company. They gathered and then spread enough straw for their beds, as one does for cattle, each one spread out his blanket, lying down on one half and covering himself with the other. The starlings watched their shadowy forms from the branches, Who can that be, beneath the tree, among the branches everything is wide awake, and with a moon like this, getting to sleep is going to be very difficult. The moon is rising swiftly, the squat, rotund crown of the fig tree transforms itself into a black and white labyrinth, and José Anaiço remarks, These shadows are not what they were, The peninsula has moved so little, a few meters, it can't have had much effect, Joaquim Sassa observed, pleased at having understood the remark, It has moved, and that was enough for all the shadows to change, there are branches there that the moonlight is touching for the first time at this hour. Some minutes passed, the starlings began to settle down, and José Anaiço murmured, in a voice that sleep finally interrupted, each word waiting or searching for the next one, Once upon a time, our King, Dom João II, known as the Perfect King and in my opinion the perfect wit, made a certain nobleman a gift of an imaginary island, now tell me, do you know of any other nation where such a thing could happen, and the nobleman, what did the nobleman do, he set out to look for it, now, what I'd like to know is how you can find an imaginary island, That's something I can't tell you, but this other island, the Iberian one, which was once a peninsula but is no longer, I find just as amusing, as if it had set out to sea in search of imaginary men. Nicely phrased, couldn't be more poetic. Well, let me assure you that I've never written a line of verse in my life, Don't worry, if all men were to become poets, none would write verses. That phrase also has a certain charm, We've had too much to drink, I agree. Silence, calm, infinite harmony, and Joaquim Sassa murmured, as if he were dreaming, What will the starlings do tomorrow, will they stay or will they accompany us, When we leave we'll find out, it's always the same, José Anaiço said, the moon is lost among the branches of the fig tree and will spend all night searching for a way out.

It was still dark when Joaquim Sassa rose from his bed of straw to go and look for Deux Chevaux, which had been parked under the plane trees in the square, right beside the fountain. To avoid being seen together by some early riser, of whom there are many in farming communities, they had agreed to meet on the outskirts of the village, at some distance from the last houses. José Anaiço would turn off the main road, take side roads and short cuts, keeping well out of sight, Joaquim Sassa, however, would discreetly take the main road used by everyone, he was one of those travelers who go neither in debt nor in fear, he set out early to enjoy the fresh morning air and to make the most of the day, tourists who are out and about early are like this, at heart troubled and restless, unable to accept life's inescapable brevity, late to bed and early to rise does not make one healthy, but it does prolong life. Deux Chevaux has a quiet engine, the ignition is as smooth as silk, only the few inhabitants who could not sleep heard anything, and these thought they had finally fallen asleep and were dreaming, in the stillness of dawn even the steady noise of a water pump can scarcely be heard. Joaquim Sassa left the village, passed the first bend, then the second, then brought Deux Chevaux to a halt and waited.

In the silvery depths of the olive grove the trunks started to become visible, there was already a touch of humidity in the air, the faintest hint of a breeze, as if the morning were emerging from a well of clouded water, and now a bird sang, or were his ears deceiving him, for not even the larks sing at this early hour. Time passed and Joaquim Sassa began muttering to himself, Perhaps he's thought it over and decided not to come, but he didn't strike me as being like that, or perhaps he had to take a much more roundabout way than he imagined, that must be the explanation, and then he's carrying a heavy suitcase, that's something I overlooked, I could have carried it to the car myself. Then, from amid the olive trees, emerged José Anaiço, surrounded by starlings, a frenzy of wings ruffling continuously, strident cries, whoever mentioned two hundred is unable to count, this reminds me more of a swarm of big black bees, but what Joaquim Sassa obviously had in mind were the birds in Hitchcock's classic film, although those were wicked assassins. José Anaiço approaches the car with his garland of winged creatures, he comes smiling, which makes him look younger than Joaquim Sassa, for, as everyone knows, a serious expression makes one look older, he has the whitest of teeth, as we discovered last night, and while there is nothing remarkable about any individual feature, there is a certain harmony in those sunken cheeks, besides, no one is obliged to be good-looking. He put his suitcase into the car, climbed in beside Joaquim Sassa, and before closing the door looked out to see the starlings, Let's go, I wondered what they would do, but you can see for yourself, If we had a rifle here and fired a few shots, two cartridges of buckshot would finish them off, Are you a hunting man, No, I'm only repeating what I've heard others say, We don't have a rifle, Perhaps there might be another solution, I'll get Deux Chevaux moving, and the starlings will be left behind, they're a species with short wings and little stamina, Try. Deux Cheveaux changed gear, accelerated on a long stretch of straight road, and, taking advantage of the flat terrain, soon left the starlings behind. The morning light became tinged with contrasting shades of pale and bright pink, colors fallen from the sky, and the air turned blue, we repeat, the air and not the sky, as we also observed yesterday evening, these hours are much the same, the one beginning the day, the other ending it. Joaquim Sassa switched off the headlights and reduced speed, he knows that Deux Chevaux was not destined for such bold exploits, its ancestry is undistinguished, anyway, the car has seen better days and the engine's tameness is nothing more than stoic resignation, Good, that's the end of the starlings, these were the words of José Anaiço, but there was a note of regret in his voice.

Two hours later, in the Province of Alentejo, they stopped for a bite to eat, coffee with milk, cinnamon-flavored sponge cakes, then they returned to the car, chewing over the same old worries, The worst thing that could happen wouldn't be to find myself barred from Spain, it would be much worse if they were to keep me there, You haven't been accused of anything, They can invent some pretext, detain me for questioning. Don't worry, before we reach the frontier we're sure to find some means of getting across, this was their dialogue, which adds nothing to our understanding of the story, perhaps it was only put here so that we would understand that Joaquim Sassa and José Anaiço are already on familiar terms, something they must have decided during the journey. Let's not stand on ceremony, one of them said, and the other replied, I was just about to make the same suggestion. Joaquim Sassa was on the point of opening the car door when the starlings reappeared, that enormous cloud, resembling more than ever some great swarm whirling overhead and making a deafening noise, one could see that they were angry, people standing beneath them stopped and looked up, pointed to the sky, someone declared, I've never seen so many birds together in my whole life, and to judge from his appearance he was old enough to have had this experience and many others, There are more than a thousand of them, he added, and he was right, at least twelve hundred and fifty birds had gathered on this occasion, They've finally caught up with us, said Joaquim Sassa, let them wear themselves out and we'll be rid of them for good. José Anaiço watched the starlings as they flew triumphantly in a great circle, he stood there transfixed, staring at them intently, Let's drive slowly, from now on we'll go slowly, Why, I don't know, it's just a premonition, for some reason these birds won't leave us alone, You could be right, so do me a favor and go slowly, and we'll see what happens.

How they crossed the Alentejo in this blazing heat, under a sky more white than blue, amid shining stubble with the occasional holm oak on the bare land and bundles of straw waiting to be gathered, beneath the incessant chirping of the cicadas, would make a whole story in itself, perhaps even harder to tell than that other one I recounted on an earlier occasion. It's true that for kilometer after kilometer along this road there is not a living soul to be seen, but the corn has been cut, the grain threshed, and all these tasks required men and women, but on this occasion we shall learn nothing about all this, all too true is the proverb that warns us, Don't count your chickens before they're hatched. The heat is oppressive, suffocating, but Deux Chevaux is in no hurry, is only too pleased to stop wherever there is a little shade, then José Anaiço and Joaquim Sassa get out to scan the horizon, they wait as long as they have to, finally it comes, the only cloud in the sky, these stops wouldn't be necessary if the starlings knew how to fly in a straight line, but because there are so many of them, each with its own disposition despite its attachment to the flock, dispersions and distractions are inevitable, some would prefer to rest, others to drink water or to peck at berries, and until their desires coincide, the flock will be scattered and its itinerary upset. Along the route, in addition to the kites, solitary raptors, and members of less gregarious species, other birds of the starling family had been sighted, but they didn't join the flock, perhaps because they were not black but speckled, or perhaps because they had some other destiny in life. José Anaiço and Joaquim Sassa got into the car, Deux Chevaux resumed its journey, and so, starting and stopping, stopping and starting, they arrived at the frontier. Then Joaquim Sassa said, And now let's see if they'll allow me to pass, you follow, perhaps the starlings will help.

Just as in those tales about fairies and enchantments, knights and damsels, or in those no less admirable Homeric epics in which, thanks to the bounty of the tree of fables or through some caprice of the gods or other superhuman beings, anything might happen, however contrary to custom or opposed to nature, it came about that Joaquim Sassa and José Anaiço had stopped at the police lookout, or frontier post in technical jargon, and God alone knows how anxious they must have felt as they presented their papers, when the next moment, like a sudden downpour of lashing rain or cyclone sweeping all before it, the flock of starlings swooped down from the heavens like a black meteor, bird bodies transformed into flashes of lightning, hissing, screeching, finally scattering in all directions when they reached the low roofs of the lookout, just like a whirlwind out of control. The terrified policemen waved their arms about, ran to take shelter, Joaquim Sassa saw his chance, got out of the car and retrieved the documents one of the policemen had dropped, there was no one to observe this infringement of customs regulations, and that was that, secret crossings had been made by many routes, but never before like this. Hitchcock is applauding from the wings, the applause of someone who is a master of the genre. The excellence of this method was soon confirmed, showing that the Spanish police, like their Portuguese counterparts, take these avian omens, these black starlings, in all seriousness. The travelers passed with no difficulty, but dozens of birds stayed behind, for there was a loaded shotgun at the customs post across the border, even a blind man would have been able to hit the target, all you had to do was to shoot into the air, and this was needless slaughter, because in Spain, as we know, no one was looking for Joaquim Sassa. Nor is it certain that this is the action the Andalusian guards would have taken, for the starlings were Portuguese by nationality, born and bred in the lands of Ribatejo, and they had come a long way only to die, let us hope that these cruel guards will at least have the decency to invite their colleagues from Alentejo to share the feast of fried starlings in an atmosphere of wholesome conviviality and comradeship.

Accompanied by the canopy of birds overhead, the travelers are heading for Granada and the surrounding region, when they are obliged to seek assistance at the crossroads, for the map they are using does not indicate the village of Orce, how very inconsiderate on the part of the cartographers, I'll bet they didn't forget to indicate their own hometowns, in future they should remember how vexing it is for someone to check out his birthplace on a map only to find a blank space, this has given rise to the gravest of problems for those trying to establish personal and national identities. Along the route, they pass Seat cars and Pegaso trucks, these can be recognized immediately by their insignia and license plates, and the villages through which Deux Chevaux passes have that sleepy air said to be characteristic of the south, the people here are accused by northern tribes of being indolent, facile and arrogant remarks of racial disparagement made by those who have never had to work with the sun beating down on them. But it is true that there are differences between one world and another, everybody knows that on Mars the inhabitants are green, while here on earth they are every color except green.

From an inhabitant of the north we would never hear what we are about to hear, if we stop to ask the man going by astride a donkey what he thinks about this extraordinary business, the Iberian peninsula's having separated from Europe, he will pull the donkey's reins, Whoa!, and reply without mincing his words, The whole thing's a joke. Roque Lozano judges from appearances, they have helped him to form his own judgment, which is easy to understand, behold the bucolic tranquillity of these fields, the serene sky, the harmony of the rocks, the mountains of Morena and Aracena, which have remained unaltered since they were born, or, if not that long, since we were born. But television has shown the whole world how the Pyrenees have split open like a watermelon, let us say for argument's sake, using a metaphor within the grasp of rustic minds, I don't trust television, unless I can see things with these eyes of mine that the earth will one day devour, I don't believe in them, Roque Lozano replies without dismounting, So what are you going to do, I've left my family to look after my business and I'm off to see if it's true, With these eyes of yours that the earth will devour, With these eyes of mine that the earth hasn't devoured yet, And do you expect to arrive there riding a donkey, When it can't carry my weight any longer, we'll both go by foot, What name does your donkey answer to, A donkey doesn't answer to anything, it's called by its master, So what do you call your donkey then, Platero, and we're both making the journey, Platero and I, Can you tell us where Orce is, No sir, I don't know, It would appear to be a little way beyond Granada, Oh, in that case, you've still got some way to go, and I must bid you gentlemen from Portugal farewell, for my journey is much longer and I'm riding a donkey, Probably by the time you get there, you won't be able to see Europe any longer, If I don't see it, that'll be because the place never existed. Roque Lozano is absolutely right when all is said and done, because for something to exist there are two essential conditions, that a man should see it and that he be able to give it a name.

Joaquim Sassa and José Anaiço spent the night in Aracena, following in the footsteps of our King, Dom Afonso III, who conquered the town from the Moors, but his victory was the briefest of false dawns, for those were the Dark Ages. The starlings disappeared into the various trees in the vicinity, being too many to stay together as a flock, as they would have preferred. In the hotel, already lying down, each in his own bed, José Anaiço and Joaquim Sassa discuss the threatening images and words they have seen and heard on television, Venice in peril, and that appeared to be true, St. Mark's Square flooded at a time when the water is not normally high, a smooth, liquid surface that reflected in every detail the campanile and the façade of the Basilica, As the Iberian peninsula gradually moves away, the announcer said in solemn, measured tones, the damaging effect on tides is certain to worsen, grave consequences are predicted throughout the entire Mediterranean basin, the cradle of civilization, we must save Venice, this is our plea to humanity, even if it means making one fewer hydrogen bomb, one fewer nuclear submarine, if it is not too late. Joaquim Sassa, like Roque Lozano, has never seen the Pearl of the Adriatic, but José Anaiço could vouch for its existence, it is true that he had not given it either its name or its sobriquet, but he had seen it with his own living eyes, had touched it with his own living hands, What a terrible tragedy if Venice should be lost, he said, and these anguished words affected Joaquim Sassa more than the agitated waters in the canals, the tumultuous currents, the encroaching tide penetrating the ground floors of the palaces, the flooded quaysides, the awesome spectacle of an entire city sinking, an incomparable Atlantis, a submerged cathedral, the Moors, their eyes blinded by water, striking the bell with their bronze hammers until seaweed and barnacles paralyze the mechanism, liquid echoes, the Christ Pantocrator of the Basilica finally in theological conversation with the seagods subordinate to Jupiter, the Roman Neptune, the Greek Poseidon, and Venus and Amphitrite, now deliberately restored to the waters from which they emerged. Only the God of Christians is without a wife. Perhaps I'm to blame, Joaquim Sassa murmured, Don't overestimate yourself to the point of thinking you're to blame for everything, I'm referring to Venice, the loss of Venice, If Venice should be lost, everyone will be to blame, and that goes for past generations as well, the city has been declining for some time through neglect and speculation, I'm not talking about that, the whole world is suffering on that account, I'm referring to what I did, I threw a stone into the sea and some people believe that that caused the peninsula to break away from Europe. If you should have a son one day, he will die because you were born, no one will absolve you from this crime, the hands that make and weave are the same hands that dismantle and undo, right engenders wrong, wrong produces right, Poor consolation for a man in distress, There is no consolation, I'm afraid, man is a creature beyond consoling.

Perhaps Joaquim Sassa, who voiced this opinion, is right, perhaps man is a creature who cannot and will not be consoled, but certain human actions, with no meaning but that of being to all appearances meaningless, sustain the hope that man will one day come to weep on man's shoulder, probably when it is too late, when there is no longer time for anything else. The television announcer mentioned one of these actions in the news bulletin and tomorrow the newspapers will debate it further, with detailed statements from historians, critics, and poets, this was the secret landing in France, on a beach near Collioure, of a band of Spanish citizens and men of letters, who in the dead hours of the night, fearing neither hooting owls nor ghosts, burst into the cemetery where the poet Antonio Machado had been buried for many years. They had a brush with the gendarmes, who, alerted by some nighthawk, pursued the grave robbers but could not catch up with them. The sack containing the poet's mortal remains was thrown into a launch waiting on the beach, its engine running quietly, and within five minutes the pirate ship was out in the open sea, on the shore the gendarmes fired into the air, just to give vent to their annoyance, not because they felt bereft of the poetic bones. In an interview with France-Presse, the *maire* of Collioure tried to discredit the deed, even going so far as to insinuate that no one could be sure after all this time that the remains were those of Antonio Machado, nor is it worth inquiring how many years have passed, only through some improbable oversight on the part of the local authorities would they still be found there, despite the particular reverence with which the bones of poets are usually handled.

The journalist, a man of much experience, but so lacking in skepticism that he did not even appear to be French, stated that in his opinion, the cult of relics requires only a suitable object, its authenticity is of no importance, for the sake of verisimilitude one asks for nothing more than a mild resemblance, consider the Cathedral of Valencia, where in times gone by the faith was promoted with a collection of precious relics, namely, the chalice used by Our Lord during the Last Supper, the shirt He wore as a boy, some drops of Our Lady's milk, locks of Her hair, fair in color, and the comb She used, and also some fragments from the Holy Cross, some indefinable object that had belonged to one of the Holy Innocents, two of those thirty pieces, made of silver after all, with which Judas allowed himself to be bought through no fault of his own, and, to end the list, one of St. Christopher's teeth, four fingers in length and three in width, dimensions undeniably excessive, that will surprise only those unaware of the saint's gigantic proportions. Where will the Spaniards bury the poet now, asked Joaquim Sassa, who had never read Machado, and José Anaiço replied, If, despite the ups and downs of life and the reversals of fortune, everything has its place and every place claims what belongs to it, what remains of Antonio Machado today must be buried somewhere in the fields of Soria, beneath a holm oak, the Castilian word is *encina*, without any cross or tombstone, nothing but a tiny mound of earth, it doesn't even have to look like a stretched-out corpse, in the fullness of time earth will turn to earth and all will be equal. And we Portuguese, what poet should we go and look for in France, if any of our poets ever stayed there, As far as I know, only Mário de Sá Carneiro, but in his case there's no point even trying, first of all, because he wouldn't have wanted to come, second, because the cemeteries in Paris are well protected, third, because so many years have passed since he died, the administration of a capital city would not commit the errors of a provincial town, especially one with the additional excuse of being Mediterranean, And besides, what purpose would it serve to remove him from one cemetery in order to put him in another, now that in Portugal it is forbidden to bury the dead in an unauthorized place or in the open air, not even his bones would rest in peace if we were to leave him in the shade of an olive tree in the Parque Eduardo VII, But are there any olive trees left in the Parque Eduardo VII, That's a good question, but I can't give you an answer, and now let's get some sleep, for tomorrow we must go in search of Pedro Orce, the man who can feel the earth shaking. They switched off the light, lay there with open eyes waiting to drop off, but, before sleep arrived, Joaquim asked another question, And what about Venice, what's going to happen there, Believe me, the easiest of all the difficult tasks in this world would be to save Venice, all they would have to do would be to close the lagoon, and link the islands together so that the sea wouldn't be able to enter so readily, if the Italians aren't capable of carrying out the job on their own, let them send for the Dutch, they could dry out Venice in no time at all, We should help, we have certain responsibilities, We are no longer Europeans, well, perhaps that's not entirely true, For the time being you are still in territorial waters, interrupted an unknown voice.

In the morning, as they were paying their bill, the manager started to unburden himself, the hotel was almost empty at the height of the season, such a pity, Joaquim Sassa and José Anaiço, absorbed in their own affairs, had not even noticed the dearth of guests. And the grottoes, no one is visiting the grottoes, the man repeated in dismay, for no one to visit the grottoes was the worst of catastrophes. On the street there was great excitement, the children of Aracena had never seen so many starlings together, not even when they went bird-watching in the countryside, but the pleasure of this novelty did not last long, no sooner had the Portuguese Deux Chevaux started off in the direction of Seville than the starlings took flight as if the entire flock were a single bird, they circled twice as if saying farewell or trying to get their bearings, and disappeared behind the castle of the Knights Templar. The morning is clear, you could touch the sky with your fingers, and today promises to be less hot than yesterday, but the journey is long, From here to Granada it's more than three hundred kilometers, and then we have to go in search of Orce, let's hope we're successful and we find the man, these were the words of José Anaiço, that they might not find the man was a possibility that only now came to mind, And if we do find him, what are we going to say to him, now it was Joaquim Sassa's turn to be doubtful. In the merciless light of another day, or perhaps as a result of night's evil counsel, he suddenly found all these events absurd, could it be true that a continent had divided simply because someone had thrown a stone into the sea, a stone that exceeded the strength of the person who threw it, yet

6 2

there was no shadow of doubt that a stone had been thrown and the continent had divided, and a Spaniard swears that he can feel the earth shaking, and a flock of demented birds is following a Portuguese schoolmaster everywhere, and who knows what else has happened or is about to happen throughout the peninsula, Let's talk about your stone and my starlings, and he will talk about the earth that shook or is still shaking, And then, Then, if there is nothing more to see, nothing to experience and learn, we'll go home, you to your job, I to my school, pretend it was all a dream, and by the way, you still haven't told me what you do for a living, I work in an office, I also work in an office, I'm a teacher. They both laughed, and Deux Chevaux, ever prudent, pointed out on the gauge that they were running out of gas. They refilled the tank at the first service station they encountered, but they had to wait more than half an hour, the line of vehicles stretched way down the road, everyone was anxious to have a full tank. They got back on the road, Joaquim Sassa was now seriously worried, There's a run on gas, very soon they'll close the pumps, and then what, We should have been prepared for this, gas is a sensitive commodity, unstable, whenever there's a crisis it's the first indication, some years ago there was a ban here on supplies of gas, I don't know if you can remember that or even heard about it, it was utter chaos, I'm beginning to think we'll never reach Orce, Don't be a pessimist, I'm a born pessimist.

They passed through Seville without stopping, but the starlings lingered for a few minutes to admire the Giralda, which they had never seen before. Had there been only half a dozen of them they could have formed a diadem of black angels for the Statue of Faith, but because there were thousands of them, in their avalanche-like descent they covered the statue, transforming it into an indefinable figure, one that could just as easily have been taken for the symbol of Doubt as for the Statue of Faith. The metamorphosis was short-lived, José Anaiço is already speeding through this labyrinth of streets, let's follow him, winged species. Along the way, Deux Chevaux drank wherever possible, some gas stations had notices saying Sold Out, but the pump attendants said Mañana, they're an optimistic bunch, or perhaps they have simply learned how to make life tolerable. But the starlings had no lack of water, thank God, for Our Lord is much more concerned about birds than about humans, nearby are the tributaries of the Guadalquivir, the lagoons, the reservoirs, more water than those tiny beaks could drink in a million years. It's already mid-afternoon when they arrive in Granada, Deux Chevaux is panting, shuddering after all that effort, while Joaquim Sassa and José Anaiço go off to investigate, as if they were carrying sealed orders and the moment had come to open them, now we shall know where our destiny awaits us.

At the tourist office, an employee asked them if they were Portuguese archaeologists or anthropologists, that they were Portuguese could be seen at once, but why anthropologists and archaeologists, Because Orce is generally visited only by the latter, some years ago a discovery was made in nearby Venta Micena, the oldest human remains to be found in Europe, A whole skeleton, asked José Anaiço, Only a skull, but ancient, going back somewhere between one million three hundred thousand and one million four hundred thousand years, And do we know for certain they are human remains, Joaquim Sassa cautiously inquired, whereupon Maria Dolores replied with a knowing smile, Whenever human remains from ancient times are discovered, they always belong to some man, Cro-Magnon Man, Neanderthal Man, Swanscombe Man, Peking Man, Heidelberg Man, Java Man, at that time there were no women, Eve still hadn't been created, she was only created later, You're being ironic, No, I'm an anthropologist by training and a militant feminist by inclination, Well, we're journalists and we want to interview a certain Pedro Orce, the one who felt the earth shaking. How does such news make it to Portugal, Everything comes in Portugal and we go everywhere, this part of the dialogue was conducted solely by José Anaiço, who always has an answer ready, undoubtedly because he's used to coping with schoolchildren. Joaquim Sassa had moved away to examine some illustrated posters of the Courtyard of the Lions, the Gardens of Generalife, the entombed effigies of the Catholic Kings, studying them he had to ask himself if there would be any point in visiting these places after having seen the photographs. Absorbed in these thoughts about perceptions of reality, he lost the drift of the conversation, what could José Anaiço have said to make Maria Dolores laugh so heartily, if every Dolores had not changed her name to Lola, each of those guffaws would have been a scandal. But she no longer showed the slightest hint of feminist aggression, perhaps because this Ribatejo Man was something more than just a mandible, a molar, and a patch of skull, and because there is plenty of evidence, in this age in which we live, that women do exist. Maria Dolores, who works in tourism because she cannot find employment as an anthropologist, draws the missing road on the map for José Anaiço, indicates with a black dot the village of Orce, and that of Venta Micena right beside it, now the travelers may proceed, the sorceress at the crossroads has shown them the way, It's a desert, a lunar landscape, but one can see in her eyes that she regrets not being able to accompany them, to practice her skills in the company of Portuguese journalists, especially that rather more discreet one who moved away to look at the posters, how often life has taught us not to judge by appearances, as Joaquim Sassa himself is now doing, his mistake, modest man that he is, If we were to stay here you would be getting it on with the lady anthropologist, let us forgive him this vulgar expression, when men are together that's how they talk, and José Anaiço, presumptuous, but also fooled, replied, Who knows.

This world, we shall never tire of repeating, is a comedy of errors. Another proof of this maxim is that the name Orce Man should have been given to some old bones found not in Orce but in Venta Micena, which would make a nice palaeontological label, were it not for that name Venta, which translates as Sale, the sign and symbol of inferior merchandise. The fate of words is truly strange. Unless Micenae was a woman's name, before it became that of a man, like that celebrated Galician woman who gave her name to the town of Golegã in Portugal, perhaps some Greeks from Mycenae, in flight from the demented Atridae, arrived in these remote parts, and anxious to reestablish the name of their native region, they happened to choose this place, much farther away than Cerbère, at the heart of hell, and never so remote as now, as we go sailing off. However difficult you may find it to believe.

*T*he devil had his first abode in these parts, his were the hooves that scorched the ground and trampled the ashes, amid mountains that shivered with fear then and continue to do so to this day, the ultimate desert where even Christ would have allowed Himself to be tempted by that same devil, had He not already experienced the wiles of Satan, as one reads in the Bible. Joaquim Sassa and José Anaiço contemplate, what do they contemplate, the landscape, but this delightful word belongs to other worlds, to other languages, you cannot refer to what one sees here as a landscape, we have called it an infernal abode, but we are not altogether sure, for in places of damnation we're almost certain to find men and women with the animals that keep them company, until the moment comes to slaughter them in order to live, amid disasters and misfortunes, this is the place of exile where the poet who never visited Granada must have written his verses. These are the lands of Orce, which must have soaked up so much Moorish and Christian blood, to speak once more of the Dark Ages, but why speak of those who died so many years ago, if it is the land that is dead, buried within itself.

At Orce, the travelers found Pedro Orce, a pharmacist by profession, older than they would have imagined him, had they given the matter any thought. Pedro Orce did not appear on television, therefore we could not have known that he is a man in his sixties, thin in features and body, his hair almost entirely white, and were it not for his sober taste, which shuns any artifice, he could make up dark and fair hair dyes at will in the secrecy of his laboratory, for he is skilled in these chemical concoctions. When Joaquim Sassa and José Anaiço enter the pharmacy, he is filling capsules with quinine powder, an old-fashioned medicament that avoids the powerful concentrations characteristic of modern prescriptions, while astutely preserving the psychological effect of awkward deglutination, followed as if by magic by immediate results. In Orce, which one must inevitably pass through to reach Venta Micena, travelers are rare now that the commotion of excavations and discoveries has passed, we do not even know where the skull of the town's oldest ancestor is kept, there in some museum awaiting a glass case with a label, normally any customers passing through buy aspirin, pills to help their digestion or to cure diarrhea, as for the local inhabitants, they probably die from their first illness, so the pharmacist will most likely never get rich. Pedro Orce has finished sealing the capsules, just like a conjuring trick, after moistening the parts that will serve to seal the capsule, the two brass plates are pressed together, then opened, and the prescription is ready, one last capsule of quinine makes a dozen, and this done he asks them, What can I do for you gentlemen, We are Portuguese, a pointless statement, one need only hear them speak to know at once where they come from, but, after all, it is only natural to declare who we are before saying why we have come, especially in situations of such importance, to travel hundreds of kilometers just to ask, although not necessarily with these dramatic words, Pedro Orce, do you swear on your honor and on the excavated bones that you felt the earth shake when all the seismographs of Seville and Granada, their needles steady, traced the straightest line you ever saw, and Pedro Orce raised his hand and said, with the simplicity of a just and honest man, I do, We would like to have a word in private, Joaquim Sassa added after they had revealed their nationality, and there and then, since there were no other clients in the pharmacy, they told him about their personal and joint experiences, about the stone, the starlings, crossing the frontier, they could not show him the stone, but as for the birds, you need only stick your head outside the door and look, there, in this square or in the adjacent one, the inevitable flock of birds, all the inhabitants staring up at the sky amazed at this unusual spectacle, now the birds have disappeared, they have descended upon the Castle of the Seven Towers, Arabic in origin. Better not to speak here, Pedro Orce said, get into the car and drive out of town, In which direction, Drive straight ahead, in the direction of Maria, keep going for three kilometers beyond the last houses, there is a tiny bridge, nearby an olive tree, wait for me there, I'll join you shortly, Joaquim Sassa had the impression that he was about to relive a scene from his own life, that morning two days ago, when he had waited for José Anaiço, beyond the last houses in town.

They are seated on the ground, under a Cordoban olive tree, the kind that, according to the popular quatrain, makes the oil yellow, as if olive oil weren't yellow, or only occasionally slightly greenish, and the first words from José Anaiço, he could not suppress them, were, This place is enough to put the fear of God into you, and Pedro Orce replied, It's much worse in Venta Micena, where I was born, an ambiguous formality that means what it appears to be saying as well as the exact opposite, depending more on the reader than on the reading, although the latter is entirely dependent on the former, which explains why we find it so difficult to know who is reading what has been read, or the effect of what has been read on the person who reads it, let us hope that, in this case, Pedro Orce will not think that the curse on the place is the result of his having been born there. Then as their discussion got under way, they gradually started to compare their experiences as discus-thrower, bird-catcher, and seismologist, and they came to the conclusion that all the events that had taken place had been, and continued to be, somehow connected, especially since Pedro Orce insists that the ground has not stopped shaking, I can feel it even at this very moment, and he stretched out his hand to show them what he meant. Drawn by curiosity, José Anaiço and Joaquim Sassa touched the hand he kept outstretched, and they could feel, oh yes, beyond the shadow of a doubt they could feel the tremor, the vibration, the drone, and although some skeptic might suggest that it is natural for people to start trembling at a certain age,

Pedro Orce is not all that old, and trembling and tremor are not the same thing, whatever the dictionaries might tell us.

Anyone watching from afar would think that the three men had just pledged themselves to some commitment or other, what is certain is that they quickly shook hands, and nothing more. All around, the stones have intensified the heat, the white earth is dazzling, the sky is an open furnace blowing hot air, even in the shade beneath this Cordoban olive tree. So far no olives have appeared, the men are safe for the moment from the voracious starlings, once December comes you will see such plundering, but since there is only one olive tree, the starlings are not likely to frequent these parts. Joaquim Sassa switched on his radio, for suddenly none of the three had anything more to say, scarcely surprising, after all, they have not known each other for very long, the announcer's voice can be heard, grown nasal from all that broadcasting and because the batteries are low, Judging from the latest measurements, the speed of the peninsula's dislocation has stabilized at around seven hundred and fifty meters per hour, the three men started listening to the news, According to the latest reports to reach the newsroom, an enormous crack has appeared between La Línea and Gibraltar, the voice droned on and on, We shall be back with more news, unless anything unforeseen should happen, in an hour's time, at this very moment the starlings passed in a flurry, *vruuuuuuuuu*, and Joaquim Sassa asked, Are they yours, and José Anaiço didn't even have to look up before replying, They're mine, he has no difficulty in recognizing them, he knows them, Sherlock Holmes would be bound to say, Elementary, my dear Watson, there isn't another flock like it in these parts, and he is right, for there are few birds in hell, only the nocturnal ones, a matter of tradition.

Pedro Orce follows the flock's flight, initially out of mild curiosity, then his eyes light up with blue sky and white clouds, and, unable to hold back the words, he suddenly proposes, Why don't we go to the coast and see the rock as it passes. This may sound absurd, nonsensical, but it is not, even when we travel by train, we think we see trees passing when they are firmly rooted in the soil, at this moment we are not traveling by train, we are traveling more slowly, on a stone raft that is sailing the sea, unfettered, the only difference being that which exists between solid and liquid. So often we need a whole lifetime in order to change our life, we think a great deal, weigh things up and vacillate, then we go back to the beginning, we think and think, we displace ourselves on the tracks of time with a circular movement, like those clouds of dust, dead leaves, debris, that have no strength for anything more, better by far that we should live in a land of hurricanes. At other times one word is all that is needed, Let's go and see the rock as it passes, and they get to their feet, eager for adventure, they don't even feel the scorching heat, they run laughing down the slope, like children given their freedom, Deux Chevaux is like a burning cauldron, within seconds the three men are bathed in sweat, but they scarcely notice their discomfort, for from these same southern parts men set out to discover the New World, rugged and fierce, sweating like pigs in their armor, steel helmets on their heads, they advanced sword in hand to fight the naked Indians, clad only in feathers and war paint, an idyllic image.

They did not go back through the village, for anyone seeing Pedro Orce and the two strangers traveling in the same car would suspect either that he was being abducted or that the three of them were involved in some conspiracy, better call the police, but some old man, one of the veterans of Orce, would say, We don't want the Civil Guard here. They went by other routes, along roads not marked on the average map, the person we need right now is the sphinx of tourism, to trace out the itinerary of these new discoveries, for she had turned out to be a sphinx, after all, rather than a sibyl, for no sibyl has ever been seen at a crossroads, even if both species are native to the peninsula. Pedro Orce said, First I must show you Venta Micena, the place where I was born, the phrase came out as if he were mocking himself or deliberately touching a sore point. They passed through a village in ruins called Fuente Nueva, if there ever was a fountain here it has dried up and vanished, and at a wide bend in the road ahead, he called out, There it is.

They take a good look and see so little that they start searching for what must be missing and can no longer be found. There, asked José Anaiço, he has cause for doubt, because there are only a few scattered houses, they merge with the color of the earth, a church tower down below, here at the edge of the road what is unmistakably a cemetery, with a cross and white walls. Under the volcanic sun, the countryside rolls like a petrified sea covered with dust, if things were already like this one million, four hundred thousand years ago, you do not have to be a paleontologist to testify that Orce Man died of thirst, the world was young once, the stream that flows over there would then have been a wide and generous river, great trees would have towered, and grasses taller than man, in the days before hell was located here. At the right season, when there is rain, some greenery will sprout on these ashen fields, nowadays the low verges are cultivated with great effort, the plants dry up and die, then revive and flourish, it's man who still has not learned how cycles repeat themselves, with him it is once and nevermore. Pedro Orce makes a gesture that embraces the blighted village. The house where I was born no longer exists, and then, pointing to the left, in the direction of some flat-topped hills, That's the Cueva de los Rosales, where the bones of Orce Man were discovered. Joaquim Sassa and José Anaiço looked at the livid landscape, one million, four hundred thousand years ago this place was inhabited by men and women who engendered men and women who engendered men and women, destiny, disaster, right up to the present day, one million, four hundred thousand years hence someone will come to carry out excavations in this poor cemetery, and since there is already an Orce Man, perhaps the skull that has just been found will now be returned to its rightful owner and be called Venta Micena Man. No one passes, no dog can be heard barking, the starlings have disappeared, Joaquim Sassa feels a shiver run all the way up his spine, as he tries in vain to suppress his uneasiness, and José Anaiço asks, What's the name of that mountain down there, That's the Sierra de Sagra, And this one here, on our right, That's the Sierra de Maria, When Orce Man died, that must have been the last thing he saw, What would he have called it when he talked with other men from Orce, the ones who left no skulls behind, Joaquim Sassa asked, At that time there were no names, José Anaiço said, How can you look at something without giving it a name, You have to wait for the name to be born. The three men stood there gazing, with nothing more to say, it was time to leave the past to its restless peace.

In order to lighten their journey, Pedro Orce repeated in greater detail the story of his adventures, the scientists had even linked him up to a seismograph in the presence of the authorities, a desperate but useful measure, for then they would be able to establish whether he had been telling the truth, the needle on the dial immediately registered an earth tremor, the line becoming straight again once the guinea pig had been disconnected from the machine. The inexplicable has been explained, declared the Mayor of Granada, who was looking on, but one of the experts corrected him, The inexplicable will have to wait a little longer, it wasn't a strictly scientific statement but everyone understood what he meant and agreed. They sent Pedro Orce home, instructing him to remain at the disposal of science and the authorities, warning him that he should speak to no one of his extra-sensory powers, a recommendation differing little from the decision made by the French veterinary surgeons concerning the mysterious disappearance of the vocal cords of the dogs of Cerbère.

Deux Chevaux has finally turned in a southerly direction, the car is already on well-traveled roads, there seems to be no shortage here of fuel, gasoline, or diesel, but little by little the car is obliged to reduce its lively pace, ahead there is an endless line of traffic crawling at a snail's pace, other cars, trucks and buses carrying freight, motorcycles, bicycles, mopeds, scooters, horse-drawn carts, people riding donkeys, but no Roque Lozano among them, and people on foot, many of these, some asking for a lift, others clearly disdaining any means of transport, as if doing penance, or fulfilling some dream, it is more likely to be a dream, and there is no point in asking them where they are going, you do not need to be called Pedro Orce to share the same thought and want to see Gibraltar pass in the distance, drifting off course, you need only be Spanish, and here Spaniards abound. They come from Cordoba, from Linares, from Jaén, from Guadix, all of them major cities, but also from Higuera de Arjona, from El Tocón, from Bular

Bajo, from Alamedilla, from Jesús del Monte, from Almácegas, delegations appear to have been dispatched from every region, these people have been extremely patient, ever since the year 1704, just imagine, if Gibraltar is not going to belong to us, if we who have become part of these waters must renounce it, then why should it go to the English. The human river grew so wide that the traffic police had to open wherever possible a third lane heading south, few vehicles are traveling north, only in an emergency, sickness or death, and even so they are looked at with mistrust, suspected of Anglophilia, perhaps they want to bury in some remote corner their distress at this geological and strategic separation.

But for most people this is a day of great rejoicing, a week as holy as the official one, and there are trucks carrying statues of Christ, the Virgins of Triana and Macarena, brass bands, their instruments shining in the sun, and on the donkeys' backs can be seen bundles of firewood and mortars, if someone were to put a lighted match anywhere near them, they would soar like Clavileño to the second and third heights of the heavens, and to that of fire, where they would singe Sancho Panza's beard, if, with his gullible nature, he allowed himself to be deceived yet again. The young girls are dressed in all their finery, with mantillas and shawls, and the elderly, when they can walk no farther, are carried by the young on their backs, son you are, father you will be, you will reap as you have sown, until some vehicle stops, any vehicle, and the journey goes on, their weary limbs relaxed, everyone making for the coast, the beaches, better still if they can find some elevation looking out to sea where they might be sure of a good view of that damned rock, what a pity it's too far to hear the monkeys screeching, disoriented because there's no land in sight. As the sea gets closer, the traffic becomes more congested, some are already abandoning their vehicles and walking, or begging a lift from those traveling in horse-drawn carts or on donkeys, the latter cannot abandon these creatures of nature, they have to tend them, water them, put the baskets of straw and bean pods to their snouts, even the police are aware of the situation, they are all countryfolk, therefore the orders are to leave the trucks and cars at the side of the road, the animals can go on, and motorcycles, bicycles, scooters, and mopeds are also permitted, the latter have ways and means of maneuvering smoothly in and out of traffic because they do not take up much space. The brass bands, on foot, rehearse the first paso dobles, an overenthusiastic vendor of fireworks, or some ardent patriot, prematurely lets off a mighty firecracker, to the annoyance of his friends, not prepared to waste their fireworks without good reason. Deux Chevaux has also come to a halt, it was the only Portuguese car in the procession, the only one with Portuguese registration, that is, watching Gibraltar drifting past does not bother Deux Chevaux one way or the other, his ancient grief is called Olivença and this road does not lead there. You can see people who are already lost, women calling for their husbands, children calling for their parents, but fortunately for all of them they will eventually be reunited, if this is not a day for laughter, it is not one for weeping either, God willing and that Cur of a Son. There are dogs too, sniffing around, few of them bark, except when they start fighting among themselves, not a single one of them from Cerbère. And when two donkeys appeared on the loose, with no sign of their owners, Pedro Orce, Joaquim Sassa, and José Anaiço unwisely decided to make use of them taking turns, one walking, the other two riding, but their comfort was short-lived, the donkeys belonged to a band of gypsies who were traveling north, these last could not have cared less about Gibraltar, and if Pedro Orce had not been Spanish, and of the most ancient and respected lineage, Portuguese blood would have been shed on the spot.

All along the coast the encampment stretches for miles, almost like a small village, thousands and thousands of people looking out to sea, some have clambered onto rooftops and up tall trees, not to mention all the other thousands who did not want to come so far and stayed behind, with spyglasses and binoculars, on the heights of the Sierra Contraviesa or on the slopes of the Sierra Nevada, here we are only interested in the more humble people, those who have to touch things in order to recognize them, they will not get all that close, but they are doing their utmost. José Anaiço, Joaquim Sassa, and Pedro Orce

have come with them, spurred by the enthusiasm of Pedro Orce and
the good-natured friendliness of the others, now they are seated on
some boulders facing the sea, the evening is drawing in, and Joaquim
Sassa, the self-confessed pessimist, remarks, If Gibraltar should pass
during the night, we will have made the journey in vain. At least we'll
be able to see her lights, Pedro Orce argued, and it might actually be
even better to watch the rock moving away like a ship all lit up, then
we'd have a real excuse for setting off fireworks, pinwheels, silver rain,
cascades, or whatever they're called here, while the rock fades away
in the distance, disappears into the darkness of night, good-bye, good-
bye, never to be seen again. But José Anaiço had spread out the map
on his lap, and with pencil and paper he made some calculations,
repeated them one by one to be absolutely certain, checked the scale
once again, double-checked his figures, and finally declared, As for
Gibraltar, my friends, it will take about ten days to get here, incred-
ulous surprise on the part of his companions, then he showed them
his arithmetic, he did not even need to invoke his authority as a
certified teacher, knowledge of this kind, fortunately, is within reach
of the simplest minds, if the peninsula, or island, or whatever, is moving at a speed of seven hundred and fifty meters per hour, we can
figure it will cover eighteen kilometers each day, okay, draw a straight
line from the Bay of Algeciras to where we are standing, it's almost
two hundred kilometers, so work that out, it's not difficult. Confronted
with this irrefutable proof, Pedro Orce bowed his head in submission,
And we have come running here with all these people thinking our
day of glory has arrived, that today we could have mocked the Evil
Stone, and now we'll have to wait ten days, no fire lasts long. And
suppose we were to go and meet it, taking the roads along the coast,
Joaquim Sassa suggested, No, no, it isn't worth it, Pedro Orce replied,
these things have to happen at the right moment, before one's enthusiasm flags, it's right now that the rock should be passing before our
very eyes, while we're still feeling excited, we were in the right mood
but not any more, Well, what shall we do, then, José Anaiço asked,
Let's go, Don't you want to stay, You can no longer live your dream

once the dream has gone, In that case, let's leave tomorrow, So soon, I have to get back to school, And I to my office, And I've always got my pharmacy.

They went to look for Deux Chevaux, but while they are searching and having some difficulty finding the car, this is the moment to mention that many thousands of people who achieved neither voice nor vote in this story, who have not made even a brief appearance at the edges of the scene, thousands of people who have not budged for the last ten days and nights, who ate from the provisions they had brought along, who then, when they ran out on the second day, went to buy whatever they could find locally, and cooked in the open air, on great bonfires that were like pyres from another age, and not even those who had run out of money went hungry, where there was food for one there was food for all, we are enjoying a revival of fraternity, if such a thing has ever been humanly possible or is likely to return. Pedro Orce, José Anaiço, and Joaquim Sassa are not about to experience this admirable fraternity, they have turned their backs on the sea, and now it is their turn to be looked at suspiciously by those hordes of people who are still descending.

Meantime darkness has fallen, the first lights go on. Let's go, said José Anaiço. Pedro Orce will remain silent, sitting on the back seat, looking sad, his eyes closed, it has to be now or never, we shall never have a better opportunity to recall the Portuguese refrain, Where are you going, I'm off to the party, Where have you come from, I've come from the party, even without the help of exclamation points and pauses, one can readily see the difference between the joyful anticipation of the first reply and the disillusioned weariness of the second, they only look alike on the page on which they're written. During the entire journey, only six words were spoken, You must have dinner with me, they came from the lips of Pedro Orce, he feels obliged to be hospitable. José Anaiço and Joaquim Sassa did not feel it necessary to make any reply, some might think they were being impolite by remaining silent, but such people know very little about human nature, those better informed would testify that the three men had become close friends.

They reach Orce in the dead of night. The roads at this hour are a desert of shadows and silence, Deux Chevaux can be left at the door of the pharmacy, and it is no bad thing that they should give it a rest, tomorrow the car will be back on the road carrying the three men, a matter about to be decided indoors as they sit round the table enjoying a simple meal, for Pedro Orce also lives alone and there is not time enough to prepare anything elaborate. They switched on the television, the news is broadcast hourly, and they saw Gibraltar, not simply separated from Spain, but already at a considerable distance, like an island abandoned in the middle of the ocean, transformed, poor thing, into a peak, a sugarloaf, a reef, with its thousand cannon out of action. Even if they should insist on opening new loopholes on the northern side, perhaps to gratify imperial pride, they would be throwing their money into the sea, in both the literal and the figurative senses. Those scenes undoubtedly made an impression, but were nothing when compared to the shock produced by a series of satellite pictures showing the progressive widening of the canal between the peninsula and France, flesh froze and hair bristled at the sight of this great catastrophe, beyond human powers, for this was no longer a canal but open sea, where ships sailed at will, over water that had truly never been sailed before. Obviously, the displacement could not be observed, at this altitude a speed of seven hundred and fifty meters per hour cannot be captured by the naked eye, but for one observing it was as if the great mass of stone were shifting in his head, sensitive people almost fainted, others complained of feeling dizzy. And there were pictures that had been taken from aboard the indefatigable helicopters, the gigantic Pyrenean escarpment, cut vertically, and the minute swarm of ants heading south, like a sudden migration, just to see Gibraltar adrift, an optical illusion, for it is we who are being carried off with the current, and also, to add a colorful detail, an entry worthy of a diary, a flock of starlings, thousands of them, like a cloud obscuring one's field of vision, darkening the sky. Even the birds are responding to the crowd's excitement, that was the verb the announcer used, responding, when we know from natural history that birds have their own good reasons for going whithersoever they choose or must, they act neither for me nor for you, at most for José Anaiço, who ungratefully confesses, I'd forgotten about them.

There were also shots of Portugal, taken on the Atlantic coast, showing the waves beating on the rocks or swirling over the sands, and lots of people watching the horizon, all with the tragic expression of someone who for centuries has been prepared for the unknown and fears that it may not come after all, or may turn out to be no different from the common, banal experiences of everyday life. There they are now, as Unamuno described them, his swarthy face cupped in the palms of his hands, *Fix your eyes where the lonely sun sets in the immense sea*, all nations with the sea to the west do the same, this race is swarthy, there is no other particularity, and it has sailed the seas. Lyrical, ecstatic, the Spanish announcer declaims, Look at the Portuguese, all along their golden beaches, once but no longer the prow of Europe, for we have left the European quayside to sail once more the Atlantic waves, what admiral will guide us, what port awaits us, the closing shot showed a young lad throwing a pebble into the sea, practicing the art of ricochet, one that requires no training, and Joaquim Sassa said, He has the strength of his years, the stone couldn't possibly go any farther, but the peninsula, or whatever it might be, appeared to be advancing with even greater vigor over the deep sea, so different from what it normally is in the summer. The final item of news was given by the announcer, in passing, as if he did not consider it very important, Some volatility has been observed among the population, lots of people are leaving their homes, not only in Andalusia, there we know the reason, but, bearing in mind that most of them are heading for the sea, we may assume that they are driven by natural curiosity, in any case we can assure our viewers that there is nothing to see on the coast, as we have just confirmed, all those Portuguese who were staring at the sea, stared and saw nothing, let us not make the same mistake. Then Pedro Orce said, If you have room for me, I'm coming with you.

Joaquim Sassa and José Anaiço remained silent, they could not understand why such a sensible Spaniard should want to visit the regions and beaches of Portugal. The question was worth raising, and as the owner of Deux Chevaux, it was up to Joaquim Sassa to ask, and Pedro Orce replied, I don't want to stay here, with the earth shaking under my feet all the time, and people telling me that I'm only imagining things, You might well feel the earth shaking in Portugal too, and very likely people there will say much the same thing, José Anaiço told him, and we have our jobs waiting for us. I won't be a burden to you, just take me with you and leave me in Lisbon, where I've never been, I'll come back here one day, And what about your family and your pharmacy, You must have gathered by now that I have no family, I'm the last survivor, the pharmacy will be all right, I have an assistant who will look after things. There was nothing more to be said, no reason for refusing, We'll be glad of your company, was the phrase Joaquim Sassa used, The worst thing would be if they were to detain you at the frontier, José Anaiço reminded him, I'll tell them I've been touring Spain, so I couldn't possibly have known that anyone was looking for me, and that I'm just about to present myself to the authorities, but it's unlikely there will be any need for explanations, they're sure to be paying more attention to those who are leaving than to those who are entering, Let's cross over at some other frontier post, I'm worried about the starlings, José Anaiço reminded them, and, having spoken, he spread out on the table a map of the whole Iberian peninsula, drawn and colored at a time when everything was terra firma and the ossified callus of the Pyrenees discouraged any temptation to venture beyond, in silence the three men stood looking at the flat area representing this part of the world as if they failed to recognize it, Strabo used to say that the peninsula is formed like the hide of an ox, Pedro Orce muttered these words earnestly, and despite the warm night Joaquim Sassa and José Anaiço broke out in goose pimples, as if suddenly confronted by the Cyclopean beast that was about to be sacrificed and skinned in order to burden the continent of Europe with yet another carcass that would go on bleeding until the end of time.

The open map showed the two countries, Portugal indented, suspended, Spain unhinged to the south, and the regions, the provinces, the districts, the thick rubble of the major cities, the dust of the towns and villages, but not of all of them, for dust is often invisible to the naked eye, Venta Micena being merely one example. Their hands smooth and stroke the paper, they pass over Alentejo and continue northwards, as if they were caressing a human face, from right to left, following the hands of the clock, the direction of time, the Beiras, Ribatejo before them, and then Trás-os-Montes and Minho, Galicia, Asturias, the Basque country and Navarre, Castile and León, Aragón and Catalonia, Valencia, Estremadura, both the Spanish and the Portuguese, Andalusia where we still find ourselves, the Algarve, then José Anaiço pointed with his finger to the mouth of the Guadiana and said, Let's enter through here.

Swept away by the volley of gunfire from Rosal de la Frontera of bitter memory, the starlings, prudent on this occasion, made a wide circle northward and crossed to where the air was clear and the circulation free, some three kilometers from the bridge, which was already built by then, and none too soon. The police on the Portuguese side expressed no surprise that one of the three travelers was called Joaquim Sassa, there were clearly more serious matters worrying the authorities, and these soon became apparent from the ensuing dialogue, Where are you gentlemen heading for, the guard inquired, For Lisbon, replied José Anaiço, who was at the wheel, and he in turn asked, Why do you ask, officer, You will run into roadblocks along the highway, follow any orders you may receive, under no circumstances should you try to force your way through or look for ways around, otherwise you'll be in trouble, Has there been some kind of disaster, Depends what you mean by disaster, Don't tell us the Algarve is also breaking away, it had to come sooner or later, they've always thought of themselves as being a separate kingdom, No, it's something else, something more serious, people are trying to occupy the hotels, they claim that if there are no tourists they ought to be given shelter, We've heard nothing about this, when did the occupation begin, Last night, Well I never, exclaimed José Anaiço, had he been French he would have said *Ça alors*, everyone has his own way of expressing the surprise the next man also experienced, listen to Pedro Orce who gave a resounding *Caramba*, while from Joaquim Sassa you could scarcely hear the echo of that, Well I never.

The police instructed them to carry on, warned them for a second time, Look out for the roadblocks, and Deux Chevaux was able to cross Vila Real de Santo António while the passengers went on discussing this extraordinary affair, Seriously, who would have believed it, there are two different types of Portuguese, those who take off for the beaches and sand dunes to contemplate the horizon despondently, and others who advance intrepidly on those hotels-cum-fortresses defended by the police, by the Republican Guard, and even, it would seem, by the army itself, Already people have been wounded, this they were told secretly in a café where they decided to stop and gather some information. This was how they learned that in three hotels, one in Albufeira, one in Praia da Rocha, the last in Lagos, the situation is critical, the forces of order are on the point of surrounding the buildings where the insurgents are digging in, barricading doors and windows, blocking all points of access, they are like besieged Moors, infidels without mercy, apostates heeding neither appeals nor threats, they know that the white flag will be followed by tear gas, therefore they refuse to negotiate, they reject the very word surrender. Pedro Orce is shaken, goes on repeating *Caramba* under his breath, and one can detect a hint of patriotic pique in his expression, deep regret that the Spanish should have failed to take the initiative.

At the first roadblock they were asked to turn off in the direction of Castro Marim, but José Anaiço protested that he had important business in Silves, it must be dealt with urgently, he said Silves to allay any suspicions, Besides, I have to travel along country roads, And keep as far off the beaten track as possible, if you want to avoid complications, the officer in charge advised him, reassured by the harmless appearance of the three passengers and the jaded respectability of Deux Chevaux, But officer, in a situation like this, with the country going adrift, and the expression could not have been more apt, here we are worrying ourselves about some hotels being occupied, this isn't the kind of revolution that warrants a general mobilization, people get impatient sometimes, that's all, the comment came from Joaquim

Sassa, scarcely diplomatic, fortunately the lieutenant was not a man to go back on his word but a soldier who upheld ancient traditions, otherwise they would have found themselves obliged to go through Castro Marim after all. Joaquim Sassa's impertinence was duly reprimanded nonetheless, The army is here to carry out its orders, what would you say if we were to abandon our uncomfortable barracks and occupy the Sheraton or the Ritz, the officer must really have been mad to condescend to giving explanations to a civilian. You're absolutely right, lieutenant, just like my friend to speak without thinking, as I'm always telling him, Well, he should make a point of thinking, he's old enough, the officer retorted sharply. With an abrupt gesture he waved them on, he did not hear what Joaquim Sassa said, and just as well, otherwise they might have ended up behind bars.

They were detained at other roadblocks manned by the Republican Guard, who were not quite so obliging, sometimes they were forced to make detours along bad roads before returning to the main highway. Joaquim Sassa was angry, not without reason, he had been reprimanded twice, That the lieutenant should throw his weight around, I can accept, but you had no right to say that I don't think before speaking, Forgive me, I was only trying to keep the situation from deteriorating, you were being ironic with the man and that was a mistake, you must never be ironic with the authorities, either they don't notice and it's pointless, or they notice, and it only makes things worse. Pedro Orce asked them to explain, slowly, what they were arguing about, and the inevitable change of tone, the repetitions, revealed that it was a matter of no importance, when Pedro Orce understood everything, everything had been understood.

After the road forked at Boliqueime, on a deserted stretch José Anaiço took advantage of a shallow ditch and with no warning drove Deux Chevaux straight into an open field, Where are you going, Joaquim Sassa called out, If we keep to the road, like obedient little children, we'll never get close to any of those hotels, and we do want to see what's going on there, don't we, José Anaiço retorted between one jolt and another, struggling with the unsteady steering wheel as the car bounced over the ruts like something demented. Pedro Orce, sitting on the back seat, was thrown from one side to another with neither pity nor mercy, and Joaquim Sassa, who had burst out laughing, replied in fits and starts, That's really funny, that's really very funny. Fortunately, three hundred meters ahead they found a hidden path among the fig trees, behind a broken-down wall of dry stones, or one that had lost its mortar with time. They were, in a manner of speaking, in the field of operations. Taking every precaution they close in on Albufeira, wherever possible they choose flat terrain, worst of all are the clouds of dust sent up by Deux Chevaux, ill-equipped to act as beater and vanguard, but the police are already far away, guarding the crossroads, the major road junctions as they are called in the current terminology of communications, besides, the effective strength of the forces of order is not so great that it could strategically cover a province that is as rich in hotels as in locust trees, if such a comparison were permissible. In fact, anyone whose next destination is the city of Lisbon would not need to venture into those parts where subversion reigns, but we might as well confirm whether our information is correct, time and time again one has seen how stories get exaggerated in the telling, there might have been the odd isolated incident, but the roadblocks might turn out in the end to be nothing more than the putting into practice of that wise proverb that warns us that prevention is better than cure. But there were already infiltrations. From among the sparse trees, eagerly tramping over the red soil, came men and women carrying sacks, suitcases and bundles on their shoulders, tiny children in their arms, their intention being to secure a place in a hotel, with these few belongings and the closest members of the family as a guaranty, wife, children, then, if all goes well, they will send for the rest of their relatives, and the bed, the chest, and the table, for want of any other belongings, no one seems to have remembered that there are plenty of beds and tables in hotels, and while there may not be all that many chests, there are wardrobes serving the same purpose.

At the gates of Albufeira preparations were under way for the decisive battle. The travelers had left Deux Chevaux behind, parked tranquilly in the shade, in a situation of this kind one cannot rely on its assistance, a car is a mechanical entity, devoid of emotions, wherever you drive it, it goes, it remains where it is parked, it does not care one way or another whether the peninsula goes sailing off, the peninsula's dislocation is not likely to make distances any shorter. The battle was preceded by a rallying speech, as was common in ancient warfare, with words of defiance and exhortation to the troops, prayers to the Virgin or to their patron, St. James, the words always sound fine at the outset, the outcome is invariably disastrous, at Albufeira, the harangue from the leader of the invading populace was to no avail, and yet how well he harangued, Guards, soldiers, friends, open your ears wide, and give me your attention, you are, and don't you forget it, sons of the people just like us, this much-sacrificed people that builds houses yet remains homeless, that erects hotels yet never earns enough money ever to stay in one, note that we have come here with our wives and children, but we didn't come here to ask for the moon, simply for a better and safer roof over our heads, for rooms where we can sleep with the privacy and respect we deserve as human beings, we're neither animals nor machines, we have feelings, don't we, and those hotels over there are empty, there are hundreds, thousands of rooms, they were built for tourists, now the tourists have gone and they're not coming back, so long as they were here we resigned ourselves to this miserable existence, but now, we beg of you, let us in, we'll pay the same rent we paid for the houses we've abandoned, it wouldn't be right to ask us for more, and we swear, by all that is holy and profane, that you will always find everything clean and tidy, for when it comes to keeping house there have never been women to match ours, I know what you're going to say and you're quite right, what about our children, it's true that kids are a mess, but we'll get ours washed and smartened up right away, there's no problem, each room has its own facilities, we hear, choice of shower or bath, hot and cold water, this should make it easy to keep clean, and if any of our children have grown up with bad habits, I promise you they'll turn into the cleanest children in the world, all they need is a little time, for that matter, time is all that man needs, the rest is nothing but illusion, this was something no one was expecting, that the rebel leader should suddenly start playing the philosopher.

It is obvious from their features, and their identity cards would confirm it, that the soldiers are truly sons of the people, but either their major has disowned his humble upbringing once he reached the benches of the military academy, or else he was born into those very upper classes for whom the hotels in the Algarve were built. It was difficult to tell from his reply, Get back or I'll smash your face in, for such coarse language is not confined to the lower orders. The troops saw there in the crowd the beloved images of their father and mother, but the call of duty is stronger, You are the light of my eyes, the mother says to her son as he raises his hand to strike her. But the rebel leader called out angrily, turning from pleas to invective in his exasperation, Race of bootlickers, you don't even recognize the breast that gave you milk, poetic license, an accusation with no real meaning or purpose, for there is no son or daughter who remembers such a thing, although there are numerous authorities ready to affirm that deep down in our subconscious we secretly preserve these and other terrifying memories, and that our whole existence consists of these and other fears.

The major was not pleased to find himself accused of bootlicking, and, beside himself with rage, shouted, Charge, just as the fanatical general of the invaders was calling out, Get them, patriots, and they all surged forward at once, fighting hand to hand in a terrible clash. This was the moment when Joaquim Sassa, Pedro Orce, and José Anaiço arrived on the scene, curious but innocent, and they walked straight into trouble, for once things got out of control the troops did not discriminate between actors and spectators, and one could say that the three friends who had no need of a new home suddenly found themselves obliged to fight for one. Pedro Orce, despite his years, fought as if this were his native land, the others did the best they could, perhaps a little less, belonging as they did to a peaceful race. People were injured, they either dragged themselves or were carried to the side of the road, the women burst into tears and cursed the enemy, the infants had been left in the safety of the chariots, for a battle of this nature can only be called medieval and described with the words of that age. A stone thrown from afar by a youth called David knocked Major Goliath to the ground, blood pouring from a deep gash on his chin, his steel helmet was no protection, this is what happens, ever since soldiers stopped using visors and nosepieces. But the worst thing was that, in the confusion of the onslaught, the rebels rushed past the troops, breaking through their ranks on all sides, only to disperse at once in an instinctive but clever tactical move, up steep roads and alleys, thus ensuring that the soldiers surrounding the occupied hotel did not rush to the aid of the defeated battalion, no one could remember such a humiliation since the time of the French agrarian revolts in the Middle Ages. One hotel manager, whether mentally disturbed or suddenly converted to the popular cause, opened all the doors of his hotel, saying, Enter, enter, I'd rather have you than have the place deserted.

With this unexpected capitulation, Pedro Orce, José Anaiço, and Joaquim Sassa found themselves occupying a room without any real struggle, and two days later they gave it to one of the needier families, with a paralyzed grandmother and wounded relatives requiring treatment. In the upheaval, the like of which had never been seen before, there were husbands who lost their wives, children who lost their parents, but the sequel of these traumatic separations, something no one could ever have invented, which, in itself, confirms the persuasive truth of the story, the sequel, as we were saying, was that members of a given family, scattered but driven by the same dynamism even when apart, ended up in rooms in different hotels, since it had proved extremely difficult to unite under one roof all those who had been demanding that everyone should be under the same roof, and people usually ended up choosing a hotel by the number of stars on its signboard. The police commissioners, army colonels, and captains of the guard asked for reinforcements, for armored cars, for instructions from Lisbon, the government, not knowing where to turn, gave orders and countermanded them, uttered threats and pleas, it was said that three ministers had already resigned. Meanwhile, from the sands and streets of Albufeira jubilant families could be seen at the hotel windows, on those fine, spacious terraces, with their breakfast tables and padded chaises longues, father was hammering the first nails into place and putting up a clothesline, while mother, singing to herself, was already doing her washing indoors in the bathroom. And the swimming pools were teeming with bathers and divers, no one had remembered to explain to the children that they must take a shower before plunging into the blue water, it is not going to be all that easy to make these people change their habits now that they have left their slums.

Bad example has always prospered and borne more fruit than good advice, and who can tell by what rapid means bad example is transmitted, for within a few hours this popular movement of occupation had jumped over the border and spread throughout Spain, you can imagine what it must have been like in Marbella and Torremolinos, where the hotels are like cities and three are enough to form a megalopolis. Europe, upon receiving these alarming reports, began shouting Anarchy, Social Chaos, Invasion of Private Property, and a French newspaper, influential in forming public opinion, prophetically spelled out in bold print across its front page, You Can't Change Human Nature. These words, however unoriginal, struck a chord in the hearts of Europeans, whenever they spoke of the former Iberian peninsula, they would shrug their shoulders and say to each other, What can you do, they're like that, you can't change human nature, the only exception to this accusing chorus came from a certain modest but Machiavellian newspaper published in Naples, Housing Problem Solved in Portugal and Spain.

During the remaining days the three friends spent in Albufeira, the riot police, bolstered by a special squad, tried to clear one of the hotels by force, but the joint and coordinated resistance of the new arrivals and the owners, the former resolved to hold out to the last, the latter fearful of the havoc usually caused by the so-called rescuers, resulted in the suspension of the operations, which were postponed until another opportunity might arise when time and promises would have weakened the rebels' vigilance. By the time Pedro Orce, Joaquim Sassa, and José Anaiço resumed their journey to Lisbon there already existed democratically elected residents' committees in the occupied buildings, with subcommittees responsible for such matters as hygiene and maintenance, kitchen and laundry, entertainment and recreation, cultural activities, education and counseling, gymnastics and sports, everything, in short, that is essential for the smooth and efficient running of any community. On their own improvised flagpoles the squatters hoisted banners and pennants of every conceivable color, they used anything that came to hand, flags of foreign countries, of sports clubs, of various associations, under the aegis, as it were, of the national colors fluttering at the top, there were even bedspreads hanging from the windows, in admirable imitation of these decorations.

However, an adversative adverb that invariably denotes opposition, restriction, or difference, and that, applied to this situation, reminds us that even the things that are good for some are precisely those that disadvantage others, the savage occupation of these hotels was the drop of water that caused the disquiet that from the outset gripped the rich and powerful to overflow. Many of them, afraid that the peninsula might sink, sweeping away their property and their lives, had fled at once during the exodus of tourists, which obviously does not mean that the former were suddenly foreigners in their own country, although people can belong in various degrees to the country that is naturally and administratively theirs, as history has shown time and time again.

Now, amid the general condemnation of these outrages, which was more universal than general, if we leave aside the incongruous attitude of that insignificant Neapolitan paper, there occurred a second emigration, so massive one feels justified in thinking that it had been carefully planned once it became clear to all that the wounds inflicted on Europe would never heal, that the physical structure of the peninsula had split, who would ever have believed it, just where it seemed strongest. The huge bank accounts suddenly dwindled, leaving a bare minimum, just a token sum, about five hundred escudos in Portugal, about five hundred pesetas in Spain, or perhaps a little more, current accounts were practically wiped out, time deposits were closed with some loss of interest, and everything, all of it, gold, silver, precious stones, jewels, works of art, bonds, everything was carried off by the strong gusts of wind that swept the fugitives' personal property over the sea, in all thirty-two directions of the compass, they hoped to recover the rest one day, with time and patience. Clearly, these great removals could not be achieved within twenty-four hours, but a week was all that was needed for the social physiognomy of these two Iberian countries to be transformed from top to bottom, from side to side. Any observer unaware of the facts and motives, and allowing himself to be taken in by appearances, would have come to the conclusion that the Portuguese and the Spaniards had been reduced to poverty from one minute to the next, when in fact all that had happened was that the rich had gone away, and without them the demographics soon showed a dramatic decline.

To those observers who can see an entire Olympus of gods and goddesses where there are nothing but passing clouds, or to those who have Jupiter Tonans before their eyes but refer to him as atmospheric vapor, we shall never tire of pointing out that it is not enough to speak of circumstances, with their bipolar division into antecedents and consequences, as one does to reduce the mental effort, but that one must rather consider what is infallibly situated between the former and the latter, let us spell them all out in the right order, time, place, motive, means, person, deed, manner, for unless we measure and ponder everything, we are bound to make some fatal mistake in the very first opinion we offer. Man is undoubtedly an intelligent being, but not as intelligent as one would like, and this is a proof and confession of humility, which should always begin at home, as one says of charity in the proper sense of the word, before you reproach us.

*T*hey arrived in Lisbon as night was falling, at that hour when the gentle light fills souls with sweet remorse, now one sees how right that admirable judge of sensations and impressions was when he maintained that landscape was a state of mind, what he was not able to tell us was what it looked like in the days when there was nothing but pithecanthropus in the world, with as yet scant soul, and not just scant but confused as well. Thousands of years later, and thanks to evolution, Pedro Orce can now recognize in the apparent melancholy of the city the faithful image of his own intimate sadness. He had grown accustomed to the company of these Portuguese who had come to look for him in those inhospitable parts where he was born and lived, soon they will have to go their separate ways, each man to his own destination, not even families can resist the erosion of necessity, so what are mere acquaintances to do, friends of recent vintage and delicate roots.

Deux Chevaux crosses the bridge slowly, at the lowest speed permitted, to give the Spaniard time to admire the beauty of the views of land and sea, and also the impressive feat of engineering that links the two banks of the river, this construction, we are referring to the sentence, is periphrastic, and is used here to avoid repeating the word bridge, which would result in a solecism, of the pleonastic or redundant kind. In the various arts, and above all in that of writing, the shortest distance between two points, even if close to each other, has never been and never will be, nor is it now, what is known as a straight line, never, never, to put it strongly and emphatically in response to any doubts, to silence them once and for all. The travelers were so absorbed in the wonders of the city, so thrilled by this prodigious achievement, that they did not even notice how the starlings suddenly took fright. Drunk on altitude, gliding dangerously close to the enormous pillars that rose from the waters to support the sky, on this side the city with its windowpanes aflame, beyond the sea and the sun, and below the great river flowing past, like a sluggish current of lava burning beneath the ashes, the birds abruptly changed course, with a rapid cascade of wing-flaps, and it was as if the earth were rotating around the bridge, the north becoming east and then south, the south west and then north, where in the world shall we end up when we ourselves are forced one day to move just as much or even more. As we have already stated, men, even when they see these things, fail to understand them, nor did these men understand what they saw on this occasion.

They were halfway across the bridge when Pedro Orce murmured, Nice city, words as amiable as these call for no reply, except perhaps for a modest, Yes, isn't it. There would still be enough time to leave Pedro Orce settled in a hotel and continue their journey, at least as far as the town in Ribatejo where José Anaiço lives, and where Joaquim Sassa could if he wished spend another night beneath the fig tree, but it would have been impolite to abandon their visitor, so the two Portuguese had made a joint decision, they would remain there for a few days, sufficient time for the Spaniard to get to know the city and once back in Orce to make his own the words of that old saying that innocently boasts, Lisbon the lovely, Lisbon the fair, Never to see her's to miss something rare, praise be to God who has given us rhymes without denying us His blessings.

Joaquim Sassa and José Anaiço are not short of money, they had gathered what they had for their excursion across the border and back, and they had managed to economize, as we know, sleeping on one occasion under the moonlight, on another spending the night at the home of an Andalusian pharmacist, and, profiting from the anarchy and disorder in the Algarve, they received no bill for their stay in a hotel. Here in Lisbon, hotels have only been besieged and occupied on the outskirts of the city, the more central hotels were spared, two countervailing factors came into play, first, this being the capital, as in most countries you are likely to find the greatest concentration of the forces of law and order, or repression, here, second, that timidity peculiar to the city-dweller, who often becomes uneasy, withdrawing once he senses that he is being observed and judged by his neighbor, and vice versa, the protozoa in the drop of water certainly disturb the lens and the eye behind it that observes and disturbs them. Because of the lack of clients, nearly all the hotels had closed their doors, for repairs, this was their excuse, but some continued to function, offering low-season tariffs and special reductions, to the point where some large families seriously considered abandoning the houses for which they were being charged colossal rents, and taking up residence in the Méridien or some such hotel. The aspirations of the three travelers did not rise to so dramatic a change of status, which is why they decided to install themselves in a modest hotel, at the end of the Rua do Alecrim, on the left as you go down, the name has no bearing on this story, once was enough and perhaps even superfluous.

Starlings are starlings, and the word is also used for people who are frivolous and giddy, in other words people who rarely reflect on their actions, who are incapable of foreseeing or imagining anything beyond the here and now, which is not incompatible with certain acts of generosity, even the sacrifice of one's own life, as we saw in the episode at the frontier, when so many tender little bodies dropped dead, shedding their blood for the sake of others, remember we're speaking about birds, not people. But frivolity and giddiness are the least one can attribute to these thousands of birds who foolishly go and perch on a hotel roof, attracting the attention of the crowd and of the police, of ornithologists and of gourmets who relish a tasty meal of little fried birds, and thus betray the presence of the three men who, with no guilt weighing on their conscience, have nevertheless become the target of some unwelcome attention from the authorities. For unbeknownst to the travelers, the Portuguese papers, on the page that regularly features unusual events, had reported the irresistible attack the starlings waged on the unsuspecting border guards, invoking, as one might have expected, though with scant originality, the Hitchcock film we mentioned earlier. Now the newspapers, the radio and television stations, informed promptly about the strange happenings at the Cais do Sodré, sent reporters, photographers, video technicians to the scene, which might have had no consequences beyond enriching the Lisbon folklore, if the methodical and, why not say it, scientific mind of a certain journalist had not led him to consider a possible connection between the starlings outside on the roof and the guests inside the hotel, either permanent or simply passing through. Unaware of the danger literally hovering over their heads, Joaquim Sassa, José Anaiço and Pedro Orce, each in his own room, were unpacking the little luggage they were carrying, within a few minutes they would be down on the street, having decided to take a quick look around the city, until it was time for dinner. But at this precise moment the quick-witted journalist is consulting the guest list, running through the names of those registered, and suddenly two of those names begin to set the wheels of memory in motion, Joaquim Sassa, Pedro Orce, he would not be much of a journalist had those names escaped his eye, the same thing might have happened with another name, Ricardo Reis, but the book where that name was once registered, many, many years ago, is stored away in the archives, covered with dust in the attic, written on a page that may never come to light, and if it should, most likely the name will be illegible, the line will be faded, or even the entire page, that's one of the effects of time, to blot out everything. To this day there has been no greater achievement in the art of hunting than killing two rabbits at one blow, from now on the number of rabbits within the scope of the hunter's skill will be increased from two to three, this will mean reversing all the books of proverbs, so where you see two, read three, and perhaps we won't stop here.

Requested to come down to reception, then installed in the lounge before the great mirror of truth, when pressed by the journalists Joaquim Sassa and Pedro Orce had no choice but to confirm that they were, respectively, the one who threw the stone into the sea and the living seismograph. But there are the starlings, it's surely not by chance that so many starlings have gathered here, the observant reporter re-marked, whereupon José Anaiço, loyal to his friends and true to the facts, made a statement, The starlings are accompanying me. Most of the questions addressed to Joaquim Sassa, and the corresponding an-swers, coincided with the dialogue he had imagined between himself and the civil authorities, which explains why they aren't repeated here, but Pedro Orce, who hadn't exactly been a prophet in his own country, talked at length about the recent events in his life, Yes sir, he could still feel the earth tremor, deep and intense, as if his bones were vibrating, and in Granada, Seville, and Madrid he had undergone multiple tests to check his emotions and intellect, his sensory reactions and movements, and here he was, prepared to subject himself to sim-ilar or different checks if the Portuguese authorities should consider them necessary. Meanwhile, darkness had fallen, the starlings respon-sible for this investigation had dispersed into the trees of the nearby gardens, the journalists, having run out of questions and slaked their curiosity, departed with their cameras and flashlights, but this did not restore peace in the hotel, waiters and porters invented excuses for coming to the reception desk and looking into the lounge to see what these freaks were like.

Worn out by the endless upheaval, the three friends decided not to go out but to dine in the hotel. Pedro Orce was worried about the consequences of having allowed himself to get carried away and of having talked so much, After they warned me over and over in Spain not to say a word about my situation, they won't like it when they find out, but perhaps if I stay on here for a few days they will forget all about me. José Anaiço was doubtful, Tomorrow our story will be in all the newspapers, they might even have it on television this eve-ning, and those newscasters on the radio won't keep their mouths shut, they never get tired, and Joaquim Sassa retorted, Even so, among the three of us, you're the best off, you can always argue that you're not to blame if the starlings follow you, you don't whistle to them or feed them, but we're both in a tight spot, people stare at Pedro Orce as if he were some crank, the Portuguese scientists won't want to lose this guinea pig, and they won't let up on me with this story about the stone, You two have the car, Pedro Orce reminded them, you can leave at the crack of dawn, or even tonight, I'm staying on, if they ask me where you've gone, I'll say I don't know, It's much too late now, the moment I appear on television someone will telephone from the town where I live just to say that they know me, that I'm the local schoolmaster, and that they've been suspicious for some time, some people thirst for glory, this is what José Anaiço had to say, and he added, It's better for us to stick together, we just won't say very much and they'll get tired pretty quickly.

As predicted, there was a full report on the final news bulletin on television, they showed the starlings in flight, the façade of the hotel, the manager making statements we know to be false, as will soon become clear, These events are without precedent in the history of this hotel, and the three prodigies, Pedro, José, and Joaquim, answering questions.

As always when it is thought necessary to have the additional backing of some reliable authority, there was an expert in the studio, in this instance a specialist in the modern discipline of psychodynamics, who, among other speculations about the nature of the matter at hand, declared that there was always the possibility that one was dealing with out-and-out charlatans. It's well known, he declared, in moments of crisis such as this, you can always rely on some impostor or other to turn up, tellers of tall tales who are out to take advantage of the gullible masses, often intent upon destabilizing the political scene or furthering plots for an eventual coup d'état. If people believe him, we've had it, Joaquim Sassa observed, And what about the starlings, what's your opinion about the starlings, the announcer wanted to know, This is indeed a fascinating enigma, either the person the birds are following is carrying some irresistible bait, or it's a question of collective hypnosis, It can't be easy to hypnotize birds, On the contrary, a hen can be hypnotized with a simple piece of chalk, even a child can do it, But here we have two or three thousand starlings all at once, how could they fly if they were hypnotized, Observe that for each bird that forms part of it the flock is already a hypnotic agent, agent and result simultaneously, Allow me to remind you that some of our viewers will have difficulty in following such technical jargon, Well, to put it more simply, I'd say that the entire group tends to constitute itself in homogeneous hypnosis, I doubt whether that will be any easier to understand, but I'd like to thank you just the same for coming to the studio, there are sure to be further developments and we'll have another opportunity to discuss the matter in greater depth, I'm at your disposal, the expert smirked. The one person who was not amused was Joaquim Sassa, who muttered, The man's a fool, He certainly looks like one, but there are times when even fools must be heeded, José Anaiço replied, and Pedro Orce confided, I didn't understand a word, this was the first time the Portuguese tongue had left him completely baffled, if we take the meaning of his words literally, what a splendid conversation there must have been between those ancient Portuguese warriors, Viriato and Nuno Alvares Pereira, heroes of the same fatherland, as we're led to believe. While these grave matters were being discussed in the hotel lounge, in his private office the manager was receiving a delegation of restaurateurs from the vicinity who had come to offer him a deal. How much would you charge us to set up some nets on the roof, sooner or later the starlings will come back and settle there again, we don't want to put nets on the trees, within everyone's reach, that would be just like getting other men's wives pregnant, these are the kind of men who believe that the only innnermost meaning of things is that they have no innnermost meaning, the manager wavers, he's afraid he might damage the roof tiles, but he finally agrees, suggests a figure, That's a lot of money, the others say, and start haggling over the price.

Early the next morning, another delegation of solemn-faced gentlemen, neatly turned out, extremely formal, came to ask Joaquim Sassa and Pedro Orce if they would be so good as to accompany them, they were acting on government orders, among the officials there was also a counselor from the Spanish Embassy who greeted Pedro Orce, but with such manifest hauteur as could only stem from outraged patriotism. They wished to carry out a brief investigation, they explained, all very straightforward, the time it takes for a routine inquiry, which will be added to the already voluminous dossier on the rupturing of the peninsula, to all appearances irremediable, if we take into account its continuous displacement, fatal, in other words. They ignored José Anaiço, probably doubting that he could be endowed with powers of attraction and enticement comparable only to those of the Pied Piper of Hamelin, besides, the starlings are nowhere to be seen, they are flying back and forth, together, getting to know the city, inside the nets that had treacherously been set up on the roof only four stray sparrows lay trapped awaiting their fate, but now destiny decreed a different end to their life, Which fate, asks an ironic voice, and thanks to this unexpected intervention we learn that there is more than one fate, contrary to what we are told, in *fados* and folk music, No one escapes his fate, it is always possible that some other person's fate might befall us, that's what happened to the sparrows, they met the fate of the starlings.

José Anaiço stayed in the hotel, quietly awaiting the return of his companions, he ordered some newspapers, the interviews made all the front pages, with explosive photographs and dramatic headlines, Enigmas Baffle Science, The Unknown Forces of the Mind, Three Dangerous Men, The Mystery of the Hotel Bragança, we had been careful not to specify the name, only to find it published by some treacherous reporter, Will Spaniard Be Extradited, question mark, We're up the creek, this is not a headline but what José Anaiço was thinking. The hours passed, it was time for lunch, there was no news from Joaquim Sassa and Pedro Orce, no message, have they been arrested, thrown into prison, a man loses his appetite with so much worry. I don't even know where they were taking them, how stupid of me, I should have asked, what am I talking about, what I should have done was to go with them, not to leave them on their own, calm down, even if I'd wanted to go, they probably wouldn't have let me, but how can one be sure, I was quite happy to be left out of it, cowardice is worse than an octopus, an octopus can both contract and extend its arms, cowardice can only contract them, from these barbed words one can see just how annoyed José Anaiço is with himself, but who can tell where sincerity lies in these contradictory impulses and thoughts, best to wait, as in all human affairs, to see what he does. First he went to ask the manager whether he had heard any revealing remark, an address, a name, but the manager replied, Nothing at all, sir, I didn't know any of the gentlemen, I was seeing them for the first time, and that goes for the two Portuguese as well as the Spaniard, suddenly José Anaiço had a brainstorm, and about time too, he would go to the Spanish Embassy, the Embassy is bound to know, and then he had another brainstorm, these never came singly, the press, of course, he need only turn to one of those newspapers and within a few hours all the sleuths of the press, be they named Argos, Holmes, or Lupin, would be on the trail of the missing men, necessity is indeed the mother of invention, in this instance the father is called caution, but not always.

Wasting no time, José Anaiço went up to his room, he wanted to change his shoes, to brush his teeth, these mundane things are not incompatible with a resolute spirit, take Othello, for example, who, suffering from a cold and without realizing what he was doing foolishly blew his nose before killing Desdemona, who, for her part, notwithstanding her dark premonitions, didn't lock her door, for a wife never refuses her husband even if she knows he is about to strangle her, and besides, Desdemona knew very well that the room had only three walls, in the present drama, then, José Anaiço is cleaning his teeth with a brush and rinsing out his mouth when he hears someone knocking, Who is it, he asked, although it doesn't sound like his voice the tone is one of happy anticipation, Joaquim Sassa is about to reply, We're back, but the deception was short-lived, May I come in, so it's the maid after all, One moment, he finished rinsing his mouth, wiped his hands and his mouth, dried them, and finally went to open the door. The maid is an ordinary hotel employee with such individual traits and so specific a role that this is the only moment in her life in which she will impinge, ever so superficially, and only for as long as it takes to deliver a simple message, on the existence of José Anaiço and his companions, both present and future, this often happens in the theater and in life, we need someone to come and knock on our door simply to tell us, There is a lady downstairs looking for you, sir. José Anaiço is taken aback and shows his surprise, Looking for me, and the maid adds what she had felt would be necessary, The lady asked to speak to all three of you, but since the others aren't here, She must be a journalist, José Anaiço thought to himself before replying, I'll be down at once. The maid retreated like someone withdrawing from life, we won't need her any more, there's no reason why we should remember her, even with indifference. She came, knocked on the door, delivered the message, which for some strange reason wasn't given over the telephone, perhaps life enjoys cultivating from time to time this sense of the dramatic, if the telephone rings we think, What can it be, if someone's knocking at our door, we think to ourselves, Who can it be, and we give voice to our thoughts by asking, Who is it. We already know it was the maid, but the question was only half answered, perhaps not even that, which is why José Anaiço is pensive as he descends the staircase. Who can it be, he has forgotten his suspicion that it might be a journalist, some of our thoughts are like this, they serve only to occupy, as if in anticipation, the place of others that would give us much more food for thought.

The hotel is so very peaceful, like an empty house bereft of restless activity, but it has not yet aged from neglect, there are still the echoes of footsteps and voices, a sob, a whispered farewell that lingers on the upper landing. The manager is on his feet, behind the counter hangs the key rack with its pigeonholes for messages, letters, and bills, he is writing in a ledger or copying figures from it onto a sheet of paper, the type of man who keeps himself busy even when there is not much work to be done. As José Anaiço is about to pass, the manager nods in the direction of the lounge, and José Anaiço responds with an assenting nod, I know, is what this nod implies, while the first nod had implied at greater length, There's a lady in there waiting to see you. José Anaiço paused in the entrance to the lounge, he saw a young woman, a mere girl, it can only be her, there's no one else here, although she's sitting in the shadow of the awnings, she seems pleasant, even pretty, she is wearing blue slacks and a matching jacket, of a color that might be described as indigo, she might or might not be a journalist, but beside the chair where she is sitting there is a small suitcase and on her lap a stick that is neither large nor small, some-

100

where between a meter and a meter and a half in length, the effect is disturbing, a woman dressed like this doesn't walk through the city carrying a stick in her hand, She can't be a journalist, José Anaiço thought to himself, at least there's no sign of the tools of that profession, notebook, ballpoint pen, tape recorder.

The woman got up, and this gesture was unexpected, for according to the rules of etiquette and good manners a lady should remain seated until the gentleman approaches and greets her, at which point she will extend her hand or offer her cheek, and depending on her confidence, degree of intimacy, and disposition, the lady's smile will be polite, insinuating, conniving, or revealing. This gesture, or perhaps not so much the gesture as the fact that four paces away a woman is standing there waiting, or rather the sudden awareness that time has stopped and is waiting for someone to make the first move, it is true that the mirror is a witness, but of an earlier moment, in the mirror José Anaiço and the woman are still two strangers, not here on this side, for they are about to know each other, they know each other already. This gesture, this gesture that could not be fully described earlier, caused the wooden floor to sway like a deck, like the pitching of a ship amid the waves, slow and wide, an impression not to be confused with the familiar tremor that Pedro Orce talks about, José Anaiço's bones don't shake, but his whole body has felt, physically and materially felt, that the peninsula, so called out of habit and convenience, is really and truly sailing away, before he only knew it from external observation, now he can actually feel it. And so, because of this woman, unless it was because of the hour when she turned up, for most important of all is the hour when things happen, José Anaiço ceased to be merely the unwilling lure of demented birds. He goes up to her, and this movement, launched in the same direction, will be added to the force that pushes, without remedy or resistance, the raft of which the Hotel Bragança at this very moment is the figurehead and forecastle, if you'll forgive the blatant inappropriateness of these terms. Is that too much to ask.

My friends aren't here, José Anaiço explained, some scientists came this morning and took them away for questioning, I'm beginning to get worried at the delay, in fact I was just getting ready to go out and look for them, José Anaiço is aware that, to say what mattered, there was no need for all these words, but he could not restrain himself. She responds, and her voice is pleasing, low but clear, What I have to say can be said just as well to one of you as to all three, in fact it might make it easier to explain things more clearly. Her eyes are the color of a new sky, What is a new sky, what color might that be, where did I dig out that idea, José Anaiço thinks to himself, while saying in a loud voice, Please be seated, there's no need to stand. She sat down, he sat down, Are you called José Anaiço, My name is Joana Carda, Delighted to meet you. They didn't shake hands, that would look silly now that they were seated, besides, in order to shake hands they would both have to lean forward in their chairs, even sillier, or perhaps only he would have to do so, which would halve the silliness, if being half silly were not exactly the same as being completely silly. She is indeed pretty, and her hair, which is almost black, doesn't clash with her eyes, the color of a new sky by day, the color of a new sky by night, they go well together, What can I do for you, his intimate thoughts were translated by this polite inquiry. I'm not sure if it's safe to speak here, Joana Carda murmured, We're alone, no one can hear us, But people are watching, look out. Walking in a somewhat unnatural manner, the manager passed in front of the entrance to the lounge, he passed then passed once more, seemingly absorbed, as if he had just invented a new task, because the previous one had proved useless. José Anaiço glared at him but to no avail, he lowered his voice, making their conversation look even more suspicious, I can't invite you up to my room, aside from the attention it would attract, it's almost certainly forbidden for guests to receive visitors in their rooms. That wouldn't bother me, I wouldn't feel threatened by someone who obviously has no intention of assaulting me, In fact nothing could be further from my mind, especially since you're carrying a weapon. They both smiled, but there was something forced about their smiles, a certain inhibition, a sudden disquiet, indeed, the conversation had become much too intimate considering that they had only known each other for three minutes, and only by name. In an emergency this stick could be useful,

Joana Carda observed, but that's not the reason why I carry it with me, to tell the truth, the stick is carrying me. This revelation, so unexpected, cleared the air, reduced the pressure, that of the atmosphere as well as that of the blood. Joana Carda rested the elm branch on her lap, waited for his reply, José Anaiço finally spoke, We'd better go out, we can talk on the street, in a café, or if you like in a public park. She reached for her suitcase, he took it from her, We can leave this in my room, along with the stick, The stick stays with me, and the suitcase too, it might be better not to come back here. As you wish, what a pity your suitcase is so small, otherwise you could have put the stick inside, Not everything is made to fit something else, Joana Carda replied, a somewhat obvious statement, which nonetheless embraces a world of meaning.

As they were leaving, José Anaiço said to the manager, If my friends should arrive, tell them I'll be back soon, Yes sir, leave it to me, the man replied, without taking his eyes off Joana Carda, but there was no desire in his eyes, only that vague suspicion one finds in all hotel managers. They went down the stairway, at the bottom, on the finial of the banister, there was an ornamental statuette in bronze, modeled on a knight or a page from some opera, here is an effigy that would look right, with its illuminated globe, on any of the great Portuguese or Galician capes, that of São Vicente, Espichel, Roca, or Finisterre, and others of less importance, which nonetheless have just as much work to do breaking the waves, but the destiny of this knight is to be ignored, perhaps once upon a time someone may have looked at him closely, but not Joana Carda or José Anaiço, undoubtedly because they have greater worries on their mind, although, if asked, they probably wouldn't know what they are. Anyone inside that hotel, with its cool atmosphere and secular penumbra, cannot imagine just how hot it is out in the street. This is August, as you may recall, the climate hasn't changed just because the peninsula has traveled a mere one hundred and fifty kilometers, assuming that the speed has remained steady as reported by the National Radio of Spain, no more than five days have passed and it already seems like a year. José Anaiço remarked, as one would expect, Walking around in this heat, carrying a suitcase in one hand and a stick in the other, isn't much fun, we'll be worn out in no time, it would be better to go into a café and have a cool drink, Better still to find a park, a bench in some quiet, shady corner, There's a park nearby, at the Praça de Dom Luís, do you know it, I'm not from Lisbon, but I know it, Oh, you're not from Lisbon, José Anaiço repeated idly. They went down the Rua do Alecrim, he was carrying the suitcase and the stick, people on the street wouldn't think much of him were he not to carry the suitcase or have much respect for her if she were to carry the stick, for we are all such relentless busybodies, malicious whenever we get the chance, and for no good reason. In response to José Anaiço's cry of surprise, Joana Carda simply told him that she had arrived that same day, by train, and had gone straight to the hotel, the rest we are about to learn.

They are seated, fortunately in the shade of some trees, and he has asked her, What brought you to Lisbon, then, why did you come to look for us, and she told him, Because it must be true that you and your friends have something to do with what is happening, Happening, to whom, You know very well what I'm referring to, the peninsula, the breaking up of the Pyrenees, this voyage, the like of which has never been seen before. Sometimes I think the same, that we're to blame, at other times I think we must all be mad, A planet that goes around a star, turning and turning, one minute day, the next night, one minute cold, the next hot, and an almost empty space where there are gigantic things that have no names other than the ones we give them, and a thing we call time that no one can really fathom, all this must also be crazy, Are you an astronomer, José Anaiço asked her, suddenly remembering Maria Dolores, the anthropologist from Granada, I'm neither an astronomer nor a fool, Forgive my rudeness, we're all rather nervous, words don't express what they're meant to, we talk either too much or too little, do forgive me, You're forgiven, I probably strike you as being rather skeptical because nothing has ever happened to me except the starlings, although, Although, Not so long ago, in the hotel, when I saw you in the lounge, I felt as if I were on a ship at sea for the first time, And I saw you as if you were coming from a distance, And yet you were only three or four paces away.

Appearing from everywhere on the horizon, the starlings suddenly alit on the trees in the park. From the nearby streets, people came running, looking upward, pointing, They're back again, José Anaiço sighed impatiently, and worst of all, we won't be able to speak with all these people around. At this moment, the starlings all took flight together, they covered the park with a great fluttering, a black cloud, people were shouting, some with annoyance, others with excitement, yet others with fear, Joana Carda and José Anaiço stared unable to grasp what was happening, then the huge flock dwindled away to form a wedge, a wing, an arrow, and after circling rapidly three times, the starlings disappeared in a southerly direction, crossed the river, vanished into the distance, over the horizon. The assembled crowd, both curious and frightened, let out cries of amazement, of disappointment too, within minutes the park was deserted, the heat was back, on the bench sat a man and a woman all alone, they had an elm branch and a suitcase. José Anaiço said, I don't think they'll ever come back, and Joana Carda replied, Let me tell you what happened to me.

Once the seriousness of the facts related had been established, prudence decreed that Joana Carda should not lodge in that famous hotel where nets had been spread out on the roof, in the vain hope that the starlings would settle there. It was a wise decision on her part, and at least forestalled any further modification of the proverb about killing two birds with one stone, in other words, it prevented this woman well versed in metaphysical skirmishing from falling into the same trap as the three suspects, if they have not already been found guilty. Putting what has been written into somewhat less baroque language and using less convoluted syntax, Joana Carda installed herself further up the street in the Hotel Borges, right in the heart of the Chiado, with her suitcase and her elm branch, which unfortunately is neither telescoping nor easily packed away, so that people stare in amazement when she passes, and the receptionist at the desk, jesting to disguise his genuine curiosity, but without being impolite, makes a discreet reference to wands that are not walking sticks, Joana Carda responded with silence, after all, there is no law to prohibit guests from taking even a branch of holm oak into their room, much less a thin little stick, not even two meters long, which fits easily into the elevator and can be neatly stored away out of sight in a corner.

José Anaiço and Joana Carda carried on their conversation until well after sunset, can you imagine, they discussed the matter from every possible angle, and invariably came to the same conclusion, since it was all so unnatural, things were happening as if a new state of normality had taken the place of what once passed for normal, but without any convulsions, shocks, or changes of color, not that these, if they were to occur, would explain anything. The mistake is entirely ours, with this taste for drama and tragedy, this need for the sublime and the theatrical, we marvel, for example, at the sight of a birth, all the moaning and groaning and shouting, the body opening up like a ripe fig to expel another body, and this is undoubtedly marvelous, but no more marvelous than what we cannot perceive, the burning discharge inside the woman, the fatal marathon, and then the protracted formation of a human being by itself, albeit with some assistance, who will that become, let us stay where we are, the one who is now writing this, inevitably ignorant of what happened to him then, and, let us be frank, not very clear about what is happening to him now. Joana Carda neither knows nor is able to say any more, The stick was lying there on the ground, I drew a line with it, if these things are happening because of what I did, who am I to swear it, you must go there and see for yourself. They went on debating and discussing and darkness was falling when they went their separate ways, she to the Hotel Borges up the street, he to the Hotel Bragança further down, and José Anaiço is smitten with remorse, he did not have the courage to try and find out what happened to his friends, what a jerk, a woman has only to appear and tell him some fairy tale or other for him to spend nearly the entire afternoon listening to her, You should go there and see for yourself, she repeated, slightly modifying the phrase, perhaps to convince him once and for all, repeating oneself in different words is often the only solution. At the entrance to his hotel José Anaiço raises his eyes, no sign of any starlings, that winged shadow that passed, fleeting and gentle as a discreet caress, was only a bat chasing mosquitoes and moths. The little nobleman on the banister has his lamp lit, he is there to welcome guests, but José Anaiço does not even give him so much as a weary glance, he is certainly in for a bad night if Pedro Orce and Joaquim Sassa have not returned.

They have returned. They are waiting in the hotel lounge, seated in the same chairs in which Joana Carda and José Anaiço had sat, and to think that there are people who do not believe in coincidences, when one is constantly discovering coincidences in the world and is beginning to wonder if coincidences are not the very logic of this world. José Anaiço pauses in the doorway of the lounge, it's as if everything were about to be repeated, but no, not just yet, the wooden floor has remained firm, the distance of four paces is no more than a distance of four paces, there is no interstellar void, no leap of death or life, legs moved by themselves, then mouths spoke to say what one might expect, Were you out looking for us, Joaquim Sassa asked, but José Anaiço cannot give a simple answer to such a simple question, Yes, No, both answers would be true, both would be false, he would need a great deal of time to explain, so he replied with a question of his own, as reasonable and natural as the other, Where the hell have you two been all this time. One can see that Pedro Orce is tired, and little wonder, the years, whatever people might say to the contrary, take their toll, but even a young and vigorous man would have come away a wreck from the hands of the doctors, one examination after another, analyses, X rays, questionnaires, tiny hammerblows on the tendons, hearing tests, eye tests, electroencephalograms, no wonder his eyelids feel as heavy as lead, I must lie down, he says, these Portuguese specialists have almost killed me off. It was decided there and then that Pedro Orce should retire to his room until dinnertime, when he could come down and have some broth and breast of chicken despite his poor appetite, he felt as if his stomach were still full of X-ray pap, But you didn't have your stomach X-rayed, Joaquim Sassa reminded him, That's true, but I feel as if I had, Pedro Orce replied, his smile as wan as a withered rose. Have a good rest, José Anaiço suggested, Joaquim and I will eat at some restaurant nearby, we'll talk things over, and when we come back we'll knock on your door and see how you're feeling, Don't knock, I'll almost certainly be asleep, all I want right now is to sleep with no interruptions until tomorrow morning, and off he went shuffling his feet. Poor fellow, what a nice mess we've got him into, this comment was made by José Anaiço, They tormented me as well, with their cross-examining and their endless questions, but that's nothing compared to what they did to him, shall I tell you what this reminds me of, a story I read years ago entitled

At the Mercy of the Quacks, Do you mean the story by Rodrigues Miguéis, That's the one.

Once outside, they decided to go for a long drive in Deux Chevaux, they had plenty of time before dinner, and they could talk freely. People are totally bewildered, began Joaquim Sassa, and if they're latching onto us like this, it's because they've nothing else to go on, or rather, now they're beginning to have almost too much, probably because of the news on television yesterday, and today's reports in the press, did you see the headlines in the evening paper, people are taking leave of their senses, they're turning up from everywhere claiming to have felt the earth trembling, saying that they threw pebbles into the river and a nymph came out of the water, and that their pet budgies are making strange noises, It's always the same, news creates news, but we probably won't see our budgies again, Why not, what's happened, I think they've gone, Just gone, just like that, after following you everywhere all week, So it would appear, Did you see them, Yes, I saw them, they crossed the river heading south and never returned, How did you know they were going away, were you standing near the window in your room, No, I was in a public park nearby, Instead of hanging around there, you might have tried to find out where we were, That was the idea, but then I strolled into the park and stayed there, Getting some fresh air, Speaking to a woman, Well, how about that, a fine friend you've turned out to be, here we are suffering the tortures of the damned and you're putting the moves on a woman, after you got nowhere with the archaeologist from Granada, you're making up for lost time, She wasn't an archaeologist, she was an anthropologist, What's the difference, This one is an astronomer, You're joking, To be honest, I don't know what she does, this business about her being an astronomer comes from something I said to her, Well, that's your business, and I've got no reason to interfere in other people's lives, You've got every reason, what she told me concerns both of us, I know what you're going to tell me, she's also been throwing pebbles, No, Then she can feel the earth shaking, You still haven't got it, Her canary has changed its color, If you start being sarcastic, you'll never find out, Forgive me, but to tell you the truth, I'm really very annoyed,

I cannot forget that you didn't bother to come and look for us, I've already explained to you that I meant to, but then this woman appeared just as I was getting ready to leave, my idea was to start making inquiries at the Spanish Embassy, then she appeared and she told me this story, she showed up carrying a stick in one hand and a suitcase in the other, she was wearing blue slacks and a jacket to match, she had black hair and the whitest of skin, her eyes were strange and difficult to describe, These are interesting details for the history of the peninsula, I suppose you're now going to tell me that this woman is beautiful, Yes, she is, Young, Yes, she does look young, although not exactly a girl. From the way you're talking, you're infatuated, Infatuation is a big word, but it's true that I could feel the floor of the hotel lounge shaking, I've never heard it described like that before, Lay off, Unless you've been drinking and you don't remember, Lay off, will you, All right, I'll lay off, but what did Lady Strange Eyes want, and what kind of stick was it, The branch of an elm tree, I don't know much about trees, what's an elm, Elm is the common word for *ulmus*, and if you'll allow me to digress for a moment, I must say you're pretty skilled when it comes to asking questions. Joaquim Sassa laughed, I must have learned something from those smartalecks who were pestering me earlier, I'm sorry, do finish telling me about the woman, does she have any other name apart from Strange Eyes, She's called Joana Carda, Now that she's been introduced, let's get to the point, Imagine that you find a stick by the road and in a moment of distraction, without any conscious aim, you draw a line on the ground, As a boy I did that quite often, And what happened, Nothing, nothing ever happened, unfortunately, Now imagine that through some magical effect, or something like that, this line produced a crack in the Pyrenees, and that the said Pyrenees split open from top to bottom and the Iberian peninsula began to sail out to sea, Your Joana is mad, There have been other mad Joanas, but this one hasn't come to Lisbon to tell us that because she drew a line on the ground the peninsula broke away from Europe, Thank God there's still some common sense left in the world. What she does say is that the line she drew can't be made to disappear, whether in the wind or by pouring water over it, by scraping it or sweeping it with a brush, or by trampling it underfoot, Nonsense, As nonsensical as your being the most powerful shot-putter of all time, six kilos hurled five hundred meters without cheating, even the great Hercules, demigod that he was, couldn't have beaten your record, Are you trying to tell me that a line drawn on the ground, you said on the ground, didn't you, can resist wind, water, and a sweeping brush, And that even if you rake the soil, the line reappears, That's impossible, You're not being very original, I also used that word, and Little Joana Strange Eyes simply replied, You Must Go There And See For Yourself or You Should Go There And See For Yourself, I can't remember her exact words. Joaquim Sassa fell silent, at this point they were passing through Cruz Quebrada, which means Broken Cross. What sacrilege might these words conceal, words that have now become so innocuous, and José Anaiço said, All this would be absurd if it weren't happening, whereupon Joaquim Sassa asked, But is it really happening.

There was still some daylight, not much, barely enough to glimpse the sea as far as the horizon, from this summit where one descends to Caxias you can judge the scale of these immense waters, perhaps that's why José Anaiço murmured, It's different, and Joaquim Sassa, who had no idea what he was referring to, asked him, What's different, The water, the water is different, life transforms itself like this, it has changed and we haven't even noticed, we were calm, we thought we hadn't changed, an illusion, pure deception, we were moving on with life. The sea pounded against the parapet of the road, and no wonder, for these waves are also different, they are accustomed to having freedom of movement, and no witnesses, except when some tiny vessel passes, not this leviathan that is ploughing the ocean. José Anaiço suggested, Let's eat a little farther down at Paço de Arcos, then we can go back to the hotel, see how Pedro is, Poor guy, they nearly did him in. They parked Deux Chevaux in a side street, went in search of a restaurant, but before they entered, Joaquim Sassa said, During the inquiries and cross-examinations I heard something we never thought of, it was only a word but that was enough, the person who let it slip may have thought I wasn't listening, What are you talking about, Until now, the peninsula, It isn't a peninsula, Then what the hell should we call it, anyway, it has dislocated itself almost in a straight line, staying between the thirty-sixth and forty-third parallels, So what, You may be a good teacher in most subjects, but you're weak when it comes to geography, I don't understand, You'll understand at once if you remember that the Azores lie between the thirty-seventh and fortieth parallels, What the hell, That's what it's going to be, hell, The peninsula is about to collide with the islands, Precisely, It will be the greatest catastrophe in history, Maybe, maybe not, and, as you said yourself a little while ago, all this would be absurd if it weren't happening, now let's go and eat.

They found a place, sat down, and ordered, Joaquim Sassa was starving, he fell on the bread, the butter, the olives, the wine, with a smile that begged for indulgence, This is the last meal of a man condemned to die, and some minutes passed before he asked, And the lady with the wand, where is she at this moment, She's staying at the Hotel Borges, the one on the Chiado, Oh, I thought she lived in Lisbon, No, she doesn't live in Lisbon, that much she did confide, without saying where she comes from, nor did I ask her, probably because I thought we would be taking her there, To do what, To examine the line on the ground, So you also have your doubts, I don't think I'm in any doubt, but I want to see the line with my own eyes, to touch it with my own hands, You're like the man with Platero the donkey, between the Sierra Morena and the Sierra Aracena, If she's telling the truth, we'll see more than Roque Lozano, who will find nothing but water when he reaches his destination, How do you know he was called Roque Lozano, I don't remember our asking him his name, the name of his donkey, yes, but not his. I must have dreamed it, And what about Pedro, will he want to come with us, A man who can feel the ground trembling beneath his feet needs company, Like the man who felt the wooden floor swaying, Peace, Poor Deux Chevaux is going to be too small to carry so many people, four passengers with luggage, even if it's only knapsacks, and the car is old, poor thing, No one can hope to live beyond his last day, You're a prophet, About time you realized it, It looked as if our travels were over, that each of us would go home, back to our normal existence, Let's turn our back on all this and see what happens. So long as the peninsula doesn't collide with the Azores, If that's the end that awaits us, our life is guaranteed until it happens.

They finished their dinner, resumed their journey without haste, at the slow pace of Deux Chevaux, there was little traffic on the road, probably because of the scarcity of gasoline, they were fortunate in having a car that got such good mileage, But we would still run the risk of grinding to a halt somewhere or other, then our journey would really be over, Joaquim Sassa remarked, then suddenly remembering, he asked, Why did you say the starlings must have gone away, Anyone can tell the difference between farewell and so long, what I saw was definitely farewell, I can't explain it, but there is a coincidence, the starlings went away the moment Joana appeared, Joana, That's her name, You could have said the lady, the woman, the girl, that's how male diffidence refers to the opposite sex, when to use their names might seem much too familiar, Compared to your wisdom, mine is rudimentary, but, as you've just seen, I spoke her name quite naturally, proof that my inner self has nothing to do with this matter, Unless, at heart, you're much more Machiavellian than you appear, trying to prove the opposite of what you really think or feel so that I will think that what you think or feel is precisely what you only appear to be trying to prove, I don't know if I've made myself clear, You haven't, but never mind, clarity and obscurity cast the same shadow and light, obscurity is clear, clarity is obscure, and as for someone being able to say factually and precisely what he feels and thinks, don't you believe it, not because he doesn't want to, but because he cannot, Then why do people talk so much, Because that's all we can do, talk, perhaps not even talk, it's all a question of trial and error, The starlings went away, Joana arrived, one form of companionship went, another took its place, you should consider yourself fortunate, That remains to be seen.

At the hotel there was a message for Joaquim Sassa from Pedro Orce, his companion in torment, Don't disturb me, and another from Joana Carda, this time by telephone, for José Anaiço, So it's all true,

he hadn't dreamed it. Over José Anaiço's shoulder, the voice of Joaquim Sassa seemed to be mocking him, Lady Strange Eyes assures you
she's real, therefore don't waste your time dreaming about her tonight.
They went upstairs to their rooms, José Anaiço said, Tomorrow, first
thing in the morning, I'll call her to say we'll go with her, if that's all
right, Fine, and don't pay too much attention to what I said, as you've
probably guessed, I'm jealous. To be jealous of what only appears to
exist is a waste of effort, My wisdom secretly tells me that everything
only appears to exist, nothing actually exists, we must be satisfied with
that, Good night, prophet, Pleasant dreams, comrade.

*P*eople neither knew nor suspected what was going on, such was the secrecy with which governments and scientific institutions set about investigating the subtle movement that was carrying the peninsula out to sea with enigmatic persistence and constancy. To discover how and why the Pyrenees had cracked was no longer a matter for discussion, any hope of redressing the situation was abandoned within days. Despite the vast amount of accumulated information, the computers coldly demanded fresh data or gave preposterous results, as in the case of the famous Massachusetts Institute of Technology, whose programmers blushed with embarrassment upon receiving on their terminals the peremptory diagnosis, Overexposure to the sun, would you believe. In Portugal, perhaps because of the difficulty, even today, of ridding everyday speech of certain archaisms, the nearest conclusion we could reach was, The pitcher goes so often to the well that the handle finally stays there, a metaphor that only served to confuse people, since it wasn't a question of handles or wells or pitchers, but it is not difficult to perceive in it a reference to the effects of repetition, whose very nature, making allowances for frequency, is such that one never knows where it might end. Everything depends on the duration of the phenomenon, on the accumulated effect of these actions, something along the lines of A steady fall of water wears away the hardest stone, a formula that curiously has never been output by a computer, although it might well be, for between the one and the other there are similarities of all kinds, in the first instance there is the heavy weight of the water in the pitcher, in the second instance there is water once more but this time drop by drop, dripping freely, and there is time, that other common ingredient.

These are popular philosophies that we could go on discussing forever, but they are of no great interest to men of science, to geologists or oceanologists. For the sake of simple souls, the matter could even be put in the form of an elementary question, one that in its ingenuousness brings to mind that of the Galician confronted by the River Irati, sinking into the earth, Where does this water go, he wanted to know, as you may recall, now we shall phrase it differently, What is happening beneath this water. Out here, where we stand with our feet firmly on the ground, looking at the horizon, or from the air where observation continues indefatigably, the peninsula is a mass of earth that seems, note the verb, seems to float on the waters. But obviously it cannot float. In order to do so it would need to have detached itself from the bottom, which means it would inevitably end up at that same bottom, this time reduced to rubble, for even supposing that under the circumstances a sufficient force could be applied without producing any greater deviation or damage, the disintegrating effect of the water and the maritime currents would progressively reduce the thickness of the navigating platform until the entire layer was dissolved. Therefore, by a process of elimination, we must conclude that the peninsula is sliding over itself at an unknown depth, divided now along a horizontal fault into two slabs, the lower one still part of the earth's crust, the upper one, as already explained, gliding slowly through the darkness of the waters, amid clouds of mud and startled fish, this is how the Flying Dutchman, of unhappy memory, must be navigating through the depths, somewhere in the ocean. The notion is intriguing and mysterious, with a little more imagination it could provide the most fascinating chapter of all for *Twenty Thousand Leagues under the Sea*. We live in another age, however, science is much more exacting, and since it has not proved possible to discover what is causing the peninsula to displace itself above the seabed, someone should go down there to witness the phenomenon with his own eyes, to film the dragging of this great mass of stone, to record, perhaps, the whale's cry, that squeaking, that interminable laceration. For this is the moment for the deep-sea divers.

As everybody knows, divers holding their breath cannot go down very deep or for very long. Fishers of pearls, sponges, or coral can dive to fifty feet, the best of them perhaps even to seventy, and they can stay under for three or four minutes, it's all a question of training and motivation. Here the depths are greater and the waters much colder, even when the body is protected by one of those rubber wet suits that transform anyone, man or woman, into a black Triton, with yellow stripes and dots. So one must have recourse to diving gear, to cylinders of compressed air, and with these more recent techniques and appa ratus, taking a thousand and one precautions, one can reach depths on the order of two or three hundred meters. Better not tempt Providence by attempting to go any farther down, but send down unmanned machines instead, equipped with film and television cameras, sensors, tactile and ultrasonic probes, all the appropriate instruments for the job at hand.

At a given hour, to enable subsequent comparison of results, simultaneous operations began on the coasts to the north, south, and west, discreetly passed off as naval maneuvers within the scope of North Atlantic Treaty Organization training programes, lest the announcement of these investigations provoke fresh outbursts of panic, for, inexplicably, it had not occurred to anyone so far that the peninsula might be sliding over what for millions of years had been its plinth. The moment has come to reveal that the experts intend to keep quiet about another nagging anxiety stemming, almost inevitably, from this same hypothesis of a deep horizontal cut, it can be summed up in this other question of terrifying simplicity, What will happen if an abyss lies in the path of the peninsula, an end to that continuous surface over which it is sliding. Judging from experience, which is always desirable for a better understanding of the facts, in this case our experience as swimmers, we will understand perfectly what this must mean if we recall the novice swimmer's panic and distress when he unexpectedly loses his footing. Should the peninsula lose its footing or its balance, it will inevitably sink, go to the bottom, suffocate, drown, who would have thought that after so many centuries of miserable existence we would be doomed to the fate of Atlantis.

Let us spare ourselves the details, these will one day be divulged for the enlightenment of all those interested in submarine life, for the time being shrouded in the utmost secrecy they are to be found in ships' logs, confidential reports, and various records, some in code. All we shall say is that detailed examination of the continental platform yielded no results, no new crack was found, no abnormal friction was picked up by the microphones. This initial hypothesis having failed, examination of the depths was the next step, and the cranes lowered instruments built to withstand high pressures, to scan and search the depths of the silent waters, but these found nothing. The research submarine *Archimedes*, a jewel of technology French-manned and French-owned, descended to the maximum peripheral depths, from the euphatic to the pelagic zone, and from there to the bathypelagic zone, deployed lamps, pincers, bathometers, sounding lines of various kinds, scanned the subaquatic horizon with its panoramic sonar, to no avail. The vast versants, the steep escarpments, the vertical precipices were exposed in their somber majesty, in their unspoilt beauty, the instruments registered continuously, with much clicking and switching on and off of lights, the ascending and descending currents, they photographed the fish, the shoals of sardines, the colonies of hake, the brigades of tuna and bonito, the flotillas of mackerel, the armadas of swordfish, and if the *Archimedes* had been carrying in its belly a laboratory equipped with the necessary reagents, solvents, and other chemical paraphernalia, it would have been able to identify the elements dissolved in the waters of the ocean, namely, in diminishing order in terms of quantity, and for the cultural benefit of the masses who have not the faintest idea how much exists in the sea where they swim, chlorine, sodium, magnesium, sulfur, calcium, potassium, bromine, carbon, strontium, boron, silicon, fluorine, argon, nitrogen, phosphorus, iodine, barium, iron, zinc, aluminum, lead, tin, arsenic, copper, uranium, nickel, manganese, titanium, silver, tungsten, gold, such riches, dear God, and with all the things we lack on terra firma, the only thing we cannot trace is the crack that would explain the phenomenon, which does exist, after all, and is plain for all to see. In desperation, a North American expert, and one of the most distinguished, went so far as to proclaim before the winds and the horizon, standing on the deck of the hydrographic ship, I hereby declare that the peninsula cannot possibly be moving, whereupon an Italian expert, much less knowledgeable but armed with a historic and scientific precedent, muttered, but not so quietly that he could not be heard by that providential Being who hears all things, *Eppur si muove*. Their researchers empty-handed and chapped by all that salt, humiliated and frustrated, the governments simply announced that under the auspices of the United Nations they had carried out an investigation of possible changes in the habitat of the ichthyic species brought about by the peninsula's dislocation. It was not the mountain that had conceived a mouse, but rather the ocean that had given birth to a tiny sardine.

The travelers heard this news as they were leaving Lisbon but did not consider it important, just one more report among others pertaining to the separation of the peninsula, which itself seemed to be of no great importance. A person can get used to anything, as can nations with even greater ease and speed, when all is said and done it is as if we were now traveling in an immense ship, so big that it would even be possible to live aboard for the rest of one's life without ever seeing the prow or the stern, the peninsula was not a ship when it was still attached to Europe and there were still plenty of people who knew no country other than that of their birth, so tell me, if you please, what's the difference. Now that Joaquim Sassa and Pedro Orce appear to have escaped at last from the obsessive prying of the scientists and there is nothing more to fear from the authorities, they can return to their respective homes, and José Anaiço too, for the starlings have unexpectedly lost interest in him, but the apparition, so to speak, of this woman has sent everything back to square one, this being fairly characteristic of women, although not always in so radical a manner. It was after a meeting in that same park where Joana Carda and José Anaiço had been the day before that the four of them decided, after reexamining the facts, to make the journey together that will take them to the spot marked with a line on the ground, one of those lines we have all had to make in life, but one with singular features, to judge from the agent and witness, coincidently one and the same person. Joana Carda had still not revealed the name of the place or even that of the nearest city, but merely indicated the general direction, We'll take the highway north, then I'll show you how to get there. Pedro Orce had taken José Anaiço discreetly aside to ask him if he thought it was a good idea to set out like this, blindly falling in with the whims of an eccentric woman with a stick in her hand, suppose this were a snare, a plot to kidnap them, a cunning ruse, On whose part, José Anaiço wanted to know, That I can't tell you, perhaps they want to take us to the laboratory of some mad scientist, as you see in films, some Frankenstein or other, Pedro Orce replied smiling, No wonder people are always talking about the Andalusian imagination, it doesn't take much water to start boiling, José Anaiço commented, It's not because there isn't much water, it's because there's so much fire, Pedro Orce replied, Forget it, José Anaiço concluded, what must be, will be, and they rejoined the others, who had started a discussion more or less in this vein, I don't know how it happened, the stick was lying on the ground, I picked it up and drew a line, Did it ever occur to you that it might be a magic wand, It seemed rather big for a magic wand, and I've always heard it said that they are made of shimmering gold and crystal, with a star on top, Did you know it was an elm branch, I know very little about trees but in this case I'm sure a matchstick would have produced the same effect, Why do you say that, What has to be, has to be, and that's something you can't fight, Do you believe in fate, I believe in what must be, Then you're just like José Anaiço, said Pedro Orce, he also believes in fate. The morning, with a light wind that blew like a playful mouthful of air, gave little promise of a warm day, Shall we go, José Anaiço asked, Let's go, they all replied, including Joana Carda who had come to look for them.

Life is full of little episodes that seem unimportant, while others at a certain moment absorb all our attention, when we reappraise them later, in the light of their consequences, we find that our memory of the latter has faded while the former have come to seem decisive or, at least, a link in a chain of successive and meaningful events, to give the example one expects, there will not be any frenetic loading and unloading, apparently so much to be expected when the luggage of four passengers is packed into a car as small as Deux Chevaux. This tricky operation engages everyone's attention, each of them makes some suggestion or proposal, tries to lend a hand, but the main question latent in all this, which may well determine the final constellation of the four people in the car, is at whose side Joana Carda will travel. That Joaquim Sassa should drive Deux Chevaux seems right, on the first leg of a journey a car should always be driven by its owner, this is an undisputed fact that bespeaks prestige, prerogative, a sense of possession. The alternative driver, when the right moment comes, will be José Anaiço, since Pedro Orce, not so much because of his age but because he lives in a terrain disturbed by excavations and his job keeps him behind a counter, has never ventured into the complex mechanics of a steering wheel or gearshift, and it is rather soon to be asking Joana Carda if she knows how to drive. In the light of these details, it seems inevitable that these two should travel in the back seat, with the pilot and copilot logically seated in front. But Pedro Orce is Spanish, Joana Carda is Portuguese, neither of them speaks the other's language, and besides they've only just met, later on, when they've had time to become acquainted, things will be different. The seat beside the driver, although considered by the superstitious and proved by the statistics to be the dead man's seat, is generally regarded as a place of honor and should therefore be offered to Joana Carda, putting her on Joaquim Sassa's right, with the other two men behind, and they should not have much difficulty understanding each other after sharing so many experiences. But the elm branch is much too big to go in front, and Joana Carda has made it clear that nothing will induce her to part with it. So, there being no alternative, Pedro Orce will sit in front for two explicable reasons, each more excellent than the other, first, as we have already said, because it is a place of honor, second, because Pedro Orce is the oldest person here, the one closest to death, on account of what we term, with black humor, the nature of life. But what really counts, more than this twofold reasoning, is that Joana Carda and José Anaiço want to ride together in the back seat, and by means of gestures, pauses, and feigned distractions they've managed it. Let us be seated, then, and get on our way.

The journey was uneventful, that's what novelists in a hurry always say when they think that, in the ten minutes or ten hours they are about to eliminate, nothing has taken place that would warrant any special mention. Strictly speaking, it would be much more correct and honest to put it like this, As in all journeys, whatever their duration and length, there have been a thousand incidents, words and thoughts, and for a thousand you could read ten thousand, but the narrative is dragging, so I'm allowing myself to abbreviate, using three lines to cover two hundred kilometers, bearing in mind that the four people inside the car have traveled in silence, with neither thought nor gesture, pretending that by the end of the journey they will have nothing to relate. In our case, for example, it would be impossible not to derive some meaning from the fact that Joana Carda had quite naturally accompanied José Anaiço when he took over from Joaquim Sassa, who wanted a rest from driving, and that she had managed, God knows how, to squeeze the elm branch into the front, without hampering the driver or blocking his vision. And needless to say, when José Anaiço returned to the back seat, Joana Carda went with him, and so wherever José happened to be Joana was there too, although neither of them could yet say for what reason or purpose, or they knew but cannot bring themselves to say it, each moment has its own flavor and the flavor of this moment has not yet been lost.

There were few abandoned cars on the roads, and those they saw invariably had parts missing, having been stripped of their wheels, headlights, rearview mirrors, windshields, a door, sometimes all the doors, the seats, some cars were even reduced to a bare shell like crabshells with no meat left inside. But the gasoline shortage meant that traffic was thin and there were long intervals between one passing car and the next. Certain incongruities also hit one in the eye, like a cart being drawn by a donkey along the highway, or a squadron of cyclists who even at full speed were far below the minimum speed the signs foolishly continued to impose, indifferent to the force of reality.

And there were also people traveling on foot, usually with a knapsack on their back, or, in rustic fashion, with two sacks loosely tied together at the top and strung over one shoulder like a saddlebag, the women with baskets on their heads. Many people were alone, but there were also families, to all appearances entire families with old and young and babes in arms. When Deux Chevaux had to leave the highway farther ahead, the number of pedestrians diminished only in proportion to the relative importance of the road. Three times Joaquim Sassa tried to ask people where they were going, and they all gave him the same answer, We're on our way to see the world. They must have known that the world, the immediate world, strictly speaking, was now much smaller than before, perhaps for this very reason their dream of knowing all of it had become much more feasible, and when José Anaiço asked, But what about your home and your job, they calmly replied, Our home will be waiting for us and work we can always find, those are the priorities of the past and they must not be allowed to hinder the future. And perhaps it was just as well that people did not ask him the same question, whether too discreet or simply too absorbed in their own affairs, otherwise he would have been forced to explain, We're accompanying this woman to examine the line she drew on the ground with this stick, and as far as their jobs were concerned they would have made a poor impression, perhaps Pedro Orce would have confessed, I've left my patients to look after themselves, and Joaquim Sassa argued, Let's face it, office clerks are a dime a dozen, I won't be missed, besides I'm enjoying a well-deserved vacation, and José Anaiço, I'm in the same situation, if I were to go back to school now I wouldn't find any pupils, until October my time is my own, and Joana Carda, I've nothing to tell you about myself, if I've revealed nothing so far to these men with whom I'm traveling, there's no reason why I should confide in strangers.

They had passed the town of Pombal when Joana Carda informed them, Just ahead there is a road to Soure, that's the one we have to follow, since leaving Lisbon this was the first indication she had given of a specific destination, until now they had felt as if they were traveling through mist, or, adapting this particular situation to general circumstances, they were ancient and ingenuous mariners, We are being carried along by the sea, where will she carry us. They would soon find out. They did not stop in Soure, they went through narrow roads that crossed and forked into two or three branches, and sometimes they seemed to be going around in circles, until they finally reached a village that had a signpost at the limits bearing the name Ereira, and Joana Carda announced, It's here.

Taken by surprise, José Anaiço, who was driving Deux Chevaux at that moment, put his foot down sharply on the brake, as if the line were right there in the middle of the road and he were about to run over it, not that there was any danger of destroying this prodigious bit of evidence, which Joana Carda had described as indestructible, but because of that holy terror that strikes even the most skeptical of men when routine is broken like the thread that broke as we ran it through our hand, confident and with no responsibility but that of preserving, strengthening, and prolonging this thread, and our hand too, as far as possible. Joaquim Sassa looked outside, he saw houses with trees above the rooftops and low-lying fields, the marshes and rice paddies are visible, it's the gentle Mondego, better that than arid rock. Had this been what Pedro Orce was thinking, then Don Quixote of the sad countenance would inevitably come into the story, the one he possessed and the one he presented, when, stark naked, he began jumping up and down like a madman amid the peaks of the Sierra Morena, it would be absurd to draw a comparison with such episodes of knight-errantry, therefore Pedro Orce, on getting out of the car and putting his feet on the ground, simply confirms that the earth is still shaking. José Anaiço walked round Deux Chevaux, went, perfect gentleman that he is, to open the door on the other side, he pretends not to notice the ironic, patronizing smile of Joaquim Sassa, and taking the elm branch from Joana Carda, he extends his hand to help her out, she gives him hers, they clasp hands for longer than is necessary in order to guarantee firm support, but this is not the first time, the first and only other time so far was on the back seat, an impulse, but they did not utter a word either then or now, in a louder or softer tone of voice that might embrace the word spoken by the other with equal force.

This is indeed the hour for explanations, but Joaquim Sassa's question demands others, like the ship's captain who opens sealed orders suspecting that he may find nothing except a blank page, Now where do we go, Now we take this road, Joana Carda replied, and on the way I'll tell you the rest of my story, not that it has anything to do with our coming here, but there's little point in continuing to act like strangers when we've traveled all this way together, You could have told us sooner, either in Lisbon or during the journey, José Anaiço remarked, I don't see why, either you came with me because you were convinced by a single word, or many more words would have been needed to convince you, and then it wouldn't have done much good, As a reward for having believed in you, It's for me to decide your reward and when it should be given, José Anaiço refrained from answering, he played for time, started looking at a row of poplars in the distance, but she heard Joaquim Sassa murmur, What a girl, Joana Carda smiled, I'm no girl, and I'm not the bitch you think I am, I don't think you're a bitch, Domineering, stubborn, conceited, affected, Good heavens, what a list, why not say mysterious and leave it at that, Well, there is a mystery, and I wouldn't have brought anyone here who didn't believe without seeing, not even you in whom no one believes, They're beginning to believe in us now, But I was more fortunate and only needed to say one word, Let's hope many more won't be necessary now. This dialogue was conducted entirely between Joana Carda and Joaquim Sassa, given Pedro Orce's difficulty in understanding and the obvious impatience of José Anaiço, who had been excluded from the conversation through his own fault. But observe how this curious situation, with the differences that always distinguish situations, simply repeats what happened in Granada, when Maria Dolores conversed with one Portuguese but would have preferred to be conversing with another, in this particular case, however, there will be time to explain everything, the man who is really thirsty will have his thirst quenched.

They are now walking along the path, which is narrow, Pedro Orce is obliged to follow the others, they will explain everything to him later, if the Spaniard is truly interested in the fortunes of these Portuguese. I don't live here in Ereira, Joana Carda began, my home was in Coimbra, I've only been here since separated from my husband about a month ago, for what reasons, well, why bother discussing the reasons, sometimes one is enough, at other times not even lumping them all together will do it, if your own lives haven't taught you this, too bad for you, and I repeat, lives not life, for we all have several, and fortunately they kill each other off, otherwise we wouldn't be able to survive. She leapt over a wide ditch, the men followed her, and when the group reassembled, now treading on soft, sandy terrain where the earth had been waterlogged, Joana Carda went on, I'm staying with some relatives, I wanted time to think, but not the usual self-questioning, have I done the right thing, have I done the wrong thing, what is done is done, I wanted time to think about life, what is its purpose, what's my purpose in life, yes, I reached a conclusion, the only possible conclusion, I simply do not understand life. The expression on the faces of José Anaiço and Joaquim Sassa is one of bewilderment, this woman, who came down to the city carrying a stick in her hand to proclaim impossible feats of land surveying, has now turned philosopher here in the fields of Mondego, a philosopher of the negative kind, and to complicate matters, in that special category that says yes after saying no, and that will say no after having said yes. Having been trained as a teacher, José Anaiço is better qualified to understand these contradictions, but this does not apply to Joaquim Sassa, he simply senses them and therefore finds them twice as bewildering. Joana Carda continues to speak, having come to a halt because they are now close to the spot she wants to show them, she still has something to say to them, other things will have to wait, I didn't go to Lisbon to find you because of the strange happenings that attracted so much attention but because I saw you as people detached from any apparent logic in the world, and that's precisely how I feel about myself, I would have been very disappointed if you hadn't accompanied me all this way, but you came, perhaps something still has some

1 2 6

meaning, or will regain it after having lost all meaning, now come with me.

They enter a clearing away from the river, a circle surrounded by ash trees that appear never to have been pruned, such places are less rare than one imagines, set foot in them and time seems to stand still, the silence seems different, you can feel the breeze all over your face and hands, no, we're not talking about witchcraft and sorcery, this is not a witches' coven or a gate to the other world, that is simply the impression created by these trees in the form of a circle and the ground that appears to have lain undisturbed since the beginning of time, the sand simply came and made it soft, but the soil is heavy beneath the humus, whoever planted the trees like this is entirely to blame. Joana Carda has nothing more to tell them. This is where I used to come to think things over, there can be no more peaceful place on earth, but it's disturbing too, you don't have to answer, but if you hadn't come here you wouldn't be able to understand, and one day, two weeks ago to be precise, as I was walking across the clearing to sit down under that tree over there, I found this branch lying on the ground, I was seeing it for the first time, I'd been here the day before and it wasn't here, it was as if someone had put it here deliberately, but there were no footprints to be seen, the marks you can see there are mine, or else were left by people who passed this way a long, long time ago. They are standing on the edge of the clearing, Joana Carda detains the men a bit longer, these are her final words, I picked up the stick from the ground, the wood seemed to be living as if it were the whole tree from which it had been cut, or rather this is what I now feel as it comes back to me, and at that moment, with a gesture more like a child's than an adult's, I drew a line that separated me forever from Coimbra and the man with whom I lived, a line that divided the world into two halves, as you can see from here.

They advanced to the middle of the clearing, drew close, there was the line, as clear as if it had just been drawn, the earth piled up on either side, the bottom layer still damp despite the warmth of the sun. They remain silent, the men are at a loss for words, Joana Carda has nothing more to say, this is the moment for a daring gesture that could make a mockery of her wonderful tale. She drags one foot over the ground, smooths the soil as if she were using a level, stamps on it and presses it down, as if committing an act of sacrilege. The next moment, before the astonished gaze of all the onlookers, the line reappears, it looks exactly as it was before, the tiny particles of soil, the grains of sand resume their previous shape and form, return to where they were before, and the line is back. Between the part that was obliterated and the rest, between one side and the other, there is no visible difference. Her nerves on edge, Joana Carda says in a shrill voice, I've already swept away the entire line, I've covered it with water, yet it keeps reappearing, try for yourselves if you wish, I even put stones on top, and when I removed them the line was still there, why don't you try if you still need convincing. Joaquim Sassa bent down, buried his fingers in the soft earth, scooped up a handful of soil, threw it into the distance, and the line reconstituted itself immediately. Then it was José Anaiço's turn, but he asked Joana Carda to lend him her stick and he drew a deep line alongside the original one, then smoothed it out along its entire length. The line didn't come back. Now you do the same, José Anaiço told Joana Carda. The tip of the stick dug into the soil, was dragged along the ground, opened an extensive wound, which closed up at once like a defective scar when they pressed it down, and so it remained. José Anaiço said, It's got nothing to do with the stick or the person, it's the moment, it's the moment that counts. Then Joaquim Sassa did what had to be done, he lifted up from the ground one of the stones that had been used by Joana Carda, similar in weight and appearance to the one he had thrown into the sea, and gathering all his strength he hurled it as far as he could into the distance, it fell where one expected it to fall, several paces away, that's as much as human strength can achieve.

Pedro Orce had witnessed these trials and experiments without wishing to participate, probably he had enough to contend with as the earth went on shaking under his feet. He took the elm branch from Joana Carda's hands and said, You can break it, throw it away, burn it, they're no longer useful, your stick, Joaquim Sassa's stone, José Anaiço's starlings, they no longer serve any purpose, they're like those men and women who were useful only once, José Anaiço is right, what counts is the moment, we only serve the moment, That may be so, Joana Carda retorted, but this stick will stay with me forever, moments give us no warning when they're coming. A dog appeared among the trees, on the far side. It gave them a long stare, then crossed the clearing, it was a large powerful animal, its tawny coat caught by a sudden ray of sunlight appeared to burst into flames. Taking fright, Joaquim Sassa aimed a stone, the first stone that came to hand, I don't like dogs, but he missed. The dog stopped in its tracks, not the least bit intimidated, not at all menacing, it simply stopped to look, not even barking. As it reached the trees, the dog turned its head, it seemed bigger when seen from a distance, then it went off slowly and disappeared. Joaquim Sassa tried to relieve the tension with a wisecrack, Joana Carda might as well hold onto her stick, it might come in handy if such huge beasts are prowling around.

They returned by the same route, now there were certain practical matters to settle, for example, since it was too late to go back to Lisbon now, where are the men going to spend the night. But it isn't all that late, said Joaquim Sassa, even without rushing we can get back to Lisbon in plenty of time for dinner, As far as I'm concerned, the best solution would be to stay here in Figueira da Foz, or in Coimbra, tomorrow we can come back this way, Joana might need something, José Anaiço said, and there was a note of deep concern in his voice. As you prefer, Joaquim Sassa said with a smile, and the rest of the sentence was no longer in words but in his look, I know exactly how you feel, you want some time to think this evening, you want to decide what to say tomorrow, certain moments arrive without any warning. Pedro Orce and Joaquim Sassa are now leading the way, the afternoon is so peaceful that one is overcome with emotion directed at no one in particular, only at the light, the pale sky, the inert trees, the gentle river whose presence one senses before it looms into sight, a smooth mirror that the birds slowly traverse. José Anaiço takes Joana Carda by the hand, and says, We're on this side of the line, together, but for how long, and Joana Carda replies, We'll soon find out.

As they approached the car they saw the dog, Joaquim Sassa

grabbed another stone, but decided not to throw it. The animal, despite this threatening gesture, did not stir. Pedro Orce went up to it, held out his hand as a gesture of peace, as if about to caress it, but the dog remained impassive, its head raised. It had a chewed thread of blue wool hanging limply from its mouth. Pedro Orce stroked its back, then rejoined his companions. There are moments that warn you when they are coming, the earth is shaking beneath the dog's paws.

Man proposes, dog disposes, this very latest maxim is just as valid as the old one, we must give some name to whoever decides in the final analysis, for decisions don't always come from God, as is generally believed. There they took their leave of one another, the men heading for Figueira da Foz, which is nearest, the woman for the home of her hospitable relatives, but when Deux Chevaux, the brake already released, started moving, to everyone's astonishment the dog was seen to stand in front of Joana Carda, preventing her from passing. It didn't bark, it didn't bare its teeth, the gesture she made with the stick made no impression, after all, it was only a gesture. José Anaiço, who was driving, thought his beloved might be in danger, and, once more the knight-errant, he brought the car to a sudden halt, jumped out, and ran to her assistance, a dramatic but somewhat ineffectual act, as he was soon to realize, for the dog simply lay down on the road. Pedro Orce drew near, Joaquim Sassa too, the latter disguising his antipathy with an air of detachment. What does the beast want, he asked, but no one could give him an answer, not even the dog itself. Pedro Orce, as he had done before, went up to the animal and laid his hand on its huge head. The dog closed its eyes in a wistful manner at this caress, should such an adjective be appropriate here, we are talking about dogs, not about sensitive people who display their sensibility, and then it got up, stared at them one by one, gave them enough time to understand, and started walking. It walked about ten meters, stopped, waited.

Now experience has taught us, and movies and romances are full of similar scenes, Lassie mastered the technique to perfection, for example, experience tells us that a dog always behaves like this when it wishes us to follow. In this instance, the dog was obviously preventing Joana Carda from passing in order to oblige the men to get out of the car, and if, now that they are together, it is showing them the way that its canine instinct suggests they must follow, it is because, pardon these further repetitions, the dog wants them to follow it together. You don't have to be as intelligent as a man in order to grasp this, if an ordinary, simpleminded dog can convey it so easily. But men, having been deceived so often, have learned to put everything to the test, principally by means of repetition, the easiest method of all, and when, as in this case, they have attained a modicum of culture, they are not content with a second experience just like the first, they introduce minor variations that do not radically alter the basic facts, to give an example, José Anaiço and Joana Carda got into the car while Pedro Orce and Joaquim Sassa stayed where they were, now we'll see what the dog does. Let us say that it did what it had to. The dog, which knows perfectly well that it cannot stop a car except by getting in front of it, but that would mean certain death and there is not a single driver whose love for our animal friends is so great that he would stop to witness its last moments or move its pitiful corpse into the gutter, the dog prevented Joaquim Sassa and Pedro Orce from passing just as it had prevented Joana Carda before. The third and decisive proof came when all four of them got into the car and started moving, because Deux Chevaux happened to be facing in the right direction, the dog got in front of it, this time not to obstruct its progress, but to lead the way. All these maneuvers took place without any inquisitive spectators looking on because, as on other occasions since this narrative began, certain important episodes have invariably befallen people entering or leaving towns and cities, and not those inside them, as happens in most cases. This undoubtedly warrants some explanation, but alas, we're unable to give one.

José Anaiço brought the car to a standstill, the dog stopped and looked around, and Joana Carda concluded, It wants us to follow.

They were slow in seeing something that had been obvious from the moment the dog crossed the clearing, let us say that this was the crucial warning, but people do not always pay attention to these omens. And even when there is no longer any reason for doubt, they still persist in ignoring the warning, like Joaquim Sassa when he asks, And why should we follow it, how ridiculous for four grown-ups to go tagging along after a stray dog without even a disk on its collar saying Rescue me, or a name tag, My name is Pilot, please return me to my owners, Mr. and Mrs. So-and-So, at such and such an address, Don't wear yourself out, José Anaiço told him, this episode is as absurd as all the others that keep happening and appear to make no sense, They don't make much sense to me, Don't worry about things not making sense, said Pedro Orce, a journey only makes sense if you finish it, and we're still only halfway there, or perhaps only at the beginning, who knows, until your journey on earth has ended I cannot tell you its meaning, Fine, and until that day arrives, what are we going to do. There was silence. The light fades, the day is drawing to a close, leaving shadows among the trees, the singing of the birds is already different. The dog goes and lies in front of the car, three paces away, resting its head on its outstretched front paws and waiting patiently. Then Joana Carda says, I'm ready to go wherever the dog may lead us, we'll find out if that's what it came for when we reach our destination. José Anaiço took a deep breath, he was not sighing, although people do sigh with relief. So am I, was all he said. And you can count on me, Pedro Orce added, If you're all in agreement, I won't be a killjoy and keep you from walking behind the pilot, we'll go together, I might as well make the most of my vacation, concluded Joaquim Sassa.

Reaching a decision means saying yes or no, the merest whisper on one's lips, the difficulties come later when one puts that decision into practice, as we learn from human experience, gained with time and patience, with few hopes and even fewer changes. We'll follow the dog, yes indeed, but one has to know how, since our guide can't give explanations, it cannot travel inside the car, telling us to turn left, then right, go straight until the third set of traffic lights, besides, and this is a real drawback, how could an animal this size fit into a car where all the seats are already occupied, not to mention the luggage and the elm branch, although the latter is scarcely noticeable when Joana Carda and José Anaiço are sitting side by side. And speaking of Joana Carda, her luggage has yet to come, in fact, it must be collected before they tackle the problem of finding rooms, she must explain her sudden departure to her cousins, but three men, Deux Chevaux, and a dog cannot suddenly appear on the doorstep, to say I'm going with them would be the innocent truth, but surely a woman so recently separated from her husband should give some explanation of her conduct, especially in a place as small as Ereira, a mere village, broken marriages are all very well in capitals and large cities, but even then God alone knows what traumas, what trials of body and soul, they entail.

The sun has already gone down, night is almost here, this is not an hour to be starting a journey into the unknown, and it would be wrong of Joana Carda to disappear without any warning, she told her relatives that she was traveling to Lisbon to attend to some business, she would go and return by train. These are difficulties and complications that we are led into by social conventions and family ties. No sooner had Pedro Orce got out of the car than the dog got up and watched him approach, and there in the twilight they held a conversation, at least that's how we describe it, although we know that this dog is not even capable of barking. When their dialogue ended, Pedro Orce went back to the car and told them, I think Joana Carda can go home now, the dog is staying with us, let's settle where to spend the night and decide how and where to meet tomorrow. No one doubted this assurance, Joaquim Sassa spread out the map and in three seconds they decided they would spend the night in Montemor-o-Velho, in some modest boardinghouse. And if we don't find one, asked Joaquim Sassa, We'll go to Figueira da Foz, José Anaiço replied, actually, better to play it safe, it's probably wiser to spend the night at Figueira, tomorrow you take the bus and we'll wait for you in the parking lot near the casino, needless to say these instructions were addressed to Joana Carda, who accepted them without questioning the competence of the person giving them. Joana said, See you tomorrow, and at the last moment, with one foot already on the ground, she turned and kissed José Anaiço on the lips, this was no little peck on the cheek or at the side of the mouth, these were two lightning flashes, one of speed, the other of impact, but the effects of the latter lingered, something that wouldn't have happened if the contact between their lips, so heavenly, had been prolonged. Her cousins in Ereira would comment, You can't imagine what people are saying, She's nothing but a slut, and to think we believed her husband was to blame, he must have had the patience of a saint, a man you've only known since yesterday and you're already kissing him, you didn't even wait for him to take the initiative, as a wise woman would, for when all is said and done, you have to think about your self-respect, and besides you said you were going and coming back on the same day but you spent the night in Lisbon away from home, what are people going to think. But when everyone's asleep, the wife gets out of bed and goes to Joana's room to ask her what happened, Joana tells her she doesn't really know, and it's the truth, Why did I do what I did, Joana Carda asks herself as she retreats into the deep shadows beneath the trees, her hands are free so that she can lift them to her lips like someone trying to suppress her feelings. Her suitcase had remained in the car to reserve a place for the rest of her luggage, the elm branch is in safe keeping, guarded by three men and a dog, the latter, summoned by Pedro Orce, got into the car and settled down in Joana Carda's seat, when everyone is already asleep in Figueira da Foz, two women will still be conversing in a house in Ereira at dead of night, How I'd love to go with you, Joana's cousin confided, her own marriage far from happy.

Next morning the sky was overcast, one cannot count on the weather, yesterday afternoon was like a foretaste of paradise, bright and pleasant, the branches of the trees gently swaying, the Mondego as smooth as the surface of the sky, no one here would think this was the same river under the low clouds, the sea throwing up spray, but the elderly shrug their shoulders, First of August, first day of winter, they say, most fortunate that the day should have come almost a month late, Joana Carda arrived early but José Anaiço was already waiting for her in the car, this had been agreed to by the other two men so that the lovers could be alone together before they all set out on their journey, in which direction we still don't know. The dog had spent the night inside the car, but it now was strolling along the beach with Pedro Orce and Joaquim Sassa, discreet, rubbing its head against the leg of the Spaniard, whose company it already preferred.

In the parking lot, among the larger vehicles, Deux Chevaux looks insignificant, that's the first point, and moreover, as has already been explained, it's a wild morning, there's no one around, and that's the second point, therefore it is only natural that José Anaiço and Joana Carda should fall into each other's arms as if they had been separated for a whole year and had been longing for each other all that time. They kissed with passion and desire, this was no single flash of lightning but one flash after another, there were fewer words, it is difficult to speak while kissing, but after several minutes they could hear each other at last, I really like you, I believe I'm in love with you, said José Anaiço in all sincerity, I really like you too, and I also believe I'm in love with you, that's why I kissed you yesterday, no, no, what I mean to say is that I wouldn't have kissed you if I hadn't felt that I loved you, but I'm capable of loving you much more, You know nothing about me, If one couldn't like another person before getting to know him, it would take a lifetime, Don't you believe that two people can get to know each other, Do you, I'm asking you, First you must tell me what you mean by knowing, I don't have a dictionary here, In this case, consulting the dictionary would simply mean discovering what one already knew, Dictionaries only provide information that is likely to be useful to everyone, I must repeat the question, what do you mean by knowing, I'm not sure, And yet you can love, I can love you, Without knowing me, So it would appear, Where did you get the name Anaiço, One of my grandfathers was called Inácio, but back there in the village they got his name wrong, they started calling him Anaiço, after a while Anaiço became the family name, and you, why are you called Carda, In the distant past, the family name was Cardo, which also means thistle, but when one of my grandmothers lost her husband and found herself with a family to support, people started calling her Carda, for she richly deserved the feminine form, a surname in her own right, I thought you might be a carder who combed wool for a living, I might have been, and something else too, for I once went to look the word up in the dictionary and saw that carder also meant an instrument of torture used for skinning animals, poor martyrs, skinned, burned, beheaded, and carded, Is that what awaits me, If I were to go back to using the name Cardo you wouldn't benefit from the change, Would you still prick me, No, I'm not the name I bear, Who are you, then, I'm me, José Anaiço stretched out his hand, caressed her cheek, murmured, You, she did the same, repeated in a whisper, You, and her eyes filled with tears, probably because she is still conscious of her wicked past, now, as was only to be expected, she will want to know about his life, Are you married, do you have any children, what do you do for a living, I was married, I have no children, I'm a teacher. She took a deep breath or was it a sigh of relief, then she said, smiling, We'd better call the others, poor things, they must be dying of cold, José Anaiço said, When I told Joaquim about our first encounter, I tried to describe the color of your eyes, but I couldn't, I told him they were the color of a new sky, difficult to describe, and he latched onto that phrase, and started to call you just that, Just what, Lady Strange Eyes, of course he wouldn't dare to say it in your presence. I adore that name, I adore you, and now we'd better call the others.

One arm waving, another waving back in the distance, Pedro Orce and Joaquim Sassa came walking slowly across the sand, the large docile dog between them. Judging from the way he waved, Joaquim Sassa said, their meeting went well, anyone listening who had any experience of life would have no difficulty in detecting a note of subdued melancholy in these words, a noble sentiment, tinged with envy, or resentment, if you prefer a more refined word. Are you in love with the girl too, Pedro Orce asked sympathetically, No, no, it's not that, although it could be, my problem is that I don't know whom to love or how one goes on loving. Pedro Orce couldn't think of an answer to such a negative statement. They got into the car, good morning, how nice to see you, welcome aboard, where will this adventure lead us, good-natured platitudes, the last of them mistaken, it would have been more appropriate to inquire, Where will this dog lead us. José Anaiço started the engine, since he's at the wheel he might as well stay there, he maneuvered the car out of the lot, Now what, do I turn right, do I turn left, he pretended to hesitate, playing for time, the dog turned completely around, then at a controlled but rapid trot, so regular as to appear mechanical, started heading in a northerly direction. With the blue thread hanging from its mouth.

This was the memorable day on which the latest recorded measurements placed the already remote Europe at a distance of some two hundred kilometers, a Europe that found itself shaken from top to bottom by a psychological and social convulsion that seriously endangered its identity, deprived at that decisive moment of its very foundations, of those individual nationalities so laboriously created over the centuries. Europeans, from the power elite to ordinary citizens, soon became accustomed, one suspects with an unspoken feeling of relief, to the lack of any territories to the extreme west, and if the new maps, rapidly circulated to bring the public up to date, still provoked some dismay, it could only have been for aesthetic reasons, that indefinable feeling of disquiet people must have experienced and still experience today when they see that there are no arms on the Venus of Milo, for that is the precise name of the island where the statue was found, So Milo is not the sculptor's name, No sir, Milo is the island where the poor creature was discovered, she rose from the depths like Lazarus, but no miracle occurred to make her arms grow again.

As the centuries pass, if they continue to pass, Europe will no longer remember the time when she was great and sailed the seas, just as we today can no longer imagine the Venus with arms. Obviously, one cannot ignore the disasters and sorrows that continue to plague the Mediterranean with high tides, the coastal cities destroyed at their maritime fringe, hotels that once had steps leading down to the beach and now have neither steps nor beach, and Venice, Venice is like a swamp, the piles supporting it threatened with collapse, the tourist boom is over, my friends, but if the Dutch should set to work quickly, within several months the city of the doges, the Aveiro of Italy, will be able to reopen its doors to the anxious public, much improved, no longer in danger of catastrophic flooding, for the systems of balancing sluice valves, dikes, locks, pressure and suction pumps will ensure a constant water level, now it's up to the Italians to assume responsibility for reinforcing the city's foundations, otherwise Venice will end up tragically, burying itself in the mud, the most difficult part, permit me to say, is under way, let us give thanks to the descendants of that brave lad who, with just the tender tip of his index finger, prevented the town of Haarlem from disappearing from the face of the earth, destroyed by flooding and deluge.

The restoration of Venice will also afford a solution for the problems facing the rest of Europe. This fascinating region has been stricken time and time again by plague and war, earthquakes and fires, only to rise again from dust and ashes, transforming bitter suffering into sweet existence, barbaric lust into civilization, a golf course and a swimming pool, a yacht in the marina and a convertible on the quayside, man is the most adaptable of creatures, especially when it is a question of moving up in the world. Although it may not be very polite to say so, for certain Europeans, seeing themselves rid of those baffling western nations, now sailing adrift on the ocean, where they should never have gone, was in itself an improvement, a promise of happier times ahead, like with like, we have finally started to know what Europe is, unless there still remain other spurious fragments that will also break away sooner or later. Let us wager that we will ultimately be reduced to a single nation, the quintessence of the European spirit, a simple and perfect sublimation, Europe, namely, Switzerland.

But if there are such Europeans, there are others as well. The race of the restless, the devil's spawn, but not so easily extinguished, however much the soothsayers may wear themselves out with prophecies, all those who watch the train passing and grow sad with longing for the journey they will never make, all those who cannot see a bird in the sky without feeling the urge to soar like an eagle, all those who, seeing a ship disappear over the horizon, give a tremulous sigh from the bottom of their hearts, in their rapture they had thought it was because they were so close, only to realize it was because they were so far apart. It was thus one of those restless nonconformists who first dared to write the scandalous words, *Nous aussi, nous sommes ibériques*, he wrote them on a corner of the wall, timidly, like someone who is still unable to express his desire but cannot bear to conceal it any longer. Since the words were written, as you can see, in the French language, you will think this happened in France, all I can say is, Let each man think what he will, it could also have been in Belgium or Luxembourg. This inaugural declaration spread rapidly, it appeared on the façades of large buildings, on pediments, on pavements, in the subway corridors, on bridges and viaducts, the loyal conservatives of Europe protested, These anarchists are mad, it is always the same, the anarchists are blamed for everything.

But the saying jumped frontiers, and once it had jumped them it became clear that the same thought had already appeared in other countries, in German *Auch wir sind iberisch*, in English *We are Iberians too*, in Italian *Anche noi siamo iberici*, and suddenly it caught fire like a fuse, ablaze all over the place in letters of red, black, blue, green, yellow and violet, a seemingly inextinguishable flame, in Dutch and Flemish *Wij zijn ook Iberiërs*, in Swedish *Vi också äro iberiska*, in Finnish *Me myöskin olemme iberialaisia*, in Norwegian *Vi også er iberer*, in Danish *Også vi er iberiske*, in Greek *Eímaste íberai ki emeís*, in Frisian *Ek Wv Binne Ibeariërs*, and also, although with ostensible reticence, in Polish, *My też jesteśmy iberyjczykami*, in Bulgarian *Nie sachto sme iberytzi*, in Hungarian *Mi is ibérek vagyunk*, in Russian *Mi toje iberitsi*, in Rumanian *Si noi sîntem iberici*, in Slovak *Ai my sme iberčamia*. But the culmination, the climax, the crowning glory, a rare expression we're not likely to repeat, was when on the Vatican walls, on the venerable murals and columns of the Basilica, on the plinth of Michelangelo's *Pietà*, inside the dome, in enormous sky-blue lettering on the hallowed ground of St. Peter's Square, that same declaration appeared in Latin, *Nos quoque iberi sumus*, like some divine utterance in the majestic plural, a *Mene, mene, tekel upharsin* of the new era, and the Pope, at the window of his apartments, blessed himself out of sheer terror, made the sign of the cross in midair, but to no avail, for this paint is guaranteed to last, not even ten whole congregations armed with steel wool, bleach, pumice stones, scrapers, solvents for removing paint would suffice to erase those words, they would have work enough to keep them busy until the next Vatican Council.

From one day to the next, these slogans spread throughout Europe. What probably started as little more than the futile gesture of an idealist gradually spread until it became an outcry, a protest, a mass demonstration. Initially, these manifestations were dismissed with contempt, the words themselves treated with derision. But it wasn't long before the authorities became concerned about this course of events, which could not be blamed on interference from abroad, also a source of much subversive activity, at least the homegrown nature of the graffiti campaign saved the authorities the trouble of investigating and naming the foreign power they had in mind. It had become the fashion for subversives to parade through the streets with stickers in their lapels or, more daringly, stuck on their front or back, on their legs, on every part of their body and in every conceivable language, even in regional dialects, in various forms of slang, finally in Esperanto, but this was difficult to understand. A joint strategy of counterattack adopted by the European governments consisted of organizing debates and roundtable discussions on television, mainly with the participation of people who had fled the peninsula when the rupture was complete and irreversible, not the unfortunate people who had been there as tourists and who, poor things, still had not recovered from the fright, but the so-called natives, more precisely those who, despite close ties of tradition and culture, of property and power, had turned their backs on this geological madness and opted for the physical stability of the continent. Speaking with deep compassion and knowledge of the facts, these people painted a black picture of the Iberian situation, they offered advice to those restless spirits who were unwisely about to put Europe's identity at risk, and each of them ended his turn in the debate with a definitive phrase, staring the spectator in the eye and assuming an attitude of utter sincerity, Follow my example, opt for Europe.

The result was not particularly productive, save for the protests of the partisans of the peninsula, who claimed that they had been the victims of discrimination, and who, if neutrality and democratic pluralism were not just empty words, should have been invited to appear on television to express their views, if they had any to express. An understandable precaution. Armed with reasons, which any discussion about reason always supplies, these youths, for it was chiefly youths who were carrying out the most spectacular deeds, could have made their protests with greater conviction, whether in the classroom or in the street, not to mention in the home. It is even debatable whether these youths, once armed with reasons, would have dispensed with direct action, thus allowing the calming effect of their intelligence to prevail, contrary to what people have believed since the beginning of time. The question is debatable but scarcely worthwhile, for in the meantime the television studios were stoned, shops selling television sets were ransacked in the presence of the dealers, who cried out in despair, But I'm not to blame, their comparative innocence did not help them, picture tubes exploded like firecrackers, packing cases were piled up on the street, set alight, reduced to ashes. The police arrived and charged, the rebels dispersed, and this standoff has lasted for the past week, right up until today, when our travelers leave Figueira da Foz led by a dog, three men, and the lover of one of them, who was his lover without yet being his lover, or who, not yet being his lover, was already his lover, anyone with experience of the affairs and intrigues of the heart will understand this muddle. As the latter are heading north, and Joaquim Sassa has already suggested, If we pass through Oporto we can all stay at my house, hundreds of thousands, millions of youths throughout the continent have taken to the streets, armed not with reasons but with clubs, bicycle chains, grappling irons, knives, awls, scissors, as if driven insane with rage, as well as with frustration and the sorrow of things to come, they are shouting, We too are Iberians, with that same despair that has caused the shopkeepers to cry out, But we're not to blame.

When tempers have subsided, days and weeks from now, the psychologists and sociologists will come forward to prove that, deep down, these youths didn't really want to be Iberian, what they were doing, taking advantage of a pretext afforded by the circumstances, was giving vent to that irrepressible dream that lasts as long as life itself, but which usually erupts for the first time in one's youth with an outburst of sentiment or violence, either the one or the other. Meanwhile, battles were fought in the field, or in the streets and squares to be more precise, hundreds of people were injured, there were several deaths, although the authorities tried to suppress reports about serious casualties by issuing confusing and contradictory bulletins, the mothers of August never got to know for certain how many of their sons had disappeared, for the simple reason that they didn't know how to organize themselves, there are some who always remain outsiders, absorbed in their grief, or caring for the son who survived, or busy gratifying their menfolk in their efforts to conceive another son, which explains why mothers always lose out. Tear gas, water cannon, batons, shields, and visors, stones dislodged from the pavements, crossbars from the roadblocks, spikes from park railings, these are just some of the weapons used by both sides, while certain new strategies of persuasion with more painful effects are tried out by the various police forces, wars are like disasters, they never come singly, the first is a trial run to test the ground, the second to improve performance, the third to secure victory, each of them being, according to where you start counting, third, second, and first. For the catalogs of memoirs and reminiscences there remained those dying words of the handsome young Dutchman hit by a rubber bullet, which because of a manufacturing fault turned out to be more deadly than steel, but legend will soon take this episode in hand and every nation will swear that the youth was theirs, on the other hand no one will be anxious to lay claim to the bullet, unlike those dying words, not so much for their meaning, but because they are beautiful, romantic, incredibly youthful, and nations relish such phrases, especially when they are dealing with a lost cause like this one, At last, I'm Iberian, and with these words he expired. The boy knew what he wanted, or thought he knew, which for want of anything better is just as good, he was not like Joaquim Sassa, who does not know whom he should love, but then he is still alive, perhaps his day will come if he watches out for the right moment.

Day turned to evening, evening will turn to night, along this winding road barely skirting the sea the guide dog trots at a steady pace, but it's no greyhound, even Deux Chevaux, decrepit as the car is, could travel more quickly, as has been proved quite recently. And this pace does not suit it at all, Joaquim Sassa is at the wheel and feeling uneasy, if there should be engine trouble, better that the car should be in his hands. The radio, its batteries renewed, reported the disastrous events in Europe, and referred to well-informed sources confirming that international pressure would be put on the Portuguese and Spanish governments to bring the situation to an end, as if it were in their power to achieve this desirable objective, as if controlling a peninsula adrift at sea were the same thing as driving Deux Chevaux. These representations were firmly rejected, with manly pride on the part of the Spanish and feminine haughtiness on the part of the Portuguese, we have no intention of shaming or exalting either sex, with the announcement that the Prime Ministers would speak that same night, each addressing his own country, of course, by mutual agreement. What has caused a certain bewilderment is the cautious attitude of the White House, usually so ready to intervene in world affairs, whenever the Americans sense it might be to their advantage, there are those who argue, however, that the Americans are not prepared to comment before seeing, literally speaking, where all this is going to end. Meanwhile, supplies of fuel have been coming in from the United States, with some irregularity, it is true, but we should be grateful that it is still possible to find the odd gas pump in remote areas. Were it not for the Americans, these travelers would have to go on foot, if they were determined to follow the dog.

When they stopped at a restaurant for lunch, the animal resigned itself to being left outside, it must have understood that its human companions needed to nourish themselves. As they finished their meal, Pedro Orce went out before the others, carrying some leftovers, but the dog refused to eat, and then the reason became clear, there were traces of fresh blood on its hair and around its mouth. The dog has been hunting, José Anaiço said, But it still has the blue thread in its mouth, Joana Carda pointed out, a much more interesting observation than the previous one, after all, our dog, if that's how we are to think of it, has been leading this vagabond existence for nearly two weeks and has crossed the entire peninsula on foot all the way from the Pyrenees to here, and who knows where else, and there couldn't have been anyone to fill his bowl regularly with water or to console him with a bone. As for the blue thread, it can be dropped on the ground and picked up again, like the hunter who holds his breath to take aim and then starts breathing naturally again. Joaquim Sassa, who after all was a kind man, said, Good dog, if you're as capable of looking after us as you are of looking after yourself, you'll do a good job of protecting us. The dog shook its head, a gesture we have not learned to interpret. It then went down to the road and started walking again without once looking back. The afternoon turns out to be better than the morning, there is sunshine, and this devil of a dog, or dog of the devil, resumes its indefatigable trot, head lowered, its nose protruding, its tail straight, its coat tawny. What breed can it be, asked José Anaiço, Were it not for the tail, it could be a cross between a setter and a sheepdog, Pedro Orce remarked, It's going faster, Joaquim Sassa observed with satisfaction, and Joana Carda, perhaps for the sake of saying something, asked, What shall we call it, sooner or later we inevitably come to the question of names.

The Prime Minister addressed the Portuguese and said, Citizens of Portugal, during recent days and most noticeably during the last twenty-four hours, our country has been subjected to pressures, which without exaggeration I consider unacceptable, from nearly all those European countries that have suffered, as we know, severe disruptions of the public order, but through no fault of ours, with vast numbers of demonstrators pouring into the streets with great enthusiasm, anxious to show their solidarity with the nations and peoples of the peninsula. These developments have exposed the serious internal contradiction in the debates among the governments of Europe, to which we no longer belong. Confronted with the profound social and cultural developments in these countries, they see in this historic adventure on which we find ourselves launched the promise of a happier future or, to put it in a nutshell, the hope of regenerating humanity. But instead of supporting us and showing their true humanity and genuine awareness of European culture, those governments decided to make us the scapegoats for their internal problems, with their absurd demands that we arrest the drifting peninsula, although it would have been more fitting and accurate to speak of navigating. Their attitude is all the more deplorable since everyone knows that with each passing hour we move an additional seven hundred and fifty meters away from what are at present the western shores of Europe, and those very European governments that in the past never showed any desire to have us with them are now trying to force us into doing what they don't really want and, moreover, know is beyond our powers. Unquestionably a place of history and culture, Europe in these troubled times has shown itself in the end to be lacking in common sense. It is up to us as the legitimate and constitutional government, entrusted with preserving the peace of the strong and just, forcefully to reject pressures and interventions of every kind and from any quarter by declaring before the world that we shall allow ourselves to be guided by the national interest alone, or, in a wider context, by the interests of the peoples and nations of the peninsula, and this I here solemnly affirm with the utmost conviction, now that the governments of Portugal and Spain have begun coordinating their efforts, as they will continue to do in order to examine and discuss the measures required to ensure a happy outcome to the chain of events set in motion by the historic separation of the Pyrenees. A word of acknowledgment is due the humanitarian spirit and political realism of the United States of America, thanks to whom reasonable levels of fuel supplies and also of foodstuffs have been maintained, which, within the framework of community relations, we previously imported from Europe. Under normal conditions, such matters would obviously be dealt with through the competent diplomatic channels, but in a situation of such gravity, the government over which I preside has decided to present the situation to the people without delay, thereby expressing its confidence in the dignity of the Portuguese, who will respond, as on other historic occasions, by closing ranks around their legitimate representatives and the sacred symbol of the Fatherland, presenting the world with the image of a united and determined people, at a particularly difficult and delicate moment in the nation's history, Long live Portugal.

The four travelers were already on the outskirts of Oporto when they heard this speech, they had gone into a café that served light refreshments and they lingered there long enough to see television coverage of the mass demonstrations and the counterattacks launched by the police, shivers ran up their spines when they saw those noble youths holding up posters and banners bearing that formidable phrase written in their own language. Why, asked Pedro Orce, should they be so concerned with us, and José Anaiço, echoing unknowingly but more directly the Prime Minister's sentiments, replied, All they're concerned about is themselves, and he probably couldn't have explained any better what he was thinking. They finished eating and left, this time the dog accepted the leftovers Pedro Orce brought him, and, having set Deux Chevaux in motion, now more slowly because the guide can scarcely be seen ahead, Joaquim Sassa said, Before crossing the bridge, let's try to coax the dog into the car, it can travel in the back on Joana and José's laps, we can't go around the city as we've been doing so far, and the dog certainly won't want to go on traveling through the night.

The forecast turned out to be correct and Joaquim Sassa's wish was gratified, as soon as it understood what was required of it, the dog got into the car, slow and ponderous, it stretched out on the laps of the passengers in the back seat, rested its head on Joana Carda's forearm, but the dog did not fall asleep, it traveled with its eyes open, the lights of the city danced over them as if over a surface of black crystal. Let's stay at my house, Joaquim Sassa suggested, I've got a wide bed and a sofa that opens out to sleep two people if they're not too fat. One of us, he was referring to the three men, of course, will have to sleep in a chair, but that's no problem, since it's my house, I'll use the chair or spend the night in a boardinghouse nearby. The others made no reply, their respectful silence indicating that they agreed, or perhaps preferred to settle this delicate matter discreetly later on, the atmosphere had suddenly become tense, there was an awkward feeling of embarrassment, almost as if Joaquim Sassa had done it on purpose, and he was perfectly capable of doing such a thing simply to amuse himself. But within minutes Joana Carda spoke up and announced, We two are sticking together. Really, what is the world coming to when women start taking this kind of initiative, in the past there were rules, one always started at the beginning, a few warm, encouraging looks from the man, a subtle lowering of the woman's eyes, a furtive glance darting from under her eyelashes, and then, until that first touching of hands, the courtship proceeded slowly, there were letters, lovers' tiffs, reconciliations, the waving of handkerchiefs, discreet coughs, naturally the final outcome was always the same, in bed with her on her back, him on top of her, in or out of wedlock, but never for a moment this outrageous behavior, this lack of respect in the presence of an old man, and if anyone thinks the women of Andalusia are hot-blooded, they should take a look at this woman from Portugal, no woman has ever dared to say in Pedro Orce's presence, We two are sticking together. But times have changed, and not for the better if Joaquim Sassa was trying to tease them, the conversation had turned sour, unless Pedro Orce had misunderstood, perhaps the words, sticking together, do not mean the same thing in Castilian as in Portuguese. José Anaiço did not open his mouth, what could he say, he would look ridiculous if he were to play the lover, even more so if he were to appear scandalized, best to keep his mouth shut, it does not take much to realize that only Joana Carda could have uttered those compromising words, imagine the bad impression he would have made if he had said those words without first consulting her, and even so, even if he had asked her if she was willing, there are certain attitudes that only a woman can adopt, depending on the circumstances and the moment, that's it, the moment, that precise second poised between two others that would result in confusion and disaster. Joana Carda and José Anaiço rest their clasped hands on the dog's back, Joaquim Sassa furtively watches the lovers through the rearview mirror, they are smiling, the joke has been well received after all. This Joana is quite a girl, Joaquim Sassa feels another twinge of jealousy, but he admits he is to blame because he can never decide whom he should love.

The house is no palace, it has a tiny interior bedroom, and an even tinier living room where there is a sofa bed, a kitchen, a bathroom, clearly a house for someone on his own, but he considers himself fortunate and at least he does not have to keep moving from one furnished room to another. The larder is empty, but they had satisfied their hunger at their last stop before arriving here. They watch television in the hope of catching up on the news, so far there have been no reactions from the European embassies, but just to remind them the Prime Minister has given another interview on the late news program, Citizens of Portugal, he said, the rest we have already heard.

Before they went to bed there was a council of war, not that there was any immediate need for decisions, those were left to the dog who was snoozing at Pedro Orce's feet, but they speculated in turn, Perhaps our journey ends here, Joaquim Sassa said hopefully, Or farther north, José Anaiço suggested, thinking of something else, I think it will be further north, added Joana Carda, who was thinking of the same thing, but Pedro Orce was right when he told them, The dog is the only one who knows, whereupon he yawned and said, I feel sleepy.

Now there was no longer any uncertainty as to who would be sleeping with whom, Joaquim Sassa opened out the sofa bed assisted by Pedro Orce, Joana Carda retired discreetly, and José Anaiço lingered for a few minutes longer, embarrassed, as if none of this had anything to do with him, but his heart was thumping in his breast like a drum beating, causing the whole building to shake to its very foundations, although this tremor is quite different from the other one, finally he said, Good night, see you tomorrow, and withdrew. There is no doubt that words never match up to the grandeur of certain moments. The bedroom is next door, the window extends almost to the ceiling, one way of prolonging daylight, and it doesn't even have a curtain, this apparent lack of privacy is understandable, the house is only for one person, and even if Joaquim Sassa were to have such perverted tastes he could scarcely spy on himself, although it has to be said that it would be very interesting as well as revealing, if we could spy on ourselves from time to time, although we might not like what we would see. With these words of caution, we're not trying to insinuate that Joaquim Sassa and Pedro Orce are thinking of playing childish games, such poor taste, but that window, now the mere shadow of a window, barely visible in the darkness of the room, is disturbing, it chills the blood, as if this were all one room, a dormitory, uncomfortably promiscuous, and Joaquim Sassa, lying on his back, prefers not to think, but raises his head from the pillow to create an aura of silence and to be better able to hear, his mouth is dry but he stoically resists the temptation to get up and go into the kitchen to drink some water and eavesdrop on the whispering on the way. As for Pedro Orce, he was so exhausted he fell asleep immediately, his face turned away from the wall, his arm reaching down to rest on the dog's back as it lay on the floor beside him, the trembling of the one is that of the other, their sleep probably one and the same. No sound comes from the bedroom, not even so much as an indecipherable word, not so much as a sigh, a stifled moan, Such silence, Joaquim Sassa thinks to himself, and he finds it strange, but he neither imagines nor is likely ever to suspect or know just how strange, for these things usually remain the secret of those who have experienced them, José Anaiço penetrated Joana Carda and she received him without any other movement, he hard, she most gentle, and there they stayed, their fingers clasped, their lips absorbing kisses in silence, as one mighty wave shakes the innermost fibers of their bodies, noiselessly, right to the very last vibration, to the last imperceptible drop, let us put it discreetly lest anyone accuse us of crudely portraying scenes of coition, an ugly word that has fortunately become obsolete. Tomorrow, when Joaquim Sassa wakes up, he will think that those two had the patience to wait, God knows at what cost, if God knows about these sublimations of the flesh, that they had waited until the other couple next door were asleep, he's deceiving himself, for just as he is about to fall asleep, Joana Carda receives José Anaiço once more, this time they won't be as quiet as before, certain feats cannot be repeated, The others must be asleep by now, one of them whispered, at last they could abandon themselves to passionate love, their patience rewarded.

Pedro Orce was the first to awaken, through a narrow chink in the window the ashen finger of morning touched his parched lips, then he dreamed that a woman was kissing him, oh how he struggled to make that dream last, but his eyes opened, and his mouth was dry, no mouth had deposited the truth of saliva, its fertile humidity, in his. The dog lifted its head, raised itself on its paws, and gazed steadily at Pedro Orce in the dense shadows of the room, it was impossible to see where the light that shone in its eyes was coming from. Pedro Orce stroked the animal, and it responded by giving his bony hand a lick. Disturbed by the noise, Joaquim Sassa woke up, initially without any idea of his whereabouts, even though he was in his own home, perhaps because he felt strange finding himself in a bed he rarely used, and because there was someone in the room beside him. Lying on his back, with the dog's head lying on his chest, Pedro Orce said, Another day begins, what's going to happen, and Joaquim Sassa thought, Perhaps he's become confused after sleeping, it's not uncommon, people fall asleep and that in itself has changed everything, we are the same as before yet fail to recognize ourselves. In this case they did not appear to have changed. The dog had got to its feet, big, heavy, and had walked to the closed door. One could see its blurred outline, its shadowy form, the gleam in its eyes, The dog's waiting for us, said Joaquim Sassa, you better call him, it's still too early to get up. The dog came when Pedro Orce called and obediently lay down, the men were now conversing in a whisper, Joaquim Sassa was saying, I'm going to take out all the money I have in the bank, it isn't much but I can borrow some more, And what happens when that runs out, Perhaps our little adventure will come to an end before the money does, Who can tell what awaits us, We'll find some means of surviving, even by stealing if we have to, Joaquim Sassa said smiling. But perhaps it won't be necessary to resort to such drastic measures, José Anaiço will also pay a visit to the bank here in Oporto where he has his savings, Pedro Orce has brought all his pesetas, and as for Joana Carda we don't know anything about her financial situation, but to all appearances she is not the type of woman who lives off charity or is kept by some man. It is doubtful whether the four of them will find any work, if work requires permanency, stability, normal residential status, when their immediate destiny is to walk behind a dog who we can only hope knows something about its own destiny, but this is not the age when animals could speak and therefore, as long as they had vocal cords, could say where they wanted to go.

In the next room, the exhausted lovers were asleep in each other's arms, sheer ecstasy but alas short-lived, as one would expect, after all, one's body is this body and not the other, a body has a beginning and an end, it begins and ends with the skin, what's inside belongs to it, but the body needs its rest, independence, autonomy in its functioning, to sleep in each other's arms demands a harmony of tongue and groove that may be disturbed by the sleep of either partner, one of them may awaken with a cramp in her arm, or because there is an elbow sticking into his ribs, whereupon we say in a whisper, with all the tenderness we can muster, Dearest, move over just a little. Joana Carda and José Anaiço are asleep from exhaustion, for during the night they have had sexual intercourse three times, their love affair has only just begun, therefore they respect the golden rule of never refusing the body what the body in its wisdom demands. Making as little noise as possible, Joaquim Sassa and Pedro Orce went out with the dog, they've gone to look for some provisions for breakfast, Joaquim Sassa refers to it as *pequeno almoço* rather like the French *petit déjeuner*, Pedro Orce as *desayuno* in the Spanish, but their mutual hunger will resolve the linguistic differences. By the time they return, Joana Carda and José Anaiço will be out of bed, we can hear them in the bathroom, the shower is running, a blissful pair, and such great walkers, for in a very short time they have come a long way.

When it was time to set out and resume their journey, the four of them started looking at the dog with the perplexed air of someone awaiting orders who is as uncertain of their reliability as of the wisdom of obeying them. Let us hope that in order to get out of Opórto the dog entrusts itself to us as it did when we came in, said Joaquim Sassa, and the others understood the reason for that observation, just imagine if the dog Faithful, faithful to its instinct to head north, were to start taking one-way streets here in the city where north was precisely the direction you couldn't follow, there would be endless trouble with the police, accidents, traffic jams, with the entire population of Oporto turning out to enjoy the fun. But this dog isn't any old sheepdog of suspect or clandestine paternity, its genealogical tree has its roots in hell, which, as we know, is the place where all knowledge ends up, ancient knowledge is already there, modern and future knowledge will pursue the same path. For this reason, and perhaps also because Pedro Orce has repeated the trick of whispering into the dog's ear words that we still have not been able to make out, the dog got into the car as if it were the most natural thing in the world, as if it had always traveled this way, all its life. But, look out, this time the dog hasn't rested its head on Joana Carda's forearm, this time it sits up attentively as Joaquim Sassa drives Deux Chevaux along curves and bends in the road, in every direction, anyone who happened to be there watching would think, They're heading south, but soon he would change his mind and decide, They're going west, or, They're going east, and these are the main or cardinal directions but if we were to mention the entire compass card we would never get out of Oporto or this confusion.

There is an agreement between this dog and these travelers, four rational beings consent to being led by brute instinct, unless they are all being drawn by some magnet located to the north, or being pulled by the other end of a blue thread identical to the one the dog won't let go. They left the city, one knows that despite its curves the road is going in the right direction, the dog gives signs of wanting to get out of the car, they open the door and off it goes, refreshed after a night's rest and the large meal it had been given at the house. The dog goes at a brisk trot, Deux Chevaux cheerfully accompanies it, feels no need to keep a tight rein. The road no longer skirts the sea, it wends inland, and for this very reason we won't see the shore where Joaquim Sassa acquired more strength than Samson at a given moment in his life. Joaquim himself remarked, What a pity the dog decided not to follow the coastline, then I could have shown you where the episode of the stone took place, not even the Samson mentioned in the Bible could have done what I did, but out of modesty he would say no more. What was and continues to be a much greater feat was that of Joana Carda there in the fields of Ereira, and even more enigmatic is the tremor felt by Pedro Orce, and if our guide here on earth is a dog from the underworld, what shall we say of the thousands of starlings that accompanied José Anaiço for so long and only abandoned him when it was time to take flight once more.

The road slopes upward, descends, then starts rising again, and goes on rising, and whenever it goes down, it is only to take a short pause, these mountains are not all that high, but they affect Deux Chevaux's heart, causing it to struggle for breath on the slopes while the dog travels on at a nimble pace. They stopped to have lunch at a snack bar at the roadside, once more the dog disappeared in search of its own food and when it returned there was blood on its mouth, but we already know why, there's no mystery, if no one is around to fill the bowl, a dog has to make do with what it can find. Back on the road, they kept heading north, at one point José Anaiço quipped, If we carry on like this we'll find ourselves in Spain, in your native country. My native land is Andalusia, Country and land are one and the same thing, No they're not, we may not know our country but we always know our own land, Have you ever been to Galicia, No, I've never been to Galicia, Galicia is the land of others.

Whether they will get there remains to be seen, because they will spend the night in Portugal. José Anaiço and Joana Carda signed the hotel register as man and wife, in order to economize Pedro Orce and Joaquim Sassa shared a room, and the dog had to sleep with Deux Chevaux, the huge beast terrified the landlady, I don't want a monster like that in my hotel, it can sleep outdoors where dogs belong, the last thing I need is to have the place infested with fleas, The dog hasn't got any fleas, Joana Carda protested to no avail, for that wasn't the main point. In the middle of the night Pedro Orce got out of bed, hoping to find that the front door wasn't locked, as indeed it wasn't, so he went to sleep for a couple of hours in the car with the dog in his arms, when one has no one to love, in this case for obvious impediments of nature, friendship is the next best thing. It seemed to Pedro Orce as he got into the car that the dog was whimpering, but he must have been hallucinating, as we often do when we dearly want something, our wise body takes pity on us, simulates within itself the satisfaction of our desires, this is what dreaming means, what do you think, If it weren't so, tell me how we could ever bear this intolerable life, comes the commentary from the unknown voice that intervenes from time to time.

When Pedro Orce returned to the bedroom, the dog followed him, but when told not to enter, it lay down in the doorway and there it remained. There are no words to describe the terror and outcry at first light of day, when the landlady arrived early to begin her daily chores, she opens the shutters to the freshness of the dawn, and lo and behold, here on the doormat the Nemean lion springs to its feet with bared fangs, it was simply the yawn of a dog that hadn't had enough sleep, but even yawns should be treated with caution when they expose such formidable teeth and a tongue so red that it appears to be bleeding. Such was the uproar that the guests' departure had all the appearance of expulsion rather than peaceful withdrawal, Deux Chevaux was already at some distance, almost turning the corner, and the landlady was still on the doorstep yelling at the silent beast, for these are the worst beasts of all if one is to believe the proverb that says, Dogs that bark don't bite, it's true that this one hasn't bitten yet, but if those powerful jaws are in direct proportion to its silence, God protect us from the beast. Once on their way, the travelers laugh at the episode, Joana Carda, out of feminine solidarity, didn't find it amusing, Had I been in that woman's position, I'd also have been terrified, and you needn't think you're all such heroes, let alone feel obliged to show how brave you are, her words made a deep impression, each man quietly pondered his own cowardice, the most interesting case was that of José Anaiço, who decided he would confess his fear to Joana Carda at the first possible opportunity, for real love means keeping no secrets from one's beloved, the worst comes later when the romance is over and the lover who has confided his secrets regrets having spoken while the beloved abuses his confidence, it's up to Joana Carda and José Anaiço to arrange their affairs so as to keep anything like this from happening.

The frontier isn't far away. By now accustomed to the scouting talents of their guide, the travelers have not even noticed the speedy manner, without a moment's hesitation or pause for thought, with which Faithful or Pilot, he'll have to be given some name or other one day, chooses the right fork in the road he must follow, and to make things even more difficult, this is not simply a fork but a crossroads. Even if this cunning animal has covered this same route from north to south, and of this no one can be sure, the experience will not be of much help, if we bear in mind the difference in the point of view, on which, as we are fortunately aware, everything depends. It is all too true that people live alongside things wondrous and prodigious, but they do not fathom even half of these marvels, they nearly always deceive themselves about the half they know, mainly because they desire with all their might, like our Lord God, that this and other worlds should be made in their own image and likeness, not that it matters who created them. This dog is guided by instinct, but we have no way of telling what or who guides instinct, and if we should ever be able to start explaining the strange episode narrated here, in all probability any such explanation would be no more than the semblance of an explanation, unless from that explanation we can derive another and then another, until there comes a moment when there would be nothing left with which to explain the primary source of the things explained, presumably beyond that there is nothing but chaos, but we are not speaking about the formation of the universe, we do know that much, we are only discussing dogs.

And people. These people who are following a dog and heading for the frontier just ahead. They are about to leave Portuguese territory, at sunset, and suddenly, perhaps because of the approaching twilight, they realize that the animal has disappeared, and they suddenly feel like children lost in the forest, Now what are we going to do, Joaquim Sassa seizes the opportunity to express his disdain for canine loyalty, but Pedro Orce's serene judgment, based on his experience of life, prevailed. The dog has probably swum across the river to wait for us on the opposite side, if these people had really paid attention to the ties and bonds that link existence and alchemy they would have realized it at once, we are referring to José Anaiço and Joaquim Sassa, for the dog's motives may be the same as those of a thousand starlings, if Faithful came from the north and passed this way, perhaps he may not wish to repeat the experience, without collar or muzzle, he could be suspected of having rabies and might even find himself being peppered with bullets.

The customs officers examine their papers distractedly, wave them on, it is obvious that these officials are not exactly overworked, as we have seen, people do a great deal of traveling, but for the moment it is more within national frontiers, they seem to be afraid of straying from their home in the wider sense, namely their native land, even if they have abandoned the family home where they have lived their humdrum lives. On the other side of the Minho there is the same boredom, all one detects is a glimmer of detached curiosity as the officials watch these Portuguese arrive with a Spaniard of another generation, were this a period of greater traffic to and fro they wouldn't even be noticed. Joaquim Sassa drove for a kilometer, drew Deux Chevaux over to the side of the road and came to a halt, Let's wait here, if the dog, as Pedro claims, knows what it is doing, it will come to look for us. They didn't even have time to become impatient. After ten minutes, the dog appeared in front of the car, its coat still damp. Pedro Orce had been right, and if we hadn't been quite so skeptical, we would have waited on the riverbank to witness the dog's heroic crossing, which we could then have described with relish, instead of this banal crossing of frontiers with guards whose only difference is their uniforms, Carry on, You may pass, this summed up the episode, even the glimmer of curiosity was no more than a feeble invention to fill out the narrative.

Further and somewhat better inventions would now be in order, to enhance what remains of the journey, with two nights and two days in between, the former spent in rural lodging houses, the latter on old roads that once went north, always toward the north, the land of Galicia and mist, with light showers announcing the arrival of autumn, this is all one feels like saying and no invention was needed. The rest would be the nocturnal embraces of Joana Carda and José Anaiço, the intermittent insomnia of Joaquim Sassa, Pedro Orce's hand resting on the dog's back, for here the dog was allowed inside the bedrooms to spend the night. And the days on the road, heading right toward a horizon that seemed to move farther and farther away. For the second time, Joaquim Sassa said that this was utter madness, trailing after a stupid dog to the ends of the earth without knowing why or for what purpose, to which Pedro Orce replied abruptly, betraying his annoyance, Scarcely to the ends of the earth, we'll reach the sea before then. The dog is clearly beginning to tire, its head is drooping, its tail has dropped, and the pads on its paws, despite their hard skin, must be hurting by now after all that rubbing against soil and gravel, that same night Pedro Orce will examine them and find open sores bleeding, no wonder he responded so sharply to Joaquim Sassa, who looks on and says, as if trying to excuse himself, Some compresses with hydrogen peroxide should do them good, it's rather like teaching your grandmother how to suck eggs, Pedro Orce is familiar with all the skills of pharmacy, he doesn't need any advice from Joaquim Sassa. Nevertheless, this conciliatory gesture was enough to restore the peace.

In the vicinity of Santiago de Compostela the dog veered in a northeasterly direction. It must be nearing its destination, this could be seen from the renewed vigor with which it was now trotting along, from its firm gait, the way it held its head, its bristling tail. Joaquim Sassa was forced to accelerate a little so that Deux Chevaux could keep up with the dog, and they got so close that they were almost touching the animal. Joana Carda exclaimed, Look, look at the blue thread. They all turned around. The thread didn't look the same. The other one had become so dirty that it could have been either blue or black, but this one was as blue as blue could be, and quite unlike the blue of the sky or the sea, who could have dyed and combed it, or who could have washed it, if it was the same thread, and put it back into the dog's mouth with the words, Off you go. The road has become narrow, it's almost like a footpath skirting the hills. The sun is about to set over the sea, which still cannot be seen from here, nature is masterly when it comes to composing spectacles attuned to human circumstances, this morning and all afternoon the sky had been overcast and somber as it sprinkled the land with Galician drizzle, and now the countryside is bathed in a coppery light, the dog glows like a jewel, an animal made of gold. Even Deux Chevaux no longer looks the worse for wear and the passengers inside are suddenly transformed, the light is shining on them and they go forth like the beatified. José Anaiço observes Joana Carda and shudders at the sight of such beauty, Joaquim Sassa lowers the rearview mirror in order to gaze into his own sparkling eyes, and Pedro Orce contemplates his wrinkled hands, they are no longer wrinkled, no, they've been restored by alchemy, they've become immortal, even if the rest of his body should die.

Suddenly, the dog stops. The sun is level with the summit of the mountains, the sea can be glimpsed on the other side. The road goes winding down, two hills appear to cut it off down below, but this is an optical illusion due to distance. In front, halfway down the slope, there is a large house, an austere building with an air of neglect, very old, despite signs that the surrounding fields are being farmed. Part of the house is already in the shade, the light is waning, the whole world appears to be sinking into inertia and solitude. Joaquim Sassa brought the car to a halt. They all got out. The silence can be heard vibrating like one last echo, perhaps it is only the distant thrashing of the waves against the rocks, that is always the best explanation, the interminable memory of the waves echoes even inside the shells, but this is not the case, what can be heard here is silence, no one should die before experiencing it, silence, have you heard it, now you may go, you know what it sounds like. But that hour still has not arrived for any of these four. They know that their destination is that house, this amazing dog has brought them here, mute as a statue, waiting. José Anaiço is at Joana Carda's side but he does not touch her, he knows that he must not touch her, she knows it too, these are moments when even love must resign itself to its own insignificance, forgive us for reducing the greatest of affections to almost nothing, that affection that on other occasions can be almost everything. Pedro Orce was the last to get out of the car, he puts his feet on the ground and feels the earth vibrating with terrifying force, here every seismograph needle would snap, and these hills appear to sway with the movement of the waves that surge one upon the other in the sea beyond, pushed by this stone raft, throwing themselves against it with the reflux of the powerful currents we are cutting through.

The sun has disappeared. Then the blue thread fluttered in the air, almost invisible in its transparency, searching for some support, grazing hands and faces, Joaquim Sassa held it, was this a coincidence or destiny, let us leave these hypotheses aside, even though there are a number of reasons for not giving credence either to the one or to the other, and now what will Joaquim Sassa do, he cannot travel in the car, with one hand outside holding and accompanying the thread, for a thread at the mercy of the wind does not necessarily follow the line of the road. What should I do with this, he asked, but while the others could not give him an answer the dog could, it left the road and began to descend the gentle slope, Joaquim Sassa followed it, his raised hand followed the blue thread as if it were stroking the wings or the breast of a bird above his head. José Anaiço went back to the car with Joana Carda and Pedro Orce, put it into gear, and, keeping a watchful eye on Joaquim Sassa, began slowly going down the road, he did not want to arrive before him, or for that matter much after him, the potential harmony of things depends on their equilibrium and the time when they occur, not too soon, not too late, which explains why it is so difficult for us to attain perfection.

When they stopped in the square in front of the house, Joaquim Sassa was ten paces from the door, which was ajar. The dog gave a sigh that seemed almost human and lay down, stretching its neck over its paws. It dislodged the thread from its mouth with its paws and let it fall to the ground. A woman emerged from the dark interior of the house, she had a thread in her hand, the same as the one Joaquim Sassa was still holding. She stepped down from the last step at the front door and said, Come in, you must be tired. Joaquim Sassa was the first to move, his end of the blue thread tied round his wrist.

One day, Maria Guavaira told them, about this hour and with much the same light, the dog appeared, looking as if it had come from afar, its coat was filthy, its paws bleeding, it came and knocked on the door with its head, and when I went to open it, thinking it might be one of those beggars who travel from place to place, who arrive tapping their stick and plead, Whatever you can give, ma'am or miss, what do I find but the dog, panting as if it had come running from the end of the world and the blood staining the ground under its paws, the most surprising thing of all was that I didn't feel frightened, though there was every reason to take fright, anyone who didn't know just how harmless the dog is would think he was looking at the wildest of beasts, poor creature, the moment it saw me, the dog lay down on the ground as if it had been waiting until it reached me before attempting to rest, and it seemed to be crying, as if trying to speak but unable to, and all the time the dog was here I never once heard it bark. It's been with us now for six days and it hasn't barked once, Joana Carda said. I took it in, cleaned it up, nursed it, it's not a stray, you can tell from its coat, and the dog's owners obviously fed it properly, showed it love and affection, if you want to see the difference you need only compare it with Galician dogs, who are born hungry and die from starvation after a lifetime of being deprived, beaten, and stoned, that's why the Galician dog can't lift its tail, but hides it between its legs in the hope of going unnoticed, it takes its revenge, when it gets the chance, by biting. This one doesn't bite, Pedro Orce assured them, As for knowing where it came from, we'll probably never know, José Anaiço remarked, perhaps it's not all that important, what surprises me is that it should have come to look for us in order to bring us here, you have to wonder why. I don't know, all I know is that one day it went off with a piece of thread in its mouth, looking at me as if to say, Don't move from here until I return, and off it went up the hill there from which it has just descended, What is this thread, Joaquim Sassa asked, as he wound on his wrist, then unwound, the end of the strand that still tied him to Maria Guavaira. I wish I knew, she replied, winding her end between her fingers and stretching the thread like the taut string of a guitar, while neither he nor she appeared to notice that they were tied together, the others did as they stood there looking on, what they were thinking they kept to themselves although it wouldn't be all that difficult to guess. For I did nothing but unravel an old sock, one of those socks people used to keep their money in, but the sock I unraveled would have given only a handful of wool, while the amount of wool here is what you would get from shearing a hundred sheep, not to say a thousand, and how is one to explain such a thing. For days, two thousand starlings kept following me, said José Anaiço, I threw a stone into the sea that weighed almost as much as I did, and it landed far off in the distance, Joaquim Sassa added, aware that he was exaggerating, and Pedro Orce simply said, The earth is trembling, and trembled.

Maria Guavaira got up and opened a door and said, Look, Joaquim Sassa was standing beside her, but it wasn't the thread that had drawn him, and what they saw was a blue cloud, of a blue that darkened and became almost black in the middle, If I leave this door open there are always ends sticking out, just like the one that went up the road and brought you here, Maria Guavaira said, addressing Joaquim Sassa, and the kitchen where they all had gathered was now deserted, except for these two, joined together by a blue thread, and the blue cloud that appeared to be breathing, firewood could be heard crackling in the hearth where some cabbage soup is on the boil flavored with scraps of meat, not as heavy as the Galician recipe.

Joaquim Sassa and Maria Guavaira must not remain tied together like this for too long, otherwise this union will begin to look suspicious, so she winds up all the thread and on reaching his wrist she pulls the thread around it as if she were invisibly attaching him to her once more, and then holds the tiny ball of wool against her breast, only a fool would be in any doubt about the gesture, but he would be an even bigger fool not to be in doubt. José Anaiço moved away from the fire burning in the hearth, Although it may seem absurd, we've come to the conclusion that there is some connection or other between what has happened to us and the separation of Spain and Portugal from Europe, you must have heard about it, Yes, I have, but in these parts no one gave it another thought, if we go over the mountains and down to the coast the sea is always the same. It was shown on television, I don't have television, It was broadcast in the news bulletin, News is nothing but words, and you can never really tell if words are news.

On this skeptical note the conversation was interrupted for several minutes. Maria Guavaira went to fetch some bowls from the shelf, ladled out the soup, the last bowl but one for Joaquim Sassa, the last one of all for herself, for a moment everyone thought there would be one spoon too few, but no, there were enough to go around, so Maria Guavaira did not have to wait for Joaquim Sassa to finish his soup. Then he asked her if she was living alone, for so far they had seen no one else in the house, and she told him that she had been a widow for three years, and that hired hands came to work the land, I'm between the sea and the mountains, without children or family, my brothers emigrated to Argentina, my father died, my demented mother is in an asylum in La Coruña, there can't be many women in this world as lonely as I am, You could have remarried, Joana Carda pointed out, but immediately regretted having spoken, she had no right to say such a thing, she who only a few days ago had broken up her marriage and was already keeping company with another man, I was worn out, and if a woman remarries at my age, it's on account of any land she may own, men are more interested in marrying land than a woman, You're still young, I was young once but I can scarcely remember that time, and with these words she leaned over the hearth

1 6 4

so that the flames lit up her face, she looked up at Joaquim Sassa as if to say, This is what I'm like, take a good look at me, you turned up on my doorstep tied to a thread I was holding in my hand, I could, if I so wished, draw you to my bed, and I'm certain you would come, but beautiful I shall never be, unless you can transform me into the most desirable woman who ever lived, that's something only a man can do, and does, but what a pity it can't last forever.

Joaquim Sassa watched her from the other side of the fire and saw that the flames as they danced kept on changing her expression, one moment making her cheeks look sunken, the next moment smoothing away the shadows, but the gleam in her dark eyes did not change, perhaps a suspended tear had been transformed into a membrane of pure light. She isn't pretty, he thought, nor is she ugly, her hands are rough and worn, quite unlike mine, the smooth hands of an office clerk enjoying paid leave, which reminds me that tomorrow, unless I'm mistaken, is the last day of the month, the day after tomorrow I'm due back at work, but no, how can I, how can I possibly leave José and Joana, Pedro and the Dog, they've no reason for wanting to come with me, and if I take Deux Chevaux they're going to find it extremely difficult to get back to their respective homes, but they probably don't want to go back, the only real thing that exists at this moment on earth is our being here together, Joana Carda and José Anaiço conversing in whispers, perhaps about their own life, perhaps about each other's life, Pedro Orce with his hand on Pilot's head, no doubt measuring vibrations and tremors no one else can feel, while I watch and go on watching Maria Guavaira who has a way of looking that isn't exactly looking but rather a way of showing her eyes, she is dressed in black, a widow whom time has consoled but whom custom and tradition restrict to wearing black, fortunately her eyes shine, and there is the blue cloud that doesn't seem to belong to this house, her hair is brown, and she has a rounded chin and full lips, and her teeth, I caught a glimpse of them a moment ago, are white, thank God, this woman is pretty after all and I didn't even notice, I was tied to her and didn't realize, I must decide whether to return home or remain here, even if I get back to work a few days late I'll be excused, with all this upheaval in the peninsula who's going to pay any attention to employees who are a few days late in returning to work, one can always say there was no transportation. One minute she looked common, the next quite pretty, and now, right now, standing beside Maria Guavaira, Joana Carda looks terrible, My woman is much more attractive, Senhor José Anaiço, how can you compare your lady from the city, and her affectations, to this wild creature who clearly tastes of the salty air the breeze carries over the mountains and whose body must be white underneath that black dress, If I could, Pedro Orce, I'd tell you something, What would you tell me, That I now know whom I should love, Congratulations, there are people who have taken much longer, or have never come to know, Do you know any such person, Take me, for example, and with this reply, Pedro Orce then said out loud, I'm going to take the dog for a walk.

Darkness has not yet fallen, but it is cold. In the direction of the mountain that hides the sea there is a path that begins to wend its way up the slope ahead in one bend after another, left and right like a winding thread until it disappears from sight. Soon the valley will be plunged into darkness, as on the night of the blackout, although it would be more accurate to say that in the valley where Maria Guavaira lives every night is like a blackout, so there was no need for all the electric cables of civilized and cultured Europe to break down. Pedro Orce left the house because he wasn't needed there. He walks on without looking back, at first as quickly as his strength permits, then, beginning to tire, he slows down. He does not feel the least bit nervous in this silence amid the great walls formed by the mountains, he's a man who was born and bred in a desert, in a land of dust and stones, where one is never surprised to find a horse's skull, a hoof with the metal shoe still attached, there are some who say not even the horsemen of the Apocalypse could survive there, the warhorse died in war, the infected horse died of infection, the starved horse of starvation, death is the supreme raison d'être of all things and their infallible conclusion, what deceives us is this line of the living along which we find ourselves, which advances toward what we call the future, simply because we had to give it a name, where we are constantly gathering in new beings while constantly leaving old ones behind, we are obliged to refer to these as the dead lest they emerge from the past.

Pedro Orce's heart is already starting to grow old and weary. He now has to rest more often and for longer, but he does not give up, the dog's presence consoles him. They exchange signs with each other, like a code that even though undeciphered is enough, for the simple fact of existing is enough, the animal rubs its back against the man's thigh, the man's hand strokes the soft skin inside the dog's ear, the world is filled with the sound of footsteps, breathing, friction, and now the muffled clamor of the sea can unmistakably be heard behind the summit of the mountain, growing louder, louder, getting clearer and clearer, until the immense surface looms up before one's eyes, vaguely sparkling beneath the night sky that is bereft of moonlight and has few stars, and below, like the living line separating night and death, the dazzling whiteness of spume constantly dissolving and renewing itself. The rocks are blacker where the waves are lashing, as if the stone there had greater density or had been soaked in water since the beginning of time. The wind comes in from the sea, on the one hand it is blowing normally, on the other it can scarcely be felt, this must be due to the peninsula's displacement on the water, it is no more than a breeze, as we well know, and yet there has never been such a typhoon since the world began.

Pedro Orce measures the dimension of the ocean and at that moment finds it small, because on taking a deep breath he feels his lungs expand so much that all the chasms of liquid could rush in and still leave space for the raft that with its stone battering rams is forcing its way through the waves. Pedro does not know if he is man or fish. He goes down to the sea, the dog goes ahead to sniff out and choose the path, and this prudent and astute guide was much needed, for without daylight, Pedro Orce on his own could not have found entrance or exit in this labyrinth of stones. At last they reached the great slabs of rock that descend to the sea, there the roar of waves breaking is deafening. Beneath this pitch-black sky and the cries of the sea, should the moon now appear, a man could die of rapture, while believing himself to be dying of anguish, of fear and solitude. Pedro Orce no longer felt cold. The night became clearer, more stars appeared, and the dog, which had been gone for a moment, came running back, it had not been trained to tug its master's trousers, but we know it well enough to be certain that it is perfectly capable of making its wishes known, and now Pedro Orce must accompany it to examine its discovery, a castaway swept up on the shore, a treasure chest, some vestige of Atlantis, the wreckage of the Flying Dutchman, an obsessive memory, and when he arrived he saw that it was nothing but stones, but since this was a dog not easily fooled, there had to be something unusual there, that was when he noticed that he was actually standing on it, the thing, an enormous stone, roughly in the form of a boat, and there was another one, long and narrow like a mast, and yet another, this must be the helm with its tiller, although it was broken. Thinking that the dim light was deceiving him, he started walking around the stones, touching and probing them, and then he was no longer in any doubt, this side, tall and pointed, is the prow, this other flat one is the stern, the mast is unmistakable, and the helm, for example, could only be made for a giant, were it not for the fact that this is definitely a stone ship standing here. A geological phenomenon, to be sure. What Pedro Orce knows about chemistry is more than enough to explain the discovery, an ancient wooden vessel brought here by the waves or abandoned by mariners, stranded on these rocks since time immemorial, then the fragments were covered by earth, their organic material petrified, once more the earth has retreated, thousands of years will be needed, until today, to blunt the edges and reduce these volumes, wind, rain, the erosion of cold and heat, the day will come when one stone will be indistinguishable from another. Pedro Orce sat right inside the boat, from where he's sitting he can see nothing but sky and the distant sea, if this ship were to pitch ever so slightly he would imagine himself to be sailing, and then, which shows you what the imagination can do, he absurdly began to imagine that this petrified ship was indeed sailing and towing the peninsula, one cannot trust these flights of fantasy, obviously it is not impossible, one has witnessed even more difficult feats, but as it happens the ship's stern is facing out to sea as if ironically, no reputable vessel would ever sail backward. Pedro Orce stood up, he now feels cold, and the dog has jumped onto the parapet, Time we were going home, master, you're rather old for these late nights, if you didn't go in for them when you were young, it's too late now.

When they reached the summit of the mountains, Pedro Orce could scarcely walk, and his poor lungs, which only a short time ago could have inhaled the entire ocean, gasped like a punctured bellows, the harsh air chafed his nostrils, parched his throat, these mountain tracks are not for a pharmacist getting on in years. He sank down onto a boulder, had to rest, his elbows resting on his knees, holding his head in his hands, the sweat glistening on his forehead, the wind ruffling loose strands of hair, he's a physical wreck, weary and dejected, alas, no one has yet discovered ways of petrifying a human being in the flower of youth and transforming him into an eternal statue. His breathing is more relaxed, the air has softened, it comes and goes without that grating noise like sandpaper. Aware of these changes, the dog, which had been stretched out waiting, made as if to get up. Pedro Orce raised his head, looked down into the valley where the house stood. There seemed to be an aura hovering over it, a diffused radiance, a kind of light without any luminosity, if this phrase, which like all others can be formed only with words, can be understood without ambiguity. Pedro Orce suddenly remembered that epileptic back in Orce who, in the wake of those fits that left him prostrate, tried to explain the confused sensations that preceded them, it could be a vibration of the invisible particles of the air, the radiation of energy, like heat in the distance, the distortion of luminous rays just beyond his reach, this night was truly filled with wonders, the thread and the cloud of blue wool, the stone ship grounded on the rocks on the shore, and now this house that is shaking, or so it appears to us, seen from here. The image flickers, the outline blurs, it appears to recede until it becomes an almost invisible point, then it returns, slowly vibrating. For an instant, Pedro Orce was afraid of being left abandoned in this other desert, but the fear passed, just enough time to realize that down there Maria Guavaira and Joaquim Sassa had got together, times have changed a lot, nowadays a man no sooner sets eyes on a woman than

he is poking the fire, if you'll pardon this crude metaphor, both ple-
beian and obsolete. Pedro Orce had risen to start going down the
slope, but sat down again and patiently waited, shivering with cold,
for the house to return to his image of a home, where there would be
no flames other than that last one still burning in the hearth, if he
lingers here too long he is much more likely to find only ashes instead
of the fire.

Maria Guavaira woke up with the first light of morning. She was in her room, in bed, and there was a man asleep at her side. She could hear him breathing deeply, as if he were drawing renewed strength from the marrow of his bones, and semiconscious, she wanted her own breathing to accompany his. It was the different rhythm within her breast that made her feel that she was naked. She ran her hands over her body, from her thighs to her crotch, then over her belly and up to her breasts, and suddenly she remembered her cry of surprise when her orgasm had dawned inside her like a sun. Now completely awake, she bit her fingers in order to suppress that same cry, but in that stifled sound she would have liked to recognize those sensations, to capture them forever, or perhaps it was reawakened desire, perhaps remorse, the anguish that utters that familiar phrase, Now what is to become of me, thoughts cannot be isolated from other thoughts, impressions are not untainted by other impressions, this woman lives in the country, remote from the amatory arts of civilization, and any moment now, two men will arrive who have come to work on Maria Guavaira's land, what is she going to say to them, her house filled like this with strangers, there is nothing like the light of day to alter the appearance of things. But this man sleeping beside her threw a stone into the sea, and Joana Carda cut the earth in two, and José Anaiço became the king of starlings, and Pedro Orce can cause the earth to tremble with his feet, and the Dog has come from who knows where to bring these people together, And it brought me

171

closer to you than to the others, I pulled the thread and you came to my door, to my bed, you penetrated my body, even my soul, for only from my soul could that cry have come. She closed her eyes for several minutes, when she opened them she saw Joaquim Sassa awake, she could feel his firm body, and sobbing with desire she opened herself to him, she did not cry out, but wept smiling, and day broke. There is no point in making indiscreet revelations about the words they spoke, let people form their own idea, try to imagine it for themselves, they are unlikely to succeed, however limited the language of love may appear to be.

Maria Guavaira got up and her body is as white as Joaquim Sassa had dreamed, she told him, I didn't want to wear my widow's clothes, but now I haven't got time to look for something else to wear, the farmhands will be here any minute. She dressed, returned to the bed, covered Joaquim Sassa's face with her hair and kissed him, then rushed out of the bedroom. Joaquim Sassa rolled over on the bed, closed his eyes, he's going back to sleep. There's a tear on one of his cheeks, it could have been shed by Maria Guavaira or it could be his own, for men also weep, it's nothing to be ashamed of, and weeping only does them good.

This is the room where Joana Carda and José Anaiço spent the night, the door is closed, they're still asleep. The other door is ajar, the dog came to look at Maria Guavaira, then went back inside and lay down again, keeping vigil over the sleeping Pedro Orce who is resting from his adventures and discoveries. One can tell from the atmosphere that it will be a hot day. The clouds are coming in from the sea and appear to be moving more swiftly than the wind. Near Deux Chevaux are two men, these are the hired laborers who have arrived for work, they are commenting to each other that the widow, who is always complaining about how little she earns from farming, has finally bought herself a car, Once the husband is out of the way, these women manage very nicely, this sarcastic remark came from the older man. Maria Guavaira called out to them, and as she set about lighting the fire and heating up the coffee she explained that she had offered shelter to some travelers who had lost their way, poor people,

You aren't safe living here all by yourself, the younger man said, but this phrase, so full of concern, is simply a variant of many others that have been spoken with somewhat different intentions, You should have remarried, you need a man to keep an eye on the house, no exaggeration, you couldn't have found a better man than me, when it comes to work and all the rest, Believe me when I say I'm very fond of you, One day you'll see me come through that door and you'd better believe I'll be here to stay. You're driving me out of my mind, You think men have no feelings, that we're made of wood, whereupon Maria Guavaira threatened him, If you come any closer, I'll know for sure, because you'll get a live coal in your face, and the younger man had no choice but to rephrase his opening sentence, You should have a man here to look after you, but even expressing it like this has not helped him to get what he wants.

The farmhands went into the fields and Maria Guavaira returned to the bedroom. Joaquim Sassa was fast asleep. Slowly, so as not to awaken him, she opened her trunk and began sorting out clothes in the light colors she used to wear before going into mourning, shades of pink, green, blue, white, and red, orange or lilac, and all the other color combinations popular with women, not that this was any stage wardrobe or that she was a wealthy landowner, but as everyone knows, two dresses are enough to strike a festive note, and two skirts with two blouses create a rainbow. The clothes smell of mothballs and staleness, Maria Guavaira will hang them out in the sun to allow the miasma of chemicals and the musty smell to evaporate, and just as she is about to go down, her arms a riot of color, she bumps into Joana Carda, who has also left her man tucked snugly between the sheets and who, seeing at once what is happening, offers to help. The two of them laugh at the display, the wind blows their hair about, the clothes make a smacking sound and flutter like flags, one feels like shouting, Long live liberty.

They go back into the kitchen to prepare food, the place smells of freshly brewed coffee, there is milk, bread, no longer fresh but edible, some hard cheese, jam, these appetizing odors will rouse the men, first José Anaiço appeared, then Joaquim Sassa, next to appear was not a man but a dog, it appeared in the doorway, had a good look, and went away. It's gone to call its master, said Maria Guavaira, who in theory has more claims to ownership, but she has already given them up. Pedro Orce finally appeared, said good morning, and sat down in silence, there's a hint of resentment in his expression when he observes the still very discreet gestures of affection with which the other four express themselves, whether as couples or all together. The world of contentment has its own distinctive sun.

Pedro Orce's resentment may look bad, he knows he is an old man, but we must try to understand his feelings if he is still not resigned to the idea. José Anaiço tries to include him in the conversation, asks if he enjoyed his nocturnal stroll, if the dog had been good company, and Pedro Orce, already mollified, is inwardly grateful for the olive branch offered, it came at just the right moment before any bitterness could further complicate the feeling of privation, I walked as far as the sea, he said, and this caused great surprise, most of all in Maria Guavaira, who knows perfectly well where the sea lies and how difficult it is to get there. But if I hadn't taken the dog with me I couldn't have managed, Pedro Orce explained, and suddenly the stone ship came to mind, he felt uneasy, incapable of deciding for a few seconds whether he had seen it in a dream or whether it had been concrete and real, If I wasn't dreaming, if it wasn't some vision in a dream, it exists, it's there at this precise moment, I'm sitting here drinking coffee and the ship is there, and, such are the powers of imagination, despite his having seen it only under the feeble light of those few stars, he could now visualize it in full daylight with the sun and the blue of the sky, the black rock beneath the petrified ship. I've found a ship, he said, and without thinking he might be deceived, he expounded his theory, explained the chemical process without always knowing the precise terms, but little by little words began to fail him, Maria Guavaira's look of disapproval had disturbed him, and he wound up defensively with another cautious theory, Of course, this could also be an unusual effect due to erosion.

Joana Carda said she wanted to go and take a look, José Anaiço and Joaquim Sassa agreed at once, only Maria Guavaira remained silent, she and Pedro Orce looked at each other, gradually the others fell silent, they realized that the last word remained to be said, if there really exists a last word for everything, which raises the delicate question of knowing how things will stand after everything has been said about them. Maria Guavaira held Joaquim Sassa's hand as if she were about to take an oath, It's a stone ship, you said, That's right, it turned to stone with time, perhaps through petrification, but perhaps it is just a coincidence that it has taken on this form because of the wind and other atmospheric agents, the rain, for example, and even the sea, for there must have been a time when the sea level was higher, It's a stone ship that was always made of stone, it's a ship that came from afar, and there it remained after all the persons sailing in it had disembarked. Persons, asked José Anaiço, Or person, of this I can't be sure, And of what you claim as being certain, what certainty is there, Pedro Orce asked skeptically, The ancients used to say, for their forefathers had told them, as their forefathers in turn had told them, some saints landed on this coast in ships of stone, coming from the deserts on the other side of the world, some arrived alive, others dead, as in the case of St. James, the ships have been stranded since that time and this is only one of them. Do you believe in any of what you're saying, It's not a question of believing or not believing, everything we go on saying is added to what is, to what exists, first I said granite, then I said ship, when I get to the end of what I'm saying, I have to believe in my having said it, that's often all that's needed, just as water, flour, and yeast make bread.

Joaquim Sassa now saw her as a wise shepherdess, a Minerva from the Galician mountains, we generally fail to notice, but the truth is that people know much more than we think, the majority of people do not even suspect how much knowledge they possess, the trouble is that they try to pass for what they are not, they lose their knowledge and wit, they would do better if they were like Maria Guavaira, who simply says, I've read a number of books in my life, the wonder is that I profited so much from them, this woman is not so presumptuous as to say this of herself, it is the narrator, a lover of justice, who cannot resist making this comment. Joana Carda is about to ask when they will go to see the stone ship when Maria Guavaira, perhaps so as to cut short this discussion, which is above her head, when, as we were saying, Maria Guavaira switched on the radio she keeps in the kitchen, the world must have some news to report, it is like this every morning, and the news is always startling, even when one has not caught the opening words, these can be reconstructed later. Since last night the speed of the peninsula's displacement has inexplicably altered, the latest measurement registers more than two thousand meters per hour, practically fifty kilometers each day, that is, three times the daily displacement recorded since the drift began.

At this moment there must be silence everywhere in the peninsula, people are listening to the news in their homes and in the public squares, but there are some who will find out only later what has happened, such as those two men who are working for Maria Guavaira, they are way out in the fields, remote from everything, I'll bet the younger one will forget the compliments and flattery and think of nothing except his own life and safety. But there's worse to come, when the announcer reads a bulletin from Lisbon, the news had to be leaked sooner or later, the secret has lasted for a long time, There is grave concern in official and scientific circles in Portugal, since the archipelago of the Azores is situated precisely on the route the peninsula has been following, the first signs of the population's anxiety are already in evidence, for the moment one cannot speak of panic, but it is expected that within the next few hours steps will be taken to evacuate people living in those cities and towns along the coast that are at greatest risk in the event of a collision, as for those of us here in Spain, we can consider ourselves safe from any immediate effects, insofar as the Azores are distributed between the thirty-seventh and fortieth parallels, while the entire region of Galicia lies north of the forty-second parallel, it is fairly obvious that unless there are modifications in the route, only our neighboring country, ever unfortunate, will suffer the direct impact, without forgetting, of course, the no less unfortunate islands themselves, which, because of their lesser dimensions, run the risk of disappearing under the great mass of stone that

1 7 6

is now being displaced, as we mentioned, at the terrifying speed of fifty kilometers each day, although it is just possible that those very islands could form a providential barrier, halting this approaching peril that has so far proved relentless, we are all in the hands of God, since human might is not sufficient to avoid the catastrophe should it happen, fortunately, we repeat, we Spaniards are more or less safe, there's no place for excessive optimism, however, the secondary consequences of the collision are always to be feared, so the utmost vigilance is called for and only those whose duties and obligations prevent them from moving inland should remain on the Galician coast. The announcer broke off, then there was music composed for an altogether different occasion, and José Anaiço, suddenly remembering, said to Joaquim Sassa, You were right when you spoke of the Azores, and such is human vanity, even when one's life is at such serious risk, that Joaquim Sassa was very pleased that his judgment should be publicly acknowledged in the presence of Maria Guavaira, albeit the merit was not his, it was just something he had picked up when he was taken around the laboratories with Pedro Orce.

As in a recurring dream, José Anaiço made some calculations, he had asked for paper and pencil, this time he would not say how many days Gibraltar would take to pass in front of the battlements of the Serra de Gádor, that had been a time of festivity, now it was necessary to ascertain how many days lay ahead before the Cabo da Roca crashed into the island of Terceira, one shudders just to think of that horrendous moment, once the island of São Miguel has been buried like a spike in the soft earth of Alentejo, truly, truly I tell you, nothing but evil can come of it. Having made his calculations, José Anaiço tells them, So far we've gone about three hundred kilometers, all right, since the distance from Lisbon to the Azores is more or less twelve hundred kilometers, we still have nine hundred to go, and nine hundred kilometers at fifty kilometers a day, rounding off, makes eighteen days, in other words, we'll reach the Azores around the twentieth of September, perhaps even sooner. The blandness of this conclusion was a forced and bitter irony that did not bring a smile to anyone's face. Maria Guavaira reminded him, But we're here in Galicia, beyond its reach, You can't rely on it, Pedro Orce cautioned her, it only needs to change course ever so slightly toward the south, and we are the ones who will take the full impact, the best thing, the only thing to do is to escape inland, as the announcer said, and even then we can't be sure, Abandon our homes and lands, If what they're telling us should happen, there won't be any homes or lands. They were seated, for the time being they could remain seated, they could remain seated for eighteen days. The fire was burning in the hearth, the bread was on the table, there were other things too, milk, coffee, cheese, but it was the bread that attracted everyone's gaze, half of a large loaf, thick-crusted and firm in the center, the taste lingered on their palates, even after a while, but their tongues recognized the crumbs that were left after chewing, when the last day of the universe comes we shall look at the last ant with the painful silence of someone who knows he is taking his leave for the last time.

Joaquim Sassa said, My vacation ends today, if I'm going to stick to the rules, I should be back at work in Oporto tomorrow morning, these objective words were only the beginning of a statement, I don't know if we'll keep on together, that's a matter we must decide here, but speaking for myself, I want to be with Maria, if she agrees and wants to be with me. And so that everything should be said at the right moment and each piece fitted into the right order and sequence, they waited for Maria Guavaira, who had been summoned, to speak first, and she said, That's what I want too, without needless elaboration. José Anaiço said, If the peninsula should collide with the Azores, the schools won't reopen all that soon, in fact they might never open again, I'll stay with Joana and with the rest of you if she decides to remain. Now it was the turn of Joana Carda, who like Maria Guavaira said no more than five words, women have so little to say for themselves, I'm staying with you, these were her words, for she was looking straight at him, but everyone understood the rest. Last of all, because someone had to be last, Pedro Orce said, Wherever we go, I go, and this phrase, which obviously offends grammar and logic with its excess of logic and very likely of grammar too, must stand uncorrected, exactly as it was said, perhaps there is some special meaning that will justify and absolve it, anyone who knows anything about words knows to expect anything from them. Dogs, as everyone knows, do not speak, and this one cannot even give a loud bark as a sign of jovial approval.

That same day they walked all the way to the coast to see the stone ship. Maria Guavaira was wearing her brightest clothes, she had not even bothered to iron them, the wind and light would smooth out the creases after their years in darkest limbo. Pedro Orce, their experienced guide, led the way, although he trusts the dog's instinct and scent more than his own eyes, to which everything in the light of day looks like a different route. While we cannot expect any guidance from Maria Guavaira, her route is another one, everything with her is an excuse to hold hands with Joaquim Sassa and draw near to him until their bodies touch long enough to steal a kiss, a variable time upon as we know, which explains why they do not so much accompany the expedition as trail behind it. José Anaiço and Joana Carda are more discreet, they have been together for a week now, have sated their initial hunger, slaked their initial thirst, desire comes to them when they summon it, and if truth be told, they do so frequently. Even last night, when Pedro Orce saw that splendor in the distance, it was not just Joaquim Sassa and Maria Guavaira who were making love, there could have been ten couples sleeping in that house and all making love at the same time.

The clouds come from the sea and speed away in haste, they form and disintegrate rapidly as if each moment lasted no more than a second or a fraction of a second, and all the gestures of these men and women are, or appear to be, at the very same instant, both slow and swift, one would think the world had gone crazy, if one could ever fully grasp the meaning of such an impoverished but popular expression. They reach the top of the hill and the sea is tempestuous. Pedro Orce scarcely recognizes these places, the enormous rounded boulders that are piled up, the almost invisible ox cart descending in stages, how could he have taken this route by night, even with the dog's guidance, this is a feat he simply cannot explain. He tries to make out the stone ship but it is nowhere to be seen, now it is Maria Guavaira who leads the group, and none too soon, because she knows these paths better than anyone. They arrive at the spot, and Pedro Orce is about to open his mouth to say, It's not here, but he has stopped himself in time, he has before his eyes the stone of the helm with its broken tiller, the great mast looks even thicker in daylight, and as for the ship, this is where he finds the greatest change, as if the erosion of which he had been speaking that morning had accomplished in one night the work of thousands of years, where is it, I cannot see it, the tall pointed prow, the concave belly, the stone certainly has the broad outline of a ship, but not even the most glorious of saints could work the miracle of keeping such a precarious vessel afloat without bulwarks, there is no doubt that it is made of stone, but somehow it seems to have lost the form of a ship, after all, a bird only flies because it looks like a bird, Pedro Orce thinks to himself, but now Maria Guavaira is saying, This is the ship in which a saint came from the east, here you can still see the marks of his feet when he disembarked and started walking inland, the marks were some cavities in the rock, now tiny puddles that the ebb and flow of the waves at high tide would constantly renew, clearly any doubts are legitimate, but things depend on what one accepts or refutes, if a saint came from afar sailing on a slab of stone, then why should it not be possible for his fiery feet to have marked the rock up to the present day. Pedro Orce has no choice but to accept and confirm, but keeps to himself the memory of another ship that he alone saw on a night almost without stars yet inhabited by sublime visions.

The sea splashes over the rocks as if struggling against the advance of this irresistible tide of stones and earth. They no longer look at the phantom ship, they look at the thrashing waves, and José Anaiço says, We're on the road, we know it but we don't feel it. And Joana Carda asked him, The road to where. Then Joaquim Sassa said, There are five of us and a dog, we won't fit into Deux Chevaux, this is a problem we must solve, one solution would be for us two, for José and me, to go and search for a bigger car among the vehicles abandoned all over the place, the difficulty will be finding one in good condition, the ones we've seen always had some part missing, We can decide what we're going to do once we get home, José Anaiço said, there's no hurry, But what about the house, the land, Maria Guavaira muttered, We have no choice, either we get away from here or we all die, these words were spoken by Pedro Orce and they were final.

After lunch Joaquim Sassa and José Anaiço set off in Deux Chevaux in search of a bigger car, preferably a jeep, an army jeep would be fine, or, better still, one of those transport trucks, a moving van that might be transformed into a house on wheels with sleeping accommodations, but just as Joaquim Sassa had surmised, they found nothing suitable, besides this region where we are is not particularly well provided with parking lots. They returned in the late afternoon along the roads that little by little became congested with vehicles traveling from west to east, it was the beginning of the exodus of the coastal population, there were cars, carts, once more the traditional donkeys, and bicycles, although not many of them on the bumpy roads, and motorcycles, and long-distance buses seating fifty or more that were transporting entire villages, it was the greatest migration ever in the history of Galicia. Some people stared in amuzement at these travelers going in the opposite direction, they even tried to stop them, didn't they know what had happened, Yes we know, many thanks, we're only going to look for some people, meanwhile there's no real danger, and then José Anaiço said, If it's like this here, what must it be like in Portugal, and suddenly the perfect way out occurred to them, How stupid we are, the solution is very simple, let's make the journey twice, or three times, as many times as it takes, we can choose some place in the interior to move into, a house, it shouldn't be difficult, people are leaving everything behind. This was the good news they brought, and it was deservedly given a warm welcome, next day they would start to sort out and put aside what they thought they should take, and to speed up the task they held a lengthy discussion after dinner, made an inventory of their needs, drew up lists, chopping and changing as they went along, Deux Chevaux had a long journey ahead and a heavy load to transport.

The following morning, the farmhands didn't appear and Deux Chevaux's engine wouldn't start. Putting it like this, we might give the impression that there is some connection between the two facts, perhaps that the absentee farmhands have stolen some essential part from the car, whether out of desperate need or with sudden malice. Not so. Both the older and the younger man had been swept away in the exodus that was depopulating the entire coastal region for more than fifty kilometers inland, but three days from now, when the inhabitants of the house have already departed, the younger man will return to this spot, the one who coveted Maria Guavaira and her land, in this order or the other way around, and we will never know if he is returning to attain his dream of becoming a landowner, even if only for a few days before he is killed in a geological disaster that will carry off both the land and his dream, or if he has decided to stay here standing guard, fighting loneliness and fear, risking everything to gain everything, the hand of Maria Guavaira and her possessions, if the terrifying threat should somehow fail to materialize, Maria Guavaira may come back here one day, if she should return she will find a man digging the soil or sleeping soundly after all that labor, in a cloud of blue wool.

All day long Joaquim Sassa struggled with the unwilling engine, José Anaiço helped as best he could, but what they knew between them was not enough to solve the problem. There were no parts missing, there was no lack of power, but somewhere deep down in the engine something had been damaged or broken, or had gradually worn out, it happens to people, it can also happen to machines, one day, without any warning, the body says no, or the soul, or the spirit, or the will, and nothing will move it, Deux Chevaux had also reached this point, it had brought Joaquim Sassa and José Anaiço all this way, it did not dump them in the middle of the road, so let them at least be grateful, there is no point in losing their temper, throwing punches solves nothing, kicking gets you nowhere. Deux Chevaux was finished. When they came indoors feeling discouraged, covered with grease, their hands filthy after struggling, in the near-total absence of tools, with nuts, bolts, and gears, and went to clean themselves up, with the loving assistance of their womenfolk, the atmosphere was tense. How are we going to get out of this place now, asked Joaquim Sassa who, as the owner of the car, felt himself not only responsible but at fault, he saw it as an ungrateful act of destiny, a personal affront, certain susceptibilities about one's honor are no less irritating simply because they happen to be absurd.

Then a family council was convened, it promised to be a troubled session, but Maria Guavaira immediately took the initiative and made a proposal, I've got an old wagon here that we could use and a horse that's seen better days, but if we handle it carefully perhaps it'll get us there. Several moments of bewilderment followed, a natural reaction on the part of people accustomed to traveling by car and suddenly finding themselves obliged in a crisis to revert to old-fashioned means of transport. Is the wagon covered, Pedro Orce inquired, being a practical man and of an older generation, The awning must be worn by now but it can be patched if necessary, I've got some strong material that will do the job, And if we need to, said Joaquim Sassa, we can always strip away the canvas from Deux Chevaux since it won't be needed any more, and that'll be the last favor I owe it. They're all on their feet, cheerful, this promises to be a real adventure, traveling around the world in a wagon, the world in a manner of speaking, and they say, Let's go and see the horse, let's go and look at the wagon, Maria Guavaira has to explain that the wagon is not a carriage, it has four wheels, an axle in front for pulling it, and under the awning that will shelter them from the weather there's enough room for a family, with a little planning and economizing, this won't be so very different from living in a house.

The horse is old, it saw them coming into the stable and turned around to stare at them with its enormous black eyes, startled by the light and commotion. The wise man's saying is true, While there's life, there's hope, so do not despair.

*F*rom our distant vantage point, we know little about the twists and turns of the present crisis, latent since the breaking away of the peninsula but becoming ever more serious in government circles, especially since the celebrated invasion of the hotels when the ignorant masses trampled on law and order, insofar as no one can see how to resolve the situation in the immediate future and restore all property to its rightful owners, as the higher interests of morality and justice dictate. Above all, because no one knows if there will be any immediate future. The news that the peninsula is rushing at a speed of two kilometers per hour in the direction of the Azores was used by the Portuguese government as a pretext for resigning in view of the seriousness of the situation, the imminence of collective danger, which leads one to believe that governments are only capable and effective at times when there is no real need to put their ability and effectiveness to the test. The Prime Minister, in his speech to the nation, saw the one-party system of his government as an obstacle to the broad national consensus he considered indispensable if this terrible crisis was to be overcome and a state of normality restored. In keeping with this line of thought, he had proposed to the President of the Republic the formation of a government of national salvation with the participation of all political forces, with or without parliamentary representation, bearing in mind that one could always find a position, deputy undersecretary to the deputy secretary to some deputy minister, to give to a political crony who in normal circumstances would not even be entrusted with opening the door. Nor did he forget to make it quite clear that he and his ministers considered themselves at the service of the nation, ready to collaborate, in whatever new or different capacity, in the salvation of the fatherland and to contribute to the prosperity of the nation.

The President of the Republic accepted the government's resignation and, complying with the constitution and the established norms governing the democratic functioning of institutions, he invited the resigning Prime Minister, as the leader of the party most often elected, a party that so far had governed alone, without alliances, he invited him, as we were saying, to form the proposed government of national salvation. Because there can be no doubt that governments of national salvation are also perfectly valid, and one could even go so far as to say they are the best governments of all, the sad thing is that countries need them only very rarely, therefore we do not normally have governments that know how to govern nationally. On this most delicate issue there have been interminable debates among constitutionalists, political analysts, and other experts, and in all this time precious little has been added to the obvious meaning of these words, namely that a government of national salvation, because it is national and concerned with salvation, is one of national salvation. That is how any simpleton would put it, and he could not do better. The most interesting thing about all of this is that the moment the formation of the aforesaid government was announced, the masses suddenly felt they had been saved, or soon would be, although certain manifestations of innate skepticism are inevitable when the list of ministerial appointments is announced and their photographs appear in the newspapers and on television. At the end of the day they are the same old faces, and why should we have expected otherwise, since we are so unwilling to put ourselves forward.

We have already mentioned the danger Portugal is facing should she collide with the Azores, and also the secondary consequences, unless they turn out to be direct, threatening Galicia, but the situation of the population of the islands is obviously much more serious. What is an island, after all. An island, in this instance an entire archipelago, is the emergence of a submarine cordillera, and very often just the sharp peaks of rocky needles that miraculously remain upright through thousands of feet of water, an island, in short, is the most fortuitous of events. And now here is something that, although no more than an island, is so enormous and fast-moving that we are in great danger of witnessing, let us hope from a distance, the decapitation of São Miguel followed by that of the islands of Terceira, São Jorge, and Faial, and other islands of the Azores, with widespread loss of life, unless the government of national salvation, which is due to take office tomorrow, comes up very quickly with a way to evacuate thousands and millions of people to regions of reasonable safety, if such places exist. The President of the Republic, even before the new government started to function, has already appealed for international solidarity, thanks to which, as we are reminded, and this is only one of the many examples we could give, famine was once avoided in Africa. The countries of Europe, where, fortunately, a certain lowering of the tone in official references to Portugal and Spain has been evident ever since the serious identity crisis that arose when millions of Europeans resolved to declare themselves Iberian, received the appeal sympathetically and have already inquired how we would like to be helped, although, as usual, everything depends on their ability to meet our needs from whatever surplus they may have at their disposal. As for the United States of America, which should always be named in full, despite having sent word that the plan for a government of national salvation is not to its liking, it has declared that given the circumstances, it is nevertheless willing to evacuate the entire population of the Azores, which is just under two hundred and fifty thousand people, although there is still the problem of where to settle all those people, certainly not in the philanthropic United States, because of the strict immigration laws. The ideal solution, if you want to know, and this is the secret dream cherished by the State Department and the Pentagon, would be for the islands to stop the peninsula in its path, at whatever cost in death and destruction, for it would then be stuck in the middle of the Atlantic, with obvious strategic benefits for world peace and Western Civilization. The people will be told that the

American squadrons are under orders to head for the Azores and upon arrival to pick up many thousands of the islanders, the rest will have to wait for the air lift that is currently being organized, Portugal and Spain will have to deal with any local problems, the Spanish less so than we Portuguese, for history and fortune have always treated the former with all too obvious partiality.

Leaving aside the case of Galicia, a case and a region that are purely peripheral, or, to adopt other criteria, appendicular, Spain is protected from the more fatal consequences of the collision, since Portugal essentially acts as a screen or buffer. Problems of some logistic complexity have yet to be resolved, such as that posed by the important cities of Vigo, Pontevedra, Santiago de Compostela, and La Coruña, but, as for the rest, the people who live in villages are so accustomed to a precarious existence that, almost without waiting for orders, advice, or information, they have started retreating farther inland, peaceful and resigned, using the means of transport already described, and others as well, starting with the most primitive means of all, their own feet.

Portugal's situation, however, is quite different. Note that the entire coast, excepting the southern part of the Algarve, now finds itself in danger of being stoned by the islands of the Azores, the word stoned is used here because the outcome is much the same whether a stone hits us or we hit our head against a stone, it is all a question of speed and inertia, not forgetting that in this case, the head, even though wounded and cracked, will reduce all the stones to splinters. Under the circumstances, with a coastline like this, nearly all of it flat, and with the proximity of the larger cities to the sea, and taking into account the unpreparedness of the Portuguese for the slightest catastrophe, earthquake, flood, forest fire, or drought, it is doubtful whether the government of salvation will know how to do its duty. The best solution, actually, would be deliberately to stir up panic, to rush people into abandoning their homes and force them to seek refuge farther inland. The worst thing of all will be if people start to run out of food, either during the journey or wherever they decide to settle, then there will be so much indignation and frustration that all hell will break loose. We are worried, naturally, but frankly we would be much more worried if we happened to be in Galicia watching the travel preparations of Maria Guavaira and Joaquim Sassa, Joana Carda and José Anaiço, Pedro Orce and the Dog, the relative importance of topics is variable, it depends on the point of view, the humor of the moment, one's personal sympathies, the objectivity of the narrator is a modern invention, we need only reflect that our Lord God didn't want it in His Book.

Two days have passed, the horse, after being near starvation, has been given extra rations of food, as much oats and beans as it likes, Joaquim Sassa even suggested giving it soup laced with wine, and the wagon, now that the holes have been patched with the canvas removed from Deux Chevaux, not only is more comfortable inside but will protect them from the weather as the light showers give way to constant rain, for September is here and we're in a region that is invariably wet. Meanwhile, one can reckon that the peninsula has sailed about a hundred and fifty kilometers since José Anaiço made his precise calculations, So there are still seven hundred and fifty kilometers to go, or fifteen days, for those who prefer more empirical measurements, at the end of which, give or take a minute, the first collision will take place, Jesus, Mary, and Joseph, those poor wretches in Alentejo, it's just as well they are used to disasters, they are like the Galicians, their skin is so tough that we would be fully justified in using another word, let us say leather instead of skin and dispense with any further explanation. Here in these northern territories, in the Elysian valleys of Galicia, there is plenty of time for our travelers to get out of harm's way. The wagon is already equipped with mattresses, sheets, and blankets, all the luggage is on board, along with basic cooking utensils, food already prepared for the first few days, omelettes to be precise, and various foodstuffs, such as white and red beans, rice and potatoes, a barrel of water, a cask of wine, two laying hens, one of them mottled, its neck bald, salt cod, a pitcher of olive oil, a bottle of vinegar, and some salt, for we cannot live without it unless we refuse baptism, pepper and saffron, all the bread they had in the house, a bag of flour, hay, bran and bean pods for the horse, the dog presents no problem, it knows how to look after its own needs, when it accepts any help, it is only to please others. Maria Guavaira, without explanation, but then perhaps she could not have explained even if asked, wove bracelets of the blue thread for them all, and collars for the horse and dog. There is such a quantity of wool there that no one noticed any difference. Besides, one must admit that, even if they'd wanted to take it with them, there's no room for the wool in the wagon, nor was it ever foreseen that there would be, otherwise where would he sleep, that young farmhand who is about to arrive.

On the last night in the house, they were late getting to bed, they sat up talking for hours on end, as if the following morning was to be one of sad farewells, with each of them going his separate way. But staying together like this was one way of keeping up their spirits, it is a well-known fact that canes start to break the moment they are separated from the bundle, everything breakable has already been broken. They spread out the map of the peninsula on the kitchen table, as drawn here it is still incongruously joined to France, and they marked out the first day's itinerary, the inaugural route, taking care to choose the least bumpy roads, in view of the feeble strength of their scraggy horse. But they would have to make a side trip to the north, as far as La Coruña, where Maria Guavaira's demented mother was in a mental institution, daughterly love decrees that she go and rescue her from that pandemonium, for one can imagine the panic in that bedlam, an enormous island bursting through the front door, hurling itself onto the city and sweeping before it the anchored boats, and all those glass-paned windows on the avenue on the waterfront shattering to smithereens at the same time, and the demented inmates thinking, if they are capable of thinking in their lunacy, that the Day of Judgment has finally come. Maria Guavaira will have the honesty to say, I don't know what life is going to be like with my mother in the wagon, even if she isn't really violent, bear with me, it's only until we reach a place of safety. They promised to be patient, they would arrange things as best they could, but as we know very well not even the greatest love can withstand its own madness, so how will it cope with another's madness, in this case that of the insane mother of one of the insane.

Just as well that José Anaiço had the fortunate idea of telephoning for information from the first place where it was possible, the health authorities might well have transferred or be about to transfer the inmates to a place of safety, for this is not one of your classical shipwrecks, the first to be rescued here are those who are lost.

The couples finally withdrew to their rooms, they did what people normally do on these occasions, who knows if we will ever come back, so let the vibrations of carnal love between humans remain, that love with no equal among the species, made as it is of sighs, murmurings, impossible words, saliva and sweat, anguish, implored martyrdom, Not just yet, one is dying of thirst yet refuses the water of freedom, Now, now, my love, and this is what old age and death will steal from us. Pedro Orce, who is old and already bearing the first sign of death, which is solitude, left the house once more to go and take a look at the stone ship, accompanied by the dog, which has every name and none, and in case you are about to say that if the dog accompanied him then Pedro Orce is no longer alone, do not forget the animal's remote origins, the hounds of hell have already seen everything, and because they have such a long life they accompany no one, it is the humans who live for such a short time who accompany dogs. The stone ship stands there, the prow is as tall and pointed as on the first night, Pedro Orce is not surprised, each of us sees the world with the eyes he possesses, and eyes see what they choose to see, eyes create the world's diversity and fabricate its wonders, even if they're only made of stone, its tall prows, even if they're only an illusion.

The morning awoke overcast and drizzly, a familiar figure of speech but one that is incorrect, because mornings do not awaken, it is we who awaken in the mornings, and then, going to the window, see that the sky is covered with low clouds and the rain is drizzling down, tiresome for anyone caught in it, but such is the power of tradition that if there were a ship's log book on this journey of ours, the clerk would inscribe his first paean as follows, The morning awoke overcast and drizzly, as if the skies were gazing down with disapproval on this adventure, the skies are always invoked in these instances, whether it rains or shines. Deux Chevaux, with one mighty heave, replaced the wagon under the tiled roof, or rather the thatch, for this is not a garage but a lean-to exposed to the elements. Abandoned like this and without its canvas hood, which was used to patch the awning on the wagon, the car already looks like a wreck, objects suffer the same fate as people, when they have outlived their usefulness they are discarded, they are discarded once they no longer serve any purpose. The wagon, on the other hand, despite being ancient, has been rejuvenated after being taken out into the open air, the wagon is restored as the rain washes it down, being put into action has always had this admirable effect, just look at the horse, covered with an oilcloth to protect its back and looking almost like a charger in a joust, caparisoned for battle.

These descriptive interludes should cause no surprise, they're ways of showing how difficult it is to uproot people from places where they have been happy, all the more so since these people are not fleeing in panic, Maria Guavaira is now closing the doors carefully, she sets free the hens that are being left behind, releases the rabbits from their hutch, the pig from the sty, these are animals accustomed to being fed and now left to God's mercy, if not to the wiles of Satan, for the pig is quite capable, should the mood take it, of attacking the other animals. When the younger of the two farmhands arrives he will have to break a window to enter the house, there is no one for leagues around to see him break in. If I break in, there's good reason for doing so, these are his words, and perhaps it is true.

Maria Guavaira climbed into the driver's seat, beside her sat Joaquim Sassa with open umbrella, his duty is to accompany the woman he loves and to protect her from the inclement weather, he cannot do her job for her, because of the five persons here only Maria Guavaira knows how to drive a wagon and horse. Later in the afternoon when the sky clears, she will teach them. Pedro Orce will insist upon being the first to receive some basic training, a thoughtful gesture on his part, so that the two couples may relax under the awning with no unwelcome separations, the driver's seat is spacious enough for three, an ideal solution that allows the other two to be together, even if this only means sitting quietly side by side, in silence. Maria Guavaira shook the reins, the horse, hitched between the shafts of the wagon with no partner at its side, gave the first pull, felt the harness tugging, then the weight of the load, memories came flooding back to its old bones and muscles, and the almost forgotten sound returned, that of the earth being crushed beneath the rotating metal rims of the wheels. You can learn, forget, and learn everything anew, when forced by necessity. For several hundred meters the dog accompanied the wagon in the rain. Then it saw that it could travel in the shelter of that great encumbrance while still on foot. It got under the wagon, fell into step with the horse's rhythm, and that is how we will see the dog for the rest of the journey, come rain or shine, since it has no wish to act as guide or to amuse itself with all those senseless comings and goings that make men and dogs seem so similar.

That day they did not travel far. They had to conserve the horse's strength, all the more so since the bumpy road demanded constant effort, whether pulling the wagon on the way up or slowing down in the descents. There was not a living soul as far as the eye could see. We must have been the last people to leave these parts, Maria Guavaira said, and the clouded sky, the leaden atmosphere, the gloomy landscape were like the dying breath of a world at its end, desolate, expiring after so much sorrow and weariness, so much living and dying, so much resolute life and subsequent death. But new loves travel in this wagon, and new loves, as those who have observed them know, are the greatest force in this world, they fear no misfortune, since by their very nature new loves are themselves the greatest misfortune of all, a sudden flash of lightning, joyful surrender, disquieting confusion. But one must not put too much trust in first impressions, in this almost funereal appearance of this departure, in the dreary rain, from a deserted country it would be better, were we not so discreet, to listen carefully to the conversations between Joana Carda and José Anaiço, between Maria Guavaira and Joaquim Sassa, Pedro Orce's silence is even more discreet, it is almost as if he were not here at all.

The first village they passed through had not been completely abandoned. Some of the elderly had reassured their worried children and relatives that dying for the sake of dying was preferable to dying of hunger or some malignant disease, if a person has been so gloriously chosen to die along with the whole of his world, be he a Wagnerian hero or not, he will accede to that sublime Valhalla to which all great catastrophes lead. Elderly Galicians and Portuguese, for they belong to the same race, know nothing about such matters, but for some strange reason were capable of saying, I'm staying put, you can leave if you're frightened, and this doesn't mean that they felt all that courageous, simply that at this point in their lives they have finally come to realize that courage and fear are the two pans on the scale that oscillate while the pointer remains still, paralyzed by amazement at the useless invention of emotions and feelings.

As the wagon passed through the village, curiosity, which is probably the last human trait to disappear, brought the elderly out in the road, they waved slowly, and it was as if they were bidding themselves good-bye. Then José Anaiço suggested that it would be wise to seize this opportunity to get some sleep by making use of one of the empty houses, here or in some other village, or in some deserted spot, they were certain to find beds and greater comfort than in the wagon, but Maria Guavaira announced that she would never set foot in a strange house without the owner's consent, some people have such scruples, while others if they see a locked window smash it in and then say, It was all for the best, and whether it is for their own good or that of someone else, there will always be some doubt about the first and ultimate motive. José Anaiço regretted having made the suggestion, not because it was a bad one, but because it was absurd, Maria Guavaira's words were enough to define a code of self-respect, Try to be self-sufficient as far as you can, then confide in someone deserving of your trust, better still if this is someone deserving of you. As matters stand, these five appear to deserve one another, in every sense, so let them stay in the wagon, eat their omelettes, talk about the journey they have made so far and the journey that lies ahead of them. Maria Guavaira will reinforce the practical driving lessons she has given with a little theory, beneath a tree the horse goes on munching its ration of hay, the dog satisfies itself on this occasion with domestic provisions, it prowls around sniffing and startling the nightjars. It has stopped raining. A lantern illuminates the inside of the wagon, anyone passing this way would say, Look, a theater, they are certainly characters but not actors.

When Maria Guavaira finally succeeds in contacting the asylum in La Coruña by telephone tomorrow, she will be told that her mother and the other inmates have already been transferred inland, And how is she, As mad as ever, but this response could refer to anyone. They will continue their journey until the land becomes populated once more. There they will wait.

The Portuguese government of national salvation was formed and got down to business without delay, the Prime Minister himself had appeared on television and uttered a phrase that will certainly go down in history, words like Blood, sweat, and tears, or, Burying the dead and cherishing the living, or, Honor your country for your country is relying on you, or, The sacrifice of our martyrs will sow the seed of future harvests. In this instance, and bearing in mind the peculiar circumstances of the situation, the Prime Minister thought it best simply to say, Sons of Portugal, Daughters of Portugal, salvation lies in retreat.

But to find accommodation deep in the interior for the millions of people who live along the coastal strip was a task of such extreme complexity that no one had the presumption, absurd to say the least, to put forward a national plan of evacuation, comprehensive and capable of integrating local initiatives. With regard, for example, to the city and region of Lisbon, both the initial analysis of the situation and the subsequently adopted measures started from an assumption, both objective and subjective, that could be summed up as follows, The great majority, let us be frank, the overwhelming majority of Lisbon's inhabitants were not born there, and those who were are linked to the others by family ties. The consequences of this fact are broad and decisive, the first being that both the former and the latter will have to betake themselves to their places of origin, where many still have relatives, with some of whom they may have lost touch through various circumstances, let them take advantage of this enforced opportunity to restore harmony to their families, healing old wounds, patching up quarrels caused by contentious inheritances and unfair allocations that resulted in brawling and cursing. The great misfortune that has befallen us will have the merit of bringing hearts together again. The second consequence, which naturally stems from the first, concerns the problem of feeding the people evacuated. For here too, obviating the need for state intervention, the extended family will play a crucial role, speaking quantitatively, one could express this with a macroeconomic updating of the old saying, Three can eat as cheaply as two, the well-known arithmetic of resignation in any family where a child is expected, now one can say with even greater authority, Ten million can eat as cheaply as five, and with a quiet smile, A nation is nothing but a great big family.

Those living on their own, whether bereft of family or merely misanthropic, would be without recourse, but even they would not be excluded automatically from society, one has to have confidence in spontaneous solidarity, in that irrepressible love for one's neighbor that manifests itself on so many occasions, take train journeys, for example, especially in the second-class compartments, when the moment comes to open the basket of provisions, the mother of the family never forgets to offer some food to the other passengers occupying the nearby seats, Would you care for something to eat, if someone accepts she does not mind, even though she may be counting on a polite chorus of refusals, Not for me, thank you, but do enjoy your meal. The most awkward problem will be that of accommodation, it is one thing to offer someone a fish cake and a glass of wine, but it is quite a different matter to have to give up half of the bed we are sleeping in, but if we can get it into the heads of people that these solitary and abandoned people are reincarnations of Our Lord, as when He wandered the world disguised as a beggar in order to test the generosity of mankind, then someone will always find them a cupboard under the stairs, a corner in the attic, or, in rustic terms, a loft and a bundle of straw. This time God, however He may multiply Himself, will be treated as someone responsible for creating humanity deserves to be treated.

We have spoken of Lisbon in terms differing only quantitatively from those we could have used in speaking of Oporto or Coimbra, or of Setúbal and Aveiro, of Viana or Figueira, without forgetting those innumerable little towns and villages one finds everywhere, although in some cases the perplexing question arises of knowing where those people must go who live in the exact place where they were born, or those who, living somewhere on the coast, were born somewhere else on the coast. After these difficulties had been discussed by the cabinet ministers, their spokesman brought the reply, The government is confident that private initiative will find a solution, perhaps something truly original that will ultimately benefit everyone, to those problems not covered by the national program for the evacuation and resettlement of the population. Having been thus authorized from on high to put aside these individual destinies, we shall simply mention, with regard to Oporto, the case of Joaquim Sassa's employers and colleagues. Suffice it to say that if he, mindful of discipline and professional integrity, had rushed from the Galician mountains at the drop of a hat, abandoning love and friends to fate, he would have found his office closed and a notice on the door with the latest instructions from the management, Employees returning from vacation should report for work at our new premises at Peñafiel, where we hope to continue to satisfy the needs of our esteemed clients. And Joana Carda's cousins, the ones from Ereira, now find themselves in Coimbra, at the home of an abandoned cousin, who was not exactly overjoyed to see them, it stands to reason, he is the one who is aggrieved, after all, he still had a glimmer of hope, he thought that his cousins had gone ahead to prepare the ground for the returning fugitive, but when nothing happened he asked them, And what about Joana, his cousins confessed sorrowfully, We don't know, She was there in our house, but she disappeared even before the commotion began, we heard no more from her, what the cousin knows about the rest of the story she cautiously keeps to herself, for if he was astonished at what little he was told, what would he say if he were to learn everything.

And so the world is in a state of suspense, anxiously awaiting what is or is not about to happen to the western shores of Portugal and

Galicia. But we must repeat, tiresome though it may be, that It is an ill wind that bloweth no man good, that at least is the attitude of the governments of Europe, because from one moment to the next, along with the salutary results of the repression mentioned earlier, they are seeing the revolutionary fervor of youth fade and almost disappear, youth whose wise parents are now insisting, Do you see what you were risking if you had insisted on being Iberian, repentant youth now dutifully responding, Yes, Dad. As these scenes of domestic reconciliation and social appeasement are enacted, the geostationary satellites, each kept in place over a single point on the equator as it circles the earth, transmit photographs and measurements to earth, the first of these naturally showing no variation in the form of the moving object, the second registering with every passing minute a reduction of almost thirty-five meters in the distance that separates the large island from the small ones. In an age like ours with its acceleration of particles, seeing thirty-five meters per minute as a cause for concern would be laughable, unless we remind ourselves that behind these pleasant, sandy beaches, this deeply etched and picturesque coastline, these jagged promontories overlooking the sea, over five hundred and ninety thousand square kilometers of surface area is approaching, and an incalculable, astronomical number of millions of tons, to count only the sierras, cordilleras, and mountains. Let us just try to imagine what the inertia of all the orographic systems of the peninsula now set in motion will amount to, not to mention the Pyrenees, even reduced to half their former size, then we can only admire the courage of these peoples, who unite so many ancestral strains, and applaud their existential fatalism, which, with the experience of centuries, has been condensed into that most notable precept, From among the dead and wounded, someone must get away.

Lisbon is a deserted city. Army patrols are still circulating, with air support provided by helicopters, just as in Spain and France when the breakaway occurred and during the turbulent days that followed. Until they are withdrawn, which is expected to happen twenty-four hours before the anticipated moment of collision, the soldiers' mission is to be vigilant, on the qui vive, although they were really wasting their time since all the valuables had already been removed from the banks. But no one would forgive a government for abandoning a city as beautiful as this one, perfect in its proportions and harmony, as will inevitably be said of it once the city has been destroyed. That's why the soldiers are here, serving, in the people's absence, as their symbolic representatives, the guard of honor that would fire the customary salvos, if there should still be time, at that sublime moment when the city sinks into the sea.

Meanwhile, the soldiers fire a few shots at the looters and thieves, they offer advice and guidance to the odd person who refuses to abandon his home or who has finally decided to get out, and when, as happens from time to time, they meet a harmless madman wandering through the streets, one who has had the misfortune to be allowed out of the asylum on the day of the exodus and, not having known about or understood the order to return, has ended up being left to his fate, they tend to adopt either of two courses of action. Certain officers argue that the madman is always more dangerous than the looter, on the grounds that the latter, at least, is as rational as they are. In such a case they don't think twice, but order the troops to open fire. Other officers, less intolerant and, above all, aware of the desperate need to relieve nervous tension in time of war or catastrophe, order their men to have a bit of fun at the idiot's expense before sending him on his way in peace, unless it happens to be a madwoman rather than a madman, for there is always someone, whether in the army or elsewhere, who is prepared to abuse the elementary and obvious fact that sex, instrumentally speaking, is not in the head.

But now that there is no longer a living soul to be seen in this city, along the avenues, in the roads and squares, in the neighborhoods and public parks, now that faces no longer appear at the windows, now that those canaries not yet dead of hunger and thirst sing in the deathly silence of the house or on the verandah overlooking the empty courtyards, now that the waters of the fountains and springs still sparkle in the sunlight but no hand is dipped, now that the vacant eyes of the statues look around in search of eyes that might be returning their gaze, now that the open gates of cemeteries show that there is no difference between one absence and another, now, finally, that the city is on the brink of that anguished moment when an island will come from the sea and destroy it, now let the wonderful story of the lonely navigator and his miraculous salvation unfold.

For more than twenty years the navigator had been sailing the seven seas. He had inherited or bought his ship, or it had been given to him by some other navigator who had also sailed in it for twenty years, and before him, if the memory does not finally become confused after such a long time, yet another solitary navigator had apparently ploughed the oceans. The history of ships and those who sail them is full of unexpected adventures, with terrible storms and sudden lulls as terrifying as the worst hurricanes, and, to add a touch of romance, it is often said, and songs have been composed on the theme, that a sailor will find a woman waiting for him in every port, a somewhat optimistic picture, which the realities of life and the betrayals of women nearly always contradict. When the lonely navigator disembarks, it is usually to get a fresh supply of water, to buy tobacco or some spare part for the engine, or to stock up on oil and fuel, medicine, sewing needles for the sails, a plastic raincoat to keep out the rain and drizzle, hooks, fishing tackle, the daily newspaper to confirm what he already knows and is not worth knowing, but never, never, never, did the lonely navigator set foot on land in the hope of finding a woman to accompany him on the voyage. If there really is a woman waiting for him in port, it would be foolish to turn her down, but it is usually the woman who makes the first move and decides for how long, the lonely navigator has never said to her, Wait for me, I'll come back one day, that's not a request he would permit himself to make, Wait for me, nor could he guarantee that he will be back on this or any other day, and, on returning, how often he finds the harbor deserted, or should there be a woman waiting there, she is waiting for some other sailor, although it often happens that if he does not turn up, any sailor who appears will do just as well. One has to admit that neither the woman nor the sailors are at fault, solitude is to blame, solitude can sometimes become unbearable, it can even drive the sailor into port and bring the woman to the harbor.

These considerations, however, are spiritual and metaphysical, we could not resist making them at some point, whether before or after relating these extraordinary events, which they do not always help elucidate. To put it simply, let us say that far away from this peninsula, now turned into a floating island, the lonely navigator was sailing with his sail and engine, his radio and binoculars, and with the infinite patience of someone who one day decided to divide his life into one part sky and one part sea. The wind suddenly stopped blowing and he lowered the sail, the breeze suddenly dropped, and the great billows carrying the ship gradually start losing their force, the surge dwindles, within an hour the sea will be smooth and calm, we find it incredible that this chasm of water, thousands of meters deep, should be able to maintain its balance, falling neither to one side nor to the other, the observation will seem foolish only to those who believe everything in the world can be explained by the simple fact that it is as it is, something one obviously accepts but which is not enough. The engine is running, chug-chug chug-chug, nothing but water as far as the eye can see, it corresponds sparkle for sparkle to the classical image of the mirror, and the navigator, despite many years' mastery of a strict routine of sleep and vigil, suddenly closes his eyes, drugged by the heat of the sun, and falls fast asleep, he woke up shaken by what seemed to be a mighty blast, thinking, perhaps, that he had slept for several minutes or hours but it was only seconds, in that fleeting moment of sleep he dreamt that he had collided with the corpse of an animal, with a whale. Startled, his heart beating furiously, he tried to discover where the sound was coming from, but did not immediately notice that the engine had stopped. The sudden silence had woken him, but in order to awaken more naturally, his body had invented a sea monster, a collision, thunder. Broken-down engines, on land and sea, are much more common, we know of one that is beyond repair, it has a broken heart and has been dumped under a lean-to and exposed to the elements, up north where it is gathering rust. But this navigator, unlike those motorists, is experienced and knowledgeable, he stocked up on spare parts the last time he touched land and woman, he intends to dismantle the engine as far as possible and to examine the mechanism. Such a waste of effort. The damage is right down in the piston rod, the horsepower of this engine is mortally wounded.

Despair, as we all know, is human, there is no evidence in natural history that animals despair. Yet man, inseparable from despair, has become accustomed to living with it, endures it to its extremes, and it will take more than an engine's breaking down in mid-ocean for the sailor to start tearing out his hair, to implore the heavens or rail at them with curses and abuse, one gesture being as useless as another, the solution is to wait, whoever carried off the wind will bring it back. But the wind that departed did not return. The hours passed, serene night came, another day dawned, and the sea remains motionless, a fine thread of wool suspended here would drop like a plumb line, there isn't the tiniest ripple on the surface of the water, it is a stone ship on a stone slab. The navigator is not greatly concerned, this is not the first lull he has experienced, but now the radio has stopped working for some inexplicable reason, all one can hear is a buzzing sound, the carrier wave, if such a thing still exists, which is carrying nothing but silence, as if beyond this circle of stagnant water the world has become silent in order to witness, unseen, the navigator's mounting agitation, his madness, perhaps his death at sea. There is no lack of provisions or drinking water, but the hours are passing, each one increasingly prolonged, silence tightens its grip on the ship like the coils of a slippery cobra, from time to time the navigator taps the gunwale with a grappling iron, he wants to hear a sound unlike that of his own thick blood coursing through his veins, or the beating of his heart, which he sometimes forgets, and then he awakens after having thought he was already awake, for he was dreaming that he was dead. The sail is raised against the sun, but the still air retains the heat, the lonely navigator is sunburnt, his lips are cracked. The day passed, and the following day is no different. The navigator finds refuge in sleep, he has descended into the tiny cabin, now furnace-like, there is only one bunk there, narrow, proof that this navigator is truly alone, and he is stark naked, the sweat pouring off him at first, then, his skin dry, covered with goose pimples, he struggles with his dreams, a row of very tall trees swaying beneath a wind that pushes the leaves back and forth, then dies away before returning to attack them once more, on and on. The navigator gets up to drink some water and the water is finished. He goes back to sleep, the trees no longer stir, but a seagull has come to settle on the mast.

From the horizon there advances an enormous dark mass. As it gets closer, houses become visible along its shores, lights resembling white fingers outstretched in midair, a thin line of spume, and beyond the wide mouth of a river a great city built on hills, a red bridge joining the river's banks, and from this distance it looks like an etching in delicate lines. The navigator goes on sleeping, he has sunk into a state of extreme torpor, but the dream suddenly came back, a sudden breeze shook the branches of the trees, the ship swayed in the choppy waters of the channel, and, swallowed up by the river, it ran aground, rescued from the sea, still immobile, while the earth is still moving. The lonely navigator could feel the swaying in his bones and muscles, he opened his eyes and thought, The wind, the wind's come back, and, almost without strength, he slipped down from his bunk, dragged himself on deck, he felt as if he were dying with each moment and with each moment being reborn, the light of the sun hurt his eyes, but it was the light of earth, bringing whatever it could extract from the green foliage of the trees, from the obscure depths of the countryside, from the soft colors of the houses. He was safe, and at first he did not know how, the air was still, the breath of wind had been an illusion. It took him some time to understand that a whole island had saved him, the former peninsula, which had sailed to meet him and opened the river's arms to receive him. This all seemed so unlikely that the lonely navigator himself, who so many years ago had heard rumors about the geological rupture, while knowing that he was in the course of the terrestrial ship, had never imagined that he might be saved in this way, for the first time ever in the history of shipwrecks and losses at sea. But on land there was no one to be seen, on the decks of the anchored and moored ships no face appeared, the silence was once more that of the cruel sea, This is Lisbon, the navigator murmured, but where are the people. The windows of the city are gleaming, cars and buses can be seen at a standstill, a great square surrounded by arcades, a triumphal arch at the far end with figures in stone and crowns in bronze, they must be bronze because of the colors. The lonely navigator, who is familiar with the Azores and knows how to find them whether on the map or at sea, then remembered that the islands are on a collision course, what saved him will destroy them, what is about to destroy them will destroy him too, unless he gets away from these parts without delay. With no wind and a broken engine, he cannot go upriver, the only way out is to inflate the rubber dinghy, to lower the anchor to secure the boat, a useless gesture, to row ashore. Strength always returns with one's hopes.

The lonely navigator had dressed to go ashore, shorts, singlet, a cap on his head, sandals, everything a dazzling white, this is a point of honor with sailors. He hauled the rubber dinghy up the harbor steps, stood there watching for several seconds, waiting too to get his strength back, but above all to allow time for someone to appear from the shadows of the arcades, for the cars and buses suddenly to start moving again, and for the square to fill up with people, who knows, perhaps some woman might approach smiling, gently swaying her hips as she walks, without overdoing it, simply that insinuating appeal which affects a man's sight and speech, mainly because he has just come ashore. But the desert remained a desert. The navigator finally understood what had to be understood. Everyone had left because of the imminent collision with the islands. He looked back, saw his boat in the middle of the river, he felt certain he was seeing it for the last time, not even a battleship could withstand the tremendous head-on collision, so what chance would there be for a sailing nutshell abandoned by its owner. The navigator crossed the square, his legs still stiff from lack of exercise, he looks like a scarecrow with his tanned skin, his hair sprouting from his cap, his sandals hanging off his feet. He looks up as he approaches the great arch, reads the Latin inscription *Virtutibus Majorum ut sit omnibus documento P.P.D.*, he had never studied Latin, but vaguely understands that the monument is dedicated to the virtuous ancestors of the people who live here, and he proceeds along a narrow street with identical buildings on either side until he comes out into another square, smaller, with a Greek or Roman building at one end, and in the middle of the square there are two fountains with naked women cast in iron, the water is playing, and suddenly he feels very thirsty, feels the urge to plunge his mouth into that water and his body into those naked forms. He walks with outstretched arms, as if delirious, sleepwalking or in a trance, he mutters as he goes, has no idea what he is saying, only knows what he wants.

The patrol appears on the corner, five soldiers under the command of a second lieutenant. They spotted the madman twitching in his madness, they heard him raving, there was no need to give the order. The lonely navigator lay stretched out on the ground, there is still some way to go before reaching the water. The women, as we know, are made of iron.

*T*hese were also the days of the third exodus. The first, which was fully reported at the appropriate moment, was of the foreign tourists who fled in terror from what then, how time passes, still seemed no more than the possible danger that a crack would cleave the Pyrenees as far down as sea level, and what a pity this unexpected misfortune didn't stop there, just imagine how proud Europe would have felt to find itself endowed, as it were, with a geological canyon compared to which the one in Arizona would look no bigger than a tiny ditch. The second exodus was that of the rich and powerful when the fracture became irreparable, when the peninsula's course, although still slow, seemed to be gathering speed, showing, in a manner we believe definitive, the precariousness of established structures and ideas. It then became clear how the social edifice, with all its complexity, is no more than a house of cards, solid only in appearance, we need only shake the table on which it stands and the house collapses. And the table in this instance, and for the first time in history, had moved by itself, dear God, let's save our precious possessions and precious lives and get away from here.

The third exodus, the one we were discussing before summing up the first two, had in a sense two components or parts, which some believe should be referred to, in view of their essential differences, as the third and the fourth exodus. Tomorrow, that is to say in the distant future, those historians who will devote themselves to the study of events that have changed the face of the earth, in both an allegorical and a literal sense, will decide, let us hope with the reflection and impartiality of whoever dispassionately observes the phenomena of the past, whether or not this division should be made, as some people now maintain. The latter claim that it betrays a serious lack of critical judgment or sense of proportion to equate the retreat of millions of people from the coastal regions inland and the flight of a few thousand people abroad, simply an account of the undeniable coincidence in the timing of the one exodus and the other. And although we have no intention of taking sides in the debate or of expressing any opinions, it costs us nothing to recognize that while the two groups of people might have experienced the same fear, their methods and means of remedying this fear were quite different.

In the first case, they were nearly all people with few possessions, who, finding themselves forced to move elsewhere by the authorities and the harsh realities of their situation, hoped at most to save their lives by trusting in some miracle, luck, chance, fate, good fortune, prayer, faith in the Holy Ghost, by wearing an amulet around their neck, the Star of David, or a holy medal, and by holding onto all those other traditional beliefs and customs too numerous to mention here but which can be summed up in that other well-known saying, My hour has not yet come. In the second case, the refugees were people with assets and wealth at their disposal who had held out to see how things would go, but now there was no longer any doubt, the planes operating the new shuttle service were full, the mail boats, cargo vessels, and other smaller craft carried their maximum load. Let us draw a discreet veil over certain unedifying episodes, bribes, intrigues, and treacherous betrayals were common, even crimes, and some people were murdered for a ticket, it was a sorry sight, but, the world being what it is, we would be ingenuous to expect anything better. In short, all things considered, most likely the history books will record a fourfold rather than a triple exodus, not for the sake of precise classification, but lest we should confuse the wheat with the chaff.

But they will nevertheless exclude anything in the summary analysis given here that might reflect, however involuntarily, a certain mental attitude tainted by Manichaeism, a tendency, that is, to give an idealized picture of the lower orders and a superficial condemnation of the upper classes, who are readily but not always correctly labeled as being rich and powerful, which naturally provokes hatred and dislike, along with base feelings of envy, the source of all evils. Of course the poor exist, and their presence cannot be ignored, but we must not overrate them. Especially since they are not and never have been models of patience, of resignation, of the self-imposed discipline needed in this crisis. Anyone remote from these events and locations, who imagined that the Iberian refugees who crowded into houses, shelters, hospitals, barracks, warehouses, or whatever army tents or huts it was possible to requisition, along with those relinquished and set up by the military, and the even greater number of people without accommodation, huddled here and there under bridges and trees, inside abandoned cars, or even out in the open, anyone who imagined that these angels were visited by God may know a great deal about angels and God, but he knows little about mankind.

Without fear of exaggeration one can say that the inferno, in mythical times, distributed uniformly throughout the entire peninsula, as we recalled in the opening of this narrative, is now concentrated into a vertical strip about thirty kilometers wide, extending from northern Galicia to the Algarve, along with the uninhabited lands to the west, which few people regard as effective buffers. For example, if the Spanish government had no need to leave Madrid, so comfortably positioned inland, anyone wishing to locate the Portuguese government will now have to travel to Elvas, which is the city farthest from the coast, if you draw a straight line, more or less latitudinal, from Lisbon. Among the starving refugees, exhausted from lack of sleep, with old people dying, children screaming and crying, the men without work, the women supporting the entire family, quarrels inevitably break out, insults are exchanged, there is disorder and violence, theft of clothes and food, people are kicked out and assaulted, and also, would you believe, there is so much loose living that these settlements are transformed into mass brothels, really shameful, an appalling example for the older children who may still know their father and mother but have no idea what children they themselves will engender, or where or by whom. This aspect of the situation is less important, clearly, than it appears at first sight, consider how little attention today's historians give to periods that, for one reason or another were somewhat similar, especially the present one. When all is said and done, perhaps in moments of crisis indulging the flesh is what best serves the deeper interests of humanity and of human beings, both habitually harassed as they are by morality. But since this is a controversial hypothesis, let's move on, the mere allusion is enough to satisfy the scruples of the impartial observer.

Amid this tumult and confusion, however, there exists an oasis of peace, these seven creatures who live in the most perfect harmony, two women, three men, a dog, and a horse, although the last of these may have to swallow several reasons for complaint regarding the distribution of labor, having to pull on its own a loaded wagon, but even this will be remedied one day. The two women and two of the men constitute two happy couples, only the third man is without a partner, perhaps he does not mind this privation given his age, so far, at least, there have been none of those unmistakable signs of edginess that betray an excess of blood in the glands. As for the dog, whether it seeks and finds other pleasures when it goes in search of food, we cannot say, for even though the dog is in this respect the greatest exhibitionist among animals, certain species are discreet. Let us hope no one takes it into his head to follow this one, certain unwholesome pryings must be curbed in the name of hygiene. Perhaps these considerations about relationships and forms of behavior would be less imbued with sexuality were not the newly formed couples, whether out of intense passion or because their love is so new, so exuberantly demonstrative, which, let it be said before anyone thinks evil, does not mean that they kiss and embrace each other without regard for their surroundings, they are restrained to this extent, what they cannot conceal is the aura that surrounds them or that they exude. Only a few days ago Pedro Orce saw the glow of the brazier from the summit of the mountain. Here on the edge of the forest where they now live, sufficiently remote from the settlements to imagine themselves alone, but sufficiently close to ensure supplies of provisions, they might believe in happiness were they not living, for who knows how much longer, under the threat of a cataclysm. But they are taking advantage of each moment, they would claim, as the poet exhorted, *Carpe diem*, the merit of these old Latin quotations is that they contain a world of secondary and tertiary meanings, not to mention the latent and undefined ones, so that when one starts to translate, Enjoy life, for example, it sounds feeble and insipid, not worth the effort. Therefore we insist on saying *Carpe diem*, and we feel like gods who have decided not to be eternal in order to be able, in the precise meaning of the expression, to take advantage of their time.

What time still remains, one cannot say. Radios and television sets are going twenty-four hours a day, there are no longer news bulletins at certain hours, programs are interrupted every second to read the latest news flash, and there are endless announcements, We're now at a distance of three hundred and fifty kilometers, We're now at a distance of three hundred and twenty-seven, We're able to report that the islands of Santa Maria and São Miguel have been completely evacuated, the evacuation of the remaining islands has been stepped up, We're at a distance of three hundred and twelve kilometers, A small team of American scientists has remained at the base in Lajes, they will leave, by plane of course, only at the last minute, in order to witness the collision from the air, let's use the word *collision* without any adjectives. A request from the government of Portugal that a Portuguese be included as an observer in the aforesaid team went unheeded. There are three hundred and four kilometers to go, those responsible for the recreational and cultural programs on television and radio discuss what should be broadcast, some insist on classical music given the seriousness of the situation, others argue that classical music is depressing, that it would be preferable to broadcast some light music, French *chansons* of the thirties, Portuguese *fados*, Spanish *malagueñas* and other popular airs from Seville, lots of rock and folk music, the top tunes from the Eurovision song contest. But surely such cheerful music will shock and upset people who are living through this terrible crisis, retort the classical buffs. It would be worse if we were to play funeral marches, the advocates of lighter music allege, and the argument raged on with neither side giving an inch, two hundred and eighty-five kilometers to go.

Joaquim Sassa's radio has been used sparingly, he has some batteries in reserve, but is reluctant to use them, No one can tell what tomorrow will bring, a popular saying that tells us a good deal, here we could almost bet on what tomorrow will bring, death and destruction, millions of corpses, half the peninsula going under. But those moments when the radio is switched off soon become unbearable, time grows tangible, viscous, it grips your throat, you sense that you are about to feel the impact at any moment although we are still far away, the tension is intolerable, Joaquim Sassa switches on the radio, *É uma casa portuguesa com certeza é com certeza uma casa portuguesa*, the delightful voice sings of life, *Dónde vas de mantón de Manila dónde vas con el rojo clavel*, the same delight, the same life, but in another language, then they all sigh with relief, they're twenty kilometers closer to death, but what does that matter, death has yet to be announced, the Azores are not in sight, Sing, girl, sing.

Seated in the shade of a tree, they have just finished eating, and they could pass for nomads in their habits and dress, they have changed so much in so short a time, the result of having no comforts, their clothes are creased and stained, the men are unshaven, but let us not reproach them or the women, whose lips are now their natural color, turned pale from anxiety, perhaps when their last hour comes they will put on some lipstick and prepare themselves to receive death with dignity, ebbing life does not warrant so much effort. Maria Guavaira is leaning against Joaquim Sassa's shoulder, she grips him by the hand. Several tears appear among her eyelashes, but not because she is afraid of what is about to happen. These are tears of love that come springing to her eyes. And José Anaiço cradles Joana Carda in his arms, kisses her on the forehead, then her eyelids close, If only I could take this moment with me where I am going, I would ask no more, only one moment, not this moment as I am speaking, but that previous one, and the one before that, now almost vanished, I failed to grasp it as I experienced it and now it is too late. Pedro Orce has got up and walks away, his white hair gleams in the sun, he too carries the aura of cold light. The dog has followed him with lowered head. But they won't go very far. They now keep together as much as possible, neither of them wishes to be alone when the disaster occurs. The horse, as the experts claim, is the only animal that does not know it is going to die, it feels contented despite the great trials it has endured on its long journey. It munches the hay, shakes off the gadflies with a shudder, sweeps its grizzled flank with the long hair of its tail, probably unaware that it had been about to end its days in the semidarkness of a dilapidated stable, among cobwebs and dung, its infected lungs gasping for breath, how true that the misfortune of some is the fortune of others, however short-lived.

The day passed, another came and went, one hundred and fifty kilometers to go. You can sense the terror growing like a black shadow, the panic becomes a flood seeking out weak spots in the dike, corroding the stone foundations until they finally give way, and those who so far had remained more or less peacefully in their camps, began to move farther eastward, now realizing that they were far too close to the coast, only some seventy or eighty kilometers away, they could visualize the islands tearing through the land as far as where they were, and the sea inundating everything, the mountain on the island of Pico like some ghostly presence, Who knows, perhaps with the impact the volcano will become active once more, But there is no volcano on Pico, but no one listened to this or any other explanation. Naturally, the roads became congested, each crossroads a knot impossible to untie, at one point one could neither advance nor retreat, people were trapped like mice, but scarcely any were willing to give up the few possessions they were carrying in order to seek salvation by taking to the fields. In order to arrest this influx by its own good example, the Portuguese government abandoned the security of Elvas and installed itself at Evora, while the Spanish government settled more conveniently at León, whence they issued communiqués countersigned respectively by the President of our Republic and by the Sovereign of their Realm, for we should have mentioned that our President and their King have accompanied their respective Prime Ministers at every stage of the crisis, even offering to go and confront the hysterical mobs with extended arms, exposing themselves to some act of violence or aggression, and to address them once more, Friends, Romans, countrymen, and so on and so forth. No Your Majesty, no Mr. President, crowds in a state of panic, and ignorant crowds to boot, would not understand, people have to be extremely cultured and civilized to meet a king or a president with extended arms in the middle of the road and stop to ask him what he wants. But there was also one who in an outburst of anger turned around and shouted, Better to be dead than to survive so briefly, let's put an end to this once and for all, and they stayed there waiting, contemplating the serene mountains in the distance, the rosy morning, the deep blue of the hot afternoon, the starry night, perhaps the last, but when my hour comes, I won't look away.

Then it happened. About seventy-five kilometers away from the easternmost point of the island of Santa Maria, with no warning, no one felt the slightest shock, the peninsula began to sail in a northerly direction. For several minutes, while observers in all the geographical institutes of Europe and America analyzed in disbelief the satellite data and hesitated about making them public, millions of terrified people in Portugal and Spain had already been saved from death, without knowing it. During those minutes, tragically, some began quarreling in the hope of being killed, and perhaps had their wish granted, and some, frightened out of their wits, committed suicide. Some implored pardon for their sins, while others, thinking there was no time for repentance, inquired of God and the Devil what new sins they might still commit. There were women who gave birth hoping that their offspring would be stillborn, and others who knew they were carrying children they would never deliver. And when a universal cry echoed throughout the world, They're saved, they're saved, some would not believe it and went on lamenting the approaching end until there could be no more doubt, governments swore to it in every tone, the experts started giving explanations, the reason advanced for their salvation was a mighty current, artificially produced, and a great debate ensued as to whether the Americans or the Russians were responsible.

Rejoicing spread like wildfire, filling the entire peninsula with laughter and dancing, especially on that great strip of land where millions of displaced persons had gathered. Fortunately, this occurred at midday, when those who still had some provisions were about to eat, the confusion and chaos would otherwise have been dreadful, the authorities maintained, but they were soon to regret this hasty judgment, for no sooner had the news been confirmed than thousands and thousands of people began the long trek home. It became necessary to circulate the cruel hypothesis that the peninsula might revert to its original route, now a little farther north. Not everyone believed the news, especially since another worry was quietly creeping into people's thoughts, in their mind's eye they could see abandoned cities, towns and villages, their own native city, town, or village, the street and the house where they once lived, their home ransacked by opportunists who didn't believe in old wives' tales or who accepted the hypothetical risk with the naturalness of the acrobat who must attempt a triple somersault night after night, these visions were not the fantasies of a sick mind, for throughout all those deserted places thieves, robbers, and scoundrels of every age were warily mustering, ready to pounce, and passing the word along. The first to arrive helps himself and anyone who comes later must look for another house to loot, don't start bickering, there's plenty for everyone. But let no one, say we, be tempted to break into Maria Guavaira's house, it's the worst thing anyone could do, for the man inside is armed with a shotgun, and he will open the door only to the mistress of the house to assure her, I've guarded your property, now marry me, unless, dazed and exhausted after so many nights of vigil, he might have fallen asleep on a pile of blue wool, and thus have wasted the best years of his manhood.

Exercising prudence, the inhabitants of the Azores still had not returned to their homes on the islands, let us try to put ourselves in their shoes, it is true that any immediate danger has passed, yet it continues to lurk there, this is like a new version of the tale about the iron pan and the clay pan, with the important difference that the clay in this case was only good for making the mugs typical of these islands, there was not enough to make the pan of a continent, which, if it ever existed, sank to the bottom and was called Atlantis. We would be very foolish were we not to learn from experience, or our memory of it, however false both may be. But the sentiment that causes the five people under that tree to linger is not prudence, now that everyone has set off in the direction of the coasts of Portugal and Galicia, in triumphant reentry, as it were, bearing branches and flowers, with bands playing, fireworks exploding, bells pealing as they pass in procession, families return to their homes, perhaps there are things missing, but they have brought life with them and that is the most important thing, life, the table where we eat, the bed where we sleep and where this night, out of sheer happiness, we will make the most wonderful love in the world. Underneath the tree, their wagon waiting and the horse's strength restored, the five who have remained behind look at the dog as if expecting some sign or mandate, You who came from we know not where, you who turned up one day so weary from your travels that you collapsed into my arms, you who passed and stared as I was showing the men where I drew a line on the ground with a stick, you who waited for us beside the car we parked beneath the lean-to, you who had a blue thread hanging from your mouth, you who guided us along so many roads and paths, you who accompanied me to the sea where we found the stone ship, tell us by some movement, gesture, or sign, since you cannot even bark, tell us where we must go, for none of us wishes to return to the house in the valley, for all of us it would mean the beginning of that final return, the man who wants to marry me would say, Marry me, the office manager where I work would tell me, I need that invoice, my husband would say to me, So you've finally come back to me, the father of my worst pupil would inform me, Schoolmaster, I've given him a few paddlings, the notary's wife who complains of headaches would plead, Give me some pills for my headache, so do tell us where we should go, arise and walk and that will be our destination.

The dog, who was lying under the wagon, lifted its head as if hearing voices, jumped up briskly, and ran to Pedro Orce, who held its head between his hands, Would you like to come with me, he asked the dog, and these were the only words he spoke. Maria Guavaira owns the horse and wagon and she still has not made up her mind, but Joana Carda looked at José Anaiço, who read her thoughts, Whatever you may decide, I'm not going back. Then Maria Guavaira said in a loud, clear voice, There's a time for staying and a time for leaving, the time hasn't yet come to return, and Joaquim Sassa asked, Where do we want to go. Nowhere in particular. Let's go to the other side of the peninsula, Pedro Orce suggested, I've never seen the Pyrenees. Nor are you likely to see them now, half of them were left behind in Europe, José Anaiço reminded them. What difference does it make, you can recognize a giant by looking at his finger. They were delighted with this decision, but Maria Guavaira warned them, The horse has carried us all this way on its own, but it can't do the rest of the journey by itself, the horse has seen better days and the wagon should really be drawn by a pair, with only one horse, it's lopsided. So what are we going to do, asked Joaquim Sassa. We'll need to find another horse, It can't be easy to find horses around here, besides a good horse costs a lot of money, and we probably can't afford it.

The problem appears to be insoluble, but here we will see further evidence of how adaptable the human spirit can be. Only a few days ago, Maria Guavaira flatly rejected the idea of spending the night in an abandoned house, her words still echo in the ears of those with a good memory, yet such is the force of circumstance that Maria Guavaira is about to turn her back on a lifetime of moral integrity, let us hope no one will taunt her with this lapse from grace, We won't buy it, we'll steal it, those were her very words, and now Joana Carda, concerned not to offend their sensibilities, tries indirectly to ease their conscience, I've never stolen anything in my life. There was an awkward silence, people need time to adapt to new codes of morality, here the first move was made by Pedro Orce, contrary to the custom of the elderly, such staunch believers in traditional values, We've never stolen anything in our life, it's always in the life of others, this could be the maxim of a cynical philosopher, but is merely a statement of fact, said Pedro Orce with a smile, but the words had been spoken. All right, we've made up our minds, let's steal a horse, but how do we go about it, let's toss a coin to see who should go on this expedition. I'd better go, said Maria Guavaira, you don't know anything about horses, and you'd never be able to get it here. I'll come with you, said Joaquim Sassa, but perhaps we should take the dog with us to protect us from any danger we might encounter.

That night the three of them left the encampment and set out for the east, a region that had remained relatively tranquil and where there was greater likelihood of finding what they wanted. Before departing, Joaquim Sassa said, We don't know how long we'll be, wait for us here. Come to think of it, perhaps we should have brought a bigger car with room for everyone and the luggage and the dog too, commented José Anaiço. There are no such cars, what we need is a truck, besides don't forget that we didn't find a single vehicle that was running and fit to put on the road, and now that we have a horse we can't just abandon it somewhere. In their time the musketeers declared, One for all and all for one, they were four, now they are five, without counting the dog. Or the horse.

Maria Guavaira and Joaquim Sassa set off, the animal trotting in front, sniffing out the winds and investigating the shadows. The expedition is faintly absurd, chasing off in search of a horse. A mule would do just as well, Maria Guavaira had said, without knowing if such an animal existed within five leagues, perhaps it would be easier to find an ox, but you don't hitch an ox and a horse to a wagon together, or a donkey, with such a heavy load it would be like trying to make something strong from combined weakness, something that happens only in parables, like the one about the rushes we quoted earlier. They walked and walked, left the road whenever they glimpsed any dwellings or farmhouses amid the fields, if there were any horses around that is where they would find them, for what we need are beasts of burden rather than horses bred for show or for bullfighting. The moment they approached dogs started barking, but they were soon quiet again, we will never know what secret powers the Dog possessed to make even the loudest and most excitable watchdog suddenly fall silent, and not because some wild beast from the underworld had savaged it, in that case there would have been signs of a struggle, cries of pain, the silence is not sepulchral simply because no one is dying.

By the early hours of morning, Maria Guavaira and Joaquim Sassa could scarcely lift their feet, they were so tired, he had said, We must go on searching, and they searched so hard that they found rather than discovered what they were looking for, and it came about in the simplest way imaginable. Dawn was already breaking, the night sky to the east had turned a deep blue, when they heard a muffled neigh coming from a hollow by the road, a sweet miracle, I'm here, they went to look and found a tethered horse, it was not the Good Lord who had put it there to enhance His catalog of miracles, but the beast's rightful owner, whom the blacksmith had instructed, Put this ointment on the sore and leave the horse out to catch the morning dew, do this for three consecutive nights starting on a Friday, and if the horse isn't cured, I'll give you back your money and stake my reputation. A fettered horse, unless one has a sharp knife to cut the rope, cannot be carried off on one's shoulders, but Maria Guavaira knows how to deal with animals, and despite the beast's nervousness at being handled by a stranger, she succeeded in coaxing it into the shadows of the trees, where at the risk of being trampled or receiving a mighty kick, she managed to untie the awkward knot. Usually in such cases one makes a simple knot, one easily undone, but perhaps that's a skill people do not practice in these parts. Fortunately, the horse also realized that they were trying to free it, and freedom is always welcome, even when we're facing the unknown.

They returned by roads well off the beaten track, trusting more than ever in the dog's ability to foresee anything suspicious coming in their direction, and in its effectiveness in dealing with any inopportune visitors. When day broke, already remote from the scene of the crime, they began meeting people in the fields and along the roads, but no one appeared to recognize the horse, and even if they did, perhaps they would not have given it another thought, for they made such a lovely and innocent picture, the damsel sidesaddle on the palfrey, to put it in medieval terms, and the knight-errant walking ahead, laboriously leading the horse by the reins they had fortunately remembered to bring. The mastiff completed this heavenly vision, which some mistook for a dream, others as a sign of the change of life, the former and latter both unaware that all they are seeing go past are two wicked horse thieves, how true that appearances can deceive, what is generally overlooked is that they can deceive twice, perhaps a reason for trusting first impressions and inquiring no further. That's why some will be claiming before the day is out, Why, this morning I saw Amadís and Oriana, she on horseback, he on foot, and they had a dog with them, It can't have been Amadís and Oriana, for they were never seen with a dog, Well, I saw it, and that's a fact, one witness is as good as a hundred, But in the lives, loves, and adventures of those two, no dog is ever mentioned, Then let their stories be rewritten, and as often as may prove necessary until nothing has been left out. Nothing, Well, almost nothing.

They reached the encampment early that evening and were received with much hugging and laughter. The gray horse looked askance at the sorrel, which was gasping for breath. It has a sore on its back that is almost dry, they've obviously rubbed on some ointment and left it outdoors for three nights, starting on a Friday, an infallible remedy.

*A*s people return to their homes and life gradually returns, as one is wont to say, to normal, the arguments rage on among the scientists about possible causes for the peninsula's deviation at the very last minute, just when it appeared that nothing could avert the catastrophe. The theories vary, nearly all of them irreconcilable, thus contributing mathematically to the irreducibility of experts locked in controversy.

A first theory considers the peninsula's new course to be entirely random, forming as it does a perfect right angle with the previous one, and thus rules out any explanation that might assume, shall we say, an act of volition. Besides, to whom could such an act be attributed, since no one is likely to suggest that the incessant swarming, on an enormous mass of stone and earth, of tens of millions of people could somehow be added or multiplied to engender an intelligence or power capable of acting with a precision one can only describe as diabolical.

Another theory maintains that the peninsula's advance or, to put it more accurately, its progression, and we shall soon see why this is the better word, will result time and time again in another right angle, which ipso facto allows for the amazing possibility that the peninsula will return to its point of departure after a succession or, we repeat, progression of displacements, which after a certain point could be less than a millimeter in length, until it finally settles in precisely the right place.

The third theory advances the existence on the peninsula of a magnetic field, or some other force, capable on approaching an alien body of sufficient volume of unleashing an aversive process of a rather special nature, since as we have seen the aversive motion does not reverse the direction of the original movement, but is instead essentially a skid, to borrow a mundane example from the familiar realm of the automobile, but what determines whether this should be to the north or to the south is something the experts forgot to consider.

Finally, a fourth and more heterodox theory has recourse to what it terms metapsychic powers, affirming that the peninsula was diverted from collision by a vector formed in less than a tenth of a second from the concentration of the stricken population's sheer terror and the desire for salvation. This explanation gained wide popularity mainly because its author, in his efforts to make the theory accessible to simple minds, borrowed an example from physics and demonstrated how the incidence of solar rays on a biconvex lens causes those rays to converge on a focal point, resulting, as one would expect, in heat, combustion, and fire, the intensifying effect of the lens having an obvious parallel in the power of the collective mind, through which so many chaotic individual thoughts are stimulated, concentrated, and worked up in a moment of crisis to a state of paroxysm. The incongruity of this explanation troubled no one, on the contrary, many people began proposing that all problems concerning man's psyche, spirit, soul, will, and creation should henceforth be explained in physical terms, even if only by simple analogy or dubious inference. The theory is even now being studied and developed with a view to applying its fundamental principles to daily life, in particular to the functioning of political parties and competitive sports, to cite two familiar examples.

Some skeptics argue, however, that the real test of all these hypotheses, since that is all they are, will be seen in a few weeks' time, if the peninsula continues to follow its present route, which will cause it to stall between Greenland and Iceland, inhospitable territories for Portuguese and Spaniards accustomed to the mildness and languor of a temperate climate that is generally warm for the greater part of the year. If this were to happen, the only logical conclusion to be drawn from all we have witnessed so far is that the journey was not worthwhile. Which, on the other hand, would, or will, be much too simple a way of confronting the problem, for no journey is but one journey, each journey comprises a number of journeys, and if one of them seems so meaningless that we have no hesitation in saying it was not worthwhile, our common sense, were it not so often clouded by prejudice and idleness, would tell us that we should verify whether the journeys within that journey were not of sufficient value to have justified all the trials and tribulations. Bearing all this in mind, we will refrain from making any final judgments or assumptions. Journeys succeed each other and accumulate like generations, between the grandson you were and the grandfather you will be, what father will you have been. Therefore a journey, however futile, is necessary.

José Anaiço studied the details of the journey they are about to make, along paths that will not be direct if they are to avoid the great slopes of the Cantabrian mountains, and he explained what he had worked out, From Palas de Rei, which is about where we are now, to Valladolid must be about four hundred kilometers, and from there to the frontier, forgive me, but on this map I still have a frontier, there are another four hundred, making eight hundred kilometers altogether, a long journey at a horse's pace, Not a horse's pace, that's a thing of the past, and it won't be so much a pace as a trot, Maria Guavaira corrected him. Then Joaquim Sassa spoke, With two horses pulling, he broke off in mid-sentence with the expression of someone on whom a light is dawning, and then bursts out laughing, Isn't it ironic, we've abandoned Deux Chevaux and now we're traveling with two horses, I suggest we call the wagon Deux Chevaux, de facto et de jure, not that I've ever studied Latin, but I've heard others use the expression, as one of my grandfathers used to say who also didn't know the language of his ancestors. The Deux Chevaux are munching hay behind the wagon, the sore on the sorrel's back is now completely healed, and the gray horse, if not exactly rejuvenated, looks fitter and stronger, it can't lift its head as high as the sorrel, but they don't make a bad pair. Joaquim Sassa repeated his question once the laughter had subsided. As I was saying, with two horses pulling, how many kilometers will we cover in an hour, and Maria Guavaira replied, About three leagues, So about fifteen kilometers as we say nowadays, Right, Ten hours at fifteen kilometers an hour makes one hundred and fifty, within three days we'll be in Valladolid, and three days after that we'll reach the Pyrenees, it won't take long. Looking dismayed Maria Guavaira replied, That's quite a schedule unless we're trying to work the horses to death in no time, But you said, I said fifteen kilometers, but that was on flat land and in any case the horses will never keep going for ten hours each day, They can rest, Just as well you haven't forgotten they need to rest. From the sarcastic tone in her voice it was clear that Maria Guavaira was close to losing her temper.

At such moments, even when horses are not at issue, men become submissive, a fact women generally ignore, they only notice what they take to be male resentment, that is how mistakes and misunderstandings arise, perhaps the root of the problem lies in the inadequate hearing of human beings, in particular of women, who nevertheless pride themselves on being good listeners. I must admit, I know nothing about horses, I belong to the infantry, Joaquim Sassa muttered. The others eavesdrop on this duel of words, they smile because it's not to be taken seriously, the blue thread is the most powerful bond in the universe, as we shall soon see. Maria Guavaira said, Six hours a day is the most we can hope for, at best we'll cover three leagues in an hour, or whatever the horses can manage. Do we leave tomorrow, José Anaiço asked her, If everyone agrees, Maria Guavaira told him, and softening her tone she inquired of Joaquim Sassa, Is that all right, and taken by surprise he smiled and said, That's fine by me.

That night they counted their money, so many escudos, so many pesetas, some foreign currency belonging to Joaquim Sassa who had acquired it when they left Oporto, only a few days ago and yet centuries seem to have passed, scarcely an original thought but as irresistible as most banal statements. The provisions they brought with them from Maria Guavaira's house have almost run out, their supply of food will have to be replenished and that will not be easy, given the chaos and disruption and the marauding horde in whose wake not even cabbage stalks remained, not to mention the plundered chicken coops, the angry response of starving people asked to pay a fortune for a scraggly chicken. Once the situation began to return to normal, prices fell a little, but not to what they were before, for as we know they never do. And now there is a shortage of everything, even finding anything to steal would be a problem, if anyone should want to resort to such wickedness. The horse's was a special case. Had it not been for that sore, it would still be adorning the stables and assisting the labors of its former owner, who knows nothing of the beast's fate except that it was taken away by two scoundrels and a dog who left abundant evidence behind. People say time and time again that out of evil comes good, it has been said so often and by so many that it might well be a universal truth, so long as we take the trouble to distinguish evil from good, and those who have experienced the one or the other. Then Pedro Orce said, We'll have to work to earn some money, it seemed a sensible idea, but after taking stock of their skills they arrived at the depressing conclusion one might have expected. For Joana Carda, after getting a degree in humanities, never taught but married and became a housewife, here in Spain there is not a great deal of interest in Portuguese literature and, besides, the Spaniards have more important things on their minds right now, Joaquim Sassa, as he declared with some annoyance, belongs to the infantry, which, coming from his lips, meant that he holds the lowly rank of office clerk, a useful profession undoubtedly, but only in times of social sta-bility and normal trading, Pedro Orce has spent his life making up prescriptions, when first we met him he was filling capsules with qui-nine, what a pity he didn't remember to bring his pharmacy with him, he could now be offering consultations and earning good money, for in these rural districts the pharmacist and doctor are one and the same, José Anaiço is an elementary schoolteacher, and that tells us every-thing, let alone the fact that he is in a country with a different ge-ography and history and how could he explain to Spanish children that the Battle of Aljubarrota was a victory when they are usually taught to forget that it was a resounding defeat. Maria Guavaira is the only person in the group who could look for work on one of these farms and be equal to it, if only in proportion to her strength and experience, which are limited.

They look at each other not knowing what to do and Joaquim Sassa says hesitantly, If we have to stop every five minutes to make some money we'll never reach the Pyrenees, money made like this never lasts, it's no sooner made than spent, the ideal solution would be for us to travel like gypsies, I mean those who wander from country to country, they must live on something, he was asking a question, expressing his doubt, perhaps manna fell from heaven on the gypsies. Pedro Orce answered him, hailing as he did from the south where the gypsy race abounds, Some of them trade in horses, others sell clothes in the market, others hawk their wares from door to door, the women tell fortunes, Let's not hear any more about horses, we'll never live this one down, besides, it's a profession we know nothing about, and as for telling fortunes, let's hope our own won't give us cause for concern, And not to mention that in order to sell horses one has to start by buying them. Their money would not stretch that far, even the horse they have had to be stolen. Silence fell, no one knew how, but when it passed, Joaquim Sassa, who is beginning to reveal that he has a practical mind, told them, I can see only one way out of this situation, let's buy clothes from one of those wholesalers, there are bound to be some in the first big town we come to, and then we can sell them in the villages at a reasonable profit, I can look after the accounts. It seemed a good idea for want of a better one, and they might as well give it a try. Since they could not be farmers or pharmacists or teachers or landlords, they might as well be peddlers and traveling salesmen, selling clothes for men, women, and children is no dishonor, and with careful bookkeeping they'd be able to live.

Having drawn up this plan for survival, they settled down for the night, the moment having arrived to decide how the five of them should accommodate themselves in the wagon, now called Deux Chevaux, which is as follows, Pedro Orce sleeps in front, lying crosswise on a narrow pallet just big enough for him, then Joana Carda and José Anaiço, lengthwise in an empty space amid some of the luggage, and the same for Maria Guavaira and Joaquim Sassa further back. Improvised curtains create imaginary compartments and some semblance of privacy, if Joana Carda and José Anaiço, who sleep in the middle of the wagon, need to go outside during the night, they pass alongside Pedro Orce, who does not mind, here they share discomfort as they share everything else. And what about the kisses, embraces, and sexual intercourse, inquisitive spirits will inquire, endowed by nature with a perverse taste for malice. Let us say that the lovers had two ways of satisfying the sweet impulses of nature, either they go through the fields in search of some lonely and pleasant spot, or they take advantage of the temporary and deliberate absence of their companions to do what need not be spelled out, the signs speak for themselves unless we choose to ignore them, and while they might lack money they are not without understanding.

They did not set out at break of day, as poetry would demand, for why get up early when they have all the time in the world now, but this was not the only or the most persuasive reason, they took their time in getting ready, the men clean-shaven, the women neat and tidy, their clothes carefully brushed, in a suitable corner of the wood, having carried a bucket to draw water from the stream, the couples washed one after the other, perhaps stark naked for there was no one to look on. Pedro Orce was the last to wash and he took the dog with him, they looked like two animals, I'm tempted to say the one laughed as much as the other, the dog pushing Pedro Orce and Pedro Orce splashing water on the dog, a man of his age should not make such a fool of himself in public, anyone passing by would have said at once, That old man ought to show more self-respect, he is certainly old enough to know better. Few traces remain of the encampment, nothing except the trampled ground, the water splashed from their ablutions under the trees, ashes among blackened stones, the first gust of wind will sweep everything away, the first heavy shower will flatten the soil and dissolve the ashes, only the stones will reveal that people have been here, and if needed they will serve for another campfire.

It is a good day for traveling. From the slope of the hillock where they had taken shelter they descend the road, Maria Guavaira is in the driver's seat for she does not trust anyone else with the reins, one has to know how to talk to horses, there are boulders and potholes in the road and if one of the axles should break that would be the end of all their endeavors, God protect us from any such misfortune. The chestnut sorrel and the gray horse still make an ill-matched pair, Chess seems uncertain about the steadiness of Grizzly's legs, and Grizzly once harnessed and yoked tends to pull outward as if trying to get away from its companion, forcing Chess to make an even greater effort. Maria Guavaira is watching their goings-on, once they are on the road she will bring Chess under control with a skillful combination of whipping and tugging on the reins.

Joaquim Sassa had dreamed up the names Chess and Grizzly, always bearing in mind that these Deux Chevaux are not like those of the car, the latter were so closely knit that they were indistinguishable and wanted the same thing at the same time, while these two differ in everything, color, age, strength, size, and temperament, so it seems only right and proper that each one have a name. But Grizzly in English usually refers to bears, Chess is a game, complained José Anaiço, whereupon Joaquim Sassa retorted, We're not in England, the gray horse has been baptized Grizzly and the sorrel Chess and I'm their godfather. Joana Carda and Maria Guavaira exchange smiles at the men's childishness. And Pedro Orce unexpectedly joins in, If these were a mare and a stallion and they had a foal, we might end up with a chess-playing bear.

On the first day they traveled no more than seventy kilometers, first because it did not seem right to put pressure on the horses after they had been idle for so long, one of them because suffering from sores, the other because awaiting certain decisions that were slow in coming, and second because, to go through the town of Lugo, where they would go to stock up on the merchandise from which they hoped to earn their living, they had to depart from their northeast route. They bought a local newspaper to catch up with the latest news, the most interesting item of all being a photograph taken yesterday of the peninsula. Its displacement to the north, one day after its departure from its previous route, was clearly indicated by a superimposed dotted line. No doubt about it, it was unmistakably a right angle. But the conflicting theories we summarized earlier had made little progress, and as for the views held by the newspaper itself, one could detect a note of caution and skepticism, perhaps justified in the light of previous disappointments but also typical of the narrow-mindedness one tends to find in the provinces.

In the wholesale warehouses the women, for naturally it was left to them to choose the clothes, with Joaquim Sassa on hand to negotiate the prices, could not decide what to buy, whether they should select garments for the approaching winter, or plan ahead for the following spring. Joaquim Sassa referred to midterm planning but Joana Carda insisted it should be mid-season, whereupon Joaquim Sassa told her curtly, Back in the office that was the expression we used, we always referred to short-, mid-, or long-term planning. The final choice was dictated by their own needs, for they were all badly in need of some new clothes for the autumn, besides it was inevitable that Maria Guavaira and Joana Carda should be tempted to buy what they themselves wanted. All in all, they completed their purchases to everyone's satisfaction, and there were healthy profits in store if demand should match up to the stock they now had to offer. Joaquim Sassa expressed some disquiet, We've tied up more than half our money, and unless we recoup half of what we've spent within a week, we'll be in trouble, in our situation, with no funds in reserve and no chance of obtaining a bank loan, we must manage our stock so as to maintain a steady turnover and bring our income into line with our investment. Joaquim Sassa delivered this little speech, in his capacity as bookkeeper, at the first stop they made after leaving Lugo, and it was benevolently received by the others.

They soon realized that this business would not be a bed of roses when a woman who knew how to strike a bargain obliged them to lower the price of two skirts so far as to deprive them of any profit. As it happened, Joana Carda was doing the selling, and she later apologized to her trading partners and promised that in future she would be the most intransigent saleswoman operating in the peninsula. Repeating his warning, Joaquim Sassa told them, Unless we're cautious from the outset, we'll find ourselves bankrupt, with neither money nor goods, and besides, it's not just a question of our livelihood, we have three more mouths to feed, the dog's and the horses'. The dog looks after itself, interrupted Pedro Orce. So far it has managed to look after itself, but should it ever be unable to hunt for its own food, it will come back to us with its tail between its legs, and if we have nothing to give it, what then, Half of everything I own is for the dog, That's a kind thought but our main concern should be to share wealth instead of poverty. Wealth and poverty is one way of expressing it, José Anaiço observed, but at this moment in our lives we find ourselves poorer than we really are, it's an odd situation, we're living as if we had chosen to be poor. If it were a matter of choice, I don't believe it would be in good faith, it was a question of circumstances only some of which we accepted, those that served our personal aims, we're like actors, or mere characters, said Joana Carda before asking, For example, if I were to go back to my husband, who would I be, the actor outside the character, or a character playing the part of an actor, and where would I stand between the one and the other. Maria Guavaira had been listening in silence and now she began speaking like someone beginning another conversation, perhaps she had not fully grasped what the others had said, People are reborn each day, but they can decide whether to go on living the previous day or to make a fresh start. But there is experience, all that we've learned, Pedro Orce pointed out. Yes, you're right, Joaquim Sassa said, but we usually live our lives as if we had no previous experience, or make use only of that part of life that allows us to go on making mistakes, quoting examples and the fruits of experience, I've just thought of something that you may find absurd and nonsensical, perhaps experience has a greater effect on society as a whole than on individuals, society takes advantage of everyone's experience, but no one wishes, knows, or is able to take full advantage of his own experience.

They debate these interesting problems in the shade of a tree while having their lunch, a frugal one as befits traveling salesmen who have not yet finished their day's work, and lest anyone find this discussion unlikely in these circumstances and in such a place, we must remind him that in general the level of learning and culture typical of pilgrims fosters without blatant impropriety, a conversation whose drift, from the exclusive point of view of literary composition in search of strict verisimilitude, should in fact betray some flaws. But everyone, independent of whatever skills he may possess, has at one time or another said or done things far above his nature and condition, and if we could remove those people from the dull humdrum existence in which they gradually lose their identity, or if they were to throw off their fetters and chains, how many more wonders would they be able to perform, how many fragments of deep knowledge would they be able to communicate, for we all know infinitely more than we think, and others know infinitely more than we are prepared to acknowledge. Five individuals are assembled here for the most extraordinary reasons and it would be most surprising if they were not to say some astonishing things.

In these parts there is rarely a car to be seen. Now and then a big truck goes by carrying provisions, mainly foodstuffs, to the villages. With everything that has happened local food supplies have been disrupted, shortages are common, with an occasional sudden glut, but there is always some excuse, remember, the human race has never experienced a similar situation. As for sailing, man has always sailed, but in small ships. Many refugees are on foot, others ride donkeys, and if the road were not so uneven there would be more bicycles around. People here are usually good-natured and peaceable, but envy is probably the one trait to be found in every social class and indeed in most human beings, so it was no surprise that the sight of Deux Chevaux passing along the road, when nearly everyone was without transport, should have provoked some jealousy. Any determined and violent gang of brigands would soon have disposed of the occupants, one is an old man, the others could hardly be mistaken for Samson or Hercules, and as for the women, once their men had been overpowered, they would be easy prey, true, Maria Guavaira is a woman who can stand up to any man, but not without a firebrand in her hand. It might well have happened, therefore, that our traveling salesmen should be suddenly attacked and then left to their fate, the poor women raped,

2 3 0

the men injured and humiliated. But the dog was there, if anyone appeared it came out from under the wagon, and whether in front or behind, stationary or walking, its nose down like that of a wolfhound, with its icy stare it transfixed the passersby, these were nearly always harmless, but they felt every bit as afraid as any would-be assailants. If we consider everything this dog has done so far, it would deserve to be called guardian angel, despite the continuous innuendo about its infernal origins. Objections will be raised that cite the traditional teachings of doctrine, Christian and non-Christian, according to which angels have always been depicted with wings, but in all those cases where the necessary angel would not be required to fly, what harm would be done if it were to appear now and then in the guise of a dog, without being obliged to bark, which would in any case be quite unfitting for a spiritual being. At least let us acknowledge that dogs that do not bark are just as good as angels.

They set up camp that evening on the banks of the river Minho, near a village called Portomarín. While José Anaiço and Joaquim Sassa untied and attended to the horses, kindled the fire, peeled the potatoes, and prepared the salad, the women, accompanied by Pedro Orce and their guardian angel, took advantage of the remaining twilight to visit some houses in the village. Because of the language barrier, Joana Carda did not say a word, it was probably the problem of communication that had foxed her last time, but she is gaining experience for the future, which is the only place where mistakes can be corrected. Business was fair and they sold their goods at the right price. When they got back the camp looked like home, the campfire crackled among the stones, the lamp hanging from the wagon cast a semicircle of light in the open space, and the smell coming from the bubbling pot was as consoling as the Lord's presence.

As they conversed around the fire after they had eaten, it suddenly occurred to Joaquim Sassa to ask, Where did you get this name Guavaira, what does it mean, and Maria Guavaira told him, As far as I know there is no one else with this name, my mother dreamed it when I was still inside her, she wanted me to be called Guavaira and nothing else, but my father insisted that I should be called Maria, so I ended up with a name I was never meant to have, Maria Guavaira. So you don't know what it means, My name turned up in a dream. Dreams always have some meaning. But not names that turn up in dreams, now the rest of you tell me your names. They told her, one by one. Then, poking the fire with a stick, Maria Guavaira said, The names we possess are dreams, what will I be dreaming about if I should dream your name.

The weather has changed, an expression of admirable concision that informs us in a soothing and neutrally objective manner that, having changed, it has changed for the worse. It is raining, a gentle rain now that autumn is here, and until the ground becomes muddy we will be tempted to stroll through the countryside in rubber boots and raincoats receiving that gentle spray of moisture on our faces, and absorbing the melancholy of the distant haze, the first trees shedding their leaves, looking bare and cold, as if they might suddenly beg to be caressed, there are some one would like to press to one's bosom with tenderness and pity, we rest our cheek against the moist bark and it feels as if the tree were covered in tears.

But the canvas of the wagon goes back to the origins of such coverings, which were solidly woven and made to last rather than to keep out the rain. It dates from an age when people were accustomed to letting their clothes dry out on their bodies, their only protection, if they were lucky, a glass of aquavit. Then there was the effect of the seasons, the drying out of the fibers, the fraying of the stitches, it is easy to see that the canvas removed from the car is not enough to patch up all the damage. And so the rain continually leaks into the wagon, despite Joaquim Sassa's reassurances that the soaking and enlarging of the threads, and the consequent tightening of the weave, will make things better, if only they would be patient. In theory nothing could be truer, but in practice it clearly does not work. If they had not taken the trouble to roll up the mattresses to protect them, it would have been some time before they could sleep on them.

When the rain turns heavy and the opportunity arises, the travelers take shelter under a viaduct, but these are rare, this is only a country road, off the main highways that, to eliminate intersections and permit high speeds, are bridged by secondary roads. One of these days it will occur to José Anaiço to buy some waterproofing varnish or paint, and he will get some, but the only suitable paint he will find is a bright red and not even enough to cover a quarter of the canvas. If Joana Carda had not come up with the better and more feasible idea of sewing large strips of plastic together to make a cover for the wagon and then a second one for the horses, once they realized that they probably would not find any more waterproof paint in the same shade of red for the next thirty kilometers, the wagon might well have found itself traveling the wide world with a hood, all the colors of the rainbow with stripes, circles and squares in green and yellow, orange and blue, violet, white on white, brown, and perhaps even black, according to the artist's whim. Meanwhile it is raining.

After their brief, inconclusive dialogue about the meaning of names and the significance of dreams, they began discussing what name they should give to the dream that this dog is. Opinions are divided, they are, as we ought to know, simply a matter of preference, we might even say that an opinion is nothing but the reasoned expression of preference. Pedro Orce suggests and upholds such rustic and traditional names as Pilot or Faithful, both very suitable if we consider the animal's character, an infallible guide and utterly loyal. Joana Carda wavers between Major and Rookie, names with military overtones that don't quite fit the temperament of the woman making the suggestion, but the feminine soul possesses unfathomable depths, Goethe's Marguerite will struggle all her life at the spinning wheel to repress the urge to behave like Lady Macbeth, and to her dying hour she will not be certain of having won. As for Maria Guavaira, although unable to explain why, and not for the first time, she proposed, somewhat embarrassed by her own suggestion, that they call the dog Guardian Angel, and she blushed as she spoke, aware of how ridiculous it would sound, especially in public, to summon one's guardian angel, and to have appear, instead of some heavenly being, garbed in white robes and descending with a flutter of wings, a ferocious mastiff, covered with mud and the blood of some poor rabbit, and respecting only its masters, if they deserve that name. José Anaiço was quick to silence the laughter provoked by Maria Guavaira's suggestion, and proposed that the dog be named Constant, For if I've understood the meaning of that word, it embraces all the qualities evoked by those other names, Faithful, Pilot, Major, Rookie, and even Guardian Angel, for if any of them should be inconstant, all trust is lost, the pilot loses his way, the major abandons his post, the rookie surrenders his arms, and the guardian angel allows himself to be seduced by the young girl he was supposed to be shielding from temptation. They all applauded, although Joaquim Sassa felt that it would still be preferable simply to call the animal Dog, for as the only dog around, there was little danger of his mistaking any summons or response. So they've decided to call the dog Constant, but they needn't have taken so much trouble christening it, the animal answers to whatever name they care to use once it knows it's being called, but there is another name that lingers in its memory, Ardent, but no one here remembers that one. The man who once said that a name is nothing, not even a dream, was right, even if Maria Guavaira believes otherwise.

Unknown to them, they are following the old route of Santiago, they pass through places that bear names of hope or past misfortune, depending on what travelers experienced there in bygone days, Sarriá, Samos, or the privileged Villafranca del Bierzo, where any sick or weary pilgrim who might knock on the door of the apostle's church received dispensation from completing the journey to Santiago de Compostela, and gained the same indulgences won by those going all the way. So even in those days faith made concessions, although nothing like today when the concessions are more rewarding than faith itself, the Catholic faith or any other. At least these travelers know that if they wish to see the Pyrenees, they will have to go all the way there and lay their hand on the crest, a foot is not enough, since it is less sensitive, and the eyes are more easily deceived than one imagines.

Little by little, the rain has started to abate, there is the odd drizzle now and then, until it finally stops altogether. The sky has not cleared, night is rapidly falling. They camp under some trees to shelter from any further showers, although Pedro Orce could quote the Spanish proverb that goes something like this, Shelter under a tree and you'll get soaked twice. The fire wasn't easy to light, but Maria Guavaira's know-how finally conquered the damp twigs, which crackled and flared up at the ends as if the sap were spilling out. They ate as best they could, enough to prevent their stomachs from rumbling with hunger during the night, for as another proverb tells us, Go to bed without a bite, you'll be restless all the night. They had their meal inside the wagon, by the light of the smoking oil lamp, the atmosphere heavy, their clothes damp, the mattresses rolled up and stacked away, their remaining possessions in a heap, any self-respecting housewife would have had a fit at such untidiness. But since there's no evil that lasts forever or rain that never stops, let's wait for a ray of sunshine to appear and then they'll tackle the washing, the mattresses opened out so that they can dry down to the last fine wisp of straw and the clothes spread over the bushes and boulders, when we gather them in they'll give off that fresh, warm smell the sun always leaves behind, and all this will be done while the women, creating a cosy domestic scene, adjust and sew the long strips of plastic that will solve all their problems with leaking rain, blessed be whoever invented progress.

They remained there, conversing with the ease and indolence of people whiling away the hours, until it was time to go to bed, and then Pedro Orce interrupts what he was saying and starts telling them, I once read somewhere that the galaxy to which our solar system belongs is heading toward some constellation, I can't remember the name, and that constellation is heading in its turn to a certain point in space, I wish I knew more, the details escape me, but what I wanted to say is this, look, we're on a peninsula, the peninsula is sailing on the sea, the sea goes around with the earth to which it belongs, and the earth spins around on its own axis but also goes around the sun, and the sun also spins around, and the whole thing is heading in the direction of the aforesaid constellation, so I wonder whether maybe we're not the last link in this chain of movements within movements. And what I'd like to know is what moves inside us and where does it go, no, I'm not talking about worms, microbes, bacteria, those living creatures that inhabit us, I'm referring to something else, to something that moves and perhaps moves us at the same time, just as constellation, galaxy, solar system, sun, earth, sea, peninsula, and Deux Chevaux move and move us with them, what is the name, finally, of the thing that moves all the rest, from one end of the chain to the other, or perhaps there is no chain and the universe is a ring, at once so thin that apparently only we and what is inside us fit into it and so thick that it can accommodate the maximum dimension of the universe, which is the ring itself, what is the name of what follows after us. The nonvisible begins with man, came the surprising answer of José Anaiço, who spoke without thinking.

Passing from leaf to leaf, large drops of water come trickling down onto the canvas. Outside, Grizzly and Chess can be heard stirring under their plastic sheets, which do not quite cover them, this is where total silence can be useful, allowing us to hear the slightest noise. Everyone here believes it to be his or her duty to contribute to this solemn council whatever knowledge they possess, but they are all terrified that if they open their mouths, what comes out, even if it is not the little toads of the fable, will be no more than random banalities about existence, ontological pronouncements, however doubtful the relevance of that word in the context of wagon, drops of rain and horses, without forgetting the dog, now fast asleep. Maria Guavaira, having the least education, was the first to speak, Perhaps we should call the nonvisible God, but it is curious how a certain note of interrogation crept into the phrase, Or willpower, suggested Joaquim Sassa, Or intelligence, added Joana Carda, Or history, and this closing remark was made by José Anaiço. Pedro Orce had no suggestion to make, he simply commented, Anyone who thinks this is easy is profoundly mistaken, there are endless answers just waiting for questions.

Prudence cautions us that any investigation of such complex matters should stop here lest those participating start saying something different from what they said before, not because it is necessarily wrong to change one's mind, but because the difference can sometimes be so great that the discussion goes back to its jumping-off point and those debating the issue fail to notice. In this instance, that first inspired statement by José Anaiço, after having circulated among his friends, degenerated into trivial and excessively obvious reminders of the invisibility of God, or willpower, or intelligence, and, perhaps a little less trivial and obvious, of history. Putting his arms around Joana Carda, who complains of feeling cold, José Anaiço tries not to fall asleep, he wants to reflect on his idea, to ponder whether history is really invisible, if the visible witnesses of history confer sufficient visibility on it, if the visibility of history, which is so relative, is anything more than a covering like clothes worn by the invisible man while he continues to be invisible himself. He could not bear to have these thoughts going around and around in his head for much longer, and it was just as well that during those final moments before he fell asleep, his mind had foolishly concentrated on making out the difference between the invisible and the nonvisible, which, as will be obvious to anyone who stops to think about it, had no particular bearing on the case. In the light of day all these entanglements seem much less important, God, the most famous example of all, created the world because it was night when He thought about it. At that sublime moment He felt that He couldn't stand the darkness any longer, but had it been day God would have left everything as it was. And just as the sky here dawned bright and clear and the sun came out unhindered by clouds and stayed that way, all the nocturnal philosophizing dissipated and all attention is now concentrated on the smooth passage of Deux Chevaux over a peninsula, whether it is drifting or not makes no difference, for even if my life's journey should lead me to a star, that has not excused me from traveling the roads of this earth.

That afternoon, as they were selling their wares, they learned that the peninsula, after having traveled in a straight line to a point due north of the northernmost island of the Azores, the island of Corvo, and from this summary description it should be clear that the extreme southern tip of the peninsula, the Punta de Tarifa, found itself on another meridian to the east, north of the northernmost point of

Corvo, the Ponta dos Tarsais, the peninsula, then, after what we have tried to explain, immediately resumed its displacement to the west in a direction parallel to that of its initial route, or rather, let us see if we are making ourselves clear, resumed it some degrees higher. When this happened, those who had put forward and defended the theory of displacement along rectilinear paths at right angles to one another were fully vindicated. And since no movement had yet been confirmed that might support the conjecture of an eventual return to the point of departure, stated, moreover, as a demonstration of the sublime rather than as a foreseeable corollary of the general thesis, which merely left open the possibility of return, there was even a possibility that the peninsula might never again come to a halt but drift forevermore over the seven seas, like the oft-cited Flying Dutchman, and the peninsula is currently going by another name, tactfully suppressed here to avoid any outbursts of nationalism and xenophobia, which would be a tragedy under the circumstances.

The village where the travelers now found themselves did not hear of these matters, the only news that came was that the United States of America had promised, in a statement made by the President himself, that the approaching countries could count on the support and solidarity, both moral and material, of the American people, If they continue to move in this direction they will be received with open arms. But this declaration, which showed remarkable perceptiveness, as much from a humanitarian as from a geostrategic viewpoint, faded somewhat from public view with the sudden bedlam in tourist agencies throughout the world, besieged by clients who wanted to travel to Corvo without delay, regardless of means or expense, and why, because unless it changed course the peninsula was about to pass within sight of the island, a spectacle not to be spoken of in the same breath as the insignificant parade of the Rock of Gibraltar when the peninsula broke away, abandoning the rock to the waves. Now it is a huge mass that is about to pass before the eyes of those privileged enough to find a spot on the northern half of the island, but despite the vastness of the peninsula, the event will last only a few hours, two days at the most, bear in mind the peculiar outline of this raft, only the extreme southern part will be visible and only if it is a clear day. The rest, because of the earth's curvature, will pass well out of sight, just imagine what it would be like if instead of that angular shape the peninsula's southern coast formed a straight line, I hope you can visualize my drawing, it would take sixteen days to watch it pass, an entire vacation, if the speed of fifty kilometers daily were to be maintained. Be that as it may, in all likelihood more money will flow into Corvo than has ever been seen there before, obliging the island's inhabitants to order locks for their doors and to hire locksmiths to fit them with crossbars and alarm systems.

From time to time there are still light showers, at worst a rapid cloudburst, but for most of the day it is sunny, with blue skies and high clouds. The great plastic cover was put up, sewn and reinforced, and now that it looks like rain their progress is arrested, and in three stages, the cover is first unfolded, then stretched, and finally tied down, the awning is protected. Inside the wagon are the driest mattresses you ever saw, the musty smell and dampness have gone, the interior is neat and tidy, things could not be cosier. But now one can see just how much rain there has been in these parts. The land is waterlogged and one has to be careful with the wagon, testing the soft ground at the edge of the road before passing, otherwise it would be a hell of a job to move it, two horses, three men, and two women are not as effective as a tractor. The landscape has altered, they have left the mountains and hills behind, the last undulations are disappearing from sight, and looming up before one's eyes is what looks like an endless plain with such a vast sky overhead that one begins to doubt that the sky is all one, more likely each location, if not each person, has its own sky, greater or smaller, higher or lower, and this has been an amazing discovery, yes indeed, the sky like an infinite succession of encrusted domes, the contradiction in terms is only apparent, you need only look. When Deux Chevaux reaches the summit of the last hill one thinks the world will come to an end before the earth rises again, and since it is quite common for different causes to have the same effect, we have to struggle for breath up here as if we had been carried to the top of Everest, as anyone will tell you who has also been there, unless he has had the same experience as we have had on this flat ground.

Pedro reckons without his host. But let it be said at once that this Pedro is not Orce, nor does the narrator know who he is, even if he admits that behind the aforementioned Pedro is the apostle of the same name who denied Christ three times, and these are the same calculations God made, probably because he was Triune, and not very good at arithmetic. In Portugal it is customary to say that Pedro knows his sums when the sums done by all Pedros come out wrong, this is a popular and ironic way of saying that some people should leave decisions to others, in other words, Joaquim Sassa was wrong when he estimated they would cover one hundred and fifty kilometers each day. Maria Guavaira was also wrong when she reduced it to ninety. The trader knows about trading, horses know about pulling a wagon, and just as one says, or used to say, Bad money drives out good, so the pace of the old horse moderated that of the young one, unless the latter was showing pity, kindness, human respect, because for the strong to brag about their strength in the presence of the weak is a sign of moral perversion. We have deemed all these words necessary in order to explain that we have been traveling more slowly than was predicted, concision is not a definitive virtue, on occasion one loses out by talking too much, it is true, but how much has also been gained by saying more than was strictly necessary. The horses go at their own pace, they had set off at a trot and they obey the whims or demands of the driver, but little by little, so subtly that no one even notices, Grizzly and Chess start reducing their pace, how they can manage it so harmoniously is a mystery, for no one heard the one say to the other, Slow down, or the other reply, When we get past that tree.

Fortunately, the travelers are not in a hurry. In the beginning, when they left the already distant lands of Galicia, they felt that they had dates to meet and itineraries to respect, there was even a certain feeling of urgency, as if each of them had to save a father from the gallows, to reach the scaffold before the executioner let the trapdoor fall. Here it is not a question of father or mother, for we know nothing about the one or the other, except for Maria Guavaira's mother, who is senile and no longer lives in La Coruña, unless she returned there once the danger had passed. About the other mothers and fathers, ancient and modern, nothing has been revealed, when children fall silent, questions must also be silenced and inquiries suspended, for when all is said and done, the world begins and ends with each one of us, although this statement might deeply offend the family spirit as showing disrespect for one's heritage and lineage. Within several days, the road became a world outside the world, as with any man who, finding himself in the world, discovers that he is himself a world, nor is this difficult, one need only create a little solitude around oneself, like these travelers who while traveling together travel alone. That is why they are not in a hurry, that is why they stopped measuring the distance they have covered, any stops they make are for selling or taking a rest, and they often feel tempted to stop for no reason other than that same appetite, for which there may always be reasons but we generally do not waste time looking for them. We all end up where we want to be, it is only a question of time and patience, the hare goes faster than the tortoise, perhaps it will arrive first, so long as it does not cross the path of the hunter and his shotgun.

We have left the barren plain of León, have entered and are traveling through Tierra de Campos where that famous preacher Fray Gerúndio de Campazas was born and flourished, whose words and deeds were recounted in detail by the no less celebrated Padre Isla, as an example to long-winded orators, relentless bores who never stop quoting, compulsive rhymers and tiresome scribblers who go on and on, what a pity we have not learned from their example, which could not be clearer. Let us therefore prune this rambling exordium right at the outset, and say quite simply that the travelers will spend the night in a village called Villalar, not far from Toro, Tordesillas, and Simancas, all of them touching closely on Portuguese history in terms of a battle, a treaty, archives. A teacher by profession, José Anaiço finds these names evocative, but little else. His knowledge of history is only general, other than the rudiments he knows only a few more details than his Spanish and Portuguese audience who must have learned something, or can't have forgotten everything, about Simancas, Toro, and Tordesillas, given the wealth of information and patriotic lore to be found in the history books of both countries. But no one here knows anything about Villalar except Pedro Orce who, although a native of Andalusia, has the enlightenment of someone who has traveled throughout the peninsula, the fact that he said he did not know Lisbon when he arrived there two months ago does not rule out this hypothesis, perhaps he simply did not recognize the place, just as the city would no longer be recognized today by its Phoenician founders, its Roman colonizers, or its Visigothic rulers, the Muslims might look on it with a glimmer of recognition, the Portuguese with increasing bewilderment.

They are sitting in pairs around the bonfire, Joaquim and Maria, José and Joana, Pedro and Constant, the night is a little chilly, but the sky is serene and clear, there are scarcely any stars to be seen, for the early-rising moon floods with light the flat countryside and the nearby rooftops of Villalar, whose friendly mayor raised no objections when this band of Spanish and Portuguese migrants sought to camp so close to the village, despite their being vagrants and peddlers and therefore likely to steal trade from local shopkeepers. The moon is not high but has already taken on that appearance we so enjoy admiring, that luminous disk that inspires trite verses and even more trite sentiments, a silken sieve sprinkling white dust over the submissive landscape. Then we exclaim, What lovely moonlight, and we try to forget the shudders of fear we experience when the heavenly body first appears, enormous, red, threatening, over the curving earth. After thousands and thousands of years, the nascent moon continues even today to dawn like a threat, like a sign of the approaching end, fortunately the anxiety lasts only a few minutes, the moon has risen, become small and white, we can breathe more easily. The animals, too, are fretful, a short time ago when the moon appeared the dog stood there staring at it, tense, rigid, perhaps it might have howled had it not been without vocal cords, but the dog bristled all over as if a frozen hand had ruffled its coat while stroking its back. There are moments when the world leaves its axis, we sense that nothing is secure, and if we could fully express what we are feeling, we would say, with an expressive absence of rhetoric, That was a close call.

What Pedro Orce knows about the history of Villalar we are about to find out once they finish their meal. As the flames of the bonfire dance in the still air, the travelers look at them pensively, stretch out their hands as if they were imposing them on or surrendering them to the flames, there is an ancient mystery in this relationship between us humans and fire, even under the open sky, as if we and the fire were inside the original cave, grotto, or matrix. Tonight it is José Anaiço's turn to wash up, but there is no hurry, the hour is peaceful, almost gentle, the light of the flames flickers on their weather-beaten faces, the color of sunrise, the sun is of another order and alive, not dead like the moon, that is the difference.

And Pedro Orce tells them, You may not know this but many, many years ago, in 1521 there was a great battle here in Villalar, greater for its consequences than for the number of dead, because had it been won by the one who lost it, those of us who are alive today would have inherited a very different world. José Anaiço is well informed about the great battles of history, and if the question were fired at him, he would be able to run off without a moment's hesitation some ten names, beginning classically with Marathon and Thermopylae and proceeding, without regard for chronology, through Austerlitz and Borodino, Marne and Monte Cassino, Ardennes and El Alamein, Poitiers and Alcácer Quibir, and also Aljubarrota, which means nothing to the world and everything to us, these were paired for no special reason, But I've never heard of the Battle of Villalar, concluded José Anaiço, Well, that battle, explained Pedro Orce, took place when the communes of Spain rebelled against Emperor Charles V, a foreigner, but not so much because he was a foreigner, for in past centuries it was the most natural thing in the world for nations to find a king sneaking in through the back door, someone who spoke another language, the whole business was left to royal houses who gambled away their own countries along with those of others, I don't mean dice or cards, but they played for dynastic interests, entering into fake alliances and marriages of convenience, which is why one cannot really say that the communes rebelled against an unwanted king, nor should anyone imagine it was the eternal war of the poor against the rich, if only things were that simple, the fact is that the Spanish nobility did not approve, not in the slightest, of the Emperor's having conferred appointments on so many foreigners, and one of the first measures taken by these new masters was to raise taxes, an infallible means of paying for luxuries and further ventures, in any event the first city to rebel was Toledo, and others soon followed its example, Toro, Madrid, Avila, Soria, Burgos, Salamanca, and so on and so forth, but the motives of some were not the motives of others, sometimes they coincided, yes indeed, but at other times they were in conflict, and if this was true of the cities it was even more true of the people living in them, certain nobles simply defended their own interests and ambitions and therefore changed sides depending on how the wind was blowing and what would benefit them. Now, as always happens, the people were involved in this for their own reasons, but especially for those of others, this has been the case since the world began, if people were all one, that would be fine, but people are not all one, that's something we cannot get into our heads, not to mention that the masses are generally deceived, how often have their representatives ridden to parliament on their votes and once there, receiving bribes and threats, voted contrary to the will of those who sent them, and strange as it may seem, despite all these divergencies and contradictions, the communes were able to organize militias and fight the king's army, needless to say battles were won and lost, the last battle was lost here in Villalar, and why, habit, mistakes, incompetence, betrayals, people got tired of waiting to be paid and deserted, battle ensued, some won, others lost, it was never discovered exactly how many members of the communes died here, by modern statistics not all that many, some put the figure at two thousand, others swore that there had been fewer than a thousand casualties, perhaps even as few as two hundred, we don't know, nor are we ever likely to know, unless the graves are moved elsewhere one day and the skulls counted, because to count the other bones would only add to the confusion, three of the commune leaders were tried the following day, sentenced to death, and beheaded in the main square of Villalar, their names were Juan de Padilla, born in Toledo, Juan Bravo from Segovia, and Francisco Maldonado from Salamanca. This was the Battle of Villalar, and had it been won by those who lost, Spain's destiny would have changed course. With moonlight such as this, one can imagine what the night and day of battle must have been like, it was raining, the fields were flooded, they fought up to their knees in mud, by modern standards, undoubtedly, few lost their lives, but one is tempted to say that the few who lost their lives in the wars of old had greater influence on history than the hundreds and thousands and millions who died in the twentieth century, the moonlight is the one thing that doesn't change, it covers Villalar just as it covers Austerlitz or Marathon, or, Or Alcácer Quibir, interrupted José Anaiço, What battle was that, Maria Guavaira asked, If that, too, had been won instead of lost, I can't imagine what Portugal would be like today, replied José Anaiço, I once read in a book that your King Dom Manuel fought in this war, said Pedro Orce, In the textbooks I teach from there's no mention that the Portuguese went to war with Spain at that time, It wasn't fought by the Portuguese themselves, but by fifty thousand crusaders lent by your king to the Emperor, I see, said Joaquim Sassa, with fifty thousand crusaders in the royal forces the communes were bound to lose, for the crusaders always win.

This night Constant dreamed that it went to unearth bones on the battlefield, it had already gathered one hundred and twenty-four skulls when the moon went down and the earth turned dark, then the dog went back to sleep. Two days later, some boys playing soldiers in the fields reported to the mayor that they had found a heap of skulls in a field of wheat, and no one ever discovered how they came to be there, all gathered into a pile. But the housewives of Villalar have nothing but good to say of those Portuguese and Spaniards who came with a wagon and have already left, For price and quality they were the most honest peddlers who had ever passed this way.

Overcome evil with good, the ancients used to say, and with good reason, at least they put their time to good use by judging facts that were then new in the light of facts that were already old. Nowadays we make the mistake of adopting a skeptical attitude toward the lessons of antiquity. The President of the United States of America promised that the peninsula would be welcome, and Canada, as we will see, was not pleased. As the Canadians point out, Unless the peninsula changes course, it is we who will be playing host and then we'll have two Newfoundlands here instead of one, little do the people on the peninsula know, poor devils, what awaits them, biting cold, frost, the only advantage for the Portuguese is that they will be close to supplies of that cod they're so fond of. They will lose their summers but have more to eat.

The spokesman at the White House hastened to explain that the President's speech had been prompted fundamentally by humanitarian considerations without aspiring to political supremacy, especially since the countries of the peninsula had not ceased to be sovereign and independent just because they had gone floating off over the waters, they will have to come to a halt one day and be like every other country, and then added, For our part, we solemnly guarantee that the traditional good-neighbor policy between the United States and Canada will not be affected by any eventuality, and as proof of America's desire to maintain friendly relations with the great Canadian nation, we propose setting up a bilateral committee to examine the various problems arising in the context of this dramatic transformation of the world's political and strategic physiognomy, which certainly constitutes a first step toward the birth of a new international community comprising the United States, Canada, and now the Iberian countries, who will be invited to participate as observers at this meeting since they are still not physically close enough for there to be any immediate prospect of specifying the eventual form of this integration.

Canada publicly expressed its satisfaction with this explanation but let it be known that it considered an early meeting to be inopportune, arguing that any terms proposed might well offend patriotic sensitivities within Portugal and Spain, and suggesting as an alternative a quadrilateral conference to examine what measures should be taken to deal with any violent opposition once the peninsula reached the Canadian coast. The United States agreed forthwith, and its leaders silently thanked God for having created the Azores, for if the peninsula had not veered northward but had moved consistently in a straight line after breaking away from Europe, the city of Lisbon would definitely have remained with its windows facing toward Atlantic City, and after much reflection they came to the conclusion that the more it veered north the better, just imagine what it would be like if Baltimore, Philadelphia, New York, Providence, and Boston were to be transformed into inland cities with the inevitable decline in the standard of living. There is no doubt that the President had been much too hasty when he made that initial statement. In a subsequent exchange of confidential diplomatic notes, followed by secret meetings of high-ranking officials, Canada and the United States agreed that the best solution would be to arrest the peninsula en route, if at all possible at a point sufficiently close for it to remain outside the European sphere of influence but sufficiently remote to avoid causing any immediate or indirect damage to Canadian and American interests, and meanwhile to set up a committee charged with amending their respective immigration laws so as to strengthen discretionary clauses and discourage the Spanish and Portuguese from thinking that they can enter the North American countries at will on the pretext that we are all close neighbors now.

248

The governments of Portugal and Spain protested at the discourtesy of these powers that thus presumed to dispose of their interests and destinies, the Portuguese government with greater vehemence in view of the oaths it swore as a government of national salvation. Thanks to initiatives on the part of the Spanish government, contact will be established between the two peninsular countries to draw up a joint plan for exploiting the new situation to the fullest, in Madrid it is feared that the Portuguese government will enter these negotiations with the tacit hope that sometime in the future it will derive special benefits from its greater proximity to the coasts of Canada and the United States, but that depends. And it is known, or believed to be known, that in certain Portuguese political circles there is a campaign in favor of a bilateral agreement, albeit of a nonofficial nature, with the region of Galicia, which evidently won't please the central powers in Spain at all, intolerant as they are of irredentism, however disguised. There are even some who cynically claim and spread the word that none of this would have happened if Portugal had been on the other side of the Pyrenees, or, better still, had clung to the Pyrenees when the rupture occurred. That would have been one way of ending once and for all this habit of reducing the peninsula to a single country, this problem of being Iberian, but the Spaniards are deceiving themselves, for the problem will persist, and we need say no more. The days before reaching the shores of the New World are counted, a plan of action is under way so that negotiations may get under way at the right moment, neither too soon nor too late, this, after all, is the golden rule of diplomacy.

Unaware of the political intrigues being played out behind the scenes, the peninsula continues sailing westward, so steadily and easily that the various observers, whether millionaires or scientists, have already withdrawn from the island of Corvo, where they had positioned themselves in the front rows, as it were, for the sight of the peninsula passing. The spectacle was breathtaking, suffice it to say that the extreme tip of the peninsula passed less than five hundred meters away from Corvo, with great seething of waters. It was like watching the climax of a Wagnerian opera or, better still, like being at sea in a tiny vessel and seeing the enormous hulk of an unloaded oil tanker passing a few meters away, with most of its keel out of the water, it was enough, in short, to strike terror into us and make us dizzy, to send us to our knees to beg a thousand pardons for our heresies and evil deeds and to exclaim, God exists. Such is the power of primitive nature over the spirit of man, however civilized.

But while the peninsula is playing its part in the movements of the universe, our travelers are already proceeding beyond Burgos, so successful with their trading that they have decided to put Deux Chevaux on the highway, which is unquestionably the fastest route. Farther ahead, after passing Gasteiz, they will return on to the roads that serve the smaller villages, there the wagon will be in its element, a cart drawn by horses on a country road rather than this unusual and startling exhibition of dawdling along a road designed for high speeds, this lazy trot at fifteen kilometers an hour, provided they are not going uphill and provided the animals are in a good mood. The Iberian world is so greatly altered that the traffic police who witness this do not order them to stop, they impose no fine, mounted on their powerful motorcycles they give them a nod to wish them a good journey, at most they ask about the red paint on the awning if they happen to be on the side where the patch is visible. The weather is good, there has been no rain for days, you would think summer had returned were it not for the autumnal wind that can sometimes be extremely cold, especially since we are so close to high mountains. When the women started complaining about the chill in the air, José Anaiço remarked, as if in passing, on the consequences of getting too close to high latitudes, telling them, if we end up in Newfoundland, our journey is finished, to live outdoors in that climate you have to be an Eskimo, but the women paid no attention, perhaps they weren't looking at the map.

And perhaps because they were talking, not so much about the cold they were feeling, as about a greater cold that someone else, but who, might be feeling, not they themselves who had the comfort of their partners every night, even during the day when the circumstances were favorable. Many a time one couple kept Pedro Orce company in the driver's seat, while the other couple lay down inside the wagon, allowing themselves to be lulled by the swaying of Deux Chevaux and then seminaked, satisfying their sudden or postponed desire. Knowing that five people were traveling in that wagon thus divided by sex, anyone with any experience of life would get a good idea of what was going on under that awning simply by looking to see who was up front in the driver's seat, if there were three men there, for example, you could be sure that the women were doing their household chores, especially the mending, or if, as we said before, there were two men and a woman in the seat together, the other woman and man would be enjoying an intimate moment, even if dressed and doing no more than talking. Clearly, these were not the only possible combinations, but neither of the women ever sat in the driver's seat unless she was with her own partner and the other woman was with her man under the awning, for they didn't want people to start gossiping. This tactful behavior came about of its own accord. There was no need to convene a family council to decide on ways and means of safeguarding morality inside and outside the awning, and working it out combinatorially, it was inevitable that Pedro Orce nearly always had to travel in the driver's seat, except on the rare occasions when the three men rested at the same time while the women took the reins, or when, all their urges satisfied, one couple sat in front while the other, their privacy restricted, refrained from engaging in any acts under the awning that might embarrass or disturb Pedro Orce, who lay stretched out on his narrow pallet arranged crosswise. Poor Pedro Orce, Maria Guavaira murmured to Joana Carda when José Anaiço spoke of the frost in Newfoundland and of the advantages of being an Eskimo, and Joana Carda agreed, Poor Pedro Orce.

They nearly always set up camp before nightfall, they liked to choose a pleasant spot with water nearby, if possible within sight of some village, and if some place took their fancy they stopped there even if there were two or three hours of sunshine left. The lesson of the horses had been well learned to the advantage of all, now the animals enjoyed a longer rest, the travelers lost that human trait of haste and impatience. But ever since that day when Maria Guavaira said, Poor Pedro Orce, a different atmosphere surrounds the wagon on its journey and the people inside. This gives food for thought if we recall that only Joana Carda heard those words being spoken and that when she repeated them only Maria Guavaira was listening, and since we know they kept them to themselves, for this was not a matter for amorous dialogue, then we can only conclude that a word, once spoken, lasts longer than the sound and sounds that formed it, the word remains, invisible and inaudible, in order to be able to keep its own secret, a kind of hidden seed below the surface of the earth that germinates out of sight until suddenly it pushes the soil aside and emerges into the light, a coiled stem, a crumpled leaf slowly unfolding. They set up camp, unhitched the horses, released them from their harnesses, lit the fire, everyday actions and gestures that all of them were now capable of doing with equal skill, depending on whatever tasks they were assigned each day. But contrary to their behavior since the journey's outset, they now conversed very little and they themselves would be taken by surprise were we to tell them, Not one of you has uttered a word in the last ten minutes, then they would be aware of the special nature of that silence, or they would reply like someone unwilling to acknowledge an obvious fact and looking for some futile justification. It sometimes happens, and frankly one cannot be talking all the time. But were they to look at one another at that moment, each would see on the others' faces, as if in a mirror, the reflection of his own disquiet, the embarrassment of someone who knows that explanations are but empty words. Although it has to be said that the looks exchanged between Maria Guavaira and Joana Carda convey such explicit meanings for them that they cannot stand it for very long and soon turn their eyes away.

After finishing his chores Pedro Orce was in the habit of going off with the dog Constant, telling the others that he was off to get to know the neighborhood. He was always gone for some time, perhaps because he walked slowly, perhaps because he wandered off the main road, or, remote from the gaze of his companions, ended up resting on a boulder watching the evening draw to a close. One day recently, Joaquim Sassa had said to him, You want to be alone, are you feeling unhappy, and José Anaiço commented, If I were in his shoes, I'd probably do the same. The women had finished washing some clothes and had hung them up to dry on a rope stretched between the frame of the awning and the branch of a tree, they listened and kept silent, for they were not included in the conversation. This was some days after Maria Guavaira, because of the frosts of Newfoundland, had said to Joana Carda, Poor Pedro Orce.

They are alone, how strange that four people should give the impression of being alone, they are waiting for the soup to be ready, there is still daylight and rather than waste time José Anaiço and Joaquim Sassa check the harnesses, while the women read over and make a tally of the day's takings, which Joaquim Sassa as bookkeeper will later transfer into the ledger. Pedro Orce has wandered off, he disappeared among the trees about ten minutes ago, accompanied as usual by Constant the dog. He no longer feels cold, the breeze that is blowing is probably the last tepid waft of autumn, at least that's what it feels like after the cold we've experienced recently. Maria Guavaira says, We must buy aprons, we haven't many left in stock, and as she spoke she looked up at the trees, she stirred as she sat there, as if repressing some urge before giving way, only the harsh noise of the horses' champing could be heard, then Maria Guavaira stood up and walked toward the trees where Pedro Orce had disappeared. She did not look back, not even when Joaquim Sassa asked her, Where are you going, but in fact, he did not even finish the question, but left it suspended in midair, as it were, for the reply had already been given and could not be amended. A few minutes later the dog appeared, it went and lay down under the wagon. Joaquim Sassa was standing some meters away, as if scanning some hills in the distance. José Anaiço and Joana Carda avoided looking at each other.

Maria Guavaira finally returned, with the first shadows of evening. She arrived alone. She walked up to Joaquim Sassa but he turned away abruptly. The dog came out from under the wagon and disappeared. Joana Carda lit the oil lamp. Maria Guavaira removed the soup from the fire, poured some oil into a frying pan that she then placed on the trivet, waited for the oil to sizzle, meantime she had cracked some eggs, she scrambled them, adding some slices of sausage, soon a smell would fill the air that at any other time would have made mouths water. But Joaquim Sassa did not come to eat. Maria Guavaira called him but he refused to come. There was food left over, Joana Carda and José Anaiço didn't feel hungry, and when Pedro Orce returned the camp was already in darkness apart from the dying embers of the bonfire. Joaquim Sassa had lain down underneath the wagon, but it was a bitterly cold night, the chill comes from the mountains, there is no wind, just a mass of cold air. Then Joaquim Sassa told Joana Carda to go and sleep beside Maria Guavaira, he didn't refer to her by name, but said, Lie down beside her, I'll stay with José, and since it seemed a good moment for a bit of sarcasm, he added, There's no danger, we're decent people, there's nothing promiscuous about us. When he returned, Pedro Orce climbed into the driver's seat, who knows how but the dog Constant managed to get up there beside him. It was the first time this had happened.

All the next day Pedro Orce traveled in the driver's seat. José Anaiço and Joana Carda sat beside him and Maria Guavaira remained alone in the wagon. The horses were kept at a steady pace. When they tried to please themselves by breaking into a trot, José Anaiço restrained their impetuous speed. Joaquim Sassa traveled on foot, lagging far behind the wagon. They covered only a few kilometers that day. It was still midafternoon when José Anaiço brought Deux Chevaux to a halt in a place that looked exactly like the other, it was as if they had never got around to leaving or had come full circle, even the trees looked the same. Joaquim Sassa did not appear until much later, as the sun was setting over the horizon. On seeing him approach, Pedro Orce withdrew, the trees soon concealed him and the dog went after him. The campfire sent up great flames, but it was still too early to prepare supper. Besides, the soup was ready and there were sausages and eggs left over. Joana Carda remarked to Maria Guavaira, We didn't buy any aprons and we only have two. Joaquim Sassa told José Anaiço, I'm leaving tomorrow, I'll need my share of the money, show me where we are on the map, there ought to be some sort of railroad around here. Then Joana Carda got up and headed toward the trees where Pedro Orce had disappeared with the dog. José Anaiço didn't ask her, Where are you going. The dog reappeared after a few minutes and went and lay down under the wagon. Time passed, and Joana Carda returned. Reluctantly, Pedro Orce came with her, but she led him gently as if there were no need for much force, or perhaps it was another kind of force. They arrived in front of the campfire, Pedro Orce with lowered head, his white hair disheveled, and the flickering light of the flames appeared to dance on top of his head. And Joana Carda, whose blouse was unbuttoned and not tucked into her slacks, said quite openly and naturally, tucking her blouse in when she realized how untidy she looked, The stick with which I drew a line on the ground has lost its power, but it can still be used to draw another line here, then we'll know who is to remain on this side and who on the other, if we cannot all be together on the same side. As far as I'm concerned, I couldn't care less, I'm leaving tomorrow, Joaquim Sassa told her. I'm the one who is going tomorrow, said Pedro Orce. Just as we came together, we can go our separate ways, said Joana Carda, but if someone has to be blamed to justify our separation, don't make Pedro Orce the scapegoat. If anyone is to blame, we are, Maria Guavaira and I, and if you think what we did calls for an explanation, then we've been wrong about each other since the day we met. I'm leaving tomorrow, Pedro Orce repeated. Don't go, said Maria Guavaira, for if you leave, it's almost certain that we'll all separate, for the men won't be able to stay with us nor we with them, not because we don't love each other, but because we don't understand each other. José Anaiço looked at Joana Carda, stretched out his hands to the fire as if they had suddenly become cold, and said, I'm staying. Maria Guavaira asked, And what about you, are you leaving or staying, Joaquim Sassa did not reply at once, he caressed the dog's head as it stood beside him, then, with his fingertips, he stroked its blue woolen collar, then the bracelet around his own arm, before saying, I'll stay, but on one condition. He didn't need to spell it out, Pedro Orce began speaking, I'm an old man, or at least getting on, I've reached that age when one isn't too sure, but let's say I'm old rather than young, Obviously not all that old. José Anaiço smiled, his smile somewhat bitter. Sometimes things happen in life that can never be repeated, he appeared to be about to continue, but sensed that he had said enough. Nodding his head, he withdrew to weep alone. Whether he wept a lot or a little, one cannot say, but to weep he had to be alone. That night they all slept inside the wagon, but their wounds were still bleeding, the two women slept together, as did the two betrayed men, and Pedro Orce, out of sheer exhaustion, slept soundly throughout the night. He had wanted to mortify himself with insomnia but nature proved stronger.

They awoke early, with the nestlings. As dawn broke, the first to emerge was Pedro Orce, from the front of the wagon, then Joaquim Sassa and José Anaiço from the back, and finally the women, as if they were all coming from different worlds and were about to meet here for the first time. At first they scarcely looked at one another, nothing but furtive glances, as if to confront another face would have been intolerable, too much to bear in their weak state after the crisis from which they had just emerged. Once they had drunk their morning coffee, an occasional word could be heard, bits of advice, a request, an order cautiously phrased, but now the first delicate problem had to be tackled, how were the travelers to accommodate themselves in the wagon, in the light of everything that now made the previous arrangement impossible. They were all agreed that Pedro Orce must travel in the driver's seat, but the men and women in open conflict could not continue to keep their distance. Try to imagine this distasteful and equivocal situation. If Joaquim Sassa and José Anaiço were to sit up front with Pedro Orce, what conversation could they possibly hold with the driver, or more embarrassing still, were Joana Carda and Maria Guavaira to ride next to the driver, what would they say to him, what memories would they evoke, and meantime, under the awning, what biting of nails would there be, the two men asking each other, What can they be saying. These are situations that make us laugh when seen from outside, but any temptation to laugh soon disappears if we imagine ourselves in the same distress that now envelops these men. Fortunately, there's a remedy for everything, death alone has yet to follow this rule. Pedro Orce was already seated in his place, holding the reins and waiting for the others to reach a decision, when José Anaiço said, as if addressing the invisible spirits of the air, The wagon can go ahead, Joana and I will walk for a bit. And we'll do the same, Joaquim Sassa announced. Pedro Orce shook the reins, the horses gave the first sharp tug, the second one was more convincing, but even had they wanted to, they could not have gone quickly this time, the road is uphill all the way, amid mountains higher on the left than on the right. We're in the foothills of the Pyrenees, Pedro Orce thinks to himself, but it's so peaceful up here that it's hard to believe this is where those dramatic ruptures we've described took place. Trailing behind come two couples, apart, obviously, for what they have to discuss is between man and woman in the absence of witnesses.

The mountains are no good for selling, especially these wares. In addition to the sparse population typical of these mountainous regions, one must take into account the terror of the local inhabitants, who still haven't got used to the idea that this side of the Pyrenees is no longer complemented or supported on the other side. These villages are almost deserted, some completely abandoned. As the wagon passes, between doors and windows that remain firmly closed, the sound of Deux Chevaux's wheels on the stony roads is lugubrious. I'd rather be in the Sierra Nevada, thinks Pedro Orce, and these magical and entrancing words filled his heart with longing, or *añoranza*, as the Spanish would say. If there is any advantage to be gained from such desolation, it will be that the travelers, after so many nights of discomfort, and some promiscuity, will be able to get a good night's sleep. We are not referring to the recent and particular manifestation of promiscuity, about which opinion is divided and which the interested parties have been discussing, but simply pointing out that they will be able to sleep in the houses abandoned by their owners. For while possessions and valuables were carried off in the general exodus, the beds were generally left behind. How remote that day now seems when Maria Guavaira vehemently rejected the suggestion of sleeping in someone else's house, let us hope this ready complacency is not an indication of a lowering in moral standards, but simply the outcome of lessons learned from hard experience.

Pedro Orce will sleep alone in a house of his choice with the dog for company. Should he decide to go for a nocturnal stroll, he's free to go out and return whenever he wishes, and this time the other men will not sleep apart from their women, Joaquim Sassa will finally be back sleeping with Maria Guavaira and José Anaiço with Joana Carda, they've probably already said all they had to say to each other and they might go on talking into the night, but human nature being what it is, out of weariness and displeasure, out of tender sympathy and sudden love, it's only natural for a man and a woman to come together, to exchange a first, uncertain kiss, and then, blessed be whoever made us so, the body awakens and desires the other body, it might be madness, it might, for the scars still throb, but the aura grows, if Pedro Orce should be walking along these slopes at this hour, he will see two houses lit up in the village, perhaps he'll feel jealous, perhaps tears will come to his eyes once more, but he will not know that at this moment the reconciled lovers are sobbing in joyful sorrow and in sudden flaring passion. Tomorrow will truly be another day, it will no longer be important to decide who should travel inside the wagon and who in the driver's seat, all combinations are now possible and none of them ambiguous.

The horses are tired, the slopes are never ending and ever upward. José Anaiço and Joaquim Sassa went to have a quiet word with Pedro Orce, using the utmost tact lest their motives be misunderstood. They wanted to know if he thought they had seen enough of the Pyrenees or if he wanted to carry on until they reached the uppermost summits, and Pedro Orce replied that it was not so much the summits that attracted him as the end of the earth, although he was aware that from the end of the earth one always sees the same sea. That's why we didn't go in the direction of Donostia, what's so special about looking at a beach that has been cut in two, of standing at the edge of the sand with water on either side. But for us to see the sea from such a height, I'm not sure that the horses can make it, rejoined José Anaiço. We don't need to climb two or three thousand meters, assuming there are actually trails all the way up, but I'd rather we went on climbing until we see for ourselves. They opened the map. Running his finger between Navascués and Burgui, and then pointing in the direction of the frontier, Joaquim Sassa said, We must be about here. There don't seem to be any great elevations on this side, the road follows the river Esca, then moves away to keep on climbing, here's where things start to get difficult, on the other side there's a peak of more than one thousand seven hundred meters. There isn't any longer. There was, said José Anaiço. Yes, of course, there was, agreed Joaquim Sassa, I must ask Maria Guavaira for some scissors to cut the map along the frontier. We could try this path and if it gets too hard on the horses we can always turn back, suggested Pedro Orce.

It took them two days to reach their destination. At night they could hear the wolves howling in the hills, and they were apprehensive. People from the lowlands, they suddenly became aware of the danger they were facing. Should wild beasts invade the encampment, they would first savage the horses, then attack any human beings. If only they had a gun with which to defend themselves. Pedro Orce confessed, It's my fault that we're running these risks, let's turn back, but Maria Guavaira replied, Let's go on, the dog is here to protect us. A dog can't do much when confronted by a pack of wolves, Joaquim Sassa reminded her, This one can, and however strange this may seem to anyone who knows more about these things than the narrator, Maria Guavaira was right. One night the wolves came fairly close, the terrified horses began neighing, such anguish, and pulling at their tethers, the men and women looked around to see where they might take shelter from an attack, only Maria Guavaira insisted, though she was trembling, They won't come, and she repeated, They won't come. They kept the bonfire blazing all through that sleepless night, and the wolves drew no closer. Meanwhile, the dog appeared to grow bigger in the circle of light. The flickering shadows created the impression that heads, tongues, and teeth were multiplying, nothing but an optical illusion, human forms expanded, swelled out of all proportion, and the wolves went on howling, but only because of their fear of other wolves.

The road had been severed, truly severed in the literal sense of the word. To both left and right, the mountains and valleys were suddenly cut off in a clean line, as if sliced with a blade or cut out of the sky. The travelers, now some way from the wagon, which the dog was guarding, advanced cautiously and in dread. About a hundred meters from the scission there was a customs post. They went inside. Two typewriters still stood there, one with a sheet of paper stuck in the roller, a customs form with some words typed on it. The cold wind penetrated an open window and rustled the papers lying on the floor. There were scattered feathers. The world is coming to an end, Joana Carda exclaimed. Then let's go and see how it's ending, suggested Pedro Orce. They left. They trod cautiously, worried that cracks might suddenly appear in the ground, a clear sign that the land is unstable. José Anaiço was the one who remembered this, but the road looked smooth and even, with only an occasional bump caused by wear and tear. Ten meters from the gap, Joaquim Sassa said, Better not get too close on foot in case we get dizzy, I'm going to crawl. They got down on all fours and advanced, at first on their hands and knees, then dragging themselves along the ground, they could hear their hearts pounding in uneasiness and fear, sweating profusely despite the intense cold, asking themselves whether they would be brave enough to reach the edge of the abyss, but none of them wished to look like a coward, and almost in a trance they found themselves looking out to sea at an altitude of about one thousand eight hundred meters, the escarpment a sheer vertical cut and the sea shimmering below, the tiniest of waves in the distance and white spume where the ocean waves thrashed against the mountain as if trying to dislodge it. Pedro Orce cried out in exaltation, jubilant in his grief, The world is coming to an end, he was repeating Joana Carda's words, and they all repeated them. My God, happiness exists, said the unknown voice, and perhaps that's all it is, sea, light, and vertigo.

The world is full of coincidences, and if one thing does not coincide with another that happens to be close to it, that is no reason for denying coincidences, all it means is that what is coinciding is not visible. At the exact moment that the travelers were leaning over the sea, the peninsula came to a halt. No one there noticed what had happened, there was no jolt as it braked, no sudden loss of balance, no impression of rigidity. It was only two days later, at the first inhabited spot they came to after descending from the magnificent heights, that they heard the astounding news. But Pedro Orce said, If they maintain that the peninsula has come to a halt, it must be true, but speaking for myself and Constant, I swear to you that the earth is still shaking. As he spoke, Pedro Orce's hand was resting on the dog's back.

Newspapers throughout the world, some putting it on the front page beneath a banner headline, published the historic photograph that showed the peninsula, which perhaps we should now definitively call an island, sitting quietly out in the middle of the ocean, maintaining its position with millimetric precision in relation to the cardinal points by which the earth is ruled and guided, with Oporto as far north of Lisbon as ever, Granada as far south of Madrid as it has been since Madrid came into being, and all the rest with the same familiar contours. The journalists concentrated their imaginative powers almost exclusively on divising bold, dramatic headlines, inasmuch as the geological displacement, or rather the tectonic enigma, continued to unfold, as indecipherable now as on the first day. Fortunately, the pressure of public opinion, for want of a better expression, had diminished, people had stopped asking questions, they were satisfied with the suggestive power of certain striking comparisons, The Birth of a New Atlantis, A Piece Has Moved on the Universal Chessboard, A Link Between America and Europe, An Apple of Discord Between Europe and America, A Battlefield for the Future, but the headline that made the deepest impression was the one in a Portuguese newspaper that read The Need for a New Treaty of Tordesilla, this is truly the simplicity of genius, the author of the idea looked at the map and verified that, give or take a kilometer or two, the peninsula would be situated on the line that in those glorious days had divided the world into two parts, one for me, one for you, one for me.

In an unsigned editorial it was proposed that the two peninsular countries adopt a joint and complementary strategy that would make them the pointer on the scales of world politics, Portugal facing west, toward the United States, Spain turned to the east, toward Europe. A Spanish newspaper, anxious to come up with something equally original, advocated an administrative plan whereby Madrid would become the political center of this entire strategy, on the pretext that the Spanish capital is situated, as it were, at the geometric center of the peninsula, which is not even true if one looks at the map, but there are people who have no qualms about the means used to achieve their objective. The chorus of protests did not come only from Portugal, the autonomous Spanish regions also rebelled against the proposal, which they saw as further proof of Castilian centralism. On the Portuguese side, as one might have expected, there was a sudden revival of interest in the occult and in esoteric sciences, this did not go very far, simply because the situation changed radically, nevertheless it lasted long enough to sell out every copy of Padre António Vieira's *History of the Future* and *The Prophesies of Bandarra*, as well as Fernando Pessoa's *Mensagem*, but that goes without saying.

From the standpoint of realpolitik, discussion of the problem in European and American foreign ministries centered on spheres of influence, that is to say on whether, ignoring the question of distance, the peninsula or island should preserve its natural ties with Europe, or whether, without entirely severing them, it should orient itself rather toward the ideals and destiny of the great American nation. With no hope of exerting any clear influence in the matter, the Russians pointed out time and time again that nothing should be decided without their participation in the discussions, and meantime reinforced the fleet that from the outset had been accompanying the errant peninsula under the watchful eye, needless to say, of the fleets of the other powers, the Americans, the British, and the French.

It was within the framework of these negotiations that the United States informed Portugal, in an audience, urgently requested by Ambassador Charles Dickens, with the President of the Republic, that the continuance of a government of national salvation made no sense whatsoever once the circumstances no longer prevailed that had been adduced, In the most dubious fashion, Mr. President, if you will allow me to express an opinion, to justify its constitution. This tactless remark became public indirectly, not because the relevant ministries of the Presidency had made any public announcement, or through any statements made by the Ambassador as he left the Palace of Belém, in fact he simply remarked that his discussions with the President had been very frank and constructive. But that was enough for the members of the governments representing the parties who would inevitably have to go, were the government to be reshuffled or a general election called, to launch an attack on the Ambassador's intolerable meddling. The internal problems of Portugal, they declared, must be solved by the Portuguese, adding with spiteful irony, Just because the Ambassador wrote *David Copperfield* doesn't entitle him to come and give orders in the land of Camoëns and *The Lusiads*. At this point, the peninsula, with no warning, started moving again.

Pedro Orce had been right when he said, there at the foot of the Pyrenees, It may have stopped, fine, but it's still trembling, and so as not to be the only one to say so, he had put his hand on Constant's back, the dog was also trembling, as the others were themselves able to confirm, repeating the unique experience of Joaquim Sassa and José Anaiço beneath the Cordovan olive tree, in the arid lands between Orce and Venta Micena. But now, and the shock was general and universal, the movement was neither westward nor eastward, neither to the south nor to the north. The peninsula was turning on itself, widdershins, counterclockwise, that is, which, once made public, immediately caused the Portuguese and the Spaniards to suffer from dizziness, although the speed of rotation was anything but vertiginous. In the face of this decidedly unusual phenomenon, which threatened to jeopardize all the laws of physics, especially the mechanical ones, by which the earth had governed itself, all political negotiations, alliances made behind closed doors or in corridors, and diplomatic maneuvers, whether direct or step by step, were broken off. And we must agree that it could not have been easy to keep calm, when one knew, for example, that the table at the council of ministers, along with the building, the street, the city, the country, and the entire peninsula, was whirling like a turntable going around and around as if in a dream. Those who were more sensitive swore they could feel a circular motion, while admitting that they could not feel the earth itself going around in space. To show what they meant, they stretched out their arms seeking something to hold onto, but they did not always succeed, sometimes they even fell down, ending up on their backs on the ground, where they watched the sky slowly turning, at night the stars and the moon, during the day, with a smoked lens, the sun. Some doctors were of the opinion that these were nothing but manifestations of hysteria.

Obviously, more radical skeptics were in good supply, go on, the peninsula turning around on itself, simply impossible, sliding would be one thing, everybody knows about landslides and what happens to an escarpment when there is a heavy rainfall could also happen to a peninsula even without rain, but all this talk about rotation would imply that the peninsula was wrenching itself from its own axis, not only is such a thing objectively impossible, but it would inevitably cause the central core to snap off, sooner or later, and then we would certainly be adrift with no moorings whatsoever, at the mercy of the whims of fate. These skeptics were forgetting that the rotation might instead resemble that of a plate revolving on top of another, note that this lamellar schist is composed, as the name implies, of thin layers of shale placed one over the other. If the adhesion between two of them should loosen, the one could revolve quite easily on top of the other, thus maintaining, theoretically speaking, a certain degree of union between them that would prevent total separation. That's precisely what's happening, asserted those who defended the theory. And for confirmation, they sent divers once more to the bottom of the sea, as far down as possible into the bowels of the ocean, and with them went the *Archimedes*, the *Cyana*, and a Japanese vessel with an unpronounceable name. As a result of all these efforts, the Italian investigator repeated those famous words, he emerged from the water, opened the hatch, and spoke into the microphones of television stations throughout the world, It cannot move and yet it moves. There was no central axis coiled like a rope, there were no layers of shale, yet the peninsula turned majestically in the middle of the Atlantic, and as it turned, it became less and less recognizable, Is this really where we've spent our lives, people asked themselves. The Portuguese coast veered to the southeast and what had formerly been the easternmost point of the Pyrenees was pointing in the direction of Ireland. Observing the peninsula had become an obligatory part of transatlantic commercial flights, although frankly to little advantage, for there the indispensable fixed point to which the movement might be related was missing. In fact, nothing could replace the image captured and transmitted by satellite, the photograph taken from a great altitude that really gave some idea of the magnitude of the phenomenon.

This movement continued for a month. Seen from the peninsula, the universe transformed itself little by little. Every day the sun emerged from a different point on the horizon, and one had to search for the moon and the stars in the sky, their own movement, proceeding around the center of the system of the Milky Way, was no longer enough, now that there was this other movement transforming space into a frenzy of flickering stars, as if the universe were being reorganized from one end to the other, perhaps following the discovery that it had not turned out right the first time around. Until one day the sun set precisely where in normal times it had risen, and then there was no point in saying that it was not true, that appearances were deceiving, that the sun was following its normal path and was incapable of any other. The man in the street simply retorted, Let me just tell you, mister, that the morning sun used to come through my front window and now it comes in at the back, so perhaps you could explain that in simple language. The expert explained it as best he could, he brought out photographs, made drawings, opened a map of the sky, but the pupil could not be persuaded and the lesson ended with him asking the good doctor to please arrange for the rising sun to go back to coming in through his front window. Seeing that he could not convince him with scientific arguments, the expert told him, Don't worry, if the peninsula turns all the way around you will see the sun as before, but the suspicious pupil rejoined, In other words, Mr. Know-it-all, you think all this is happening so that things can go back to being the same as before. And in fact they did not.

It should already have been winter, but winter, which seemed at one point to have arrived, suddenly backed away, that is the only verb to describe it. It was neither winter nor autumn, certainly not spring, not remotely like summer. It was a season in suspension, without a date, as if the world were just beginning and the seasons and their timing had still to be decided. Deux Chevaux proceeded slowly along the foothills and the travelers now stopped from time to time, astonished above all at the spectacle of the sun, which no longer appeared over the Pyrenees but rose from the sea, casting its first rays on the uppermost slopes of the mountain as far as the snow-covered peaks. Here, in one of these villages, Maria Guavaira and Joana Carda realized that they were pregnant. Both of them. There was nothing surprising about their situation, one might even say that these women had done their utmost to become pregnant during these months and weeks, giving themselves wholeheartedly to their men without the slightest precaution on either side. Nor should anyone be surprised that both women became pregnant at the same time, this was simply another of those coincidences that constitute life on this earth, the good thing being that they can sometimes be clearly identified for the enlightenment of the skeptics. But the situation is embarrassing, it leaps to the eye, and the embarrassment stems from the difficulty of ascertaining two dubious paternities. The fact is, were it not for the false step taken by Joana Carda and Maria Guavaira when, moved by pity or some other more obscure sentiment, they went into the woods and forests in search of the solitary Pedro, whom, such was his confusion and disquiet, they almost had to beg to penetrate them, to impregnate them with his last seeds, were it not for this lyrical and far from erotic episode, Maria Guavaira's child would undoubtedly be accepted as that fathered by Joaquim Sassa and Joana Carda's child as that efficiently fathered by José Anaiço. But then Pedro Orce had to cross their path, although it might be truer to say that the temptresses waylaid him, and decency overcome by shame concealed its face. I don't know who the father is, said Maria Guavaira, who had set the example, Neither do I, said Joana Carda, who later followed her example, for two reasons, first to prove that she was no less heroic, and second to correct error with error, making exception the rule.

But neither this argument nor another, however subtle, can help them to evade the main problem. José Anaiço and Joaquim Sassa must be told. How will they react and what expression will come over their faces when their respective women tell them, I'm pregnant. Were the situation more harmonious, they would be, as one is wont to say, overcome with joy, and perhaps even now, with the initial shock, their faces and expressions would betray the sudden jubilation that springs from the soul, but their faces would soon cloud over, their eyes would darken, foretelling a dreadful scene. Joana Carda suggested that they say nothing, with the passing of time and the swelling of their bellies, the evident fact of the matter would soothe ruffled susceptibilities, would appease offended honor and reawakened resentment. But Maria Guavaira did not agree, she felt that it would be sad for the courage and generosity shown on all sides to end in a feeble deception, in a cowardice worse than tacit complacency. You're right, Joana Carda conceded, we must take the bull by the horns, she answered, without realizing what she was saying, that is the danger of using certain expressions without paying enough attention to the context.

That same day the two women each called her man aside and walked out with him into the country, there where the wide open spaces reduce the most choleric and rending cries to mere whispers, that unfortunately is the reason why human voices fail to reach heaven, and there, without beating about the bush, as they had agreed, the women said, I'm pregnant and I'm not sure whether you're the father or Pedro Orce is. Joaquim Sassa and José Anaiço reacted as one might have expected. There was the furious outburst, the violent gesticulations, the poignant sorrow, they were out of sight of each other, but their gestures were identical, their words equally bitter, Not satisfied with what has happened, you have the nerve to come and tell me you're pregnant and you don't know who's responsible, How can I be expected to know, and in any case when the child is born there won't be any doubt, What on earth are you talking about, There will be some resemblance, Of course, but suppose it only resembles you, If it only resembles me then it will be my child and no one else's, Are you trying to make a fool of me, I'm not making a fool of anyone, that's something I never do, So how are we supposed to solve the problem, If you could accept that I might have slept with Pedro Orce for one night, then you can put up with waiting nine months before making any decision, if the child resembles you then it's yours, and if it resembles Pedro Orce then it's his and you can disown it and me as well, if that's what you want, and as for only resembling me, don't you believe it, there's always some physical trait that comes from the other partner. And what about Pedro Orce, how do we deal with him, are you going to tell him, No, for another two months nothing will show, especially in these floppy blouses and loose jackets, I think it's best to say nothing, I must say that it would make me angry to see Pedro Orce looking smugly at you, at both of you, with the expression of a champion stud, that was the expression José Anaiço used, with his superior command of language. Joaquim Sassa was much more down to earth, I'd hate to see Senhor Pedro Orce strutting around like the cock of the walk. So in the end the two men resigned themselves to this affront, encouraged by the thought that their worst fears might be proved groundless once nature took its course and the mystery was cleared up.

It did not even dawn on Pedro Orce, who had never known what it meant to have children, that his semen might be germinating in the wombs of the two women. How true that man never gets to know all the consequences of his deeds, here is an excellent example, the memory of the happy moments he enjoyed begins to fade, and their possible effect, modest as yet, but more important in itself than all the rest, should it come to pass and be confirmed, is invisible to his eye and concealed from his knowledge. God Himself made men, yet does not see them. Pedro Orce, however, is not entirely blind, he can see that something has upset the harmony within the couples, a certain remoteness has crept in, not exactly coldness, more a note of reserve without hostility, but causing long periods of silence, the journey had begun so well and now it is as if they had nothing more to say to each other, or as if they were too frightened to utter the only words that would have made any sense. It was over and done with, what had been alive was now dead, if that is what it is all about. It could also be that the fire of those first jealous moments had been rekindled with the passage of time. And perhaps because no one saw me passing, Pedro Orce started going for long strolls again into the surrounding neighborhood whenever they set up camp. It is almost incredible how much this man can walk.

One day, after they'd already left behind the first foothills that announce the Pyrenees from afar, Pedro Orce had gone ahead along secluded roads, feeling almost tempted never to go back to the camp, these are thoughts that come into one's head in moments of weariness, when he came across a man resting by the roadside. He looked about his own age, if not older, but worn out and tired. Beside him stood a donkey with packsaddle and load, nibbling at the sun-bleached grass with its yellow teeth, for the weather, as we mentioned earlier, is not very favorable for fresh growth and causes what new shoots there are to sprout out of place and out of season, nature has lost its way, as any lover of metaphors would say. The man was chewing a lump of stale bread and nothing else, obviously in bad shape, a tramp without food or shelter, but he seemed peaceful and harmless and, besides, Pedro Orce is not easily intimidated, as he has clearly shown on these long walks through deserted countryside. The dog hasn't left him for a moment, or rather it has left him twice, but in better company and out of sheer discretion.

Pedro Orce greeted the man, Good afternoon, and the other replied, Good afternoon, both men noted a familiar pronunciation, a southern accent, that of Andalusia, to put it in a nutshell. But the man eating the stale bread found it highly suspicious to come across a man and a dog in these parts, remote from any habitation, and looking as if they had been dropped there by a flying saucer, as a precaution, and without trying to conceal it, he reached out for his stick, which had a metal tip and was lying on the ground. Pedro Orce observed this gesture and the tramp's uneasiness, he was probably afraid of the dog as it stood there watching him, its head lowered, without moving a muscle. Don't worry about the dog, it's quite gentle, well, not exactly gentle, but it won't attack unless it thinks it's in danger of being harmed. How can the dog tell when someone is going to harm it. Now that's a good question and I wish I knew the answer, but neither I nor my traveling companions have been able to discover the dog's breed or where it came from. I thought you were on your own and lived nearby, I'm traveling with some friends, we have a wagon and because of what's happened we set out along the road, and we've never left it. You're from Andalusia, I can tell from your accent. I'm from Orce in the province of Granada. I hail from Zufre in the province of Huelva. Pleased to meet you, The pleasure's mine. May I join you for a moment, Make yourself comfortable, but I'm afraid all I can offer you is some stale bread. Many thanks, but I've already eaten with my companions, Who are they, Two friends and their women, the two men and one of the women are Portuguese, the other woman is Galician, And how did you all meet up. Ah, that's a long story.

The other did not insist, saw that he should not, and said, You must be wondering how someone from the province of Huelva landed up here. In times like these, you rarely find people where you would expect to find them. I come from Zufre and have relatives living there unless they've gone elsewhere, but when the rumor spread that Spain was about to break away from France, I decided to go and see for myself. Not Spain, the Iberian peninsula. Yes, of course. And it wasn't from France that the peninsula broke away but from Europe, that may sound like the same thing but there's a difference. I don't understand these niceties, I only wanted to go and see for myself. And what did you see. Nothing, I reached the Pyrenees and saw only the sea. That was all we saw. There was no France and there was no Europe, now in my opinion, something that isn't there is the same as something that never was and I had wasted my time traveling league after league in search of something that didn't exist. Well, that's where you're wrong. Wrong in what way. Before the peninsula separated from Europe, Europe did exist, naturally there was a frontier, and you had to cross from one side to the other, the Spanish went, the Portuguese went, foreigners came, did you never see tourists in your region. Sometimes, but there was nothing to see there. They were tourists coming from Europe, But if I never saw Europe when I was living in Zufre, and if I've now left Zufre and I still haven't seen Europe, what's the difference. You haven't been to the moon either, yet it exists. But I can see it, at the moment it's off course, but I can still see it. What's your name. Roque Lozano at your service. I am Pedro Orce, Are you named after the place where you were born. I wasn't born in Orce, I was born in Venta Micena, which is nearby. That reminds me, when I began my journey I met two Portuguese who were traveling to Orce. Perhaps they are the same two. I'd really like to know. Come with me and you'll find out. If that's an invitation, I'll gladly accept it, I've been traveling alone for such a long time. Get up slowly in case the dog thinks you're going to attack me, I'll hand you your stick. Roque Lozano put his bundle on his back and pulled the donkey's rein, off they went, the dog at Pedro Orce's side, perhaps this is how it should always be, wherever there is a man there should be an animal with him, a parrot perched on his shoulder, a snake coiled around his wrist, a beetle on his lapel, a scorpion curled up, we might even say a louse in his hair, if this bug did not belong to that detested race of parasites, a tribe not tolerated even by insects, although they, poor creatures, are not to blame, for God willed them as they are.

Traveling at the same aimless pace, the wagon had penetrated the heart of Catalonia. Business flourished, it was a brilliant idea to have launched themselves into this branch of commerce. Fewer people are to be seen on the roads now, which means that, although the peninsula is still rotating, people are returning to their normal habits and pursuits, if that is the right word to describe their former habits and pursuits. Villages are no longer deserted, although one cannot be sure that all the houses are now lived in by their previous occupants, some men are now with other women, some women with other men, and their children are thrown together. This is the inevitable outcome of all great wars and migrations. That very morning José Anaiço had suddenly announced that they must come to a decision about the group's future, since there no longer appeared to be any danger of collisions or clashes. On the most likely or at least most plausible hypothesis, in his opinion, the peninsula would go on rotating on the same spot, which would not inconvenience people's everyday existence, and although it might no longer be possible to know where the various cardinal points are, what does it matter, for there's no law that says that we cannot live without the north. But now they had seen the Pyrenees, and what a wonderful thrill they had experienced, looking down at the sea from such a height, Just like being in an airplane, Maria Guavaira had exclaimed, only to be corrected by the experienced José Anaiço, There's no comparison, no one feels dizzy looking out the window of an airplane after all, but up here, unless we hold on with all our might, we'd be tempted to throw ourselves into the sea. Sooner or later, said José Anaiço, referring to the warning he had given that morning, we shall have to decide about our future, unless we mean to spend the rest of our lives on the road. Joaquim Sassa agreed but the women were reluctant to express any opinion, they suspect there may be some ulterior motive in this sudden haste, only Pedro Orce timidly reminded them that the earth was still trembling, and if this was not a sign that the journey had not reached its end, then perhaps they could explain to him why they had made it in the first place. At another time, the wisdom of this argument, however speculative, would have made some impression, but one must bear in mind that the wounds of the soul are deep, otherwise they would not be of the soul, but now whatever Pedro Orce says, he is suspected of some ulterior motive, this is the thought one can read in the eyes of José Anaiço as he says, Immediately after dinner, each person will say what he thinks ought to be done, whether we should return home or carry on, and Joana Carda simply asked, Which home.

Now here comes Pedro Orce bringing another man with him. From this distance he looks old, just as well, we have quite enough problems of cohabitation already. The man is leading a donkey harnessed with packsaddle and load, as old-fashioned a donkey as you have ever seen, but this one is an unusual silvery color, were it called Platero, it would, like the scraggly Rocinante, be worthy of its name. Pedro Orce comes to a halt on the invisible line that marks the boundary of the encampment, he must observe the formalities of presenting and introducing the visitor, something that must always be done on the other side of the threshold, these are rules we do not have to learn, the historic man within us observes them, one day we tried to enter the castle without permission and we were taught a lesson. Pedro Orce says emphatically, I came across this fellow countryman and I've brought him along to have a bowl of soup with us, there is obvious exaggeration in the term fellow countryman, but it is understandable at a time like this, a Portuguese from Minho and one from Alentejo feel nostalgia for the same fatherland, even though five hundred kilometers had separated the one from the other, and now they are both six hundred kilometers from home.

Joaquim Sassa and José Anaiço do not recognize the man, but the same cannot be said regarding the donkey. There is something unmistakable and familiar about it, in a manner of speaking, which is not surprising, for a donkey does not change in appearance over a few months, while a man, if he is dirty and unkempt, if he has let his beard grow, has become thin or fat, or has lost his hair, would need his own wife to strip him to see if that special mark is in the same place, sometimes much too late, when everything is over and repentance will not gather the fruit of pardon. Observing the rules of hospitality, José Anaiço said, You are welcome, do join us, and if you'd like to unload the donkey and give it a rest, there's enough fodder there for all of them, the donkey and the horses. Without its packsaddle and load the donkey looked much younger, and its coat was now seen to be in two tones of silver, the one dark, the other light, and both quite striking. When the man went to tether the beast, the horses looked askance at the newcomer, doubting whether it could be of much assistance to them with its scraggly frame that would be difficult to harness. The man returned to the campfire and before pulling over the stone on which he would sit, he introduced himself, My name is Roque Lozano. As for the rest, the most elementary rules of narrative demand that it avoid repetition. José Anaiço was about to ask if the donkey had a name, if it was named by any chance Platero or Silver, but the final words uttered by Roque Lozano, which in the end always repeat themselves, I came to see Europe, caused him to fall silent. His memory was suddenly jolted and he muttered to himself, I know this man, just as well he remembered in time, it would be nothing less than offensive if it took a donkey for people to recognize each other. Similar thoughts must have been stirring in Joaquim Sassa's head when he said hesitantly, I have the impression that we've met before, Me too, replied Roque Lozano, you remind me of two Portuguese I met at the beginning of my journey, but they were traveling by car and they had no women with them, Life takes so many turns, Senhor Roque Lozano, and one gains and loses so much that one could just as easily lose a Deux Chevaux car as find a wagon with two horses, two women, and yet another man, quipped Maria Guavaira, And there's more on the way, interrupted Joana Carda. Neither Pedro Orce nor Roque Lozano had any idea what she was talking about, but José Anaiço and Joaquim Sassa knew, and they did not much like this allusion to secrets of the human body, especially women's bodies.

They had recognized each other, any doubts had disappeared. Roque Lozano was the man they had encountered between the Sierras Morena and Aracena, traveling with his donkey Platero toward Europe, which in the end he had not seen, although that was still his intention and his hope of salvation. And now where are you heading, Joana Carda asked him, I'm going back home, because despite all these turns the earth has taken it's bound to be in the same place. You mean the earth. No, my home, one's home is always where the earth is. Maria Guavaira started to ladle the soup into bowls after adding a little water to ensure that there would be enough for everyone. They ate in silence, except for the dog, which methodically gnawed a bone, and the beasts of burden, which munched and chewed the hay. Now and then you could hear a dry bean pod snap. These animals have nothing to complain about as far as their rations are concerned, if one considers the prevailing difficulties.

Some of the more personal difficulties will be resolved by the family council scheduled for tonight. The presence of a stranger will be no impediment. On the contrary, for now that Roque Lozano has said he is returning home, what are we going to do, wander at random like gypsies, buying and selling clothes off the rack, or shall we return home, go back to work, to a normal existence, for even if the pen- insula should never again come to a halt, everyone will start getting used to it, just as mankind got used to inhabiting the constantly mov- ing earth. We're not even capable of imagining how much it must have upset everyone's balance to go whizzing around an aquarium with a sunfish inside. Forgive me for correcting you, said the unknown voice, but there's no such thing as a sunfish, there's a moonfish but no sunfish. In that case I won't argue with you, but if there isn't one there ought to be. Alas, you can't have everything, José Anaiço con- cluded, comfort and freedom are incompatible, this wandering exis- tence has its charms, but four solid walls with a roof overhead give more protection than a wagon covered with canvas and bouncing along over potholes. Joaquim Sassa suggested, Let's start by taking Pedro Orce home, and then, he broke off in mid-sentence, unable to finish, and at this point Maria Guavaira intervened and said clearly what had to be said, Very well, let's drop Pedro Orce off at his phar- macy and then go on to Portugal, José Anaiço can return to his school, wherever it is, while we continue in a direction once referred to as north, Joana Carda will have to decide whether she prefers to stay behind in Ereira with her cousins or go back to her husband in Coim- bra, once this matter has been settled we can head for Oporto and drop Joaquim Sassa off outside his office, his bosses must be back from Peñafiel by now, and finally I'll make my own way home where a man is waiting to marry me, he'll say he's been guarding my property while I've been away, Now marry me, and with a torch I'll set this wagon on fire, as one burns a dream, and perhaps I will finally manage to push the stone vessel out to sea and embark.

Such a long speech leaves the person speaking breathless, not to mention those who are listening. For a moment they all remained silent, then José Anaiço reminded her, We're already traveling on a

276

stone raft. But it's much too big for us to feel like sailors, rejoined Maria Guavaira, and Joaquim Sassa observed smiling, How true, nor has traveling through space above the world turned us into astronauts. There was further silence, then it was Pedro Orce's turn to speak. Let's do one thing at a time, Roque Lozano can join us and we'll take him to his family, who must be waiting for him in Zufre, and then we can decide about our own future. But there isn't any room for anyone else to sleep inside the wagon, José Anaiço insisted. Don't let that worry you, if that's the only reason why I shouldn't accompany you, I'm used to sleeping out in the open, just so long as it doesn't rain, and if I can sleep under the wagon that will be as good as having a roof over my head at night, I was beginning to get tired of being on my own, believe me, Roque Lozano confided.

Next day they resumed their journey. Grizzly and Chess grumbled at the good fortune of donkeys, this one is trotting behind the wagon, comfortably attached with a rope and relieved of any burden, as naked as it came into the world, with its nice silvery sheen, its master is in the driver's seat, chatting about the past with Pedro Orce, the couples are talking under the canvas, the dog walks ahead, on patrol. From one moment to the next, almost miraculously, harmony has been restored to the expedition. Yesterday, after the final deliberation, they drew up an itinerary, nothing very precise but just so as not to go blindly. First they would descend to Tarragona, then travel along the coast as far as Valencia, move inland through Albacete as far as Cordoba, go down to Seville, and finally, less than eighty kilometers away, arrive at Zufre, where we shall say, Here comes Roque Lozano, back safe and sound from his great adventure, he left poor and poor he returns, he has discovered neither Europe nor El Dorado, not everyone who has gone in search of them has found them, nor is the traveler always to blame. Time and time again, there are no riches whatsoever where, out of malice or ignorance, we were promised we would find them. Then we will look on and see how he is received, Dear grandfather, Dearest father, Beloved husband, What a pity you've returned, I thought you might have perished in the wilderness or been devoured by wolves, not everything can be said aloud.

Then at Zufre the family council will convene once more, now where are we going and what will they say about us when we arrive, where, for what, for whom, Your questions are false if you already know the answer. Within so short a time, the unknown voice had spoken twice.

*A*fter turning from east to west until a perfect semicircle had been traced, the peninsula began to incline. At that precise moment, and in the most rigorous sense, if metaphors as a vehicle of literal sense can be rigorous, Portugal and Spain were two countries with their legs up in the air. Let us leave to the Spaniards, who have always disdained our assistance, the task and responsibility of evoking to the best of their ability, the structural changes in the physical space in which they live, and let us say here, with the modest simplicity that has always characterized primitive peoples, that the Algarve, a southern region on the map since time immemorial, became in that supernatural moment the most northerly part of Portugal. Incredible but true, as a Father of the Church preached, and has continued to preach even unto the present day, not because he's alive, for all the Fathers of the Church are dead, but because people are constantly borrowing the phrase and using it indifferently, as much for spiritual profit as for human expediency. If the fates had decreed that the peninsula should be immobilized once and for all in that position, the consequences, social and political, cultural and economic, not to mention the psychological aspect, which people tend to overlook, the various consequences, as we were saying, and their aftermath would have been drastic, radical, in a word, earth-shattering. One need only remember, for example, that the famous city of Oporto would find itself stripped, with no hope of recourse, whether logical or topographical, of its precious title of Capital of the North, and if this reference in the eyes of some cosmopolites smacks of provincialism and lack of vision, then let them imagine what would happen if Milan were suddenly to end up in Calabria in southern Italy, and the Calabrians were to prosper from the commerce and industry of the north, a transformation not entirely impossible, if we bear in mind what happened to the Iberian peninsula.

But it lasted, as we were saying, only for a minute. The peninsula was falling but went on rotating. Therefore, before proceeding any further, we must explain what we mean by the word fall in the present context. The meaning here is clearly not the immediate one, as in falling bodies, which would imply that the peninsula had literally started to sink. After all, if throughout all those days at sea, often deeply troubled and overshadowed by the threat of imminent catastrophe, no such calamity occurred, nor anything comparable, it would be the greatest misfortune for the odyssey to end now in total submersion. However much it may cost us, we are now resigned to the possibility that Ulysses may not reach the shore in time to encounter sweet Nausicaa, but may the weary sailor at least be allowed to touch the coast of the island of the Phaeacians, or failing that one, some other, so that he may rest his head on his own forearm, if no woman's breast awaits him. Let us be calm, then. The peninsula, we promise, is not about to sink into the cruel sea, where, should such havoc ensue, everything would disappear, even the highest summit of the Pyrenees, such is the depth of these chasms. Yes, the peninsula is falling, there is no other way of describing it, but southward, for that is how we divide the planisphere, into north and south, top and bottom, upper and lower, even white and black, figuratively speaking, although it may seem surprising that the countries below the Equator do not use different maps, of a kind that might present an appropriately inverted image of the world, one complementary to our own. But things are what they are, they have that irresistible virtue, and even a schoolchild understands the lesson the first time around with no need for further explanation. Even the dictionary of synonyms, so easily dismissed, confirms as much, one descends or falls downward, fortunately for us this stone raft is not sinking to the bottom, gurgling through a hundred million lungs, blending the sweet waters of the Tagus and the Guadalquivir with the bitter swell of the infinite ocean.

There is no lack, there never has been, of those who affirm that poets are truly superfluous, but I wonder what would become of us if poetry were not there to help us understand how little clarity there is in the things we call clear. Even at this point, after so many pages have been written, the narrative material can be summed up as the description of an ocean voyage, albeit not an entirely banal one, and even at this dramatic moment when the peninsula resumes its route southward, while continuing to turn around on its imaginary axis, we would certainly have no way of surpassing and enhancing this simple statement of facts were it not for the inspiration of that Portuguese poet who compared the revolution and descent of the peninsula to the movement of a child in its mother's womb as it takes its first tumble in life. The simile is magnificent, although we must deplore this yielding to the temptations of anthropomorphism, which sees and judges everything in an essential rapport with human beings, as if nature had nothing better to do than to think about us. It would all be much easier to understand if we were simply to confess our infinite fear, the fear that leads us to people the world with images resembling what we are or believe ourselves to be, unless this obsessive effort is nothing other than feigned courage or sheer stubbornness on the part of someone who refuses to exist in a void, who decides not to find meaning where no meaning exists. We are probably incapable of filling emptiness, and what we call meaning is no more than a fleeting collection of images that once seemed harmonious, images on which the intelligence tried in panic to introduce reason, order, coherence.

Generally speaking, the poet's voice is not understood, but there are nevertheless some exceptions to this rule, as can be seen in that lyrical episode whose felicitous metaphor, stated and restated, was on everyone's lips, even if one cannot include in this popular enthusiasm the majority of the other poets, something that need not surprise us if we bear in mind that they are not exempt from all these human feelings of spite and envy. One of the most interesting consequences of that inspired comparison was the resurgence of the maternal spirit, of maternal influence, however mitigated by the changes modernity brought to family life. And if we reconsider the known facts, there are many reasons for believing that Joana Carda and Maria Guavaira were precursors of this broader renewal, through innate sensitivity rather than deliberate premeditation. The women undoubtedly triumphed. Their genital organs, if you'll pardon the crude anatomical reference, finally became the expression, at once reduced and enlarged, of the expulsive mechanism of the universe, of all that machinery that operates by extraction, that nothingness that will become everything, that uninterrupted progression from the small to the large, from the finite to the infinite. It is satisfying to see that at this point the commentators and scholars got into deep water, but no surprise, for experience has taught us all too well how inadequate words become as we get closer to the frontiers of the inexpressible, we try to say love and the word will not come out, we try to say I want and we say I cannot, we try to utter the final word only to realize that we have gone back to the beginning.

But in the reciprocal action of cause and effect, another consequence, at once fact and factor, has come to alleviate the graveness of these discussions and to leave everyone, as it were, smiling and embracing. It so happened that from one moment to the next, allowing for the exaggeration always implicit in these simplified formulas, all, or nearly all, the fertile women of the peninsula declared themselves pregnant, although no significant change in the contraceptive practices of these women and their men had been observed, we are referring, of course, to the men with whom they slept, whether regularly or by chance. As things stand, people are no longer surprised. Several months have passed since the peninsula separated from Europe, we have traveled thousands of kilometers over this violent open sea, the leviathan just missed colliding with the terrified islands of the Azores, or perhaps, as later emerged, it was never meant to collide with them, but the men and women did not know that as they found themselves obliged to flee from one side to the other, these were only some of the many things that happened, such as waiting for the sun to rise on the left only to see it appear on the right, not to mention the moon, as if its inconstancy ever since its breaking away from the earth were not enough, and the winds that blow on all sides and the clouds that shift from all horizons and circle above our dazzled heads, yes, dazzled, for there is a living flame overhead, as if man need not, after all, emerge from the historic sloth of his animal state and might be placed once more, lucid and entire, in a newly formed world, pure and with its beauty intact. All of this having happened, and the afore-mentioned Portuguese poet having declared that the peninsula is a child conceived on a journey and now finds itself revolving in the sea as it waits to be born in its watery womb, why should we be astonished that the wombs of women should be swollen, perhaps the great stone falling southward fertilized them, and how do we know if these new creatures are really the daughters of men rather than the offspring of that gigantic prow that pushes the waves before it, penetrating them amid the murmuring waters, the blowing and the sighing of winds.

The travelers learned of this collective pregnancy from radio reports and newspaper stories, and television programs spoke of nothing else. Journalists had only to catch a woman on the street and they were shoving a microphone into her face and bombarding her with ques-tions, how and when did it happen, what name was she going to give the baby, poor woman, with the camera devouring her alive, she blushed and stammered, the only thing she did not do was to invoke the constitution because she knew they would not take her seriously. Among the travelers on the wagon there was renewed tension, after all, if all the women of the peninsula are suddenly pregnant, these two women here are not saying a word about their own mishap and one can understand their silence, if they were to confess that they are pregnant, Pedro Orce would include himself on the list of possible fathers and the harmony they restored with such difficulty last time might not survive a second blow. One evening, then, as Joana Carda and Maria Guavaira were serving dinner to the men, they said with a wry smile, Just imagine, all the women in Spain and Portugal are pregnant and here we are with no hope at all. Let us accept this momentary pretense, let us grant that José Anaiço and Joaquim Sassa may disguise their annoyance, the annoyance of the male who sees his sexual potency called into question, and the worst of it is that the women's feigned sarcasm may well have struck a nerve, for if it is true that they are both pregnant, it is also true that nobody knows by whom. With so many unanswered questions, this pretense has certainly not relieved the tension, in the fullness of time it will become clear that Maria Guavaira and Joana Carda were pregnant after all, despite their denial. What explanation will they offer, for the truth always awaits us, the day arrives when it must be faced.

Visibly embarrassed, the Prime Ministers of both countries appeared on television, not that there was any reason to feel awkward when speaking of the demographic explosion that would be evident in the peninsula nine months hence, twelve or fifteen million children born almost at the same hour, crying out in chorus to the light, the peninsula transformed into maternity ward, happy mothers, smiling fathers, at least in those cases where there appears to be sufficient certainty. It is even possible to gain some political advantage from this aspect of the situation by pointing to the population figures, by appealing for austerity for the sake of our children's future, by going on about national cohesion and comparing this fertility with the sterility prevailing in the rest of the western world. One can only rejoice at the thought that the demographic explosion had been preceded by a genetic explosion, since no one can believe that this collective pregnancy is of a supernatural order. The Prime Minister now speaks of the health measures to be taken, of maternity services on a national scale, of the teams of doctors and midwives who will be hired and deployed at the appropriate time, and his face betrays conflicting emotions, the solemnity of his official statement vies with his urge to smile, he appears to be on the point of saying, any minute now, Sons and daughters of Portugal, the benefits we reap will be great and I trust that the pleasure has been just as great, for to bring forth children without indulging the flesh is the worst punishment of all. The men and women listen, exchange smiles and glances, they can read each other's thoughts, recall that night, that day, that hour, when driven by a sudden urge they came together and did what had to be done, beneath a sky that was slowly turning, a demented sun, a demented moon, the stars in turmoil. The first impression is that this might be illusion or dream, but when the women appear with swollen bellies, then it will be clear that we have not been dreaming.

The President of the United States of America also addressed the world. He declared that notwithstanding the peninsula's diversion toward some unknown place lying to the south, the United States would never abdicate its responsibility to civilization, freedom, and peace, although the nations of the peninsula cannot count, now that they are passing through contested spheres of influence, They cannot count, I repeat, on aid equal to what awaited them when it seemed likely that their future would become inseparable from that of the American nation. This was, more or less, his utterance to the wide world. In private, however, in the secrecy of the Oval Office of the White House, ice cubes clinking in his bourbon, the President would have confided to his advisers, If they were to be stranded in the Antarctic our worries would be over, but what will become of us, countries roaming from one place to another, no strategy can cope with it, take the bases we still have on the peninsula, what good will they be except for firing missiles at the penguins. One of his advisers would have then pointed out that if one considered it carefully, the new route was really not all that bad, They are moving down between Africa and Latin America, Mr. President, Yes, this route could be advantageous, but it could also encourage further insubordination in the region. And perhaps because of this annoying thought, the President thumps the table, upsetting the smiling portrait of the First Lady. An elderly adviser jumps with fright, looks around, and says, Do be careful, Mr. President, you can never tell what a thump like that might do.

It is no longer the flayed skin of the bull but a gigantic stone in the shape of one of those flint artifacts used by men in prehistoric times, chipped away patiently, blow by blow, until it becomes a working tool, the upper part compact and rounded to fit into the palm of the hand, the lower part pointed for the tasks of scraping, digging, cutting, marking, and designing, and also, because we have not yet learned to resist the temptation, to wound and kill. The peninsula has stopped rotating and is now falling southward, passing between Africa and Central America, as the President's adviser would have explained, and its form, to the surprise of anyone who might still have in mind or on his map its former position, matches that of the two continents on either side, we see Portugal and Galicia to the north, occupying the entire width from west to east, then the great mass starts becoming narrower, Andalusia and Valencia still jutting out on the left, the Cantabrian coast on the right, and continuing the line, the great wall of the Pyrenees. The tip of the stone, the cutting edge, is the Cape of Croesus, carried from Mediterranean waters to these threatening seas, so far from the native sky of one who was the neighbor of Cerbère, that little French town so often mentioned at the beginning of this narrative.

The peninsula is descending, but descending slowly. The experts, albeit with the utmost caution, predict that the movement is about to stop, trusting in the obvious and universal truth that if the whole, as such, never stops, the constituent parts must stop at some time, this axiom being demonstrated by human life itself, which abounds as we know in potential comparisons. With this scientific statement, the game of the century got under way, with an idea that must have emerged practically at the same time everywhere in the world, and that consisted of establishing a system for placing a double wager, on the time and place in which the suspension of movement would be verified. To take a hypothetical case to clarify the point, at 5:33:49 A.M., local time of the person betting, obviously, and the day, month, and year, and the position, this being limited to the latitude in degrees, minutes and seconds, the aforementioned Cape of Croesus serving as a point of reference. There were trillions of dollars at stake, and if someone were to guess both answers correctly, that is to say, the precise moment and the exact place, which according to the calculation of probabilities was little short of unthinkable, that person endowed with almost divine foresight would find himself in possession of greater wealth than has ever been gathered on this earth, which has seen so many riches. Nor has there ever been a more terrible game than this one, for with each passing moment, with each kilometer covered, the number of gamblers with any chance of winning is gradually reduced, although one should note that many of those eliminated come back to wager once more, thus increasing the prize money to an astronomical figure. Of course not everyone manages to raise the money for another bet, clearly many of them find no way out of their financial ruin but suicide. The peninsula is falling southward leaving behind a trail of deaths of which it is innocent, while in the wombs of its women are growing millions of children that it innocently engendered.

Pedro Orce goes around looking restless and ill at ease. Scarcely speaks, spends hours away from the encampment, comes back exhausted and refuses to eat, his companions inquire if he's feeling ill and he tells them, No, no, I'm not ill, without further explanation. Any conversation he makes is reserved for Roque Lozano, they are always reminiscing about their native parts as if there were no other topic of conversation. The dog accompanies him everywhere and one senses that the man's restlessness has affected this animal, once so placid. José Anaiço has already commented to Joana Carda, If he thinks that history is about to repeat itself, the poor man alone and abandoned who finds compassionate women ready to comfort him and bring him sexual relief, he's sorely deceived, and she answered with a wan smile, You're the one who's deceived, Pedro Orce's trouble, if that's the right word, is something quite different. What trouble. I don't know, but I can assure you he's not yearning for us this time, a woman is never in any doubt about these things. Then we should talk to him, make him speak, perhaps he really is ill. Perhaps, but even that isn't certain.

They travel along the Sierra de Alcaraz, today they will set up camp near a village that, according to the map, is called Bienservida. At least in name, it is indeed well served. Perched in the driver's seat, Pedro Orce tells Roque Lozano, From here we should soon be arriving in the Province of Granada, if that's where we're heading. But my land is still far away, You'll get there, Oh yes, I'll get there, but the question is whether there's much point, These are things we only discover afterwards, give the gray horse a prod, it's slowing down. Roque Lozano shook the reins, flicked his whip over the horses' rumps, the merest graze, whereupon Grizzly obediently adjusted its trot. The couples travel inside the wagon, they converse in whispers, and Maria Guavaira says, Perhaps he'd rather go back home but doesn't like to say so in case we take offense. You could be right, replied Joaquim Sassa, we'd better ask him straight out, tell him we understand, no hard feelings, no promise or agreement need last a lifetime, after all, friends we are and friends we remain, one day we'll come back and visit him. God forbid, Joana Carda muttered under her breath. Have you something else in mind. No, not at all, just a premonition. What premonition, Maria Guavaira asked her. That Pedro Orce is going to die. We can all expect to die sooner or later. But he'll be the first to go.

Bienservida lies off the main road. They had gone there to sell their wares, they bought some provisions, renewed their supply of water, and returned to the road still early, But they did not get far, stopping a little farther on at a small country church known as Turruchel, a pleasant spot to spend the night. Uncharacteristically, José Anaiço and Joaquim Sassa jumped down from the wagon as it came to a halt and went to assist Pedro Orce in his descent from the driver's seat, making him say, as he held on to their outstretched hands, What's this, my friends, I'm not an invalid. He failed to notice that the word friends immediately brought tears to the eyes of these men who harbor the sorrow of mistrust in their hearts even while they receive this weary body, which falls into their arms despite the old man's proud statement, for there comes a time when pride has nothing but words, is nothing but words. Pedro Orce puts his feet on the ground, takes a few steps, and pauses with an expression of amazement on his face, in his every gesture, as if intense light were paralyzing and blinding him. What's wrong, asked Maria Guavaira, who had drawn near. Nothing, it's nothing. Do you feel unwell, Joana Carda asked him. No, it's something else. He bent down, spread out his hands on the ground, then summoned the dog Constant, placed one hand on its head, ran his fingers along its neck, its spine, back, and rump. The dog did not move, it stood stock-still as if trying to dig its paws into the earth. Now Pedro Orce had stretched out, his head resting on a tuft of grass, his white hair mingling with fresh shoots, flowering at a time when it should have been winter. Joana Carda and Maria Guavaira knelt beside him and held his hands, What's the matter, tell us what you feel, for he was clearly suffering some great pain, to judge from the expression on his face. He opened his eyes wide and stared at the sky, at the passing clouds. Maria Guavaira and Joana Carda did not need to look up to see them, they floated slowly in Pedro Orce's eyes just as the street lamps of Oporto had played in the dog's eyes so long ago, in some other existence, perhaps, and now they are together, reunited with Roque Lozano who has as much experience of life as of death. The dog appears to be hypnotized by Pedro Orce's expression, it stares at him, head lowered and hairs bristling, as if it were about to confront all the wild beasts in the world, and then Pedro Orce said distinctly, word by word, I no longer feel the earth, I can no longer feel it. His eyes darkened, a gray cloud, the color of lead, passed slowly across the sky, slowly, very slowly. With the utmost delicacy Maria Guavaira lowered his eyelids and announced, He's dead, whereupon the dog came running and let out a howl that was almost human.

A man dies, and then what. His four friends weep, even Roque Lozano, whom he had known for such a short time, rubs his eyes furiously with clenched fists, and the dog, which has howled only once, now stands beside the corpse, soon it will lie down and rest its enormous head on Pedro Orce's chest. But we must decide what to do with the body, José Anaiço remarked. Let's take it to Bienservida and inform the authorities, we can do no more for him. But Joaquim Sassa reminded him, You once told me that the poet Machado must have been buried under a holm oak, let's do the same with Pedro Orce, but Joana Carda had the last word, Neither to Bienservida nor underneath a tree, let's take the body to Venta Micena, let's bury him in the place where he was born.

Pedro Orce lies on the bier stretched crosswise in the wagon. Beside him kneel the two women holding his cold hands, those same eager hands that scarcely became familiar with their bodies, and in the driver's seat are the two men. Roque Lozano leads the horses by the reins, they thought they were going to have a rest, and here they are on the road, after all, and in the middle of the night, such a thing has never happened to them before, perhaps the sorrel remembers another night, perhaps it was asleep and dreaming that it was shackled so that a painful sore might be cured with ointment and the morning dew, a man and a woman came looking for it accompanied by a dog, they untied it from its trappings and the horse did not know if the dream began or ended there. The dog walks underneath the wagon and below Pedro Orce as if it were carrying him, such is the weight it feels pressing down on its neck. There is a burning oil lamp hanging from the steel arch that supports the canvas in front. They still have one hundred and fifty kilometers to go.

The horses can feel death pursuing them and need no other whip. The silence of night is so deep that the wagon's wheels can scarcely be heard as they turn on the rough surface of these old roads, and the horses' trot sounds muffled as if their hooves were clad in rags. No moon will appear. They travel among shadows, there is a total blackout, an *apagón* or *negrum*, like the first night of all before those words were spoken, Let there be light, to no great wonder, for God knew that the sun would inevitably appear two hours hence. Joana Carda and Maria Guavaira have been weeping since they set out. Out of compassion they had given their bodies to this man whose corpse they all now escort, with their own hands they had drawn him to them, shown him what to do, and perhaps the unborn children forming inside their wombs and being made to tremble by their sobs are his offspring, dear God, how all things in this world are linked together, and here we are thinking that we have the power to separate or join them at will, how sadly mistaken we are, having been proved wrong time and time again, a line traced on the ground, a flock of starlings, a stone thrown into the sea, a blue woolen sock, but we are showing them to the blind, preaching to the deaf with hearts of stone.

The sky was still covered in darkness as they reached Venta Micena. Not a soul had they met along the entire route, almost thirty leagues, and slumbering Orce was a ghost, its houses like the walls of a labyrinth, their windows and doors firmly closed. Rising above the rooftops, the Castle of the Seven Towers was like a mirage. The streetlamps flickered like stars about to disappear, the trees in the square, reduced to trunks and thick boughs, might well have been the remnants of a petrified forest. The travelers passed in front of the pharmacy, this time there was no need to stop, the details of the route were still fresh in their memories, Go straight in the direction of Maria, continue for three kilometers after the last houses, you'll come to a little bridge there with an olive tree nearby, I'll catch up with you shortly. He has already arrived. After the last bend they saw the cemetery with its whitewashed walls and enormous cross. The gate was locked, they had to force it open. José Anaiço went in search of a crowbar, pushed the claw between the gate and the post, but Maria Guavaira grabbed him by the arm, We're not going to bury him here. She pointed toward the white hills in the direction of the Cueva de los Rosales where the skull of the most ancient man in Europe had been excavated, the one who had lived more than a million years ago, and she said, The body will rest over there, that's the spot Pedro Orce himself might have chosen. They took the wagon as far as possible, the horses could scarcely walk, their hooves dragging in the loose dust. There is no one living in Venta Micena to attend the funeral, all the houses have been abandoned, nearly all of them are in ruins. On the horizon the shadowy outline of the mountains can scarcely be seen, those same mountains that Orce Man must have watched as he lay dying. It is still night, Pedro Orce is dead, in his eyes only a dark cloud remains and nothing more.

When the wagon could go no farther, the three men removed the corpse. Maria Guavaira helps them while Joana Carda carries the elm branch in one hand. They climb a flat-topped hill, and the dry soil crumbles under their feet, scattering down the slope. The corpse of Pedro Orce sways, comes close to slipping and taking its bearers with it, but they manage to hoist it to the top, where they rest it on the ground. They are bathed in sweat, covered in white dust. Roque Lozano starts digging the grave, having asked the others to leave the job to him. The soil comes away easily, the crowbar serves as a spade and their hands as shovels. Light begins to dawn to the east, the blurred form of the sierra has turned black. Roque Lozano emerges from the hole, shakes the soil from his hands, kneels and starts to lift the corpse with the help of José Anaiço, who takes it by the arms. They lower the body slowly into the ground, the grave is not deep, should anthropologists ever return to these parts they would have no difficulty in finding it. Maria Dolores will say, Here's a skull, and the leader of the expedition will take a quick look, It's of no interest, we have plenty of those. They covered the body and smoothed out the ground until it merged with the rest of the terrain, but they had to remove the dog, which was trying to scratch at the grave with its claws. Then Joana Carda stuck the elm branch into the ground where Pedro Orce's head lay buried. It is not a cross, as one can see, nor a sign of mourning, it is only a branch that has lost any value it ever had, yet it can still be put to this simple use, a sundial in a fossilized wilderness, perhaps a resuscitated tree, if a piece of dry wood stuck in the ground is capable of working miracles, of creating roots, of ridding Pedro Orce's eyes of that dark cloud. Tomorrow the rain will fall over these fields.

The peninsula has stopped. The travelers will rest here until tomorrow. It is raining as they are about to leave, they have called the dog, which has not left the grave all this time, but it will not come. It's only to be expected, observed José Anaiço, dogs cannot bear to be separated from their master, sometimes they actually pine away. He was mistaken. The dog Ardent looked at José Anaiço, then moved off slowly, head lowered. They would never see it again. The journey continues. Roque Lozano will remain in Zufre, he will knock on the door of his house saying, I've come back, that's his story and perhaps someone will tell it one day. As for the others, they will travel on their way, who knows what future awaits them, how much time, what destiny. The elm branch is green. Perhaps it will flower again next year.